SHE IS A PRIESTESS OF THE SACRED FLAME, SWORN TO CHASTITY ON PENALTY OF DEATH...

"I could kill you now," Nero said. "But I have other plans for you." He drew the blade over his palm then took her hand in his, gently as a lover, and drew the blade again.

Blood beaded in Elissa's hand.

Pressing his palm against hers, he said, "My great-grandfather worshiped an Egyptian queen, dark and powerful like you. Be Cleopatra to my Antony."

He's madder than Caligula, Elissa thought...

PRAISE FOR VESTAL VIRGIN:

New York Times bestselling author Terry Brooks says, "...a writer of real talent...a promising new voice."

New York Times bestselling author Tess Gerritsen says, "Suzanne Tyrpak weaves a spell that utterly enchants and delights. Her writing is pure magic."

VESTAL VIRGIN
SUZANNE TYRPAK

VESTAL VIRGIN

SUZANNE TYRPAK

SUSPENSE IN ANCIENT ROME

For more information about the author, please visit
http://www.facebook.com/pages/Suzanne-Tyrpak/144232238928903.

For more information about the artist, please visit www.jeroentenberge.com.

Interior book layout and formatting: TERyvisions www.teryvisions.com

ISBN-13: 978-1460943144
ISBN-10: 1460943147

First Trade Paperback Edition
Published in the United States of America

for
My Father

FOREWORD

I'm always on the lookout for a great read, and nothing engrosses like well-researched historical fiction with a killer of a story and characters you both love and hate. All that and more lies waiting in the following pages of Suzanne Tyrpak's phenomenal debut, VESTAL VIRGIN.

Picture this: a gripping story set against ancient Rome and peopled with the major players of the time...a prophet named Paul, our hero, Elissa—a vestal virgin sworn to chastity—and of course, the psychopathic, megalomaniac Nero.

To say more would spoil the joy of discovering all that this novel has up its sleeve, so just trust me...you've never read classic Rome done like this, a fully-evoked world, meticulously researched, yet compulsively readable.

Only do yourself a favor and don't start reading until you've got some time on your hands.

Because you won't be able to stop.

—Blake Crouch, December 2010

AUTHOR'S NOTE:

Vestal Virgin takes place A.D. 63-64. My research includes extensive reading, two trips to Italy, consulting with scholars, and a life-long fascination with ancient cultures. The story is rooted in history, and although some of these events did occur, and some are conjecture, the story is fiction. Any resemblance to people currently alive, or those who have been alive in the last 1900 years, is coincidence.

—*Suzanne*

Main Characters

Elissa Rubria Honoria—Vestal Virgin (there is a record of a Vestal Virgin whose family name (*gens*) was Rubria

Marcus—Elissa's brother, an intellectual and former friend of Nero's (fictional)

Angerona—Vestal Virgin (fictional)

Olfonius Tigellinus—Praetorian Prefect and advisor to Nero

Nero Claudius Caesar Augustus Germanicus—Emperor of the Roman Empire, the princeps, Pontifex Maximus (high priest)

Agrippina—"The Younger," Roman Empress and mother of Nero, married to the Emperor Claudius, sister of the Emperor Caligula

Gallus Justinus—an Equestrian (knight) and war hero (fictional)

Akeem—an Egyptian slave, servant to Justinus (fictional)

Lucan—a poet, and nephew of Seneca

Mother Amelia—Vestal Maxima, the high vestal (fictional)

Honoratus Rubrius—Elissa's father, member of the aristocracy, a senator (fictional)

Constantina Rubria Honoria—Elissa's mother (fictional)

Flavia Rubria Honoria—Elissa's sister (fictional)

Paul of Tarsus—the prophet Paul, a follower of "The Way," and Jesus

Poppaea Sabina—Empress of Rome, Nero's wife

PART I

The Silent Dead

I give you tears, and words of sorrow at our parting,
but this ground cares not for my salt, the dead remain silent.
Fate stole you, took you from me, heart and soul,
beloved brother, dead, long before you grew old,
these rituals I perform, were passed down from our ancestors,
I weep for you, the dead, for tears are my inheritance.

—Catullus

CHAPTER I

The Kalends of October

Year IX, reign of Nero Claudius Caesar Augustus Germanicus

...though they may condemn me, the words I write are heartfelt. I no longer trust Nero, no longer trust the gods. I don't fear death, but life. This life devoid of passion. My fate has never been my own—my destiny decided ten years ago when I was pledged to thirty years of chastity. Keep this letter close, for I trust only you.

Elissa

She set down the stylus and read what she'd written. Could a person be condemned merely for thinking?

Through the narrow window of her chamber, a breeze brought the scent of roses, the last of autumn. Soon it would be winter, but sequestered within the House of Vestals the world seemed seasonless.

"Elissa—" a voice called from beyond the doorway's curtain.

She snatched the papyrus, thrust it into the bodice of her stola, and turned on her stool. Angerona, her fellow priestess, swept open the curtain. Unfettered by her veil, her auburn tresses fell over her shoulders in a wild cascade of curls. Beside her, Elissa felt small and dark. She ran her tongue over her teeth, the tip lingering on her deformity.

"I've been looking for you everywhere." Angerona's face was flushed, which only made her prettier. She sounded breathless, "I thought I'd find you working in the garden then I checked the library—"

"Why aren't you at the agora?" Elissa wiped ink from the stylus, replaced it in the jar with others, hoping Angerona wouldn't ask what she'd been writing. "All you've talked about for days is that gold bracelet. I thought you'd be haggling with the merchant. Did you finally get your price?"

"So you haven't heard—" Angerona's voice trailed off.

"Heard what?"

"All of Rome is whispering. I thought, by now, you would have known." She touched Elissa's shoulder, and something in her touch made Elissa shiver. "Your brother has been charged with treason."

"Treason?" The word passed Elissa's lips, but didn't register.

"They say, Marcus has been plotting Nero's assassination. They say—"

"They say!" Elissa stood, toppling her stool. "You've been listening to idle gossip, and now you're spreading rumors."

"My source is reliable."

"Who?"

Angerona shook her head.

Elissa seldom raised her voice, but now she did, "Gossip will be your ruin, Angerona. Vicious lies."

Angerona looked close to tears. She reached into the folds of her stola and withdrew a scroll. "This came for you by messenger."

Hands trembling, Elissa broke the imperial seal, read aloud:

"I, NERO CLAUDIUS AUGUSTUS GERMANICUS, PRINCEPS OF THE ROMAN EMPIRE, BELOVED OF APOLLO, SUMMON THE VESTAL VIRGIN, PRIESTESS ELISSA RUBRIA HONORIA, TO WITNESS HER BROTHER'S DEATH—"

Her mouth went dry. The gods had acted swiftly, punishing her hubris. "There must be a mistake," she said. "A Roman citizen, the son of a senator, can't be treated like a common criminal."

"I'm sorry," Angerona said, tears spilling from her eyes.

"First your father, now my brother—Nero holds himself above the law." Elissa took a breath and willed her heart to beat more slowly. "I've got to hurry."

"You're going to the circus?"

"The emperor requests my presence. Perhaps Nero's forgotten how my family has supported him."

"You can't go unescorted—"

"No?"

"Let's speak to the Vestal Maxima," Angerona said, "request she file a petition and ask your brother's life be spared. Even Nero can't refuse a vestal's intervention on behalf of a prisoner—"

"There's no time. Marcus fights at noon."

"I'll call for the coach—"

"I'll walk. It's faster."

"At least, change your robe. Your hem is stained from pulling weeds."

"I don't want to be recognized."

Angerona thrust white slippers at Elissa. "Your shoes."

"Yes." Elissa slid them on her feet, barely noticed. She had to get to Nero soon, and with no pompous retinue. Digging through her cedar chest, she found her oldest palla. She flung the shawl over her head and wrapped it around her shoulders.

"You look like a beggar," Angerona said.

"Good. No one will notice me."

Elissa ripped open the doorway's curtain. The cubicles where the six virgins slept stood empty, the inhabitants occupied elsewhere with their work—invoking blessings for the sick, copying documents, tending the sacred fire. She glanced at the closed door of the Vestal Maxima's private chambers. At this hour Mother Amelia would be busy contracting wills and legal documents, conferring with dignitaries from the farthest reaches of the empire, downstairs in the library.

Angerona followed at Elissa's heels. "At least take a lictor."

"No bodyguard. I don't want to be recognized."

"You must follow protocol—"

15

Lifting her soiled hem, Elissa hurried down the marble stairway. Sun poured through the open ceiling of the atrium, dancing on the central pool. Serving women, carrying baskets heaped with linen, made their way along the pillared hallway and out into the courtyard where vats of water boiled. Laundry day kept the household busy—and made it easy to escape.

She opened a side door, which lead out to the street.

Angerona stepped in front of her. "You can't go to the Circus Maximus alone—"

"Come with me."

Elissa and Angerona faced each other, their breath mingling, their thoughts transparent. Torn from their families at an early age, bound by vows, they were closer than blood sisters.

Angerona had lost her glow. Her tear-streaked face looked pale as leaden powder. Of course she wouldn't come. For all her bluster and emotion, she possessed a strong instinct for self-preservation. And to confront Nero bordered on insanity.

Elissa brushed a damp curl away from Angerona's forehead. "Don't worry, sweet. Nero loved my brother once. I'll remind him, and you know I can be convincing."

"What shall I tell the Vestal Maxima?"

"Tell her what you want." Elissa's laugh sounded hollow. "Tell her I've accepted Nero's invitation."

She left Angerona gaping and walked briskly toward the forum.

CHAPTER II

On the far side of Palatine Hill, a mile from the House of Vestals, the urban mob squirmed on stone benches at the Circus Maximus. The chariot races had ended and clouds of grit settled on the arena, coating the spectators. Women poured out of the gates leaving men to watch the afternoon's more gruesome entertainment.

Horns squealed and a water organ moaned, announcing the procession of gladiators.

The Retiarii carried tridents and nets; Thracians, square shields and swords; Secutors, oval shields and daggers. Schooled in combat, massive in their builds, gladiators stood a chance for victory. A chance to live.

Not so for Marcus. He would face wild beasts unarmed. A death more shameful than crucifixion.

Beneath the spectator stalls, he waited to be summoned. Grasping the wooden bars, he stared out of his cage and recalled the fate of a prisoner of war from Germania. Destined to fight the lions, the captured soldier had gone to the latrines—a stinking row of holes in a long bench—and, using the stick meant for wiping away excrement, he rammed the salty sponge into his throat.

Beasts or suicide. The only choice.

Out in the amphitheater the crowd stamped their feet, shaking Marcus to his bones. He prayed he wouldn't shit himself.

Wooden tiers towered over the arena and held more than 150,000 people. As noon approached, the spectators devoured goat cheese and barley bread, apples and pickled eggs—while they waited for dessert.

"Answer when you hear your name," the lanista shouted.

Taskmaster of gladiators, the lanista filled his purse by treating men like animals. Society did not respect him, although his barrel of a stomach proved he ate lavishly.

"Marcus Rubrius Honoratus."

"Present."

Marcus slid his hands along the wooden bars, splinters prickling his palms. His back was broad from wrestling, his arms knotted with muscle from lifting lead weights in the gymnasium, but he was no gladiator. His thoughts turned to Socrates. Soon he'd have the chance to test that great philosopher's theory of immortality, to learn firsthand if his soul would perish or cross into the Plain of Oblivion and continue to the River of Forgetfulness.

The lanista unlocked the cage. Tugging Marcus by a leash, he dragged him into the torch-lit hallway and ordered him to kneel. Squaring his shoulders, Marcus reminded himself of the dignity with which Socrates had faced his execution.

"I said, kneel." The lanista cracked his whip, and two brutes forced Marcus to his knees amid steaming camel dung. "Rome has no tolerance for treason."

"Or truth."

The barbed whip scored welts across his back.

Marcus clenched his teeth, refusing to register the pain, searching his mind for words of wisdom. That which destroys and corrupts is evil, Socrates had said. That which preserves and benefits is good.

Above him, in the amphitheater, the crowd roared for blood.

⁂

The sun crept toward noon.

Elissa climbed the road leading from the forum, the soles of her leather slippers slick against the flagstones. Although the temperature was cool and left no doubt that it was autumn, a rivulet of sweat ran down her face. She pushed onward, glancing at the seven hills as she reached the pinnacle. A patchwork of terra-cotta rooftops gave way to parkland girded by six miles of gray tufa blocks. Beyond the Servian wall, golden fields and olive groves offered the promise of freedom. A false promise, Elissa thought—all Romans were slave to Nero.

"Jupiter," she said, tears choking her voice, "Ruler of the heavens, protector of the empire, I beg you to spare my brother's life."

She swiped her eyes, angry with herself for showing weakness. Ten years ago, when she had been wrenched out of her childhood, she'd sworn all her tears were spent. Ten years ago, when she had been nine, a golden coach drawn by four white geldings had arrived at her parents' house. They'd hoisted her into the coach. One doll, her comb and hairbrush—no other belongings.

The Vestal Maxima sat in the coach. Her voice floated from beneath snowy veils, "Are you frightened, child?"

Trembling, tears streaming down her face, Elissa shook her head. Through the coach's window, she saw her parents. Her new position was an honor. She would be rich and powerful, but her parents' faces appeared solemn as if witnessing a funeral.

The wheels of the coach squeaked, began to roll.

Elissa craned her neck in order to keep her brother in her sight. He ran alongside the coach, yelling, "Bring her back!"

"Marcus!" she called out to him, until her throat was raw.

"Drive on," the Vestal Maxima ordered the coachman. "The sooner we depart, the sooner she'll forget."

But Elissa never forgot that day, never forgot crying out to Marcus as he disappeared within a cloud of dust.

Redoubling her pace, she hurried toward the Circus Maximus.

Marcus was no traitor. The idea was preposterous. He had loved Nero, only too well. His fault had been to question the princeps, attempting to steer him away from disaster. Hopes had been high for Nero when at age seventeen he'd come into power. Initially, advisors kept him on an even keel, but now Burris was dead, Seneca banished, Agrippina murdered, and Nero charted his own course.

If only I had prayed more, Elissa thought, perhaps the gods would have protected Marcus. She wondered if her hubris had led to her brother's plight, her questioning of the gods' power—the damning words she'd written. She reached into her stola, seeking the letter, words she must destroy before they wreaked more havoc. As her fingers touched the papyrus, two boys raced around a corner, forcing her into the gutter and a stream of putrid water.

"Look out," one of the boys shouted, without pausing to offer help.

"I hear music." The other motioned for his friend to hurry. "The procession is starting."

They bolted down the hill toward the Circus Maximus.

Stumbling from the flow of waste, Elissa followed. Her slippers, soaked and no longer white, slapped the paving stones.

Down by the river, the air felt humid, smelled of fish. She saw the boys far ahead, skipping, laughing, as if going to a carnival. Gathering her robes, she clomped along the riverbank, sinking in the mud.

The fish market, usually a hub of excitement with boats docking to unload their catch and fishmongers arguing with customers, stood empty. Screeching gulls swooped over abandoned tables.

It seemed as if all of Rome were at the Circus.

Elissa sought a shortcut through an alleyway, wide enough to accommodate only one donkey. A baker had thrown fermenting bran into the gutter where pigs now feasted. A woman, a toddler secured on her hip, stepped onto an overhanging balcony. The boards groaned, threatening to collapse. Hoisting a bucket over the railing, the woman dumped out slops, and the pigs groveled happily in the rain of excrement. The stench stung Elissa's nostrils, burned her eyes. Regretting her decision not to come by coach, she hurried on.

A donkey-cart laden with earthen tiles clattered around the corner, forcing her against a fire-blackened wall. During daylight hours the only carts permitted on Rome's streets were those bearing construction materials—nothing would deter Nero's voracious building plans. The cart rattled through the gutter, splashing filth.

"Watch where you're going," Elissa wanted to shout but, accustomed to the hushed confines of the House of Vestals, her voice came out as a whisper.

She wiped something sticky from her eye.

Spattered with mire, she might have been a common prostitute. She continued past a fire-gutted tenement. Once painted brilliant yellow, the plaster walls were charred and stained with soot. Amidst scrawling graffiti, a poster announced:

GLADIATOR GAMES TODAY

Gathering her skirts, Elissa ran.

❦

The lanista's kick left Marcus gasping.

Blood trickled down his back, the result of the barbed whip. Marcus gritted his teeth, refusing to acknowledge that he suffered, refusing to give Nero that satisfaction. He felt certain his former friend was watching. Even now he felt Nero's gaze.

They had grown up together, raced horses, caroused in taverns, bedded women...known each other. Anguish of the body was nothing compared to Nero's treachery.

The lanista's thugs grabbed Marcus, jerking him onto his feet, forcing him to stand in a small two-wheeled wagon. They tied a plaster mask over his face, bound his back against a plank, fettered his arms and ankles with iron chains.

His legs felt weak, but Marcus steeled himself.

"Still some fight in him." The lanista belched fumes of garlic. "The lions are sure to find the traitor appetizing."

Traitor.

The word stung Marcus more than barbs.

He was guilty, yes, of loving Nero too much. Guilty of trusting him. He'd committed the crime of speaking bluntly, the crime of speaking truth without anticipation of retaliation. What a fool! Was he a traitor to propose a return to the Republic? A traitor to suggest the government reestablish democracy? A hundred years had passed since Julius Caesar had been proclaimed dictator for life, decreed a god—since that time democracy had become a forgotten concept, and the rights of Roman citizens had dwindled.

The wagon rolled through a tunnel that ran beneath the spectator stalls. Spine pinned to the plank and unable to turn his head, Marcus stared through the mask's eyes at his future—the little that remained of it. The wagon hit a rock and the wheels vacillated. A jolt of pain shot through his back. The cart rolled past cage after cage of angry beasts and growling men.

A fellow prisoner begged for mercy, others called his name. The crack of a whip drew an agonizing scream.

The cart bumped around a corner, and sunlight poured through an archway.

Drums rolled and the water organ blared as jugglers and acrobats led the procession into the amphitheater. The archway grew wider, taller, allowing Marcus to see into the arena. The crowd's roar echoed through the tunnel, pounding in his ears.

Acrobats were followed by minor fighters: errant slaves, captured fugitives, young men and even women anxious to prove themselves worthy opponents. Marcus wished he might be one of them. They, at least, carried weapons. They engaged in sport and would die with glory. But he, armed only with a length of rope, would face a half-starved lion.

The crowd's shouting made thinking impossible. It grew in intensity, filling up the tunnel, drowning all other sound, flooding Marcus like a tidal wave as the gladiators entered the arena. Not long ago he would have led their cheers, rising to his feet, climbing onto his bench, shouting slogans as confetti showered the arena. Gladiators were heroes, heroes to whom Nero awarded palaces and treasure—men who had faced death and survived. They rivaled gods.

The cart moved forward into the arena's blinding light.

Last in the procession were the criminals. Something hard hit Marcus in the chest and exploded with the stink of sulfur. That rotten egg was followed by fish heads, apples, anything the crowd could hurl. His wagon paraded around the arena, wheels sinking in the sand. Where were the philosophers? The artists and intellectuals? Through squinting eyes Marcus peered from his mask, and saw only a bloodthirsty mob. Had justice and democracy become foreign concepts?

The procession came to a halt before the imperial box, a tiny jewel of a palace overlooking the arena. Marcus scanned the balcony, but saw no sign of Nero. The princeps preferred to watch the games, unobserved, from within his private chambers. Through a peephole. How many times had they sat side-by-side, the best of friends, watching together?

"Show yourself," Marcus shouted.

But Nero was too cowardly to face his former lover.

Crimson pennants gashed the sky, announcing the festivities at the Circus Maximus. Elissa held her palla over her nose to stem the stench of the latrines—although, after her tramp through the slums, she didn't smell much better.

Outside the arena, merchants hawked their pickled fish and sacks of olives, figurines of gods and goddesses, colored flags for spectators to wave in support of their favorite chariot team. Marcus favored the greens. Elissa elbowed her way through the crowd, unused to the press of humanity, the heat of bodies, the stink of the mob as people shoved and pulled.

An old woman, a figurine of Venus clutched against her concave chest, smacked into her. From beneath her tattered palla, rheumy eyes peered into Elissa's.

"Rome burns," the woman said, clawing at Elissa's hand, "and from union unholy the sister will bring forth a son."

"Thief!" A merchant stormed from his stall.

Before he could stop the old woman, she slipped into the crowd.

The merchant shook his fist and cursed.

"Let an old woman have her Venus," Elissa said, attempting to calm him.

Reaching beneath her palla, she found her money pouch and came up with a silver denarius—ten times the statue's worth.

The merchant pocketed the coin, eyeing Elissa with suspicion.

She hurried toward the amphitheater. Weaving through the crowd, she thought of the old woman—her deranged eyes, her mutterings. Somehow she seemed familiar. At last, Elissa reached the entryway at the far end of the oblong arena opposite the starting gates.

"No women allowed." A guard blocked her entry.

Shifting her palla, Elissa revealed her medallion inscribed with the insignia of Vesta. Unlike other women, vestal virgins were privileged to watch the gladiators and had a designated box just below the emperor's. The guard studied her medallion, glanced at her ragged clothing. Before he could object, she dropped a coin into his palm.

The procession of gladiators had finished, and the arena had been cleared. Workers set the stage for a wild beast hunt—dragging potted palms onto the sand, erecting backdrops of painted jungle scenes on the central spina. Cages carrying lions, bears, and strange striped cats, rolled through the archways. A trench, ten feet wide, ten feet deep, and filled with stagnant water, separated Elissa from the spectacle. Flies buzzed above the moat, indifferent to the scummy water. Midway along the tiers of benches, Elissa spotted her destination: the imperial box.

Her step faltered.

Facing Nero might not be the wisest of decisions, especially without protection. To secure the throne he had poisoned his half-brother, murdered his mother. What would stop him from harming her? Seeking clemency for Marcus might only whet his appetite for cruelty. But within the arena, lions stalked the blood-soaked sand, reminding Elissa why she'd come.

Wooden steps descended to a torch-lit corridor beneath the spectator stalls. Young toughs huddled in the tunnel, inscribing fresh graffiti on the walls, jeering at Elissa as she passed. She hurried through the corridor. Even October's chill could not suppress the smell of unwashed bodies, stale wine and urine. She emerged from the tunnel blinking at the sun amid thousands of people.

"I place my money on Marcus," she heard someone say.

"I'll wager on the lion."

Two grubby men sat on a stone bench in a nearby stall. The uglier winked at her.

She hurried toward the imperial box.

Praetorian Guards in dress uniform stood at the foot of a marble stairway, breastplates gleaming over short red tunics, heads crowned with tufted helmets.

A gangly guard, a member of Nero's private army, stood in Elissa's path. Peering up at him, she said, "Don't you recognize me, Celsus?"

She knew the guard from prior visits, and she had invoked blessings for his family, casting spells for his sick child. But today, dressed in rough cloth instead of white robes, Celsus failed to recognize her.

"How is your little boy?" she asked. "Has Crispus fully recovered from the fever?"

"Priestess Elissa Rubria." The guard's face flushed, and he bowed with the reverence due a vestal. "Please, forgive me. Crispus is much improved. I thank you for your prayers. Of course you may pass."

Elissa hurried up the steps, aware that running was improper for a vestal virgin, but there was no time for propriety.

She glanced around the balcony, hoping to see Nero.

Esteemed guests of the princeps sat on ivory curule chairs, their bottoms resting in curved seats, preparing to watch the games in shaded comfort from under a midnight-blue canopy embroidered with silver stars. Tables, laden with bowls of purple grapes and figs, platters of all kinds of breads and ripened cheeses, ran along the perimeter. The scent of spiced meat, cooking on an open flame, wafted toward Elissa. Guests sipped wine from gilded chalices, while flute-girls played. A concubine wandered toward Elissa, trailing silk and jasmine perfume.

"Have you seen Nero?" Elissa asked.

The concubine smiled, eyes dreamy with opium, and nodded toward Ofonius Tigellinus.

Nero's constant watchdog looked up from his plate of food as Elissa approached. He sat by the stairway which led down to the imperial chambers. The horsehair crest of his helmet, dyed red as blood, and his scarlet toga, denoted his position as Prefect of the Praetorian Guard, Nero's personal assassin. Though weapons weren't allowed in Rome, Elissa knew within his robes Tigellinus carried a dagger.

"Elissa Rubria Honoria," he said, a sausage poised at his teeth. "What brings you here?"

As if he didn't know.

"Where can I find Nero?"

"I haven't seen you at the Circus since the Ludi Romani." Tigellinus bit into the sausage, squirting fat.

The Ludi Romani. Fifteen days of brutal games culminating in near riot when Nero showered the stalls with rubies and pearls, laughing as spectators crushed each other in their scramble for the gems.

"The princeps sent for me," she said.

"Hungry?" Tigellinus wolfed another bite.

"Tell me where he is."

Using the battered knuckles of his hand, a hand that had killed scores of men, Tigellinus wiped grease from his mouth. A purplish scar cut through his upper lip and gave him the appearance of a snarling dog. He glanced toward a narrow stairway that led down to Nero's private quarters.

"He's busy."

The concubine giggled.

Tigellinus stuffed the remainder of the sausage into his mouth.

Attempting to calm her voice, Elissa said, "The princeps requested my presence. Would you defy his wishes?"

Tigellinus shot her an angry glance, threw his plate against a wall and clambered down the steps.

Elissa gazed back at the arena, wondering how much time she had before the games commenced.

The sound of heavy footsteps announced the return of Tigellinus.

"The princeps will see you shortly—"

Pushing past him, Elissa hurried down the stairway. She found herself in a small, circular hall. No guests. No guards. Nero's private sanctuary. An oil lamp smoldered on a granite table. Carved doors surrounded her, closed and heavy. One door stood ajar. Nero's laugh boomed out from it, ricocheted around the walls.

CHAPTER III

Gallus Justinus had no intention of accepting Nero's invitation to attend the games. As a soldier in Britannia, he'd had his fill of war and had lost his taste for violence. Lost his taste for Nero's atrocities. With every passing year his childhood friend grew more perverse.

Within the courtyard of his domus, Justinus examined his apple trees. He breathed in the aroma of ripened fruit, sweet and heavy, the scent of encroaching winter. Shorter days. Long, lonely nights.

"A visitor has come," Akeem announced.

The slave stood, shivering, in the doorway leading to the house. He peered into the courtyard, unwilling to step outside. Akeem came from the warmer clime of Alexandria and bore the haughtiness of an Egyptian prince.

"Master, come inside," he said, his Latin immaculate. "Attending to horticulture is no fitting pastime for a hero—"

"I think these trees have mites." Bending a branch, Justinus searched the leaves. "I see their evidence."

"Those gardeners don't do their job. I will summon them again."

"Who's my visitor, Akeem?"

"That troublemaker, Lucan, back from Greece. The one who calls himself a poet. I will send him on his way."

"Too late!" Lucan's thunderous voice was followed by a boom of laughter. His frame filled the doorway. Before Akeem could stop him, he barreled through the threshold. Three strides brought him halfway across the courtyard. With a grip worthy of a bear, he clasped Justinus. "Dear friend, how are you?"

"Better, now that you've turned up."

"Like weighted dice, you can count on me."

The poet's laughter was infectious.

The two men clamped each other in a hug, and for the first time since his return from Britannia, Justinus felt at home.

"Have you grown taller?" he asked as he broke away from Lucan. Justinus wasn't short by any measure, but he felt dwarfed beside the poet.

"Maybe broader." Lucan patted his stomach. "Greek wine acts as fertilizer. Golden piss they call it, but its taste never slowed my drinking."

Akeem sniffed.

"When it came to women," Lucan said, "I found Athens dry. No wonder the Greeks favor boys." He winked at Akeem, and the slave left in a huff. "They let their women wither on the vine, keep them locked away like vestal virgins."

Justinus turned away from Lucan, forcing himself to think of other topics. He ran his hand over the trunk of a tree and wondered if the soil might benefit from ground fish bones. "It's a good year for apples," he said. "Despite a few mites, the crop has been abundant."

"You still have feelings for her, don't you?"

"Feelings?"

"For Elissa."

Justinus gazed through the branches at the cool October sun. Past noon. And what had he accomplished? Today or in his life? Not much. Death and destruction was his trade. And what use was a warrior who despised violence? The one person he trusted, the one person who truly understood him was Elissa.

"I have feelings. Yes."

A breeze rustled the apples trees. Justinus kicked at a fallen leaf.

"How long have you been back in Rome?" Lucan asked.

"Six months."

"How fares the Druid Queen?"

"Boudicca died three years ago in battle. As fierce a warrior as any man I've ever fought. I can still see her, driving her chariot, red hair streaming to her knees, as she led blue-faced men, shrieking women, even children into war. 'Justice,' she called out as she faced her death. 'My people fight for justice.'"

"As should all of us," Lucan said. "These days Rome is short of justice."

"Nero takes too much pleasure in the role of king."

"The role of tyrant, you mean."

The two friends stood side-by-side, watching leaves swirl to the ground. A nightingale trilled its melancholy song, long past mating season.

"I feel old," Justinus said.

"Don't be absurd, we're twenty-four and in our prime."

"I couldn't stop my men. It was a blood-bath, not a battle." In his mind's-eye Justinus still heard the battle cries, still smelled the stench of death. "When the Britons advanced, our infantry charged. So did the cavalry. Our lances spared no lives. No women. No children. Not even animals."

"Another glorious victory for Rome," Lucan said.

"I wish I could take back that day—"

"Time heals, they say."

"Does it?"

Lucan laughed.

"According to Horace," Justinus said, "the perfect meal begins with eggs and ends with apples. Green or red?"

"Who am I to disagree with that illustrious poet? I'll take red."

"My father planted these trees years ago."

Each tree stood twenty paces from the other and lined the courtyard's perimeter. Now they formed a canopy of green tinged with yellow. Justinus reached for a branch laden with fruit, winced when the old war wound twitched his back.

Lucan had no need to stretch. With ease, he plucked two apples and handed one to Justinus.

"Forget her."

"I can't."

"Find another girl. Marry. Raise a family."

Justinus rubbed his thumb over the apple. Smooth skinned without blemish. Perfect. The result of his devotion. In theory, Lucan spoke the truth. But how could he forget Elissa? She was honest, pure, and infinitely good. No other woman met her measure. Only work that had some meaning might drive her from his mind, his heart. But these past months he'd found little in Rome to occupy an Equestrian, a knight of the empire. He had no use for politics. Since the fall of the Republic the senate served only as a mouthpiece. And he wanted no part of Nero's tyranny.

"What will you do, now that you're back?" he asked Lucan.

"Nero has appointed me quaestor."

"A great honor for one our age."

"He wants me close, so he can keep his fingers in the treasury."

"Not as close as your uncle, Seneca, I hope."

"I plan to keep my distance," Lucan said. "Nero has the habit of killing off his intimates. What of you, Justinus? Will you seek a civil appointment? Overseer of the Roads? Master of the Aqueducts?"

"My father left me extensive properties—apartment buildings, store fronts, farmland beyond the city walls—without tremendous effort, I live quite comfortably. But if I had my choice I'd be tilling fields."

Justinus bit into his apple.

"A man needs something to believe in," Lucan said.

Justinus took another bite and chewed. "I've met a philosopher named Paul. He speaks of a kinder world, a world ruled by compassion."

"What world is that?"

"Paul says a man's soul is his greatest possession, that a single soul holds more value than a treasury of gold. He follows The Way of Jesus of Nazareth."

"Jesus of Nazareth!" Lucan spat chunks of apple. "Don't tell me you've taken up with wayward Jews."

Akeem appeared at the entryway.

"Another visitor," he said. "Someone important." He glanced at Lucan, his dark eyes flashing with disdain. "A vestal virgin."

"Which one?" Justinus asked, his heart quickening.

"Priestess Angerona. She requests to see you—privately."

Justinus failed to suppress his disappointment. "What does she want?"

"The priestess claims it's urgent."

A visit from a vestal virgin had to be a matter of importance, but Angerona had been known to overstep her bounds. She flaunted her body, pursuing men as if she were a prostitute. So unlike Elissa. Elissa, Justinus felt certain, never entertained a lustful thought.

Lucan slapped him on the back. "Perhaps I'll see you later at the baths. This evening I'm going to the theater with some friends. You're welcome to—"

"Priestess Angerona waits for you," Akeem said.

"I'm leaving, but I'll soon return." Lucan grinned at Akeem, and the slave made a sour face. Ducking through the doorway, Lucan left.

"Akeem," Justinus said, "must I remind you to treat your betters with respect?"

Akeem pursed his lips.

Justinus tossed the half-eaten apple against a wall. The core bounced along the peristyle, struck a bright blue pillar, and settled on the tiled walkway.

Akeem sniffed, loudly.

"Are you ill?" Justinus asked.

"I'll tell Priestess Angerona you will see her now."

Justinus sucked juice from his fingers, but felt no pleasure at its taste.

For years, Angerona had set her sight on Elissa's brother, hunting Marcus whenever she had a chance: dinners of state, imperial games, even public rituals. At every turn, Marcus shunned her. Finally she'd given up, but not without a fight. And, recently, she'd taken aim at a new target.

"Gallus Justinus." Her voice carried through the courtyard, too loud for a any proper Roman matron. "It's impolite to keep a woman waiting."

"Since when do vestal virgins visit men alone?"

"This is a dire circumstance."

He tried not to notice how her hips swayed as she walked. Burnished curls, the color of chestnuts, escaped her suffibulum

31

and the scent of perfume, seductive and no doubt expensive, preceded her.

"Bring wine and folding chairs," he said, snapping his fingers at Akeem.

"We have no time for niceties." She stood closer than appropriate, her breasts teasing Justinus. Lowering her voice, she said, "Marcus Rubrius has been arrested."

"For what?"

"For being a traitor. No trial. Nero has condemned him to be a gladiator."

"Has Nero lost his senses?"

"Marcus may be wrestling lions as we speak."

Justinus felt the blood drain from his face. He'd known Marcus all his life, thought of him as a brother. "Did you have something to do with this?"

"Of course not. I care about Marcus—though he insulted me. Some might think I have good reason to be angry."

"I've heard rumors about you—"

"Lies! I would never harm Marcus."

Tears threatened Angerona's eyes, but Justinus doubted their validity. Rumors claimed she played two sides and relayed information to Nero.

"How is Elissa taking this?" he asked.

"Elissa, of course," Angerona said, her voice harsh and all trace of tears vanishing. "It's always about her."

"Is she all right?"

"You know how stubborn she can be, how irrational. I warned her not to go to the circus, but did she listen? No! "

"She went to the circus?"

"By herself to speak to Nero. The Vestal Maxima sent me after her, and I've come for your help. I brought a lictor and the coach."

"We must leave at once."

Justinus knew too well the games Nero liked to play, especially with innocents.

CHAPTER IV

E lissa moved toward the open door, peered into the chamber. Light fell through a high window, illuminating the jewel tone colors of a Persian carpet, one of many strewn across the alabaster floor. Along muraled walls, slaves stood in attendance, their eyes widening at her appearance. At the far end of the chamber Nero reclined on a couch, his curls buoyed by silk cushions, his robe bunched around his gut. He grimaced.

Whether in pleasure or pain, Elissa wasn't certain.

A concubine knelt before him, yellow hair streaming over Nero's lap.

Elissa stood, overcome by shock, rooted by curiosity. Of course, she had seen paintings, heard whispered tales of lust, but her imagination had not come close—

Nero glanced at her, and tried to sit. The concubine's head bobbed frantically and Nero fell back on his cushions. "I told Tigellinus not yet."

"I've come about my brother."

Nero cuffed the concubine. "Hurry up and finish."

The concubine complied and Nero gasped.

The head of yellow curls turned toward Elissa. A grin split the bearded face.

Eyes wide, Elissa backed toward the door.

"No need to leave." Amusement played on Nero's face. "Corrupting a vestal virgin, whatever would my mother say? Thank Jupiter she's dead."

"Rome is better off without Agrippina," the whore said.

Nero slapped the concubine, and he yelped. "Now, fetch my robe like a good bitch."

The whore jumped to his feet and retrieved the garment.

"Excuse me, Priestess Elissa," Nero said. "I wasn't expecting you just yet." He draped himself in shimmering brocade and cocked an eyebrow. "Elisssaaah," he said, opening his mouth so wide she stared into the cavity. "Your name is most unusual. Phoenician, I believe."

"I took the name of my great-grandmother. She came from Athens."

"A daughter of Apollo. How divine." Nero resettled on the couch and two slaves fluffed the cushions behind his neck. "Your name refers to Elysium, dwelling place of happy souls. Are you a happy soul, Elissa?"

"I want you to pardon my brother."

"The traitor?"

"After all my family has done for you—"

"Nothing lately."

"—you treat my brother like a common criminal."

The whore poured rose-scented oil into his palms, reached for Nero's foot.

"Not now." Nero kicked him.

Elissa wanted to escape, but forced herself to forge ahead. "By my authority as a vestal virgin," she said, "I demand that you—"

"Demand?"

Nero squinted at her through the emerald monocle he wore around his neck, a polished stone as large as an apricot. He sniffed and made a face.

"What's that unpleasant smell?"

"I came by foot. A wagon splashed—"

"Douse yourself." He tossed the flask of scented oil to her. "How old are you, Elissa? Nineteen, maybe twenty? Vestals are known for their perfection, but your nose is too long, your eyes too wide, your lips too narrow, and your complexion freckled."

"From working in the garden."

"I've watched you. My palace affords me a fine view of the House of Vestals, of the courtyard and the gardens."

"I'd better go."

"What of your dear brother? Forgotten already?"

The question stopped her.

Nero crooked his finger. "Come closer." She took a step toward him. "Open your mouth."

"Why?"

"Because I tell you to."

She clamped her lips shut.

"You're a she-wolf like my mother. Like her, you bear the double fangs—the mark of Fortuna."

"You flatter me."

She-wolf was another name for whore. Elissa ran her tongue over her gums and felt the deformity, the sharp point of a second incisor above her right canine. The tooth was an embarrassment. More so, the comparison to Agrippina. In order to gain power, Nero's mother had bedded scores of men including her brother, Caligula. Many of the men she coupled with died suspiciously. Her second husband lived only long enough to change his will in Agrippina's favor; the third—her doddering uncle, Claudius—died swiftly after naming Nero heir to the empire.

"Women should be savored like fine wine," Nero said. "I prefer full-bodied red to insipid white. My mother was dark and spicy, begging to be drunk. Like you."

He grabbed Elissa's wrist.

"Remove your hand," she said.

"Forbidden fruit is so enticing."

"Remove it."

"Rules are made for commoners. That's what Uncle Gaius always said."

Before wise men murdered him. If Nero considered Gaius Caligula a fine example of a princeps, Rome was headed for disaster.

Nero tightened his grip and Elissa flinched. He drew her down onto the couch, so close to him that she could taste the mint leaves on his breath.

"What is the life of Marcus worth?" he said.

"Let me go or I'll report you to—"

35

"Is that a threat?"

"No man may touch a vestal."

"No mortal man." Nero snapped his fingers at the whore. "Tell Tigellinus to call off the lions. Tell him I will spare Marcus Rubrius from fighting, in honor of his sister. Go now, all of you."

The whore and the slaves backed out of the room.

"Thank you, Caesar," Elissa said. Worry lifted from her heart. She wanted to dance, to shout.

Nero pulled her back onto the cushions. "Not you, Elissa."

"My brother—"

"Is tiresome. But everyone has their price." Nero plucked a fig from a bowl of fruit, shoved it in his mouth.

Elissa thought of a stuffed pig, imagined Nero, plump and pink, roasting on a spit. She said, "Your clemency is legend, Caesar."

"You put me in a quandary Elissa. Lately, I've been puzzling, what does it mean for a vestal virgin to be sacrosanct? I concede vestals must remain pure in order to uphold the purity of the sacred fire for the good of the empire. They must be held in reverence, untouched by any man, but surely not untouched by gods."

He selected a plum. His fingers—elegantly manicured, more like a woman's than a man's—pressed the fruit between her lips.

She spat it on the floor.

"Don't care for plums?" Nero sighed. "I find it close in here, don't you? Allow me to remove this rag." He pushed aside her palla, exposing her hair. "Your best feature. Blacker than obsidian."

Gooseflesh rose along Elissa's arms as he drew the palla from her shoulders, allowing the shawl to slip onto the floor. Within the bodice of her stola, she felt the page of the letter, felt the heat of her words. It gave her strength to know she'd written the truth— words only a friend would understand.

Nero loosened the fillet of white ribbons that held her curls in place.

"You no longer wear the shorn locks of a novice."

"I'm fully consecrated."

He lifted her chin.

She gazed into his face—eyes cold as the winter sea, lips well-formed yet cruel. If not for his petulant expression, he might be handsome.

"I take after my father," he said. "Bronze curls, gray eyes, a classic nose."

"I notice the resemblance." Elissa couldn't help but smile.

Dometius had been a swindler and a cheat. Once, when driving his coach through a sleepy village, he'd whipped up his horses and trampled a small boy for sport. Upon seeing his newborn son, Dometius had stated that, like him, Nero was destined to be loathsome.

"You find me amusing?" Nero asked.

"Not in the least."

"You lack humility."

"That makes two of us."

"Did the Vestal Maxima grant you permission to visit me alone?"

"I came at your request."

"You came because you wanted to."

His stare unsettled her.

"You're shivering." He handed her the palla.

She wrapped the shawl around her shoulders, drew the wool over her head. "I must go."

"Not yet."

Nero poured wine into a chalice, added water and a pearl. He handed her the cup. "Seawater lends the tang of salt, the pearl a hint of mystery. Did you really believe I'd throw your brother to the beasts? My dearest friend."

She sipped the blood-red liquid, imagining the lions, torn from their home in Africa, starving as they paced their cells. The wine tasted brackish.

"Does your brother plan to have me assassinated?"

Nearly choking on the wine, Elissa sputtered, "No."

"Perhaps I have been misinformed."

Nero headed for the door.

"Where are you going?"

"To see your brother." Nero's mouth twisted in a smile. His eyes cut through her like a blade. "Please join me."

Elissa peeked through curtains, into the arena. Nero stood beside her, observing the spectacle through the green twilight of his monocle.

The door opened behind them. Hoping to see Marcus, Elissa turned.

Tigellinus entered. A snarl tugged at his upper lip, distorting the scar.

"Is my brother coming?"

"Soon."

Elissa gazed through the window. Slaves were dragging firewood across the sand. They lay down kindling, crisscrossing branches, stacking logs to build a pyre.

Mimes circled the arena, holding up placards:

THE DEATH OF HERCULES

"A play is to be performed?" Elissa glanced at Nero.

He nodded. "A reenactment. I'm sure it will prove amusing."

"I adore theater."

"Excellent. I offer this performance as a gift to you. It will be memorable, I promise." Nero ran his fingers through his waves of hair. The signet ring that had once belonged to Julius Caesar glistened on his hand. "Tigellinus," he said, "Is everything in order?"

The prefect gave a thumbs-up sign.

The clash of cymbals, followed by a drum-roll, announced the beginning of the theatrical. Elissa parted the curtains to gain a better view. Armed guards led an elephant across the sand, the largest animal she'd ever seen. When they reached the imperial box, they paused.

"The pachyderm represents Nessus the centaur," Nero said. "I chose the beast myself. See how the tusks are serrated and filed to points? I think it will provide more drama than a common horse. Don't you agree Elissa?"

"The poor beast seems docile."

"Not for long."

Elissa glanced at Nero then the elephant. With one thrust those tusks could gore a man, and the trunk might fling him to his death. The armored guards encircled the beast, goading it with javelins, scorching its hide with glowing irons. The elephant stamped its mammoth feet and kicked up dust. With a battle-cry, the men raised their javelins and let them sail.

The great beast reared and bellowed.

Elissa turned her face away and said, "This is horrible."

"You're missing the best part." Nero grabbed her chin, forcing her to look at the arena. A man, wearing only a loincloth, was being rolled around the arena in a small two-wheeled cart, his back strapped to a plank, his arms and legs fettered with iron chains.

From the front row to the bleachers the mob stamped their feet and yelled, "Hercules! Hercules! Hercules!"

Aristocrats, seated closest to the action, leaned forward on their padded benches. A well known Equestrian stumbled toward the railing, teetered over, and splashed into the moat. Arms thrashing, he showered onlookers with muck. Others, equally as drunk, dove in after him.

The prisoner rolled toward the Imperial box and the cart stopped. A mask depicting Hercules hid his face, yet he seemed familiar. His build, the tilt of his head, the flaxen curls—the same color as Flavia's.

"Bastard!" Elissa turned to Nero, raised her hand to slap his face.

He caught her wrist and wrenched her arm behind her back. She tried to scream, but he clamped his hand over her mouth. Tigellinus closed the curtain so there would be no witnesses.

"Your brother is a natural." Nero pulled Elissa's arm until she winced. "And I've saved a special role for you: Deianira—the wife of Hercules who kills her husband by mistake. I'm sure you'll play her to perfection."

He nodded at Tigellinus and he retrieved a gilded box. The prefect lifted the lid.

A garment lay inside, a shirt of linen.

"Designed by Locusta," Nero said.

Elissa felt sick.

Locusta was a sorceress, notorious for lethal recipes. Stews seasoned with Fool's Parsley, rabbits that had feasted on Belladonna, sweet Physic nuts from Africa that left a deadly aftertaste.

Elissa shook her head, trying to free herself from Nero. She couldn't talk, could barely breathe.

"As Deianira," Nero said, "you will present this robe to your beloved Hercules."

Elissa bit Nero's palm until she tasted salt.

"Bitch! The she-wolf's bitten me."

Elissa ran for door. Before she reached it, Tigellinus had drawn his dagger.

"No need for violence," Nero said, "just yet." He sucked his wounded palm. "You will cooperate, Elissa Rubria Honoria, or I'll eat your whole family for dinner starting with your little sister."

"Flavia is just a child."

"Your choice. Play the part or sacrifice your sister. Either way your brother dies."

CHAPTER V

The lanista undid the fetters, and iron clattered to the ground. Legs numb from the bindings, Marcus stumbled from the cart.

Through the slits of his mask he saw a behemoth, tusks sharpened to deadly points and serrated, so they might saw a man in half. Fear shot through his legs, making it difficult to stand.

The lanista thrust a length of rope at him, handed him a dagger, and said, "Here you go, Hercules."

The rope was no longer than a forearm and, against an elephant's hide, the dagger would do no more damage than a needle. Goaded by hot irons, the beast raised its trunk and trumpeted. The blast sent Marcus reeling back. The elephant raised its tree-stump of a foot, and Marcus imagined his skull splintering beneath the weight.

He thanked the gods that his family wasn't present to witness his desecration. The arrest and sentencing had happened so quickly, he wondered if they even knew.

The elephant lowered its tusks, preparing to charge. The serrated ivory, glistening in the sunlight, made the snap of a shark's jaws seem inviting.

Marcus ripped off his mask, prepared to meet his executioner. In one hand he gripped the rope, in the other the dagger.

The elephant raised its head, stopped pawing the sand and stood still, calmly regarding Marcus—its eyes surprisingly intelligent. Marcus could have sworn that he saw tears. He let the rope slip from his hand.

"Coward," the lanista called from a safe distance. "Hercules stood up to Nessus."

"I refuse to fight."

"I'll show you how it's done."

Armed with a branding iron and a shield, the lanista charged.

Marcus lunged at him, his dagger aimed for the lanista's chest. But the shield deflected him. The dagger flew into the air and landed somewhere in the sand.

The lanista jabbed the poker at the elephant, searing the beast's underbelly.

The elephant roared. Its trunk, swinging wildly, knocked the iron from the lanista's hand. The trunk swung again, slamming the lanista to the ground. The trunk snaked around his body, picked him up as if he were a sack of barley, and raised him high into the air. A stain bloomed down the front of lanista's tunic as he swung back and forth, screaming for help. The crowd cheered as he plummeted.

"Kill the beast," he called out in a rasping voice.

The elephant lowered its tusks, eyes focused on its enemy.

The lanista stumbled to his feet, sandals slipping in the sand as he staggered toward the moat, his face a mask of terror. Before he reached the water, a tusk ripped through his gut and his screams shot through the amphitheater.

The crowd pushed and shoved, scrambling over benches, surging toward the moat, to gain a better view.

With a fling of its massive head, the elephant tossed the lanista as if he were a broken doll. He somersaulted toward the moat, clawing at the air, shrieking as he crashed into the water. His shrieking stopped, but now the mob was screaming. The corpse floated to the surface, pink foam bubbling from the gash.

Gladiators fell upon the elephant, stabbing it with javelins, hacking at its hide with swords.

Marcus looked around the arena, saw his fellow countrymen, the cream of the empire, shouting, cheering, reveling in the bath of blood. His gaze fell on a boy who sat beside his father, eating honey cake. Their eyes met—the boy's expression mildly curious as if viewing a puppet show. Popping the last bite of cake into his mouth, he licked his fingers.

Through a haze of dusty sand, Marcus stumbled toward the exit. If he could make it to the archway, make it to the corridor that ran beneath the stalls, the dim light of the passageway might serve as protection.

A hand clamped his shoulder.

"Your performance isn't over yet."

Tigellinus dragged him back to the arena.

A girl ran toward him, her hair in disarray, her face distraught. "Elissa?"

His sister always had more bravery than sense. This past year she'd become a woman, the type to turn men's heads. Until that moment Marcus had managed to feign courage, but now his voice faltered, "You shouldn't be here."

"I had to come." Her eyes darted toward Tigellinus. He grasped Marcus by the shoulder, in the other hand he held a gilded box.

"And our parents?"

"I don't think they know."

Tigellinus forced the box into Elissa's hands. "Give Hercules his gift."

She let the box fall to the sand, and Marcus stooped to pick it up.

"Don't touch it," Elissa said.

"What is it?"

Tigellinus handed the box to Marcus. Crafted of bronze and painted with gold leaf, the box felt leaden.

"A gift from the emperor," Tigellinus said. "Open it, if your care for your family."

Marcus lifted the lid, expecting a nest of vipers. "It's a robe." The tunic was made of the finest linen, pale as moonlight. A robe fit for a hero.

"The robe of Hercules," Tigellinus said.

Marcus knew the story well. His eyes met Elissa's. "And you're to play Deianira."

"Don't put it on, I beg you."

"And risk our family?" Marcus saw despair in his sister's eyes, and knew no way to comfort her. "It's a gift from Nero, self-declared god of Rome. We mortals don't possess the power to change the storyline, Elissa."

"It's my fault. I could have stopped him. I could have given myself—"

Marcus touched his sister's lips. "Save that for the one you love." Her face blanched. "Your heart shines in your eyes, little sister. There are few people I trust, but you are one, and Justinus another. Now let's see how this story ends."

He lifted the tunic from the box, displaying the robe so even spectators on the highest benches could see its splendor. The people looked like colored dots set against the sky—so small, so insignificant, in the grand scheme of things. Blood rushed through his arms as he raised the robe over his head, turning slowly in a circle, taking in the whole arena. The sun warmed his back, and heat flooded his body, transforming him, just for this moment, into a hero.

"Hercules," the mob shouted. "Hercules! Hercules!"

Ignoring his sister's protests, Marcus drew the robe over his head. It fit to perfection. The fabric, smooth and silken, embraced his skin. He felt a prickling sensation, and then a sting. As poison seeped into his pores, the people in the bleachers blurred. A drilling noise shot through his ears and shards of light split his vision. Better to stare directly at the sun, even at the cost of being blinded, than remain shrouded in lies. "I'm paying for the privilege of speaking truth," he tried to shout, even as his throat was closing.

The crowd yelled and stamped their feet, standing on the benches, climbing on each others' shoulders. The world spun crazily, a swirling collage of color, a cacophony of sound. Marcus stumbled.

Elissa reached for him, but Tigellinus lowered his sword separating her from her brother. "For the gods' sake," she shouted, "for the sake of our parents, take off the robe."

Sweat poured down her brother's face and his eyes shined unnaturally. She stood by helplessly as the heat from his body warmed the fabric, releasing Locusta's venom. His face deepened to scarlet. Welts erupted on his arms and legs, pustules the size of grapes. With a moan, he fell to his knees. Scooping up sand, he rubbed the grit against his skin until the sores oozed blood.

Risking the sword of Tigellinus, Elissa lunged at Marcus. She clawed the robe tearing fabric from her brother's body, but the cloth adhered to his skin and came away with strips of flesh.

"Hercules," the crowd roared. "Hercules! Hercules!"

"Call for a physician," she yelled at Tigellinus. "There must be an antidote."

Marcus lifted his face toward the sun, his pupils dilated, bile gurgling from his lips. He clutched his throat, his body trembling, digging his fingernails into his skin—scratching, ripping.

"Lean on me," Elissa said, gathering him into her arms.

"I'm cold," he whispered as he fell against her warmth, curling into a fetal position.

She wrapped him in her palla, rocked him like a child.

The mob's chant grew deafening.

"Let him go," Tigellinus said, his voice almost gentle. "Your brother dies a hero."

Guards entered the arena, carrying a bier.

Elissa held onto Marcus as they lifted him, but finally she had to let him go. He no longer struggled. The guards set the bier on their shoulders and carried him toward the center of arena where the pyre waited. Carefully, they climbed the scaffolding. Ten feet above the ground, they placed Marcus on the pyre, upright so the crowd could watch him burn.

"A torch," Tigellinus ordered.

The amphitheater grew quiet.

Elissa raised her arms to speak, all eyes focused on her—a woman in a filthy robe, an unknown actor who played the part of Deianira so convincingly. She shouted, "I, Elissa Rubria Honoria, vestal virgin, priestess of the sacred flame—"

A rumbling sound ran through the mob.

"—declare my brother, Marcus, is not a traitor. He planned to restore the Republic, put an end to tyranny, injustice—" Her voice broke with a sob.

"I know Marcus," someone shouted from the crowd. "He's a man of learning."

"A man of honor," called another.

"A hero."

"Hercules!"

"Marcus Rubrius Honoratus! Marcus Rubrius Honoratus!" the crowd chanted—a conclamatio as at a proper funeral.

Drums rolled and trumpets blasted, and all eyes turned to the imperial box.

Nero stood on the balcony, resplendent in spangled robes. Crowned by a golden diadem, he looked like a god. He raised his hand, and the chanting ceased.

"Marcus Rubrius Honoratus has been found guilty of treason," Nero said, in the booming voice of a trained actor. "He plotted to assassinate me, Princeps of The Roman Empire. Those who would have him live are traitors to the state."

"My brother is innocent!" Elissa's protests were drowned by booing. How easily the mob turned.

"Shall the traitor live or die?" Nero gave the death sign, and the mob mimicked him. "The vote of the people stands."

With a torch, Tigellinus ignited the pyre.

Wind raced across the arena, acting as a bellows. Elissa's screams were swallowed by the roar of the crowd, the roar of flames, her brother's howls. She couldn't watch. She listened to the crack of fire, fed by her brother's bones, fueled by Nero. The princeps stood above crowd, watching from his balcony.

A gust of wind sent sparks swirling toward the indifferent heavens. If Marcus could be murdered, the gods were powerless. And if the gods were powerless, who would mete out justice?

"Pay to the dead what to the dead is due," Elissa said aloud.

And vengeance was due Marcus.

She moved toward the inferno, heat scalding her eyes, singeing her hair. Had not the gods appointed her a vestal virgin—keeper of the sacred flame, symbol of Rome's purity? If the gods refused to act, she would.

She smeared her face with sand and ash.

Nero must receive retribution, and she would deliver it.

CHAPTER VI

Justinus charged through the imperial box, prepared to challenge anyone. Ignoring the harlot who batted bleary eyes at him, pushing past the emperor's guests, he headed for the stairway leading down to Nero's lair. Angerona hurried after him, tripping on her robes.

Tigellinus blocked the stairs, arms folded across his chest, his expression begging for a fight. He disgusted Justinus. He was no true Equestrian, more thug than soldier. He'd spent little time in battle and had risen through the ranks by murder and deceit.

"Stand aside," Justinus said.

Tigellinus reached beneath his arm, his scarred lip curling, and withdrew a sica, the curved blade favored by street gangs. Perfect for slitting throats.

Justinus might have used force to turn the blade on Tigellinus, but he had no taste for violence. He shouted down the stairwell, "Nero Claudius Augustus Germanicus, come greet your visitors!"

Somewhere below, a door creaked open. A moment later a slave peered at Justinus from the bottom of the steps. Nero followed, his voice booming up the stairwell, "Who in Hades has the audacity to interrupt my music practice?"

"Me," Justinus said.

In one hand, Nero held a wine-cup, in the other a lyre—his favorite instrument of torture. "Justinus, old friend," he said. "And Priestess Angerona. To what do I owe this honor?"

"Call off your hound."

At a nod from Nero, Tigellinus re-sheathed his sica. Taking his time, he searched Justinus and found a pugio. He slipped the knife into his toga. Weapons might be illegal in Rome, but anyone with common sense carried a dagger.

"I'm delighted that you came," Nero said as he ushered Justinus and Angerona through the hall toward a chamber. "I've been rehearsing, and you can be my audience." He cleared his throat. "I think you'll find my singing much improved. I've been taking lessons."

"Glad to hear it." Justinus said.

At the door, he told Tigellinus. "Stay out here and keep watch."

"But, Caesar—"

"This wine is disgusting. Finish it." He handed the prefect his cup.

They entered a twilight world. Slaves stood at attention along the walls, but they had lit no oil lamps. A lone window, near the ceiling, allowed light into the chamber, and the sun had moved past it. As his eyes adjusted to the darkness, Justinus noticed a woman seated in a high-backed chair. Her head bowed as if in prayer, her hair disheveled, white ribbons trailing down her back.

"Elissa?"

Her eyes met his—her face appeared not only drawn, but haunted.

"What's happened?" Justinus asked

She opened her mouth as if to speak, but made no sound.

Nero steered Justinus away from her. "Come," he said, "let's drink a toast to old times." He snapped his fingers at a slave. "Bring more wine, and not that piss."

Justinus glanced at Elissa. Barely visible within the dim light, she might have been an apparition.

"We have so much to talk about," Nero said. "You've been a recluse since your return to Rome."

"Where is Marcus Rubrius?"

Nero frowned. "Gone. He committed suicide."

"Suicide?"

"Liar!" The word exploded from Elissa's mouth, her eyes riveted on Nero. Though slight of frame her fury filled the chamber. When she stood, Justinus saw her robe was stained with blood.

Nero strummed his lyre. "Perhaps you'd like another song, Elissa," he said. "Something enlivening to lift your mood."

"You murdered my brother."

"I find it puzzling that you blame me for his death. Marcus chose to die, when he plotted my assassination." Nero struck a chord for emphasis.

Angerona swooped across the room, steering Elissa back to the chair. "Sit," she said. "You've had a shock."

The slave brought a tray of wine.

Nero helped himself and offered Justinus a cup. "A toast to friendship."

Justinus refused the drink. "You killed the man I called my brother."

"It's his sister's fault he's dead. If she'd been more amenable, I might have pardoned him."

Nero's words wrapped around Elissa's throat making speech impossible. She sat rigid in the chair. Hands locked together, she stared straight ahead. Perhaps what Nero claimed was true. Perhaps she could have saved her brother. The noose she felt around her neck grew tighter. Edges faded into darkness. Nothing seemed real. Except the pain she felt. At the corners of her eyes, she noticed movement, figures forming in the shadows. Lemures.

"Where's the body?" Justinus asked.

Nero motioned toward the door. "In an urn. Not the most expensive, but acceptable."

"Cremated?"

"Burned," Elissa's voice sounded strangled. "Burned alive."

"I should have thrown that traitor's ashes in the sewer," Nero said, "let the filth of his remains wash into the Tiber. But I'm known for my clemency, so I've had the traitor's urn delivered to The House of Rubrius."

Elissa dug her fingernails into the chair, attempting to control her rage. She couldn't bear to think about her parents, could not begin to imagine their anguish.

"And to think I once called you my friend," Justinus said, his voice rising. "Angerona, Elissa—let's go now."

"Not so fast," Nero said. "We need to talk."

"I have nothing to say to you."

"I want to hear about the plot to murder me."

"What plot?"

"Perhaps you're in on it. Marcus was, and I suspect Elissa." Nero held up his hand, displaying red marks. "She bit me like an animal. By rights, she should be punished. No, my friend, you're not leaving yet."

Turning from Justinus, Nero ordered slaves to light the lamps and serve more wine.

Shadows jumped along the walls and flickered over Nero's face. Elissa couldn't bear to look at him. Eyes closed, she floated down the River Styx, descending into Hades. The dead surrounded her.

Remember us, they whispered.

Sosianus, beaten with hooked whips for reciting a poem insulting to Nero; Octavia, Nero's first wife, wrongly accused of adultery then put to death; Britannicus, half-brother of Nero and true heir to the empire, sodomized and poisoned. And his mother, Agrippina—when drowning failed, she had been bludgeoned.

Remember us!

Some called Elissa's ability to see lemures—to hear them and to speak to them—a gift. Supplicants came to the temple, seeking contact with lost souls, hoping for a moment of connection. But, to Elissa, the gift often seemed like a curse. The dead gave no warning, arriving when they chose.

Mist rose from the river as she drifted. On the far bank the shade of Agrippina beckoned. The queen called out, her voice high-pitched as winter's wind, "You hold the key, Elissa—the key to truth."

Angry voices dragged Elissa back into the chamber. Nero and Justinus were arguing.

"You've gone too far, Ahenobarbus," Justinus shouted.

"How dare you call me by that name?"

"It's your name by birth. Or have you forgotten? Forgotten your humanity?" As he spoke, it seemed to Elissa that Justinus grew taller. "What happened to the young man who despised violence," he said, his voice gaining strength. "The man who lost himself in scholarly pursuits. The hope of the empire."

"I might ask the same of you. You're an old man at twenty-four. Remember how we ran wild in the streets—you, me, and Lucan? Disrupting taverns, playing havoc in the brothels. Do you deny it?"

"That was a long time ago. I've grown up since then."

"You've grown old."

"And wiser."

"Time takes its toll on all of us." Nero placed his hand over his heart, his face a tragic mask. "I should have been a poet. My lyric verse exceeds Lucan's. Some claim it rivals Virgil's. But destiny demands I play the role of emperor."

"I pity you," Elissa said.

"What?" Nero turned to her. "Did you say something, Elissa? You look tired. Worn. But just last week I noticed your sister—"

"I pity you."

"*You* pity *me?*"

Justinus caught Nero by his arm. "Hear me as your friend. Once you had high ideals, but now you act like a tyrant. Horse races and debauchery are all you think about. You ignore your official duties, and—"

"—waste your time pretending you can sing," Elissa finished.

The slaves gasped, so did Angerona.

The light died in Nero's eyes. Like a cat, he had been toying with his prey, but now he moved in for the kill. He grabbed Elissa, drew her to his chest, holding her so tight she thought her ribs would crack. "I will sing a tune you never wished to hear, belt out notes to shatter glass, trill arias to pierce your heart. Sing with me, Elissa, or I will have you here and now. Sing for your virginity."

Slaves held onto Justinus, but with a roar he broke from them and dove at Nero.

Breaking free, Elissa ran to Angerona.

Justinus pinned Nero to the floor and locked his fingers around Nero's throat.

"My voice," Nero gasped.

Slaves surrounded the two men and shrieked for help.

The chamber door flew open, and Tigellinus burst into the room. Sica in hand, he rushed at Justinus. He yanked him off Nero, dragged him to his feet, and pressed the blade against his heart. Sentries appeared in the doorway, their swords drawn.

"Shall I kill him?"

"Not yet." Nero rubbed his neck. "I wouldn't want to mess the rugs."

"Release him," Elissa said. "I command you." Fog drifted through the chamber, cold and damp. She heard Nero shouting, as if from a distance, his words meaningless. Behind him, through the mist, she saw Agrippina. "Release Justinus, or I will call upon your mother."

"My mother." Nero laughed. "You'll have to raise her from the dead."

"The dead walk among us and between us. Your mother is here now."

Nero glanced at Angerona.

"It's true," she said. "The dead speak to Elissa, and she speaks to them."

"I have no belief in apparitions, shades, lemures."

Elissa's smile was born of grief. How clearly she saw through him, this little man, this frightened boy. "Is that why you fear visiting your mother's tomb?"

Nero's face paled.

"I'll let her sleep," Elissa said, "if you release Justinus."

Nero motioned to Tigellinus. "Let him go."

"But Caesar—"

"Release him."

Despite her triumph, Elissa felt defeated. No conjuring the dead would bring Marcus back to life.

"Take care, Ahenobarbus," Justinus said, "I fear for your mortal soul."

"My mortal soul." Nero snorted. "This conversation has become tiring." He swept out of the room followed by Tigellinus, the sentries, and the slaves—their footsteps fading as they clambered up the stairs.

Angerona squeezed Elissa's hand. "This time you escaped, but next time you may not. In future, you must appease Nero."

"Is that your tactic?"

"I do what's necessary. And I'd do anything to save my family. Use cunning, Elissa. Or Nero will destroy all of us. Remember my father."

"Of course. You're right. We must tread lightly."

Elissa kissed Angerona's cheek. Nero had forced Angerona's father to slit his veins. Weakened by a steam-bath and loss of blood, fluid had filled his lungs until he'd suffocated. The official decree had been suicide.

"Nero won't stop at Marcus," Justinus said. "He'll go after your father, even your mother and sister. You must convince your family to flee Rome."

"Listen to him," Angerona said. "Nero stops at nothing. None of us are safe. And now *we'd* better fly or the House of Vestals will be locked up for the night." She squeezed Elissa's hand again. "Besides, you sorely need to bathe."

It was only later, when, exhausted and dazed, Elissa prepared to soak in a steaming tub, she remembered the letter she'd written to Justinus. She searched her clothes, but it was missing.

CHAPTER VII

I day after the Kalends of October

Year IX, reign of Nero Claudius Caesar Augustus Germanicus

Dear Gallus Justinus,

Last night I dreamt of skulls, cracked and yellowed, lining a long corridor—warm stickiness dripped from the ceiling, and the joists were human femurs, flesh clinging to the bones.

Elissa read what she had written. The man would think her mad. She tore the page in half, began again.

Dear Gallus Justinus,

I'm delighted to hear your apple trees are thriving. Ground fish bones should enhance your crop—

"Elissa?"

She glanced toward the doorway. "Coming."

The curtain opened, revealing Angerona.

"Entering unannounced has become your habit," Elissa said. She blew on the page, willing the ink to dry before Angerona had a chance to read the words.

"The Vestal Maxima requests your presence."

"Why?"

"She said you're to come at once."

Thoughts raced around Elissa's head like chariots. The missing letter flashed through her mind. She'd prayed it had been swept under a table, tossed into a fire, but someone must have found the damning words. Nero? Tigellinus?

"Tell Mother Amelia I'll be there shortly."

Angerona peered over Elissa's shoulder. "What are you writing?"

Elissa folded the papyrus, hiding what she'd written. "Just a note to a friend of my family."

"Gallus Justinus?"

"No." Elissa wasn't certain why she lied.

Taking care to hide her nervousness, she wiped her stylus, recapped the inkpot, and drew off her leather writing glove. She needed time to think, time to make a plan. She needed time she didn't have.

⁂

"Are you listening?"

Elissa nodded.

Honeycombs of scrolls lined the library from floor to ceiling. Usually she reveled in the scent of parchment, but today the smell was suffocating. She often turned to books for comfort—Virgil for solace, Aristotle for wisdom, Sappho for oblivion. But now their words floated through her thoughts like dust.

"Did you hear what I just said?"

Elissa hadn't, but she answered, "Yes, Mother Amelia."

The Vestal Maxima sat behind her marble desk, feet planted together like an Egyptian statue, her spine straight as a pharaoh's scepter, proud as a goddess with the power to show mercy or wield punishment. Her hands, knotted from years of scribing documents, rested on the ivory arms of her curule chair. She might have retired ten years ago, at the age of thirty-seven, but like most vestals, she chose to retain her position as one of the most influential women in the empire. Coils of snowy wool wrapped around her forehead

56

like a turban, securing the shoulder-length suffibulum that veiled her graying hair. Her eyes remained sharp, and now they focused on Elissa.

"You've broken my trust."

Elissa bit her inner cheek, preparing her rebuttal regarding her letter to Justinus.

"Your family has suffered a great loss," the high vestal said. "But even death does not allow a priestess to neglect protocol and run off unescorted to the Circus Maximus."

"I'm sorry, Mother Amelia. But Marcus—" she choked on her brother's name.

"A tragedy, but no excuse." Mother Amelia shook her head. "You not only endangered your own life, but you compromised the reputation of the order. Give me one good reason why you shouldn't be interrogated by the Collegiate of Pontiffs."

Elissa dug her teeth deep into her cheek, biting so hard she tasted blood. Willing away tears, she studied the carpet, the intricate design of birds and flowers, sapphire blues, ruby reds. Her gaze came to rest on the clawed foot of the massive desk, and she felt the weight of her circumstance.

"Nero summoned me," she said, her voice wavering.

"So you decided to go to him alone, without seeking my permission?"

"There was no time."

"And, despite breaking rules, despite risking your well-being, did your actions save your brother?"

"No." A tear rolled down Elissa's face.

"If you had come to me, if I had intervened, perhaps—" Mother Amelia sighed.

"Thank the gods you're safe. Who knows what might have happened if I hadn't sent Angerona after you." The high vestal shifted in her chair. Lips straining against her teeth, she said, more to herself than to Elissa, "Though why she deemed it necessary to include Gallus Justinus, I don't understand."

"She hoped Justinus might convince Nero to spare my brother."

"Your brother committed suicide."

"He did not!"

"Don't raise your voice." Mother Amelia removed a stylus from a bronze pot of pens and tapped it on the desk.

A pale vein ran through the green marble, a stream meandering through a verdant field of stone, as pure as the River of Forgetfulness. But Elissa would not forget.

"Suicide is the official decree," Mother Amelia said. "And it's your duty, Elissa, to concede—"

"Nero murdered Marcus."

The high vestal stopped tapping the stylus. "I know you think me harsh," she said, "but there's much that you don't understand."

"Such as?"

"Things I can't discuss right now. I'm speaking to you as a mother, as one who cares for you. In the future you should be more prudent. Show restraint." She resumed tapping. "You were in the arena at your brother's death?"

"At Nero's command."

"Beast," Mother Amelia spoke softly. Despite her stern expression, moisture glistened in her eyes.

"He made me watch my brother die."

Swiping at her eyes, Elissa refused to cry. Crying meant triumph for Nero, and she would not be defeated.

Mother Amelia reached into a cubbyhole within her desk.

Elissa held her breath, expecting the worst.

The high vestal's hand emerged, not with the missing letter, but with a bowl of candied nuts. She offered it to Elissa.

"No thank you."

"I hope you've purified yourself," Mother Amelia said. "Bathed your body, burned your robes, thrown salt. The taint of death mustn't touch this sacred ground."

"Yes."

"Rules are necessary, especially in times of tribulation." Mother Amelia selected an almond from the bowl. Sucking on the sweet, she said, "It's not always possible to distinguish right from wrong. That's why we must obey the rules laid down by the Collegiate of Pontiffs and the Pontifex Maximus."

"Nero isn't fit to call himself Pontifex Maximus."

"Elissa—"

"He says rules are made for common people."

"Nevertheless, we are bound by oath to obey him." Mother Amelia rubbed her brow, dislodging the coils of wool and setting her suffibulum askew. "We must follow protocol."

Elissa stopped herself from saying something rash. Mother Amelia might look as if her spine were made of iron, but she lacked the backbone to stand up to Nero. In reality, she was spineless as a sea cucumber.

"You're a good girl, Elissa. Gifted in many ways. But you're headstrong to the point of stubbornness." Mother Amelia popped a walnut into her mouth. "You must learn to deny yourself. Practice obedience."

"I would like to see my parents."

"Of course. I'll arrange for lictors and the—"

"Thank you." Without waiting for dismissal, Elissa headed for the doorway.

"One thing more, Elissa."

She paused, her hand on the curtain.

"After your family's ten days of mourning, you're to meet in private with the Pontifex Maximus."

"Why? Does Nero plan to torture me?"

Mother Amelia reached for another nut, then thought better of it and pushed the bowl away.

"You've heard of the Sibylline Oracles?"

"Prophesies made by the Sibyls of Delphi centuries ago, scribed in Greek hexameter. I've heard of them," Elissa said, "but I've never seen the scrolls."

"They're kept within the library at the Regia, secured by the Collegiate of Pontiffs. 'Beginning with the generation first of mortal men down to the last, I'll prophesy each thing, what erst has been, and what is now—'"

"—and what shall yet befall the world through the impiety of man," Elissa completed the famous sentence. "The opening of Book One."

Mother Amelia handed Elissa a scrap of vellum, curled like a leaf and no bigger than her little finger. "Do these words mean anything to you?"

Elissa squinted at the tiny writing.

ROME BURNS AND
FROM UNION
UNHOLY
THE SISTER

WILL BRING FORTH

A SON

The same words the strange woman at the circus had spoken. Remembering the old woman made Elissa shiver.

"Where did you get this?" she asked.

Mother Amelia's eyes probed hers. "You understand that sorcery is an offense?"

"Of course."

"You've never dabbled in the dark arts, never bent another to your will?"

Elissa thought of Justinus. She often knew exactly what he was thinking, sensed what he felt. And sometimes, by her will, she seemed to influence his actions. Might love be a kind of magic?

"Answer me, Elissa."

"I've never practiced sorcery."

"Nero is convinced you have."

"If I were a sorceress I'd transform Nero into a donkey. Better yet, a worm, and make him dinner for an eel."

"He wants you to decipher the meaning of the Sybils' words."

"Nero gave this to you?" Elissa dropped the scrap of vellum on the desk as if it were infected with the plague.

"Meditate on the hexameter," Mother Amelia said. "Perhaps its meaning will come to you."

Elissa turned to leave.

"You would be wise to keep the contents of this conversation close, Elissa. Say nothing to anyone. Not even Angerona. There have been rumors—"

"Rumors?"

"Be careful whom you trust, that's all."

"Yes, Mother Amelia."

Elissa escaped through the curtain. She felt exhausted. She wanted to sleep, to die and find her way to Marcus. Most of all, she wanted nothing to do with the Sibylline Oracles and even less to do with Nero.

CHAPTER VIII

Relieved to be free of the House of Vestals, the confinement of its walls and rigid rules, Elissa and Angerona sat within the covered coach usually reserved for state occasions. Drawn by four white geldings and preceded by two lictors carrying sacred axes—the only weapons allowed within the city walls—the small procession evoked curiosity.

Elissa peered out of the coach's window, taking in the merchants and the beggars, the men of state flanked by bodyguards, the school boys—some of them about her age—gathered along the wide avenue of the Via Sacra to watch the vestals pass. She followed the progress of four slaves bearing the weight of a litter, and through fluttering curtains she glimpsed a wealthy prostitute. She imagined herself, pampered and perfumed, her body draped with silk and jewels, carried through the streets of Rome to meet her lover, to meet Justinus. And she wondered what would ensue.

"Thinking about Marcus?" Angerona asked.

Elissa felt a pang of guilt. "When I close my eyes, I hear his screams."

"It's not your fault."

Wasn't it? If she had given in to Nero, his lustful desires, her brother might still be alive. Or she might have murdered Nero when she had the chance—

She forced herself to stop that violent train of thought. After all, she was a vestal virgin, upholder of morality, not a criminal or, as Nero accused, a practitioner of dark arts.

"Marcus made his choices," Angerona said.

"What do you mean?"

"I mean, we all make choices." Angerona stared out of the window. "And I choose to live."

Elissa glanced at Angerona, couldn't read her face. "What do you know about the Sibylline Oracles?" she asked.

"Not much. A set of crumbling scrolls the priests keep under lock and key in their library."

"Have you seen them?"

"I have no use for ancient prophecies. I'm interested in the here and now. Besides, most of the books were demolished in a fire over a century ago." Angerona leaned out the window, pointing. "Look! My father's domus."

"His former house?"

"Former, of course. Nero confiscated all our property, supposedly for unpaid taxes."

The sprawling complex of the imperial palace, Nero's Domus Transitoria, his never-ending building project, had gobbled up Palatine Hill, former residence of Rome's aristocrats. For centuries, Angerona's domus had been one of them. These days most senators lived in houses clustered along the forum. Elissa's father preferred trees and a garden, and so he chose to live outside the center of the city. But even at that distance, no estate was safe from Nero's appetite. Determined to connect the Domus Transitoria to his parkland on the Esquiline, Nero devoured intervening property, engaging in a battle with the aristocracy. He even hoped to raze the forum.

The coach clattered east toward Esquiline Hill and the House of Rubrius.

Angerona sat back from the window, her full attention on Elissa. "What makes you ask about those musty prophesies?"

"Just curious."

"You're a pathetic liar. Come on, tell me."

"I don't want to talk about it."

"Not with me, you mean." Angerona stared at Elissa, her eyes penetrating. "All right, keep your thoughts to yourself."

"It's nothing, really."

"You've become secretive."

For as long as Elissa could remember she'd confided in Angerona, all her thoughts, all her dreams. But lately Angerona had been asking questions about Marcus, about his friends, Justinus in particular. Mother Amelia's warning loomed in Elissa's mind.

"I thought we were close," Angerona said. "Close as sisters."

"Of course we are."

Angerona's face settled into a mask, cold and indecipherable. They rode in silence, allowing Elissa time to think.

Rome burns and from union unholy the sister will bring forth a son.

The phrase kept running through her head, but the words meant nothing. *Rome burns.* Fire presented a constant hazard and buildings burned on a regular basis. What made Nero think she could decipher that line of gibberish? He'd probably written it himself. She thought about her meeting with Mother Amelia. It had been difficult, but at least no one had found her letter to Justinus.

The coach came to a lurching halt. Perspiration crept down Elissa's neck, and the linen of her stola clung to her back. The narrow street was crowded with pedestrians at this hour as workers returned home for their evening meal. The smell of rotting hay and fresh manure filled the air. A sheep bleated. A rooster crowed. People pushed and shoved, trying to get closer to the coach.

"Grant me health," a stooped man called out in a wheezing voice.

A woman, two ragged children clutching at her robe, hung onto the coach's window frame. "Will my husband return to me?"

"I'll pray for you," Elissa said, although she doubted prayers would have much effect. What had prayers done for Marcus?

The white geldings snorted and the iron wheels began to roll, creaking as the coach climbed the Esquiline. Here—above cramped tenements and alleyways—stood estates of the wealthy, as removed from the city's squalor as the gods were from mortality. The coach wound slowly up, passing landscaped gardens and shade trees imported from as far away as Kashmir. The coach rattled to a stop in front of the House of Rubrius.

Without waiting for assistance, Elissa stepped out, glad to feel solid ground. Her family's land. The setting sun drenched the seven hills in gold, setting ablaze late blooming roses and yellow calendula. Palms rustled overhead and boughs of cedar swept the garden path. She kicked at leaves and inhaled the rich scent of earth.

Angerona reached for Elissa's hand. Preceded by the lictors, they walked hand-in-hand toward the house.

"Promise me," Elissa said, "no matter what the future brings, we will remain the best of friends."

"Closer than blood sisters."

Their footsteps lightened, and they scampered up the path, giggling like children.

Barking greeted them.

"Cerberus!"

A mastiff bounded toward Elissa. His hair was turning white around the chin and his eyes were rheumy, but she had raised him as a puppy. He growled at the lictors, sniffed at Angerona. Standing on powerful hind legs, the dog placed his massive paws on Elissa's shoulders, and they exchanged a sloppy kiss.

"Come on, Cerberus."

The mastiff trotted happily beside her as they approached the stucco domus. The house was large by Roman standards, two stories, almost a villa. Unlike most city dwellings, windows looked out to the street, out to the garden and the trees. The shutters had been drawn, a black mourning wreath secured upon the door. A branch of cypress hung above the lintel as warning that death tainted the family.

Elissa raised the lion-headed knocker, and the brass fell with a thud.

The peephole slid open. The iron bar scraping as it released. The door groaned, and Spurius peered out. A trusted slave since before Elissa's birth, Spurius served as steward, the highest position of any servant. The fact that he answered the door, a task considered menial, offered testimony to the household's state of disarray. Upon seeing Elissa his lined face brightened then quickly fell into a frown.

"Thank the gods you've come," he said, ushering her and Angerona into the foyer. The lictors and Cerberus remained outside. With a grunt, Spurius slid the iron bar back into place. "Can't be too careful these days."

Their footsteps echoed through the quiet, and the house felt damp.

Angerona squeezed Elissa's hand. "You look pale. Are you all right?"

"I sense Marcus watching us."

They followed Spurius, keys jangling at his waist like temple bells. Pausing at the household altar out of habit, Elissa said a prayer for her brother, for his safe passage to the underworld. A stick of cedar smoldered beside a bowl of grain—gifts for gods who had ignored her. Gods who favored Nero.

Spurius drew aside a scarlet curtain, and they walked along a vestibule.

In deference to the dead the oil lamps remained unlit. Busts of ancestors set in niches along the walls peered into the dark. Avoiding their accusing eyes, their whispered denunciations, Elissa followed Angerona, her gaze focused on the floor.

Angerona stopped abruptly. "Gallus Justinus," she said. Her voice dropped in register, "Good to see you."

Elissa's eyes met his, and her heart jumped. Beneath his soldier's fringe of curls his face reflected sorrow. In him she saw a kindred soul.

"I—I wasn't expecting you," she said.

"I've come to pay my respects to your parents. After all, they've been like family to me."

He started toward Elissa as if to embrace her, then stopped himself.

"How kind you are," she said, her face becoming hot for no good reason.

"First you're pale and now you're almost purple," Angerona said.

"I feel a little feverish." Elissa's eyes did not leave Justinus. Seeking a safe haven on which to perch her gaze, she settled on his nose. Broken on the battlefield and slightly crooked. "Have you seen my parents?" she asked him.

"Not yet. I've just arrived." He handed her a package wrapped in silk.

"What is it?"

"Your belated birthday gift. A collection of poetry."

"Ovid? I've read all his work."

"Catullus."

Justinus smiled, and she smiled back. Remembering her deformity, she covered her mouth.

"Love poems." Angerona raised an eyebrow. "No wonder you feel feverish."

Spurius led them to the atrium, a spacious room in the center of the house. A fountain splashed cheerfully and birds hopped along the pool. But darkness steeped the room in shadows. Usually at this hour the atrium would be aglow with lamps, a fire would be burning in the brazier. This afternoon the frescoed walls were lit only by the dying sun which spilled in from the open ceiling. A ray of light fell across a painting of Venus reclining on a scalloped seashell. Her sad eyes followed Elissa.

A glass urn, surrounded by cut evergreen, sat upon a marble slab. Constantina, Elissa's mother, stood weeping beside the bier. Elissa's father stood beside her, his hand resting on her back. Elissa swallowed, trying to dislodge the lump that formed within her throat, trying to dispel a fresh onslaught of tears. Her parents appeared stooped and gray, older than the last time she had seen them—only several weeks ago.

"Daughter," her father's voice quavered, though his face betrayed no emotion. Honoratus practiced the stoic philosophy, refusing to succumb to feelings. "Your brother is—"

"I was there, Pater."

"Of course." The furrows in his forehead deepened. "And you did nothing to prevent his death?"

"I tried." The lump in Elissa's throat grew hard. "I'm sorry, Pater." She approached the bier, ran her fingers over the urn. The glass felt smooth and cold.

Her mother looked at her with swollen eyes. "It's not your fault Marcus committed suicide."

"Is that what you believe?"

"That's what we were told."

Her father's shoulders sagged. "Suicide is the decree."

"Lies." Elissa led her mother to a chair and sat her down, but Constantina would not stop trembling. "Spurius," Elissa called, "bring torches and light the brazier."

"No fire." Constantina shook her head. "This house is in mourning."

"Rules are made for com—" Elissa stopped herself, mortified that her words mimicked Nero's.

"For the gods' sake, Wife, let the servants light a fire," Honoratus said. "You're shivering."

Slaves rushed through the atrium, placing bronze lamps on sconces set into the walls, igniting stanchions at the entryways. Spurius lifted the brazier's iron grate, added coal, and rekindled the flame. Light flooded the atrium. But beyond the central pool the dining room and library remained dark.

A girl stood in the shadows.

"Flavia," Elissa said, moving toward her. "Dear sister."

She appeared older than her fourteen years, taller than Elissa, and over the past months she'd developed curves. Unlike Elissa, she'd inherited Constantina's beauty: a fair complexion, malachite-green eyes, flaxen curls. Her regal nose was red from crying, and the drab stola she wore in honor of her brother's death colored her complexion sallow.

Elissa took her sister in her arms, felt her body shaking.

"To bed, Flavia," Honoratus said. "You are unwell."

Ignoring her father's order, Flavia held onto Elissa. "Will you stay the night?" she asked, her voice a child's.

"I must return to the House of Vestals with Angerona."

"Priestess Angerona is here?" Honoratus glanced toward the entryway where Angerona stood, far too close to Justinus. "And Gallus Justinus! Come in! Come in! Forgive me for neglecting you." He turned to Spurius and said, "Bring wine for our guests. Not the Flavian. I'm saving that—"

"For a wedding or a funeral?" Elissa said, more sharply than intended.

"You're right, Daughter," Honoratus said, his surge of joy deflating. "By all means, serve the Flavian."

Justinus stepped forward, placed his hand on the older man's shoulder. "I'm sorry for your loss, Honoratus. For *our* loss. Marcus would have followed in your footsteps and made a fine senator."

"These are troubled times," Honoratus said.

"Troubled times," Constantina echoed. She sat before the brazier warming her hands, delicate as frozen birds.

"May I offer my heartfelt condolences?" Angerona said.

Honoratus turned to her. "My dear Avita Angerona, how fares your mother? I haven't seen her in some months."

"She's retired to our family villa. Since my father's demise, she finds the countryside—" Angerona hesitated, "—beneficial to her health."

"Pater," Elissa weighed her words, "have you considered leaving Rome?"

"Why?"

"You may not be safe here, considering…" Her father's expression told her to tread lightly. "Perhaps you and Mater should retire to the countryside."

"And do what?" Despite his stoic stance, her father's face was turning red and his words came out jumbled, "Plant sheep? Grow rocks? Herd cabbages?"

"Nero has declared a vendetta against our family. He intends to destroy the House of Rubrius."

"Nonsense. The princeps has shown generosity," Honoratus said. "His family and ours have always been aligned."

"You were on good terms with his mother, weren't you, Dear?" Constantina held her hands over the brazier and Elissa saw they trembled.

"I knew the Empress Agrippina, yes—that was a long time ago. My dear, be careful not to burn yourself. That brazier is hot."

Constantina paid no attention to her husband's warning. "To console us in our grief," she said, "the princeps has bequeathed our family twenty talents of gold."

"Blood-money to buy your silence," Elissa said.

"In many ways you're still a child," Honoratus said, "but one day you'll understand—"

"I'm an adult, Pater."

"And there are things you don't know about, things—"

"Husband," Constantina said. "This is not the time or place."

Elissa glanced from her mother to her father. They were hiding something. "Not the time or place for what?"

"For argument," Honoratus muttered, twisting his citizen's ring around his finger. "I will not flee Rome. Duty demands that I remain."

"But, Pater, your estate may be the next Nero claims."

Constantina dabbed her eyes with a linen handkerchief. "Perhaps we should consider moving to the countryside."

"Nonsense, Constantina!"

"I agree with Elissa," Justinus said. "Your family would be safer in the countryside."

"Enough! I won't leave Rome for any reason."

The gens of Rubrius had sprung from plebian roots, and Elissa's father was proud of their hard won nobility, proud of his afinity with the descendants of Julius Caesar. But pride clouded his reason.

"Pater, hear me out," Elissa pleaded. "Nero will stop at nothing." She glanced toward Flavia who leaned against a pillar, listening.

Her father's gaze followed. "What are you suggesting?"

"Not suggesting, stating."

Honoratus turned to his youngest daughter. "To bed, Flavia, and take your mother with you."

A pall of silence descended on the atrium. Despite the oil lamps, shadows scored the chamber. Elissa sensed the presence of her brother, felt his lemur hovering beside her, urging her to speak.

"We must stand up for truth, Pater."

"She's right," Justinus said. "Nero will stop at nothing."

"If only it were possible to stop him," Angerona said.

Honoratus gazed through the open ceiling at the deepening sky as if hoping for divine intervention. "By Jupiter," he finally said, "I will tolerate no talk of treason in this house. Rome is a great empire, the greatest of all time. We've built roads and aqueducts, erected monuments to honor the gods, civilized the world. We must stand unified."

Elissa pointed to the urn. "He killed Marcus."

"My son committed suicide."

"Lie to me, if you want, but don't lie to yourself, Pater."

Her father's sturdy frame seemed to shrink, and he sounded weary, "If Marcus was a traitor, his death was merited."

"You condone your own son's murder?" Elissa felt sick, not only to her stomach, but deep within her soul.

"What can I do?" her father said. "If we go against the state, chaos will rule."

"Chaos *does* rule! His name is Nero."

"Nero can't be trusted," Justinus said. "Rome's citizens must find a way to overcome his tyranny."

"What way?" Honoratus sputtered. "The way of treachery?"

"Perhaps the way of Jesus."

Angerona stared at Justinus with disbelief. "The Jewish zealot?"

Elissa said nothing. She'd heard Justinus speak of this prophet, Jesus of Nazareth, before. Heard him speak of, "The Way." Rome was tolerant of all religions, even Jews and devotees of Jesus, but what Justinus proposed was blasphemous. The family of Rubrius, a respected gens, could not follow an upstart sect that refused to sacrifice to Roman gods.

Her father's face flushed red as beetroot. "Do I understand," he said to Justinus, "you suggest we follow superstitious wanderers? Paupers, slaves, and wayward Jews who bow down to a criminal?"

"Followers of Jesus believe in one almighty God," Justinus said quietly. "We believe, Jesus, his son, died for our salvation."

"Outcasts of society! I've always thought of you as a son, part of this family. And now, as a father, I'm warning you—"

Spurius returned, bearing a tray of goblets, and talking abruptly ceased. Spurious uncorked a flagon and poured wine.

Elissa glanced from her father to Justinus. In many ways they were alike—stubborn, courageous. She admired Justinus for speaking his mind and standing up to her father. He feared no one. Not even Nero.

Honoratus drank from his goblet in awkward silence.

After a few minutes, Elissa said, "It's warm in here."

"I feel cold," Angerona said. "In any case, we need to leave. Soon it will be dusk, and we'll be late for the evening ritual."

"I'll escort you," Justinus said.

"My slaves will light your way with torches," Honoratus offered, his civility returned. "The streets of Rome are dangerous."

Not as dangerous as Nero's court, Elissa thought. She glanced at Justinus. Not as dangerous as her own heart. Clutching the book of poetry, she said, "Goodnight, Pater."

"Goodnight, Daughter. Pray for your brother's safe passage and offer sacrifice."

"I will, Pater."

What good was offering sacrifice, she wondered, to gods whose power faded in the presence of a tyrant? And what sacrifice would that tyrant demand of her family? Once she'd thought of her father as invincible, a hero among mortal men, but now he appeared as tired as a defeated gladiator. He would remain in Rome, not out of courage, but exhaustion, endangering his life and the lives of his family.

CHAPTER IX

Flavia lay on her sleeping couch, staring at the ceiling, blue sky and wisps of painted clouds. But she imagined thunderheads rumbling in the distance, bolts of lightning striking her father's domus, setting the heavy beams ablaze. Her fingers touched the plaster wall, solid and invincible.

A breeze clattered the shutters of the window, disturbing her turtledoves—secure within their cage. Fellow prisoners. Romulus and Remus had been a gift from Marcus in celebration of her four-teenth birthday. The birds flitted from perch to perch, restless and unsettled, as if they knew the fate that had befallen him.

She focused on a painted cloud, told herself she wouldn't cry. Not for a traitor.

Marcus had been ten when she was born, four years older than Elissa, and he hadn't had much use for a baby sister. But Flavia had thought the world of him. He filled the house with friends and laughter, sang songs and told stories. When Marcus was at home, loneliness did not exist.

Unlike now.

Her vision blurred, and a tear fell on the bedcover staining it a darker shade of white. Elissa had left home when Flavia was too young to remember—they were almost strangers. In truth, Marcus had been her only sibling.

Romulus and Remus pecked at their cage.

Flavia tossed aside the coverlet, got up, and peered at the birds through iron bars. Romulus, the larger dove, fluffed his gray feathers.

"Go to sleep," she said, draping a black cloth over the cage.

The room felt close. She threw open the shutters, resting her elbows on the sill, breathing cool night air. Through tangled branches of the fig tree, she peered down at the courtyard. Moonlight spilled onto paving stones catching a small creature, probably a mouse, as it scurried to the colonnaded walkway. Crickets chirred halfheartedly, bidding their short lives farewell. She breathed in the scent of moldering leaves and fallen apples. Music drifted on a breeze from the twisting lanes of the Subura far below, and she caught the smell of frying onions.

The doorway's curtain rustled. She hurried back to bed, drew the coverlet over her head, and pretended to sleep.

"Still awake?" her mother said.

Flavia burrowed deeper. Her nose tingled, and she fought the urge to sneeze. She yawned, but the sneeze erupted—not just once, but three loud bursts.

The coverlet was drawn away, and Flavia stared at her mother's face—worry lines tugged at Constantina's mouth. She placed an icy palm against Flavia's forehead. "You feel feverish."

"I'm fine, Mater."

"Why is the window open?"

"This room is stuffy."

Constantina pulled the shutters closed. "You'll catch your death."

"We all die. What difference does it make if it's now or later?" Flavia kicked aside the coverlet. "Was Marcus really a traitor?"

"Go to sleep, child."

Constantina alighted on the edge of the sleeping couch, her face pinched and tired. Usually, she kept her hair pulled back, every plait neatly secured, but now a silvery strand fell across her forehead.

"Tell me," Flavia said. "Did Nero really murder Marcus? Elissa told Pater—"

"Eavesdropping is unbecoming in a girl."

"Is it becoming in a man?"

"Don't twist my words." Constantina stood, drew the coverlet around Flavia's chin. "Close your eyes and go to sleep."

"If I don't listen to what others say, how will I learn the truth? No one tells me anything. Was my brother murdered or did he commit suicide?"

Doubt flickered over Constantina's face, and for a moment Flavia thought her mother's barricade of platitudes might crack. But taking a deep breath, Constantina fortified herself. "Things will appear different in the morning," she said, tucking in the coverlet. "You're too young to concern yourself with the world of men."

"I'm old enough to wed."

"And some day soon you will."

"Who?"

"We'll leave that for your father to determine."

"Not Egnatius!"

Constantina picked up a cushion from the floor. "Why is your chamber such a mess?"

"Don't change the subject."

Constantina sighed. "Your cousin is quite suitable."

"He's a pompous idiot. And he's done worse than eavesdropping. One night he sneaked into my room."

The cushion fell from Constantina's hands.

"He what?"

"When Marcus gave that dinner party, Egnatius thought I was asleep, but—"

"He must have lost his way."

"No, Mater. He knew exactly where he was. He slid his hands beneath my bedcovers— "

"You must have been dreaming."

"—pushed up my tunica, and forced his fingers between my thighs, insisting, as my future husband, it's his right. He said if I told anyone, he'd claim he'd ruined me."

Constantina sank onto the bed. "If this is true—"

"It's true, Mater. I swear on Venus."

Constantina touched Flavia's cheek, gazed at her with frightened eyes. "Say nothing of this to your father."

"Now do you understand why I despise Egnatius?"

"Say nothing to anyone," Constantina rubbed her temples as if hoping to erase what Flavia had told her. "Reputations are so easily destroyed."

"Why should I care about his reputation?"

"Not his, yours."

"Mine? I didn't do anything. That isn't fair!"

"Lower your voice, Flavia. It's time you learned life isn't always fair, and you must make the best of it."

"The best of it?"

With lips as cool as melted snow, Constantina kissed Flavia's forehead. Straightening her robe, she headed for the door.

"Did you marry for love, Mater?"

Constantina paused, her expression troubled. "Your father is a good man, a fine husband—"

"But do you love him? Passionately? Would you die for him?"

"Enough, Flavia."

"I won't marry Egnatius. Ever. Not in a hundred, hundred years."

Constantina's tone was hard as granite, "As the daughter of a senator, and a member of one of Rome's leading families, it's your duty to set an example and abide by your father's authority."

"If I can't marry for love, I won't marry at all."

"You will marry whom your father chooses. I expect you to serve your husband well and run an efficient household." Her voice softened. "At your age I was frightened too."

Flavia pushed off the coverlet, threw it on the floor. "This room is stifling."

"When you're older you will understand."

"Understand that I'm a slave to men?"

"Goodnight, daughter." Constantina snuffed the lamp.

Flavia stared into darkness.

Why did her father have the final say over everything? He might be paterfamilias, but even he couldn't force her to marry stupid Egnatius.

Slipping her hand between her thighs, her fingers sought the place Egnatius had pillaged. His touch had left her dry and raw, but her fingers brought liquid shivers. She breathed the scent of her own musk, closed her eyes, squeezing them, till she saw stars— a whole universe. There had to be more in this world besides marriage, childbearing and drudgery. She thought of Elissa: powerful, respected, yet doomed to live a loveless life.

Swearing on the gods, Venus in particular, Flavia vowed her life would be different. She would be an actress and perform in pantomimes. She would be famous and travel to distant lands. She would be pursued by countless men.

Her fingers rubbed harder, faster.

She would be the envy of every woman in the empire.

Her back arched, and waves of heat rippled through her thighs, her groin, building into lightning bolts, until she thought she'd split in half. She moaned.

A gurgle rose from her throat and she began to giggle—at first the sound a girl would make, then deepening into the robust laughter of a woman.

Spent, she lay on the tussled linens and stared at painted clouds.

The doves cooed.

Weak-kneed, Flavia crawled from her bed, and lifted the cover of the cage.

Romulus and Remus cocked their heads.

"I will die," she swore to them, "before I marry Egnatius."

CHAPTER X

VII days after the Nones of October

Year IX, reign of Nero Claudius Caesar Augustus Germanicus

Dear Gallus Justinus,

Today, on Fontinalia, I should be weaving garlands to honor the god of springs and fountains. But I feel no cause to celebrate. On this day, nine years ago, Nero claimed the throne. And, since that day, the Tiber flows with blood.

E lissa dipped her stylus into the ink pot.

Today I meet with Nero in his guise as Pontifex Maximus, high priest of the collegiate. An abomination. Proof that, if the gods exist, they have lost their potency.

If the god you follow offers greater strength, please pray for me.

Elissa Rubria Honoria

With a heavy hand she blotted the papyrus.

❦

"We mustn't keep the Pontifex Maximus waiting," Mother Amelia called over her shoulder. She walked briskly toward the Regia, official residence of the Collegiate of Pontiffs.

Elissa trailed after her, measuring each step, attempting to appear composed.

The Regia stood across from the House of Vestals, a small palace built by King Numa, bordering the forum. Sentries stood vigil at the gates. She glanced at the marble pilasters inscribed with the Fasti—records of Rome's history—a history now tainted by the tyranny of Nero.

Dragging her feet, Elissa followed Mother Amelia past the sacred spring, wishing she had come to collect holy water, wishing she had come for any reason other than to meet with Nero.

Guards escorted them up granite steps flanked on either side by columns.

At the door the Major Flamine, high priest of the pontiffs, greeted them and led them through the vestibule. It wasn't often that a vestal was summoned by the Pontifex Maximus. Marking the solemnity of the occasion, the high priest wore his sacramental robes—the purple-trimmed toga praetexta.

He led them to a tablinum where high-backed chairs stood beside low marble tables and shuttered windows overlooked the Via Sacra.

"Refreshment?" he asked.

Before Mother Amelia or Elissa could answer, he snapped his fingers and two servants appeared. One of them offered a tray of sweets to the priestesses while the other poured pomegranate juice into jewel-studded goblets.

Elissa took a goblet, but didn't drink.

If she must see Nero, she was anxious to be done with it.

Mother Amelia settled onto a cushioned chair. She sipped her pomegranate juice, dabbed her lips, and helped herself to a date stuffed with pistachios.

"I'll inform the Pontifex Maximus of your arrival," the high priest said and left the room.

Elissa ran her tongue over her gums, worrying the double incisor.

"Stop fidgeting, Elissa. Sit. Have a sweet."

Elissa remained standing. She gazed around the room. The walls were frescoed with exquisite murals. One panel depicted the twins, Romulus and Remus, suckling the she-wolf. Another panel showed the brothers fighting; a third showed Romulus victorious and crowned as king. Rome had been founded on the blood of brothers, and Nero held to the tradition.

She wandered to a window. The shutters had been drawn, muting sounds of the street. Through the slats she saw a man, shaggy haired and bearded, hawking bits of cloth.

"How simple life would be if I were a rag-picker."

"Thank the gods you're not." Mother Amelia perused the tray of sweets and selected a honey cake encrusted with poppy seeds. "Try not to be willful when you see the Pontifex Maximus. Practice obedience."

The mention of Nero made Elissa cringe. She stared at the rag-picker, envious.

The high priest returned. "The Pontifex Maximus will see you now."

Mother Amelia smiled, a poppy seed caught in her teeth.

"Not you, Mother," the high priest said. "The Pontifex Maximus requests a private interview with Priestess Elissa."

The high priest closed the door against Mother Amelia's protests and escorted Elissa out into the vestibule. They walked along a white marble corridor.

"Where is the library?" Elissa asked.

The high priest nodded toward an ornate double door.

"Is that where the Sibylline Oracles are housed? I'd like to see them."

"Women are not permitted to view The Book of Fates," the priest said, curtly.

"But women wrote the books."

"The Sibyls merely spoke the prophecies. Priests of Apollo translated them to hexameter."

Elissa glanced at the door and wondered if they kept it locked.

"Come along," the priest said. "The Pontifex Maximus awaits you." At the far end of the corridor he paused before a door, raised his hand and knocked three times.

"Enter," a voice called from within.

Through a smoky haze of frankincense, Elissa stared in wonder. The chamber was large, at least twenty paces from one end to the other, but it was dimly lit and choked by clutter. Armaments covered the walls: swords, double-headed axes, javelins—not the kind of decoration expected in a sanctuary. Through a high window, the only window in the room, light fell upon a statue of Anubis, the jackal-headed god of the Egyptians, guide to the underworld.

The door shut behind her.

"I come here to contemplate," said a disembodied voice.

Elissa squinted, trying to decipher who spoke. Beneath the window, Nero sat on an alabaster throne unmoving as a statue. He wore the white toga of the Pontifex Maximus, folds of fine cotton falling with arranged perfection. His curls were crowned with gilded laurel leaves like a Greek Olympian. In one hand he held the eagle-headed scepter, symbol of the empire, in the other hand he held a lyre.

"Apollo welcomes you, Lord of the sun and music's muse."

Elissa stared, unsure of how she should respond.

"Bow, when We address you," Nero said. "And repeat these words: Oh, Great One, how insignificant am I in the glory of Your presence."

Had he gone completely mad?

"Speak!" He pounded his scepter, startling cobwebs from the ceiling.

"Oh, Great One—" Elissa stammered unable to complete the sentence.

"How insignificant am I—" Nero prompted.

"In the...something...of your presence."

"Glory! Glory! Glory of My presence!" Nero pounded his scepter, so hard even the floor trembled. "You are disobedient and must be punished."

"How am I disobedient?"

"Silence!"

Nero hurled the scepter at the wall, narrowly missing Elissa. It clattered to the floor.

She edged toward the door.

"We've frightened you." Nero leaned back in his throne, his face composed and almost pleasant.

"Why have you summoned me?"

"As We said, you're disobedient. And We believe you doubt Our power."

"I'm sorry, I—"

"I? There is no you. There's only me. I *am* The Roman Empire. The Pontifex Maximus, your king, your ruler. Your very thoughts are mine. Do you understand?"

"I…yes."

"We thought you might." Nero smiled.

Elissa bit her lip, angry at herself for agreeing, but what recourse did she have?

"I'm waiting for your apology," Nero said.

"Apology for what?"

"You have insulted Us. Your emperor. Your god."

"How?"

"You said that I can't sing, but I intend to prove you wrong." Nero picked up his lyre, cleared his throat and ran a scale.

Was this her punishment?

"I will sing a song, made popular by Menecrates, the famous citharode. Do you know him?" He didn't wait for an answer. With a strum of his lyre, he broke into the song. His voice was shrill. Midway through, the words escaped him.

When the ordeal finally ended, Elissa clapped half-heartedly.

Nero's face lit up. "So you agree that We have talent."

She nodded. It took every bit of her resolve not to rip the lyre from his hands and smash it over his diadem. She imagined the satisfying sound of splintering wood, the pop of catgut strings.

He continued strumming, and when he spoke he sounded cheerful, "Now We will perform a ballad—I composed the lyrics."

"Then maybe you'll remember them," Elissa muttered.

"What?"

"I said your voice rivals Apollo."

Elissa warned herself she must tread carefully. Nero's moods were changeable as mercury.

He chuckled. "You're a goddess among women, Elissa. Enchanting. Have I mentioned you remind me of my mother?"

He struck a melancholy chord. His ballad was heartfelt, if not masterful, a tribute to an unnamed queen who seduced her son then murdered his stepfather to secure the throne. Overcome by guilt, the queen had taken her own life.

"Lovely," Elissa said, afraid his mood might change again. "I should go."

"One more." He dove into a bawdy tune.

Elissa swallowed, her mouth parched. She glanced at the closed door, regretting her decision to forgo the pomegranate juice. Studying the walls of armaments, she tried to imagine which weapon would produce the gravest injury.

The music, although Elissa wouldn't call it that, came to a halt.

"You're not listening," Nero said.

Her eyes snapped to him. "When will this interview end?"

"I want you to summon that whore I call my mother from the dead."

"What?"

"Bring the she-wolf here right now."

"I can't—"

"Can, can, can, you cunt!" Nero stood up from his throne. "Do these words mean anything to you: Rome burns and from union unholy the sister will bring forth a son?"

Elissa's throat felt raw, and when she spoke her voice sounded strangled, "The Sibylline Prophecy."

"I found the hexameter tucked inside my mother's diary."

"It means nothing to me."

"It meant something to the whore." Nero leaned close to Elissa. "I think she spawned a bastard whose bloodline rivals mine. I believe I have a long-lost sibling."

"If Agrippina bore another child, surely all of Rome would know."

"She spent ten years in exile far away from Rome. Ten years in obscurity. But that chimera wouldn't last a week without a snake to plug her hole. The prophecy speaks of unholy union, 'the sister will bring forth a son.' What if my mother, sister of Gaius Caligula, conceived a child with him? Gaius banished her for ten years— why?" Nero's eyes glittered as if he'd eaten opium. "I'll tell you why. To keep her and his bastard safe from enemies! What if she bore his son, but before the child could be named heir to the throne, Caligula was murdered?"

"I suppose it's possible."

Everybody knew Caligula had bedded each of his three sisters—Agrippina, Livilla, and his beloved Drusilla.

"Not just possible, but probable. Like me, my uncle longed for an heir. If you remember, he was a most expectant father, so anxious for Drusilla's bastard to be born he plucked the infant from her womb."

"By disemboweling her."

"Unfortunate."

"For the mother and the child."

"But not for my long lost brother. I'm his only rival."

Elissa measured her words, "If this long-lost brother does exist, surely he would have laid claim to the throne by now."

"Did I ask for your opinion?" Spittle flew from Nero's mouth. "My queen is barren. Since the death of our daughter, Poppaea's womb has been a desert. She's dry as dirt, at least with me. Why should my bastard brother risk his life by declaring his existence, claiming he's the rightful heir, when he need only bide his time until my death? What if it's *he* who masterminds my assassination?"

Elissa eyed him warily.

"Help me." Hands open like a supplicant, he approached her. "Conjure up the stinking whore. She knows the truth."

"I—" Elissa's voice caught in her throat.

"Do it!"

He moved toward her, pushing her against the wall, the heat of his body causing her to sweat, his breathing, rapid and uneven, rasping in her ear. Reaching above her head, he removed a knife from his collection. A pearl handled secespita, the narrow blade designed for sacrifice.

Elissa opened her mouth to scream.

"Don't." Nero pointed the secespita at her throat. "Your brother plotted with my long-lost brother, didn't he?"

Elissa shook her head, her eyes focused on the knife.

"I could kill you now," Nero said. "But I have other plans for you." He drew the blade over his palm then took her hand in his, gently as a lover, and drew the blade again.

Blood beaded in her hand.

Pressing his palm against hers, he said, "My great-grandfather worshiped an Egyptian queen, dark and powerful like you. Be Cleopatra to my Antony."

He's madder than Caligula, Elissa thought.

"I'll make you immortal. Declare you a goddess, and together we'll conceive the heir to Rome."

She tore out of his grasp, ran to the door and flung it open. Blood dripping from her hand, she bolted down the corridor.

End of Part One

PART TWO

A HOLY BOND

My darling, my life, you say our love is eternal,
Ours will be a love of never-ending joy.
Gods, I pray you, lend my love the power to speak truly,
and if she speaks the truth, let this vow come from her heart.
So, for all time, we shall remain true to each other,
Bound by faith and joy, in love forever.

—CATULLUS

CHAPTER XI

The Ides of October

Year IX, reign of Nero Claudius Caesar Augustus Germanicus

Dear Priestess Elissa Rubria Honoria,

I hope this missive finds you and your family well.

I saw you at the chariot race as dawn broke this morning, but I found no opportunity to speak with you. Please advise me, if your family is in need, of any help I may provide. And please give my regards to your father. I fear I've angered him.

Your friend,

Gallus Justinus

Elissa touched the book of poetry Justinus had given her—leaves of vellum bound in leather, a new technique imported from the Orient. The binding felt smooth, soft as skin. She folded his letter and tucked it into her stola.

She must write to him.

Clenching her fist, she felt the cut Nero had rendered. The wound made writing difficult. Cleopatra to his Antony, the idea sickened her. Tightening the bandage on her hand, she told herself that she had work to finish.

She sat at the high vestal's desk, pages of papyrus stacked in front of her, demanding to be completed. It was the job of the six vestals to scribe legal documents. Over a million scrolls from throughout the empire were stored within their archives. Along the library's walls, sheets of papyrus hung on racks allowing ink to dry. The last will and testament of Aulus Severus, a wealthy patron of the temple, was due today. She would receive hefty payment for the work, in addition to the vestals' generous stipend, but three copies were required, and the documents had to match exactly.

Laughter drifted through the window. Out in the forum, flutes and drums began to play. Elissa tapped her foot in time to the music. Ignoring the last will and testament, she dipped her stylus into ink.

Dear Gallus Justinus,

Thank you for the book of poetry. Thus far I've had little time to read it. We have been busy preparing for the harvest celebration.

I'm sorry I missed you at the chariot race this morning. I thought of you, for I know you love horses. The victor's steed was stunning, don't you think? A sleek black gelding. Seeing that beauty sacrificed, the creature's entrails smeared upon the altar of the Regia, upset me—as it has not before. It was my job to collect blood from the severed genitals in order to ensure protection of the flocks. In the past, I've felt honored to perform that ritual, but today I felt disgust. When I saw that butchered horse, I thought of Marcus—

She stared out the window. What was the point of writing? No words would bring her brother back. Yet, expressing her thoughts, confiding in a kindred soul, somehow eased her pain.

She blotted the papyrus.

Stretching her arms, she attempted to loosen the cramp that settled in her shoulders. She glanced at the window. Lively music invited her to join the celebration. Usually she looked forward to the festival of Meditrinalia, but this year she had no cause to celebrate.

Her gaze drifted from the stack of papyrus to the book of poetry. She picked it up, intending to place the book in a cubbyhole somewhere between the writings of Aeschylus and Zarathustra. Would it hurt to peek inside? She cracked open the binding and sheepskin pages fluttered beneath her fingers, releasing musk.

When all hope has fled, and the empty heart meets its desire,
Fulfillment of the heart—that—that is the greatest joy.

Angerona strolled into the library, the veils of her suffibulum wafting on the breeze. "Burying your nose in work?" she asked.

Elissa closed the book of poetry. "Copying legal documents."

"What are you reading?" Angerona plucked the book from Elissa's hands. "*Poems of Catullus.* Love poems from Gallus Justinus. What would Mother Amelia say?" She plunked herself into the curule chair reserved for the Vestal Maxima.

Elissa reached for the last will and testament and set it squarely on the desk, taking care to cover the letter she'd written to Justinus.

"That's Mother Amelia's chair," she said to Angerona.

"So?"

"Do you hold nothing in reverence?"

Angerona wrapped a strand of hair around her forefinger. "I hold you in reverence," she said. "I revere your ability to shut yourself away on such a day as this. Come out and celebrate."

"I have work to finish. I hope to save enough to buy a farm." Elissa reached for her stylus.

"A farm, how exciting."

"We're no longer children. Someday I hope to retire."

"Someday, twenty years from now, when we're old women. I've been a prisoner here since the age of seven. Remember when you arrived?" Angerona kicked Elissa's shin.

Elissa kicked her back. "We were nine-years-old."

"I was nine-and-a-half," Angerona corrected her. "Your elder by six months. You were so scared you wet yourself."

"I didn't." Elissa dipped her stylus into ink. "In any case, that was ten years ago. We're women now."

"And I'm ready for a man. Aren't you?"

"Angerona!"

"What?"

Elissa shook her head. "You forget our place."

"You think I can forget this prison of perpetual virginity?"

Elissa attacked the papyrus, her stylus scratching out neat letters. "I have to complete this document."

"Finish it this evening."

"Tonight's my night to tend the fire."

"The fire in the temple? Or the flame between your thighs?"

Elissa's fingers tightened, and the letters she scribed grew constricted.

Angerona threw a stylus at her. "Where's your sense of humor?"

"Don't you have something else to do?"

"On this grand stage of life?" Angerona stood. Throwing out her arms, she said, "Act One: the forum and the pantomimes. Act Two: a dazzling stroll along the Via Sacra. Act Three—" She pressed her hands into the desk and leaned toward Elissa. "Come nightfall, a hundred barges lit with lanterns will float down the Tiber, carrying lovers, and I intend to be one of them."

Elissa concentrated on an A, the beginning of a paragraph.

"Where does Mother Amelia keep her sweets?" Angerona chuckled. "She likes those honeyed nuts, and so do I." With no regard for Elissa, Angerona rummaged through the desk's cubbyholes. She found the bowl, scooped a handful of candy, and dropped several nuts into her mouth.

Elissa straightened the papyrus, drew the ink pot closer.

Angerona grabbed Elissa's wrist with sticky fingers. "And then, the Grande Finale: Nero's feast."

Elissa pulled away from Angerona. "I have no use for Nero."

"But he has use for you."

"What, exactly, do you mean?"

"I mean, exactly—" Angerona licked the honey from her fingers. "How did your meeting go with him?"

Elissa stared at Angerona, wondering how much she knew. In a house of women, few secrets remained hidden. "He wants me to call forth his dead mother."

"Perfect."

"Perfect?"

"Allow his mother's lemur to speak through you, and you'll have him in your power. He'll give you anything."

"Can he bring back Marcus?"

"Life goes on, and we must make the most of it." Angerona helped herself to another handful of nuts. "Really, Elissa, you must learn to be more politic."

"Like you?"

"Why not, like me? I take care of myself, and—more importantly—I take care of my family. Someone has to protect them."

Elissa stabbed her pen into the inkpot, spattering the papyrus. Using a rag, she attempted to blot the sooty mess. "Now I'll have to start again."

"Come out with us. We may run into Gallus Justinus."

Elissa felt her face turn red.

"You'd like to see him, wouldn't you?" Angerona goaded. "In any case, you owe him an apology."

"An apology for what?"

"For your father's rude behavior. He nearly threw Justinus out when he mentioned that Jew."

"You take uncommon interest in my affairs."

"I'm merely looking out for you. Justinus keeps strange company these days. Jews and renegades like Lucan. He's getting money from somewhere. That book he gave you must have cost him—"

"A birthday gift."

"What, exactly, is Justinus to you?"

"He's a—a family friend, a sort of brother."

"They say incest has its merits." Angerona laughed, but it rang false. "Be careful," she said. "You know how people love to talk."

Elissa snatched away the bowl of nuts. "You should go."

"Admit it. You're in love with him."

"We're vestals, Angerona. Married to the sacred flame."

"As if I might forget. You're so chaste. So good. So pure. So utterly boring." Angerona set the book of poetry in front of Elissa. "I'll leave you to your...copying." She headed to the doorway, then turned back. "By the way, I hear your sister has whet Nero's appetite."

"Flavia?"

"She's been invited to attend his Meditrinalia feast tonight."

Angerona swept out of the library, the curtain swaying in her wake.

Elissa rooted through her cedar chest, tossing aside silk veils, digging through finely woven pallas, in search of the rough garments she'd worn at her brother's death. She hadn't had the heart to burn them. Hiding the blood-drenched robes from servants, she'd stolen into the baths and scrubbed the wool until the stains had faded. Now the clothes would serve a purpose, allowing her to brave the crowds and make her way, unnoticed, to her father's domus.

Under no circumstance could Flavia attend Nero's feast.

No doubt Angerona had latched onto a scrap of gossip and cooked it up into a meal, but Elissa refused to see her sister on the menu.

She drew the drab stola over her tunica and belted it loosely at her waist. Instead of wearing her white suffibulum, she threw a shabby palla over her head, wrapped it around her shoulders and draped the end over her arm.

She glanced toward the doorway. All the other priestesses were out, even the servants had gone off to the festival. Lifting the pallet of her bed, she placed the letter from Justinus with the others, wrapped in silk and tied with a blue ribbon.

Parting the doorway's curtain, she peered into the dormitory. Empty. No one stirred in the other cubicles. A floorboard creaked under her weight, and she heard water hissing as it passed through lead pipes, otherwise the house was quiet.

She paused before the door of Mother Amelia's chambers. Nothing disturbed the Vestal Maxima's routine, not even Meditrinalia, and she had opted for a nap. Elissa told herself, if Mother Amelia were awake, of course she would seek permission to leave the house. But the high vestal hated having her naps disturbed. Besides, asking for permission might lead to being denied. Remembering Mother Amelia's warning. *You must practice obedience to the Pontifex Maximus*, only served to drive Elissa faster down the stairway.

The atrium's black floor glistened like a lake. Soundlessly, Elissa glided over the polished tiles. Passing the well-appointed tablinum, where the priestesses met visitors, she entered the foyer. Thais, an elderly Greek slave, slumped on a bench beside the double doors, nodding in her sleep.

Elissa gently touched the slave's shoulder and she woke with a start.

"Who is going there?" Thais asked in stilted Latin.

"Deliver this," Elissa said, handing Thais the letter she'd written to Justinus.

Thais secured the letter within her robe.

"I'm going out," Elissa said.

"Alone?" Thais sounded grumpy. She rubbed her eyes. "There is no lictor and no coach. The others have all gone. Only me they leave, poor, *poor,* Thais."

Elissa dug into her money pouch and found a denarius. Pressing the silver coin into the slave's palm, she said, "For your trouble."

And her silence.

The streets of Rome were always lively, but during Meditrinalia people from the countryside poured into the city and city residents flooded out of doors—feasting, dancing, drinking. The revelry continued through the night, until it reached a frenzied peak, and finally fizzled out by dawn.

Whichever way Elissa turned she was met with bawdy songs and raucous dancing. Gambling was forbidden, except at festivals, and on every corner people rolled knucklebones and placed bets. Fighting her way through the mob, she crossed the Via Sacra and walked toward the Regia. The horse's head, from that morning's race, was mounted on the wall, proof that the aristocrats had won the competition. Flies buzzed around congealing blood. She hurried past.

Someone tugged at her stola. Afraid she'd been recognized she prepared an explanation and turned to see a boy disappearing in the crowd. She felt for her money pouch. Gone. Wanting to avoid a scene, she hurried on. But without money to hire a litter, she'd have to walk. She massaged her forehead, felt a headache coming on.

Smoke billowed from an alleyway, and the greasy smell of burning flesh made her stomach turn. Rome was prone to fires, and fire laws were strict, but during festivals people ignored regulations. Braziers were set out in the street and slabs of spiced mutton, beef, and pork roasted over open flames, reminding her of funeral pyres.

The throbbing in her temples became a splitting ache.

A band of bodyguards marched down the center of the street, forcing pedestrians into the gutter. Pressed against the wall, Elissa watched a litter pass, slaves groaning under the weight.

Usually, she didn't notice the disparity between rich and poor, but lacking means to ride gave her a new perspective. Head bent, as she trudged along the road leading to the Esquiline, she considered what it must be like to live in poverty, to starve while others feasted, to perform back-breaking labor for a pittance, to suffer illness until life's drudgery became impossible. By the time she reached her father's domus pain pressed deep into her skull.

The day was warm for mid-October. She longed to rest beneath a cedar tree, breathe the scent of pine. Wearily, she climbed the steps, lifted the bronze knocker. Before it fell, the door opened.

Cerberus leapt through the entryway, jumping up to lick her face.

"Down, boy," she scolded, but she returned the Mastiff's kisses.

"Thank the gods you've come," Spurius said. The old slave slumped against the doorframe. "Your father is close to dead."

CHAPTER XII

Elissa stood in the doorway of her father's bedchamber. Honoratus lay on his sleeping couch, eyes closed and barely breathing. She expected him to push aside the coverlet, abandon his bed and reprimand his family for making such a fuss. "Open the shutters!" he would say. "A man needs to breathe."

But he didn't stir.

She might call her father tenacious, proud to the point of arrogance, bullheaded, but never, until now, would she have called him frail.

Constantina sat beside him. "Come, daughter, sit with us," she said, her voice weary. Her eyes, once green as Flavia's, appeared clouded. Flavia knelt beside the bed. She seemed to be praying—though Elissa never knew her sister to be pious. Her hair, half loosened from the bone pins securing it in place, fell in pale gold tendrils around her shoulders.

Elissa bent to kiss her mother.

Constantina's hands fluttered in her lap. She clasped them together as if preventing them from taking flight. "Did Justinus send for you?"

"No," Elissa answered quickly, her heart jumping at his name. "I came on my own. I need to speak with Pater."

Flavia looked up, her face expectant.

"You have something to say?" Elissa asked her.

Flavia shook her head.

"Out of respect for your father, your sister has taken a vow of silence," Constantina said. "She was with him when he fell ill. One minute he was fine and the next—"

"What upset him?"

Flavia shook her head so violently the remainder of her hair came undone. She bowed her head and escaped Elissa's scrutiny.

Elissa had no doubt her sister's silence served a purpose.

Constantina sighed. "Pray that Justinus returns soon."

"Justinus is coming here?" Elissa asked, trying to control her racing heart.

"With Doctor Karpos," Constantina said. She poured water from an earthen ewer into an alabaster bowl then sprinkled in a handful of white powder.

"Feverfew?" Elissa asked. She often used the flowers as a remedy for pain.

"The last from my garden."

"May I have some?" Elissa placed the bitter herb on her tongue, and hoped it would ease her headache.

Constantina dipped a linen cloth into the bowl and gently placed the compress on her husband's forehead. "Your sister lacks your interest in cultivating herbs."

"The interests she cultivates lie elsewhere." Flavia squirmed under Elissa's gaze. "You'll have to break your vow of silence soon," Elissa said. "Doctor Karpos will want to ask you questions."

"About what?" Flavia clamped her hand over her mouth, then shrugged. "Pater hates physicians. He says first they drain your veins, and then they bleed your purse."

Honoratus moaned, restless in his sleep.

Elissa straightened his coverlet, smoothing the soft wool. Then she saw it—a sheet of papyrus of the finest quality lay on the floor, half hidden by bed linens. She recognized the broken seal.

Flavia snatched the letter as Elissa reached for it. "I'll fetch fresh water," she said and hurried from the chamber.

Elissa followed her out into the atrium. Sun streamed through the open ceiling, and birds chirped by the fountain. A cat, startled from its nap, stretched and yawned.

"Give me that invitation," Elissa said.

"What makes you think it's an invitation?"

Elissa held out her hand. "Give it to me."

"It's not yours. It's addressed to Pater."

"You read it, didn't you?"

"What if I did?"

"What does it say?"

Flavia edged toward the fountain. "That's not your concern."

"Yes, it is. I'm concerned about you, concerned about our family."

"Hah! You left this family years ago. You only care about your reputation."

Elissa grabbed for the papyrus, but Flavia moved faster. She ran to the fountain and tossed the missive into the water. It floated out of reach.

Gathering her robes, Elissa hoisted herself onto the fountain's rim, wondering what she might use to retrieve the papyrus. She was taken by surprise when her sister slammed into the back of her knees. Elissa tried to regain her balance, but her foot caught on her hem and she tumbled into the water. Gasping from cold and shock, she surfaced from the shallow pool—Flavia's laughter ringing off the walls.

The invitation, Elissa felt certain that's what it was, drifted beneath the spewing fountain. Weighted by her skirts, she waded toward it. Ink ran down the page. All she could decipher was, "east of Meditri...the other words were washed away.

east of Meditri, east of Meditri...the Meditrinalia feast!

Water swirling at her hips, she turned to Flavia. Holding up the sodden papyrus, she said, "I was right."

Her sister's eyes shone green and bright. She said, "I've been invited to the feast, and I intend to go."

"To be served as dessert?"

"You can't stop me."

Elissa studied her sister's full lips, her budding breasts. Nero's banquets were infamous, orgies of food where wine flowed freer than the Tiber and dining couches served as beds.

A rush of footsteps made the sisters turn. Spurius and several other servants burst into the atrium. The old slave stopped, stared at Elissa—still standing in the fountain.

"We heard shouting," he said.

"My sister went for a swim," Flavia said, waving him away. "Bring towels."

Spurius clapped his hands, and the other servants hurried off. "I'll ask the cook to heat mint tea," he said, glancing from Elissa to Flavia before heading to the kitchen—no doubt to share the latest news.

Ignoring her sister's extended hand, Elissa climbed out of the fountain, water dripping, slippers squeaking. She wrung the hem of her robe, and rivulets ran across the mosaic floor.

"I'll lend you a dress," Flavia offered.

"Your best. You won't need it for some time. Go to your chamber." She pointed to the stairway. "Attempt to leave this house tonight, and by the gods, I'll have you prosecuted for dishonoring a Priestess of Vesta."

"I hate you," Flavia shouted as she ran from the atrium.

Elissa's shoulders sagged. She wanted to weep, but tears were not allowed a vestal virgin, not in public. And this house was no longer her home.

Voices echoed through the foyer. A moment later, Justinus and Doctor Karpos appeared, heads bowed together in conversation. Upon seeing Elissa, their talking ceased. The wet robe clung to her body, making her feel naked.

She clapped her hands, and called for the slaves.

They came running with towels, hot drinks and honey.

But not before Justinus had stripped her with his eyes.

And she had done the same to him.

Doctor Karpos had attended the Roman Medical Academy and, though he was Greek and had once been a slave, he was now a well respected freedman.

"Domina," he addressed Constantina, "you must make a sacrifice to appease the gods. Something substantial."

Honoratus grunted, seemed to be waking.

Lowering his voice, Doctor Karpos said, "Not just the usual fowls or pig, but three ewes for Jupiter and a bullock for Mars."

That woke Honoratus. "A bullock for Mars?" Through slits of eyes, he glared at the physician.

"The gods are pleased at the suggestion." Doctor Karpos said cheerfully. "Already, the patient is improving."

Elissa smiled. Her father's frugality would rouse him from the dead.

Honoratus struggled to sit, his breath ragged gasps.

Elissa rearranged the cushions at his back. "Relax, Pater," she coaxed him.

"Relax?" He shot an angry look at the physician. "Who brought this charlatan into my house?"

"Pater, calm yourself."

"A bullock for Mars!"

"Perhaps a goat will do," Constantina offered.

"For the gods' sake, Pater," Elissa touched her father's hand. "I'll provide the bullock, two bullocks if necessary."

"Waste. Women shouldn't handle money."

"Two bullocks will ensure complete recovery," Dr. Karpos said.

"Then it's settled." Elissa squeezed her father's hand. Unlike most women, vestals controlled their own finances and Honoratus held no sway. Defeated, he shook his head.

"I must speak with you, Pater"

"Maybe tomorrow," Doctor Karpos said. "Right now your father requires rest."

"But this is important. It concerns Flavia—"

"Not now," said Constantina.

Elissa had no desire to defy her mother, but she felt compelled to speak. If not now, then when? An invitation to the imperial palace would turn the head of any girl, especially a girl as foolish and naive as Flavia. Had she already forgotten her brother's death?

Honoratus spat into a cup and Doctor Karpos peered at the resulting phlegm. He measured the patient's pulse. Muttering in Greek, he prepared a tincture of fennel root, mustard seed and leaves of rosemary. He presented the physic to Constantina.

"To be dissolved in water and administered three times a day," he instructed her.

"This so-called physician poisons me," Honoratus grumbled.

Constantina escorted Doctor Karpos from the room.

"Pater," Elissa glanced toward the doorway, making sure they were gone. "We must discuss Flavia."

"I'm tired," Honoratus said. And, with that, he closed his eyes.

❦

Justinus had been waiting in the atrium for over an hour. The drip of the water-clock told him time was passing, but he would wait till nightfall, if necessary, to see Elissa. He glanced toward the tablinum hoping she'd appear.

The water-clock continued dripping.

He threw a pebble into the fountain, watched it sink. He lost the stone among the mosaic at the bottom of the pool, and then found it—at rest on Neptune's nose. Carp flashed across the sea-god's beard, darted past his trident and disappeared among a mermaid's tresses.

"You must deliver this message in person," Elissa's voice issued from the library. "I can't chance writing. Do you understand?"

The curtain opened, revealing a heavy desk and a wall of cubbyholes crammed with scrolls. Honoratus was an educated man, and he housed an impressive library. He'd taught not only his son, but his daughters, to read and write. Elissa appeared in the doorway, followed by Spurius.

She carried the clothing she had been wearing earlier and now wore a fine stola, a deep rose color that complemented her jet hair.

"Answer me, Spurius. Do you understand?"

The old slave seemed disgruntled. Frowning, he said, "Your father won't approve of lying to the princeps."

"It's not a lie. Flavia *is* to be betrothed. In the meantime, I want her watched. Under no circumstance may she leave this house tonight." Elissa came to a halt, her cheeks turning the color of her robe, when she saw Justinus. "I thought you'd left," she said.

"Your sister is betrothed?" Justinus watched with fascination as Elissa's face flushed redder.

"Not really, but—she will be soon."

"Will you be staying for the midday meal?" Spurious asked.

"No," Elissa answered, before Justinus could say yes.

"In that case," Justinus said, "allow me to escort you back to the House of Vestals."

"As you wish." She withdrew a ragged palla from her bundle, threw the shawl over her head and wrapped it around her shoulders, destroying the lovely robe's effect. "All right," she said, "I'm ready."

They followed Spurius, keys jangling at his waist, through the vestibule and into the foyer.

Elissa turned to the slave and said, "Don't forget."

Spurius nodded, half-heartedly. "Flavia Rubria Honoratus has been betrothed," he recited, his nose turning crimson at the lie.

"That's right," Elissa said. "Consequently, she is unable to attend the feast. Remember?"

"Yes, mistress." The slave looked as if he'd swallowed rotten fish.

He peered through the peephole, before opening the front door.

Cerberus lay at the bottom of the steps soaking up the heat. He raised his head, hoping to be petted. Spurius called the dog inside and closed the door on Elissa, with unnecessary force.

Justinus squinted at the sun, just past its zenith. He wandered toward the garden. The flowers had begun to fade. Roses lined the path, their petals open to the point of dropping, and yet they retained their fragrance.

Elissa seemed preoccupied.

"It's a fine day," Justinus said. "Let's walk along the riverbank and enjoy the Meditrinalia festivities."

"I've had a change of plans." Elissa drew her palla tight around her shoulders. Despite the afternoon's warmth, she shivered. "I want to pay a visit to the Domus Transitoria. I can't rely on Spurius."

"To inform the princeps that your sister intends to marry? Even if that weren't a lie, why would Nero care?"

Lines formed between Elissa's eyebrows. "He's invited Flavia to the feast tonight."

"Surely your parents won't allow her—"

"Of course not. But, my parents are preoccupied and, on my family's behalf, I must speak to him."

"And say what?"

"I don't know!"

They stood closer than they had for years. Justinus breathed in her scent, a crisp perfume of rosemary and olive soap. He remembered playing hide-and-seek with her in this garden. She'd been nine, and he fourteen. He'd found her cowering behind a statue of Venus, tears running down her face. When he asked her what was wrong, she only shook her head. Soon after that day, the family announced she'd been chosen as a vestal virgin.

"We're still playing hide and seek," he said.

"Are we?"

"Have you read the book of poetry I gave you?"

"A little." She bent to smell a rose.

" 'Once suns of gold shone bright for you'," he quoted Catullus, " 'and you wandered only where you pleased, more beloved than any girl—'"

"Don't."

Justinus studied her face, the face he adored—powerful and strangely beautiful—her eyes, dark and intense, the high forehead denoting intelligence. Her lips, usually set in a determined line, quivered.

"I feel his death as much as you, Elissa."

"Marcus loved roses." She snapped off the head of a flower and one-by-one plucked off the petals. "Nero wants me to play Cleopatra to his Antony."

"What?"

"He wants to bed me."

Justinus grabbed her wrists, squeezing so hard she dropped the savaged flower.

"You forget yourself," she said. "No one is allowed to touch a vestal virgin—except Nero, apparently."

"Is that why you want to see him?"

"Don't be absurd."

"Then why?"

"I'd like to stab him in the heart, hold a pillow to his face, feed him tainted mushrooms as his mother did Claudius."

"Elissa, don't—"

"I'd like to see him dead."

Justinus released her wrists. The years had changed not only him, but her. Perhaps not for the better. "Take care, Elissa. You sound as cruel as Nero."

"Do I?" She turned from him and, clutching her bundle of rags, walked along the garden path.

He followed her.

They paused at the statue of Venus. "Remember when I found you crying all those years ago?"

"You kissed me." She raised her face to his, her eyes filled with tears. "I live outside life, more witness than participant."

He wanted to comfort her, to hold her in his arms, but he stopped himself. "Violence leads to violence," he said. "Take a higher road Elissa."

"All roads in Rome lead to the gutter," she said.

"Not mine."

He headed down the path, and she followed him.

CHAPTER XIII

Flavia fell onto her sleeping couch. Claiming to have stomach cramps, she'd refused the midday meal and remained in her room. Elissa had ruined everything. Luckily she hadn't found the new green stola—the one Flavia planned to wear tonight. Oh yes, she would attend the feast, no matter what Elissa said.

Her stomach growled.

Sunlight stole through the shutters, and fell in lines along the walls, painting bars across the floor. Despite the afternoon's brilliance the ceiling's painted clouds seemed ominous. Thanks to Elissa a servant stood outside the door preventing Flavia's escape. At least within her chamber she had privacy.

She listened to the silence of the house. No laughter. No music. No Marcus. If Marcus were alive, the house would be bustling with preparations for a Meditrinalia celebration. If Marcus were alive, servants would be arranging banquet tables in the courtyard. Cooks would be preparing roasted meats and honeyed fruits, delicious smells seeping through the walls from the kitchen. When night fell there would be music and dancing. His death had ruined everything. And now, instead of feasting at the palace, another evening would be wasted spinning flax.

She crushed a cushion against her chest, but couldn't ease the ache. Why had Marcus spoken out against Nero? Why had he made himself a traitor? He should have considered his family. Considered her.

He'd once told her a story about a Persian princess who spent her life locked within a tower. Each night her father bolted the door, and each night the princess pushed aside her bed to descend a secret stairway that led to an enchanted world. There, she danced till dawn. But no magic stairway lay beneath Flavia's sleeping couch.

She threw the cushion at the wall.

Startled, the doves flew up in their cage. She'd forgotten to feed them.

"I'm hungry too," she said.

She opened the cage door and scattered a handful of seeds. Remus pecked her fingers, but Romulus allowed her to hold him in her palm. She felt the down of his feathers, the quick pulse of his tiny heart. It would take little effort to wrench his neck and end his life. To Romulus she held the power of a god.

The bird cooed.

She returned him to his cage.

Hearing voices, she went to the window. She unlatched the shutters and, leaning her elbows on the sill, peered down at the courtyard. Through a fig tree's cluster of leaves she saw linen sheets fluttering on the line. Her father's toga lay stretched on a rack, bleaching in the sun.

Servants carried a copper vat of steaming water from the baths while Constantina supervised. Her face, usually unblemished, was blotched from boiling potash. She might have been a household slave of the lowest order.

In my domus, Flavia thought, laundry will be sent out to a fullery, bread sent in from a bakery, and slaves will spin the flax. She picked at a callus, the result of last night's spinning. Her father was ailing, her brother dead, and today was a holiday, yet her mother insisted dirty linen must be washed, floors had to be swept, and tiles scrubbed. You'd think she was a farmer's wife, not a senator's.

A servant threw an armload of linen into the vat of boiling water, then added an amphora of urine for whitening. A smudge-pot of burning sulfur enhanced the stench. Another servant mixed together potash, carbonate of soda, and fuller's earth before dumping the resulting mess into the vat. Scalding water splashed the servant's face and she cried out. Blindness, scars, and injury without glory of battle.

Flavia sighed. Housework bored her.

She wandered to her vanity, picked up a sandalwood comb and ran it through her hair. Yanking at a knot, she clenched her teeth and ripped it out. She rolled the hair between her thumb and forefinger, curious to see how tight she could make the ball. Losing interest she flicked it to the floor. The wad landed next to a pile of dirty underclothes. The maid would sweep it up.

Yawning, not from exhaustion but tedium, she removed the key she wore around her neck and unlocked the box in which she kept her treasures. Fishing through earrings, bracelets and pendants, she found her mirror. She stared into the polished silver at her reflection—skin pale as ivory without the use of lead or arsenic, rosy cheeks without benefit of red ochre. People called her beautiful, but she wished for raven curls thick as Elissa's. She bared her teeth. No particles of food, but Elissa's were whiter. Her mother had suggested rinsing her mouth with urine to bleach them.

Flavia stuck out her tongue.

She opened her cedar chest and found her new robe. Holding it against her body, she smoothed the silk over her hips and imagined how she would look. The color accentuated her green eyes and set off her hair to perfection. She pursed her lips in imitation of an actress she had seen. In pantomimes women played any role they wanted: whores, queens, goddesses. Even men.

She let the robe slide to the floor.

What use was beauty if she was locked away in her parents' domus?

Angry voices summoned her back to the window.

Below in the courtyard Constantina shook her fist at a crow perched on the laundry line. "Get away from my clean clothes!"

The bird spread its wings, flapped several times, and flew into the fig tree. If Flavia reached out her hand, her fingers might have grazed his blue-black feathers. He cawed and more crows appeared, swooping through the courtyard, alighting in the tree. The racket made the women furious. Led by Constantina they waved their arms and yelled.

Flavia found it funny to see her mother, usually so staid and proper, clapping her hands, even cursing at the birds.

The women gathered round the tree and tried to shake the trunk, but the tree proved too stout. They pelted the crows with bits of soap. A screeching cloud ascended from the branches, flew skyward and disappeared over the roof.

Still sputtering obscenities, Constantina and the servants returned to their work.

Flavia laughed so hard tears rolled down her cheeks. The crows, her mother, and the laundry struck her as ridiculous. What difference did it make if wash was done today, tomorrow or never? As soon as the linens were folded and neatly put away they would pile up again. Surely there was more to life than endless laundry.

Her tears fell faster and her laughter became sobs. She would spend her days locked in her parents' domus until they married her to some dull senator.

Worse yet, stupid Egnatius.

If she had wings she'd sail away, escape her destiny. If she had wings, she'd soar to Olympus where the gods were said to dwell. Then she'd look down on the world and choose a fate that suited her.

But she was not a bird.

Wiping moisture from her eyes she leaned over the windowsill.

The washing was done, and her mother had retreated to the house. Servants poured the vat of steaming water onto the courtyard's paving stones.

Flavia studied the fig tree's twisting branches. Reaching out her hand, her fingertips brushed the smooth bark of a sturdy limb. The tree stood taller than the two-story house. How difficult could it be to grab hold of a branch and scale the roof? Escape to Nero's feast.

She couldn't fly, but she could climb.

CHAPTER XIV

E lissa stayed close to Justinus, clutching her bundle of clothes, as they pushed through Meditrinalia revelers. On every corner there was drinking, gambling, music. They turned down one street and another, traveling deep into the Subura's maze. The stola she'd borrowed from Flavia was ruined, the hem caked with mud, and her white slippers were filthy from the gutter. She drew the ragged palla close. At least, in her forlorn state, she wouldn't be recognized. A squeak came from a pile of garbage and she almost screamed. A cat shot out of nowhere in pursuit of a rat.

Justinus smiled at her, oblivious of any drama.

"Are we almost there?" she asked.

"I promise you this will be worth it."

They came to a row of shops, closed due to the holiday. Justinus stopped in front of a four-story tenement, an insula housing a number of small apartments. Once lemon yellow, soot had darkened it to mustard. Most of the ground floor served as a tavern where apartment dwellers, lacking a kitchen, might purchase a hot meal. A phallus, spewing beads of red, had been painted on the wall and scrawled beneath it: *Tigellinus squeezes blood from stones.* Beside the tavern stood a cobbler's shop. A CLOSED sign hung on the door.

Justinus tried the latch, but it was locked.

107

"Your friend lives here?"

"Not here, in the Hebrew Quarter. He's a tentmaker by trade and lives above his shop, but he preaches where he can."

"Preaches what?"

Justinus knocked three times.

The cobbler's door cracked open. A man wearing a leather apron stood in the doorway, his face as tan as ox-hide.

"Peace be with you," he said. Eying Elissa, he added, "What brings you here?"

"The gathering," Justinus replied. "She won't cause any trouble."

The cobbler hesitated, then opened the door wider. "No one saw you?"

"And no one knows we've come," Justinus said.

The cobbler looked up and down the street before allowing them inside. They walked through a workshop, passing a table piled with scraps of leather, shelves crammed with boots and saddlebags. Fox pelts hung from the rafters. Elissa recognized the hide of an ox, and a deerskin dangled from the ceiling. Tools for scraping, stretching, cutting, were arranged on hooks along the walls. An acrid smell permeated the room. She peered into a vat where a lamb wallowed in brine.

She stared at the lamb with horror and fascination. The men continued talking, and she caught snippets of their conversation.

"Many will die?" Justinus asked.

"...crucifixions and worse..."

Elissa gripped the vat and hung onto the rim, sickness rising to her mouth, transfixed by the lamb's dead eyes. The shape morphed into something human. A baby. It was breathing, bubbles rising to the surface, tiny hands reaching toward her from the brine, the small mouth open in a wail.

The child she might have borne.

"Elissa?"

She blinked, attempting to bring Justinus into focus.

"Come," he said. His voice, calm and reassuring, drew her.

At the rear of the shop, they passed through a door and into a courtyard—if you could call it that—a shaft between buildings littered with discarded furniture and slops. The cobbler pointed toward a stairway. "Fourth floor," he said. "Today's watchword is Jerusalem."

They climbed the steps, half-rotten and encrusted with pigeon droppings. Bypassing apartments on the lower floors, where residents might hope for running water, they reached the fifth floor and walked along a hallway. Justinus stopped at a door inscribed with a dove and an olive branch. He knocked three times.

"Why so secretive?" Elissa asked.

"Informants."

"Whose?"

"Agents of Tigellinus."

"Why should he care about your friend?"

"Since the time of Claudius, Jews are not permitted to gather due to infighting in the synagogues."

"This is a gathering of Jews?" Elissa felt faintly sick.

"Not Jews, really, followers of Jesus. Tigellinus will use the slimmest excuse to make them scapegoats for any trouble."

Elissa's heart began to pound. "Do they really drink blood?" she asked, watching Justinus intently. She had known him all her life, considered him a brother, but perhaps war had changed him. "I've heard they devour human flesh."

Justinus chuckled.

The peephole slid open.

"Jerusalem," Justinus said.

A soldier stood in the doorway. Now, Elissa thought, we'll be arrested, hauled off to jail for attending this forbidden meeting. But the soldier merely nodded. "Peace be with you," he said, admitting them into a one room apartment.

"And with you, brother," Justinus replied. Lowering his voice, he said to Elissa, "Tigellinus sends soldiers to hold Paul prisoner, but they soon become his followers."

Paul of Tarsus. Elissa had heard of him. Her heart beat faster.

The room might have held ten comfortably, but at least thirty men and women stood pressed against the mud-brick walls and sat huddled on the sagging floor. Many wore the simple garb of plebs and slaves, and some wore the felt caps of freedmen. Several wore fine robes. Elissa felt certain she recognized a senator. Someone bumped into her, and she turned to see a small, bald man with a grey beard. He smiled at her, and she couldn't help smiling back. His eyes glowed with warmth, and instantly she felt she knew him. A beaklike nose overwhelmed his face and his eyebrows joined in the middle, but his smile was beautiful. He nodded at Elissa and continued through the crowded room.

"Who is he?" she asked Justinus.

"The prophet Paul."

Elissa had expected the notorious prophet to be tall, his face haunted like a fugitive's, not this crooked little man. Paul appeared serene, incapable of hurting anyone. "Why is he held a prisoner?" she asked.

"His preaching caused a riot in Jerusalem. Soldiers rescued him from an angry mob, and when he claimed to be a Roman citizen King Agrippa sent him here."

"He's not a citizen?"

"He was shipwrecked, and his papers lost at sea. We Romans don't know what to do with him, so he's kept under guard and when he ventures out he's chained. But Paul is a respected scholar. Even Seneca reveres his writings."

Elissa nodded toward two men dressed in white robes. "Who are they?"

"The younger is Timothy, the older Luke. They accompanied Paul from Antioch."

Luke, a stocky man with the swarthy complexion of a Greek, scrutinized the crowd as if expecting trouble. Timothy, clean-shaven and open-faced, smiled beatifically.

Paul joined them. Luke nodded, and Paul said, "Friends." His gentle voice was difficult to hear above the chatter.

"Silence," Luke bellowed. "The prophet speaks."

"Shalom," Paul said, and the crowd grew quiet. "Shalom, my friends, and peace be with you." A calm descended on the crowd, peace so profound it was palpable.

Elissa sank into the feeling.

Paul spoke in a soothing voice, "I bring a message from the Lord."

What lord, she wondered.

"Not our lord and master, Nero," a young man called out.

Elissa glanced at the soldier, expecting him to pounce. But he was laughing, as were others.

"There is but one true Lord," Paul said. A murmur ran through the crowd, a collective sigh of relief. Paul spoke as if he were a messenger from a world beyond this one. "There is but one God, almighty and all powerful."

One god instead of many? The idea seemed unfathomable. But many people claimed their god to be most powerful. Elissa listened for a name, expecting to hear Jupiter, god of thunderbolts and war, or maybe Zeus, Jupiter's Greek counterpart. She would not have been surprised if the prophet named a foreign god: The Babylonian's, Shamash, rising from the mountain, rays of light pouring from his shoulders, or the Egyptian sun-god, Re.

Paul looked around the room. His eyes met Elissa's, flooding her with peace. "The one true God is love," he said, as if speaking only to her.

Love.

The word left her stunned. Love, the most dreaded of conditions, a sickness she wrestled with in secret. How could this odd, little man call that madness highest of all gods? Love was treacherous. Love brought grief and led to disaster. Better to worship hate. Malice proved a wiser god.

"Do you think I don't know hate?" Paul said, as if in answer to her thoughts. "Before I knew the Lord, I believed myself to be a righteous man. A Pharisee. I followed every law set down by the temple priests, detested those who broke the rules. Hatred ruled my heart. Hatred seeped into my blood like poison, seeped into my bones and weakened me until I stood before the gates of Hell. But my Lord Jesus provides the antidote: Love your enemies."

Elissa nearly laughed. Love your enemies, the idea was ridiculous. She thought of Nero. Instead of attending this meeting, she should be plotting his annihilation.

Paul's eyes locked on hers. "In the name of righteousness," he said, "I even committed murder."

She inhaled sharply. Did the prophet read her thoughts?

"Before I knew the Lord, these hands—" he held his hands before his face, his expression mortified, "—these hands held Stephen down as he was stoned to death."

Elissa stood dumbstruck, soaking up Paul's words.

"In the name of righteousness," he spoke softly, but his voice rumbled through her soul, "I made my heart a stone."

Her chest ached, and she found it difficult to breathe.

"Elissa, what's wrong?"

She heard Justinus, knew he spoke, but she couldn't answer. Sorrow poured out of her heart, bursting through her eyes. Through tears, she stared at him.

And then Paul stood in front of her, gently touching her face. "God loves you," he said. "Let God in, and you will heal."

The concept of a loving god, a god that cared about mere mortals, was inconceivable. Gods were fickle. They looked down on the world and used humans for their amusement.

"My words sound strange to you," Paul said, sorrow apparent in his eyes. "Rome gained an empire by use of ruthless power, but God's Kingdom can be won only with compassion. If I speak the tongue of angels, but speak without love, my words mean no more than clanging cymbals." His voice crashed over her like waves, drawing her into his depths. "If I am gifted with prophetic powers, if I comprehend life's deepest mysteries, if I possess the faith to move mountains, but lack the ability to love—my vision is clouded, my understanding false—"

Elissa surfaced, breathing heavily, sweat pouring down her neck. The fabric of her tunica stuck to her back. Bodies pressed against her, holding her afloat. Justinus stood by her side. He broke bread from a loaf and offered her a piece.

She placed the morsel in her mouth, tried to chew. But the bread felt dry against her tongue.

He handed her a chalice.

She sipped the wine, allowing it to soak the bread.

"Flesh of His flesh. Blood of His blood."

Voices echoed through the room, repeating what the prophet said. "Flesh of His flesh. Blood of His blood."

"Drink, and become one with God."

The bread grew warm and slippery. Elissa tried to swallow. Gagged. She spat the bread into her palm.

"I feel sick."

Justinus led her from the room, pushing through the swarm until they escaped into the hallway. Feeling faint, Elissa leaned against the wall.

"The way of love is powerful," Justinus said.

"Love is a weakness."

"Love gives us strength—the strength to have faith. Love brings light to life's darkest hours. I love you, Elissa. You are my light."

His words rushed through her like a fever, coursing through her veins, her limbs. Justinus leaned toward her. She turned her head, and his lips brushed her cheek.

"I have to go."

She ran along the hallway, and prayed he would catch up with her. His touch caused her knees to buckle. She wanted to be swept into his arms, to feel his body against hers. Flesh of my flesh, blood of my blood. She wanted to be one with him.

"My vows," she whispered.

"Give yourself to love, Elissa. Give yourself to me."

He lifted her chin, gently pressed his lips on hers. Her mouth parted. Fire shot through her body, a melting heat that sealed her wounds. But the vow of chastity she'd pledged to Vesta was branded on her soul. And now it burned.

"I can't," she said, drawing away. "I have been chosen."

Justinus slammed his fist into the wall and chips of plaster rained from the ceiling. "Chosen to live a loveless life? To follow gods who have no power? Let's leave Rome together, start a new life—"

"That's foolishness." She saw that she hurt him, but what he proposed was madness. "I'm a servant of the empire."

"You mean you serve Nero?"

"I must go *now*." She started for the stairway.

Justinus caught her by the arm. "Do you believe in miracles?"

She shrugged.

"You have been chosen, Elissa, not by Rome, but by a greater power. You've been chosen by the one true God. As a vestal you can gain the ear of Nero, convince him to follow Jesus."

"Is that why you brought me here?" She would have laughed, but saw he spoke in earnest. "You want me to persuade Nero to become a Messianic Jew? Nero believes himself a god."

"Miracles are possible," Justinus said quietly.

Elissa doubted it. Gathering her palla, she attempted to regain her composure. Justinus had lost all reason to this foreign god. He was a fool to hope that Nero might follow Jesus, a fool to believe that she might run away with him.

And she'd been a fool to consider, even for one moment, breaking her vow of chastity.

CHAPTER XV

Elissa tugged the handles of the massive doors, but the doors were locked. The sky deepened to a dusky blue and Venus winked, warning her that she was late for the evening ritual. She pounded the heavy knocker so hard she bruised her knuckles.

Finally the doors of the House of Vestals opened, and Thais peered out.

"The evening meal has finished," she grumbled in her broken Latin. "Trouble follows you."

Elissa hurried through the foyer, still carrying her bundle of ragged clothes. Lifting her skirts, she sprinted across the atrium, ran along the colonnaded vestibule and up the marble steps.

"There you are." Angerona stood at the top of the stairway. "Mother Amelia sent me to find you."

"I feel ill." Elissa headed for her cubicle.

"Where have you been?"

"Visiting my father." Elissa slipped through the curtain of her cubicle and Angerona followed.

"You're lying. I saw you."

"Where?"

"With Gallus Justinus."

"He walked me home."

"By way of a cobbler's shop in the Subura?"

"You followed us?"

Elissa sank onto her bed. A rotten taste surfaced from her stomach. She wanted to run, get away from Angerona. But that wasn't possible. She had to maintain protocol.

Angerona hovered over her, like a bird of prey. "I can guess what you've been doing," she said. "Meanwhile you pretend to be so good, so pure."

Elissa felt the contents of her stomach churning. "You're making assumptions, Angerona. You know me well enough—"

"Not any more."

Elissa stared at Angerona. "Maybe I don't know you either. Maybe I never did. Maybe you're a spy."

"What if I am?" Angerona set her jaw, her eyes impenetrable.

"You'd better go," Elissa said.

"And you'd better watch yourself."

Elissa sat, listening, until Angerona's footsteps faded. She stared at the space where Angerona had just stood. Nothing in this world was solid, nothing safe. Exactly what did Angerona know? If she had learned of Paul's illegal gatherings the prophet's life might be in danger, and if she knew Elissa and Justinus had attended a meeting of Messianic Jews, she might use that information to lord it over Elissa. But if she had witnessed the *kiss*, she would be uncontrollable.

She touched her chest, her throat, her lips, recalling the scent of him.

The temple bells sounded the call to evening ritual.

Elissa stood, tore off her stola, tossed it on the stool. Bending over the water basin, she stared at her reflection. Her eyes held a new light, a fire. She splashed icy water on her face attempting to extinguish it. Then she donned her sacramental robes and hurried to the evening ritual.

The vestals stood, encircling the sacred fire—a copper cauldron of flames. Elissa tried to take her place unnoticed.

"You're late." Mother Amelia's voice echoed off the temple's domed ceiling.

Ancient Junia, her eyes hooded and rheumy, stood beside the high vestal. Covering her mouth, she coughed. Even at the age of sixty-three she refused to retire, preferring to retain her status as a vestal virgin, rather than live under the roof of resentful relatives. Next to Junia stood Cornelia, barely eight years old. She smiled at Elissa, and Elissa winked at her. Most girls of Cornelia's age spent their days playing with dolls, arguing with siblings. Elissa felt sorry for the child. But she felt no pity for Marcia, a beefy woman in her thirties. Marcia came from a wealthy family, and she liked to throw around her weight—making everyone's business her concern. She and Angerona exchanged a knowing look as Elissa took her place.

"Your slippers are filthy," Mother Amelia said, "your robe in disarray. Where have you been, Elissa?"

"Visiting my father—"

"You left this house again without permission. Your behavior is unacceptable."

"I apologize, but—"

"Come here."

Head bowed, Elissa approached the high vestal.

Mother Amelia lifted Elissa's chin. "You eyes shine unnaturally and your cheeks are flushed." She pressed her palm against Elissa's forehead. "Yet, you don't seem feverish."

"My father isn't well and—"

"Go back to your place."

Grasping an amphora by both handles, the high vestal raised the vessel over the granite altar. "Goddess, Vesta, Daughter of the Hearth, Keeper of the Sacred Flame, we call on you to purify your servants." Pointedly, she glanced at Elissa before pouring wine into the stone basin.

"So may it be," the priestesses recited in unison.

Mother Amelia dipped her hand into the basin, sprinkled wine over the fire.

Elissa chanted incantations and performed the rituals, as if in a trance. Her thoughts dwelled on Justinus. Until recently she had accepted her fate, accepted her role as a vestal virgin, but now she wondered what it would be like to lie beside a man. To be his wife. To bear his child. Was her destiny to be the same as Junia's? Would she spend her days, withered and unloved, unknown, except within the sisterhood?

Frankincense filled the temple, smoky and resinous. Clouds of incense drifted to the ceiling and out through the latticework walls, carrying the vestals' prayers and blessings to the sick and dying—and beyond to the netherworld.

Elissa's thoughts wandered to Flavia. Ambition ruled her sister's heart. She prayed that Spurius had delivered her message to Nero. It wasn't a lie. Flavia *would* be married soon. If she lacked a groom, that would be rectified. Meanwhile, betrothal was a sacred vow which made her untouchable. Even to Nero. He would be furious, of course. *Let him be.* If he continued to pursue Flavia, he would bring the wrath of Vesta down on Rome.

Mother Amelia's voice rang out, waking Elissa from her trance. "We invoke you, goddess, to grant Rome your protection."

"So be it," the vestals proclaimed.

Elissa wished she could believe in Paul's almighty God, wished she could have faith like Justinus. But the idea of blindly following a formless, nameless God seemed impossible. And yet, Paul's message haunted her.

We are nothing without love.

One by one, the priestesses retrieved an olive branch from a carefully stacked pile. People made substantial donations to receive mention in the vestals' prayers. As each priestess placed her olive branch upon the fire, she spoke those prayers aloud.

"May Magia Decimitia receive—" Junia cleared her trembling voice before continuing, "—the blessings of the goddess in her recovery from childbirth and—" Her words were garbled in a fit of coughing. She seemed more ill than usual.

Marcia was next to place a branch upon the fire. Inevitably, her prayers included Galeria Fundana, an heiress (and childhood friend) who endured a troubled marriage. "May Galeria Fundana find relief from creditors." Marcia's jowls jiggled when she spoke. "And may her wastrel husband, the drunken philanderer and gambler, receive the misfortune he so richly—"

"Enough," Mother Amelia said. "Please extend my thanks to Galeria Fundana for her continued generosity."

Was it good work to offer prayers only for the rich? Elissa recalled the poverty she'd seen that afternoon in the Subura. Promising salvation to the wealthy in return for payment seemed hypocritical.

When her turn came to speak, she measured her words. "May Rome be purified," she said, hesitating before adding, "and may the gods rid us of all plagues."

Nero in particular.

The branches burned to coals as they sang in praise of Vesta. Then Mother Amelia closed as she always did. "May the goddess grant us strength to turn our backs on evil and courage to do good."

One-by-one the priestesses bowed to Mother Amelia and kissed her ring. They departed, leather slippers shushing on the stone.

"Elissa, stay. I want to speak with you."

"Yes, Mother?"

"What troubles you?"

"Nothing."

"You have nothing to confess?"

Elissa shook her head.

"I'm told you spent the afternoon with Gallus Justinus."

Trying not to panic, Elissa said, "He walked me from my father's house."

"I trust you know the punishment for consorting with a man."

"Yes, Mother."

A vestal's blood could not be spilled, but if she broke her vow of chastity her suffering would exceed any pain rendered by a sword. After an inquisition and condemnation by the Collegiate of Pontiffs, she would be severely flogged. Bound and enshrouded, she would be carried through the streets as if she were already dead and taken to the Field of Iniquity where she would be entombed. Scant provisions would prolong her torment while, slowly, she asphyxiated.

"Don't allow your heart to rule your mind, Elissa."

"No, Mother."

"There are many forms of love—the love of a parent for a child, love of country, compassion." The high vestal shook her head. "The love you dally with is untamed passion, a stirring in the groin. Think of Helen of Troy, think of Jason and Medea, think of Persephone and her eternal bond to Hades—"

"Yes, but—"

"Stay away from Gallus Justinus. Do you understand?" Lines etched Mother Amelia's forehead. "You are a guardian of the sacred fire, highest of the elements. Nothing impure may touch your body, your heart, your mind."

Elissa saw her glimpse of happiness fast fading.

The furrows in the high vestal's forehead softened. "You must tame your emotions," she said. "Despite your brother's death, I cannot make allowances for your behavior. Tonight, while you tend the fire, ponder my words."

"Yes, Mother Amelia."

The high vestal started for the door, then paused. "One thing more," she said. "I'm told Angerona is in communication with Tigellinus."

"Tigellinus?"

"Take care, Elissa. I cannot protect you from everything."

Fear raced through Elissa as the doors swung shut after the Vestal Maxima. If Angerona reported to Tigellinus, she was a spy of the worst sort. Not only could she not be trusted, but she must be avoided.

For ten years Elissa had dedicated herself to the goddess, but now she felt like an outsider. Angerona had deserted her, Marcia shunned her, Cornelia was too young to understand, Junia too old. She had no one in whom she could confide. Except for Justinus.

She sank onto a stone bench and stared at the cauldron—wide and deep, supported by four legs—the womb of the Great Mother cradled by the four winds. Each night a priestess sat vigil by the fire. Once a year, on the Kalends of March at the new moon, the flame was permitted to spend itself. The Pontifex Maximus then rekindled the fire using a quartz crystal and the sun to create a divine spark. Otherwise, allowing the fire to die was considered an offense against the state. Through flakes of ash, the embers glowed. Fire might be damped, but it was not easily extinguished.

Her thoughts returned to Justinus.

She added several lumps of coal and watched the flames ignite.

Too restless to sit, she wandered the temple's perimeter. Latticework adjoined the circle of pillars allowing her to see out to the forum. Night had fallen and the streets teemed with traffic. The ban on carts was lifted and wooden wheels clattered on cobblestones. She heard shouting, laughter, music. On Palatine Hill lights from the Domus Transitoria glittered, welcoming Meditrinalia revelers to Nero's feast.

"Jesus," Elissa said softly. "If you're listening, protect my sister."

Feeling guilt at having invoked a foreign god, she quickly said a prayer to Vesta.

She wandered to the doorway of the inner-sanctum, and stepped into the cool, dark chamber. Here lay all the secrets, earthen jars said to house ashes from Troy; divining stones, so polished you could peer into the future; and holy of holies, the Palladium. Elissa had never seen it, but she'd heard the stories—to look directly at the relic would cause instant blindness. Carved by the goddess Athena for her mortal friend, Pallas, legend claimed that upon Pallas's death the Palladium fell to earth along with Athena's tears. At the fall of Troy, Aeneas salvaged the relic from the flames and carried it to Rome.

Elissa glanced at the temple doors. No one would be coming here tonight, not on the night of the feast.

Lifting the veil carefully, she stared in wonder, not at a statue of the goddess as she'd imagined, but at a phallus. Carved from ebony, black and smooth and intricately detailed. She reached out her hand to touch it, ran her fingers down the shaft, and felt heat rising through her body, a surge like she had never known. She waited, expecting to be blinded. But, if anything, her vision grew sharper. Her senses intensified—touch, smell, hearing.

The taste of Justinus.

She ran her hands over her breasts and her nipples grew taut. Sliding her hands down her belly, and then lower, she sought the forbidden place.

She should be tending the fire.

Reciting a prayer.

Thinking about what Mother Amelia had told her.

What had the high vestal said?

But the only thing she could remember was his kiss.

CHAPTER XVI

"More lentils, Master?"

Akeem's manner made it obvious that he found saying "Master" difficult. Sometimes Justinus wondered why he put up with the slave, but he reminded himself, as a follower of Jesus, he must practice tolerance.

Akeem offered him the bowl of lentils.

"I've had enough." Justinus reclined on his dining couch and held out his chalice. "But more wine would be welcome."

"You haven't touched the milk-fed calf." Akeem pointed to a platter. "The cook especially prepared it with honey and coriander."

"Remove the food," Justinus said. The dish was his favorite, but tonight he desired the oblivion of wine.

"You need to eat."

"I'm celebrating Meditrinalia, the harvest of grapes."

Akeem gave Justinus a surly look as if he, not the cook and kitchen slaves, had prepared the dinner. He removed items from the table and set them on a wooden tray, carefully arranging each piece of crockery, each bronze plate, each copper bowl and silver spoon with irritating deliberation.

Justinus reached for the wine jar and Akeem snatched it away.

"Must I remind you that I'm your master?"

"You've had enough."

"Pig's balls," Justinus grumbled. "Can't a man drink at his own table?"

"Wine won't drown thoughts of that girl."

"What girl?" Justinus splashed wine into his cup, adding only a dash of water.

"You know which." Akeem picked up a bowl of olives and popped a green olive into his mouth. "In Egypt the act of copulation is considered sacred, priestesses are encouraged to have conjugal relations. The union of Mother Sky and Father Earth maintains the world's balance." He spit the pit into his hand.

"What else would one expect of sand-lovers?" Justinus said, vaguely aware the wine was creeping up on him. "Egyptians worship animals—cats and dogs, and some kind of river-horse. I think the desert sun has fried your brains."

"And wine has pickled yours." The bowl slipped from Akeem's hand, crashed on the mosaic floor, and olives scattered like marbles. He made no attempt to retrieve the olives or the shattered bowl. "Roman gods might appear human, but they act like beasts and argue like fishmongers."

"Forgive me for insulting you, Akeem." Justinus waved his empty chalice. "I'm not myself. I need to think."

"Wine muddles your thoughts." Akeem whisked away the serving tray and, dishes rattling, swept out of the dining room.

Justinus punched a cushion, shoved it under his head, and resettled himself. He poured another cup of wine and sipped.

He studied the frescoed walls, remembering when his mother had commissioned one of Pompeii's finest artists to paint the lavish murals. She had taken great care to see their home was immaculate, as she had taken care of him. He remembered how she'd listened to his childish woos, kissed his bruises when he fell, nursed him through fevers. He remembered how she'd told him stories late at night, tales of courageous sailors, terrifying monsters, magical princesses.

She'd promised him a baby sister.

But on the night his sister was due to arrive, his mother had screamed—so loud and long, her shrieks still echoed through his memory. There had been no baby sister. No more nighttime stories, no more mother. His father, claiming Justinus was coddled, had sent him to school and trained him for the military.

In Britannia, most of the men placed under Justinus had exceeded him in age by ten or even twenty years. Tough and experienced professional soldiers—they didn't trust members of the aristocracy, didn't trust him. He held himself responsible for the massacre of Boudicca. His men had refused to heed orders barked out by a novice in his twenties. He'd lacked the strength to properly direct them. Lacked their respect. They'd whispered that his friendship with Nero had earned him rank, not his merit. Maybe that was true.

His war wound ached. He changed position on the couch and took another gulp of wine, trying to forget the day he had received the battle-scar. But memories came rushing back.

Autumn, an afternoon of golden light. Haystacks in neat rows. A flock of sheep. The boy appeared, as if from nowhere, eyes blazing, shouting obscenities. Justinus didn't have the heart to fight, and he turned away. But the boy charged him with a pitchfork. Not even a javelin. Stabbed him in the back.

He'd had no choice but to kill him.

Justinus adjusted his cushion, but found no comfortable position.

If the boy had lived, what would he be doing now? Tilling fields? Seeing to his flock of sheep? Tending apple trees? He might be old enough to take a wife.

Chubby cupids stared from the walls. They hovered in a blood-drenched sky above two lovers. The lovers embraced heart to heart, limbs intertwined, lost in eternal bliss.

Or eternal damnation.

And he was damned to love a woman sworn to chastity.

Akeem was right. Wine did nothing to drown thoughts of Elissa.

Justinus closed his eyes and saw her face. Solemn, proud. Sensual as Venus. What was she thinking now? She was stubborn. She would never forgive Nero for her brother's death. Never forgive his insult to the House of Rubrius. And now Nero planned to sink his teeth into Flavia. Or, even worse, Elissa.

Justinus sat up. He had to act. He had to stop the princeps. He couldn't be responsible for another slaughter, another Boudicca.

He drank more wine, felt its warmth slide down his throat. Akeem was wrong on one account: wine didn't muddle him. On the contrary, it clarified his thoughts. He swung his feet onto the floor and stared at the mosaic pattern, waiting for the tiles to come back into focus. Placing one hand on the couch, he steadied himself and got up. Blood rushed to his head, and through a wine-red haze the cherubs watched.

But his path was clear.

He would confront Nero, convince him to offer an apology to the House of Rubrius and declare Marcus a hero, demand that Nero put aside his lust for Flavia. His lust for Elissa. He had seen the way Nero looked at her.

Justinus downed the dregs of his cup for fortitude. Tonight he would convince Nero that Rome's fate lay in the hands of the one true God, in the hands of Jesus.

"Akeem," he called, "my chariot."

❧

Flavia unlatched the shutters.

Music from the festival drifted through the window of her chamber, but her father's domus was silent and stultifying. The servants had gone out to celebrate while her parents slept. She would have left too, but Spurius stood guard.

Careful not to make a sound, she placed a footstool beneath the window. Romulus and Remus stirred in their cage, cooing and ruffling their feathers.

Hiking up her stola, the new green silk, she climbed onto the stool and then onto the windowsill.

Clinging to the shutters, she tottered.

The paving stones seemed far away. Further than she remembered.

She recalled a story the servants whispered about an actress falling to her death. Her lover found her body the next morning, but no one knew if it had been an accident.

Refusing to look down, she steadied herself.

"Venus, protect me."

The goddess of love might not be the most dependable, Venus could be fickle, but Flavia relied on her.

Reaching out her hand, she leaned out of the window, as far as she dared, and touched the fig tree's closest branch. The slippery bark escaped her fingers. She tumbled backward, falling off the window-ledge and back into her chamber. The footstool skidded, crashed against the wall.

Romulus and Remus fluttered in their cage, wings batting the iron bars.

Flavia sat on the floor, listening, attempting to determine if the noise had roused her parents. Except for the doves, the house remained quiet.

She rubbed her buttocks. No doubt there would be a bruise.

Her bed seemed inviting. Safe. But the feast offered her a chance for life, a chance for freedom. The thought of marrying Egnatius propelled her to the window. She brushed off her stola and climbed back onto the ledge.

To escape, she'd have to jump, grab hold of a branch. She tucked her stola around her waist, studied the tree, and found a sturdy branch. She imagined grabbing hold of it, imagined swinging easily over the roof.

She bent her knees, took a deep breath, and froze.

Looking down, she felt dizzy.

She considered sneaking down the stairs, but Spurius waited by the door along with Cerberus, and she'd never get past them.

She focused on the tree, bent her knees and jumped.

The branch groaned, and she thought it might snap. Scrambling for a foothold, she wrenched herself higher and locked her hands around another branch. Her weight dragged the branch down, and then it rebounded nearly throwing her off. She prayed to Venus as she dangled over the courtyard and bobbed like a fish caught on a line.

The moon had not yet risen and the night was dark. Below, not far from where she hung, a lower section of the roof jutted off at an angle. If she could maneuver her way over it, she could drop to safety.

Her arms ached and sweat poured down her back. Her palms felt slick against the bark. Humming a song she used to sing with Marcus, pretending this was just a game, she swung her legs, willing herself toward the roof. With every swing, she got closer. Just a few feet more—

The branch gave way with a crack. Breaking from the tree, she tumbled toward the tiles. It didn't feel like flying.

She landed with a thud, arms outstretched to break her fall. The terracotta tiles cut into her palms, her knees. She moved her arms, her legs. Blood trickled down her thighs. Her hair had come undone and fell in sweaty strands around her face. She'd survived the jump without broken bones, but her stola had ripped from the shoulder broach. She managed to refasten it.

Barking echoed through the courtyard.

Digging her fingernails between clay tiles, Flavia wedged her sandaled toes into a crevice and dragged herself toward the pinnacle. A tile broke free, slid down the incline, and clattered in the courtyard below.

She heard the jangling of keys, followed by the voice of Spurius.

She lay still, her body flat against the roof, willing herself to be invisible.

"These old tiles need to be replaced," Spurius spoke to the dog. "Probably a squirrel." She heard him kick the broken tile across the courtyard.

Cerberus whined.

"Come on boy, you'll catch that squirrel in the morning."

Flavia listened to the slave's shuffling footsteps until she was certain he and Cerberus had left.

She raised her head and surveyed the courtyard. It appeared empty. No noise came from the house. She imagined Romulus and Remus pecking at their cage, hoping to escape.

Inch by inch, she crawled to the roof's pinnacle.

Houses of the aristocracy surrounded her like Roman matrons, boring and respectable. But in the distance, the Subura's tenements winked like bawdy actresses. The lights of Rome studded the seven hills, mirroring the heavens. Lantern-lit barges floated down the Tiber like stars in the Via Lactea.

On her hands and knees, Flavia crept along the rooftop, then carefully began her descent down the far side of the house. Finally, she reached the eaves and found the water-drain. She tossed her palla from the roof, watching the shawl as it billowed and twirled and toward the garden. Then she hiked her stola around her waist and shinnied down the thick lead pipe. The drain stopped several feet from the ground. She jumped into a hedge of rosemary, falling to her knees—a little worse for wear, but free. She brushed off her stola and tied the belt beneath her breasts.

Her father's domus remained dark. Protected by the night, she headed for the Domus Transitoria.

A riot of coaches, donkey carts, litters, and pedestrians choked the narrow streets. Justinus snapped the reins, urging his horses through the crowd. Heads turned and people gawked at the matched black stallions. Justinus cared little for luxury, but he took pride in his horses, Numidian, imported from North Africa.

The chariot veered, narrowly missing a wagonload of hay. The jolt unsettled Justinus. Drinking wine without benefit of food muddled his reflexes, but the need to speak to Nero acted as a stimulant.

At the forum's gate, Justinus brought the stallions to a halt. From here he would walk to the Domus Transitoria. A young tough leaned against the wall, chewing on a stalk of straw.

Justinus knew the type—seventeen and full of piss. Justinus jumped from the chariot, but the wine made him clumsy and he caught his toga.

The young man rushed to his aid. His laughing eyes and long dark curls made him appear innocent, but the tattoo on his arm told Justinus he was a member of a street gang.

"Want me to water your horse, sir?"

"No thanks." Justinus jerked free the fabric of his toga, nearly ripping it.

The young man patted one of the stallions. "Be a shame if they broke free."

Justinus read his meaning. "You'll be here for awhile?"

"Depends..."

The young man's smile reminded Justinus of Marcus, and he handed him several coins. "There'll be more when I return, and if my horses aren't here, make no mistake, I'll find you."

Feeling a bit unsteady, Justinus crossed the forum, careful to avoid the Well of the Comitia. Tonight no crowds of thousands gathered in the circular pit to hear a politician speak. Tonight, screaming children ran down the steps in pursuit of a mongrel dog, while a soothsayer stood on the rostra ranting about the apocalypse.

Taking the long way round, Justinus approached the Temple of Vesta. He stopped, attempting to see through the latticework. The sacred fire cast light on the walls, but he saw no priestesses. No Elissa. It was useless, he told himself, to dwell on hopeless fantasies.

Feeling the weight of Atlas on his heart, he headed toward the steps of the Temple of Castor and Pollux—the sons of Jupiter. Gaius Caligula had knocked out the back wall, transforming the temple into the entrance of the Domus Transitoria. In his day, Caligula had found it amusing to pose alongside statues of the gods and receive tribute from terrified supplicants.

Flaming stanchions lined the temple's stairway, and Praetorian Guards stood at attention. A guard saluted and said, "Good evening, Captain Gallus."

"Evening." Justinus saluted back.

"I've never had a chance to thank you, sir," the guard said. "You saved my life in that wretched hole."

Justinus had no recollection of the soldier, but he clapped him on the back. "You're a brave man."

They had all been brave. The Romans. The Britons. The dead.

Weighted by memories of war, Justinus trudged up the steps toward the massive Corinthian columns. Music spilled from the temple's entryway, along with shrieks of laughter. The air stank of rich perfume and rotting fruit, reeked of decadence. Every sinew of Justinus's body begged him to go home and make this an early night, but he steeled himself. Like Jesus and the moneylenders, he would confront Nero, steer Rome back to righteousness.

He walked briskly through the temple's sanctuary trying to ignore the grunts and groans that emanated from darkened corners.

The sight of Tigellinus, sitting before the palace doors, strengthened his resolve. The prefect sat in a chair, feet propped on a table inlaid with semi-precious stones. He gnawed on a boar's rib, cracked the bone and made sucking sounds as he extracted the marrow.

"Gallus Justinus," he said.

"Good evening Ofonius."

Tigellinus removed the bone from his mouth, frowned, and ran his fingers down a list of names. "You're not on the list."

"I'll take the place of Flavia Rubria Honoria."

Tigellinus swung his feet onto the ground and let out a protracted belch. "You're not much of a substitute for a pretty girl."

Justinus slammed his fist on the table, and said, "Don't bother getting up."

He entered a colonnaded courtyard. Exotic flowers perfumed the air—lilies, night jasmine and camellias raised in Nero's steam-heated, sunken garden. Fueled by wine and opium, Nero's guests didn't seem to notice the evening's dropping temperature. Scantily clad bodies lay entangled on carved benches; couples kissed beneath the portico, writhed against the walls, and slid to the mosaic floors.

Two pavilions stood at the garden's center. Within one of the pavilions a flutist played, providing accompaniment for a dancing courtesan. She removed her remaining veil and threw the sash at Justinus. Cupping her ample breasts, she pinched her nipples till they blushed, and Justinus felt a twinge within his groin.

He hurried on, walking along the portico. Footsteps tapped behind him. He turned to see who followed, and a man drew behind a pillar.

Justinus felt every muscle in his body tighten, and instantly his mind grew lucid as if he'd been transported back to the battlefield.

The man leaned against the pillar, ignoring Justinus, and stared at the courtesan.

Justinus continued walking, weaving through small groups of people, nodding at the guests he knew without stopping to chat. At the courtyard's far end, fountains splashed in Nero's famed nymphaeum. Sheets of glistening water cascaded over walls of rose-veined marble and sea-green serpentine. A scalloped fountain stood between two stairways. In the center of the fountain Venus spouted crimson wine from milk-white marble breasts. Two boys, not much older than eleven, stood beneath the goddess, their mouths open as they guzzled her offering. A gray-bearded senator stood by the fountain admiring the boys.

The man from the pillar stood nearby.

Justinus headed toward the stairway on the right, then abruptly turned the other way and ducked into a chamber adjoining the nymphaeum. He slipped through the crowd, hoping to lose his pursuer. The room was one of Nero's favorites—a vaulted ceiling and sky blue walls, bordered by glass tiles the color of indigo. On the far wall frescoed windows gave way to frescoed views, and painted porticos stretched endlessly through halcyon gardens. On the adjacent wall a mural depicted the adventures of Odysseus. Justinus hoped he might run into Nero, but the princeps was not to be found.

"Gallus Justinus," a woman's voice purred. "My, my, how you've grown up."

Justinus recognized Vibia Petilia, a widow with an appetite for younger men. Lead powder caked the wrinkles of her face. The starkness of her complexion contrasted with the slash of her vermilion mouth and made her appear more gorgon than human. Talon-like fingernails dug into his arm.

"You look well," Justinus said, attempting to be polite.

"Donkey piss!" Vibia chuckled. "I rival an Egyptian mummy." Her kohl-rimmed eyes ran down his body, lingered at his crotch.

"Have you seen our host?" Justinus asked.

She nudged her sagging chin toward the ceiling. "Upstairs in the banquet hall."

Escaping Vibia, Justinus headed back to the nymphaeum. He climbed one of the double stairways, pausing at the second story to look down at the garden and didn't see the man who had been following him.

He hurried along the vestibule, rehearsing what he planned to say to Nero. When he reached the banquet hall's entrance, powerful fingers snagged his shoulder.

"Let me pass Ofonius," Justinus said quietly.

"One move and I'll have your cock."

"In your dreams."

Tigellinus barked out an order and guards appeared, their daggers drawn. Within the banquet hall, all heads turned and whispers stirred the crowd.

"Gallus Justinus!" Nero's voice rang out above the others. "I see Tigellinus has found you. Welcome to my humble gathering. You're just in time for my next song."

The prefect's paw remained clamped on Justinus's shoulder.

Justinus wrenched himself away and entered the banquet hall.

Torches cast Nero's guests in ever-changing light. Rome's elite reclined on couches clustered around small tables littered with exotic foods: peacock tongues on a bed of asparagus, mint-fed snails, baby eels served in aspic with crushed pearls. More usual fare also graced the menu: eggs pickled with honey and liquamen, a pungent sauce devised from salted fish entrails. The delicacies were served in precious glassware from Nero's extensive collection. Half-naked slaves wandered through the crowd serving wine and fruit, while in the corner of the banquet hall, elevated on a dais, a musician strummed a cithara.

Larger than a lyre, the instrument's rich notes accompanied the tenor voice of Menecrates. Nero stood beside the master, draped in Tyrian purple silk spangled with glittering suns, a gilded laurel wreath crowning his curls.

Nearby, Poppaea Sabina, a deadly beauty who'd arranged to have her predecessor's head served on a platter, languished on a rose-pink couch in the center of the room. She wore a stola, blue as lapis-lazuli, embroidered with silver stars. Amber tresses cascaded down her neck, flirting with lush breasts. She appeared youthful, Justinus observed, for a woman who'd discarded two husbands and now made Nero her third.

She smiled as Justinus approached, displaying sharp white teeth.

Poppaea might prove useful. Known to favor Jews, she had become an ear to Flavius Josephus, the Judean philosopher. She might provide the foothold Justinus required for the teachings of Jesus to scale the walls of the palace.

She extended a pampered hand for Justinus to kiss, her eyes thirsty.

Breaking off his song mid-verse, Nero leapt from the dais and stalked toward his wife and Justinus. "I thought you didn't care for soldiers," he said, glancing at Justinus and back at Poppaea.

"Brains combined with brawn are quite delicious," she said.

"Then perhaps you should feast on Justinus tonight."

Poppaea's expression soured. "Meaning you have other plans?"

"Fill my friend's cup." Nero snapped his fingers, and a slave lifted a double-handled amphora. Nero smiled at Justinus. "My select vintage. Only the finest for an old friend."

Justinus said. "I'd like to speak with you about Flavia."

"Flavia who?" Poppaea asked.

"Just a girl I invited," Nero said.

"A girl you plan to—"

"To Meditrinalia," Nero said, cutting her off. He raised his cup. "To old friends and new wine."

Justinus tried again, "About Flavia—"

"Drink up, while I down my tonic. It soothes the throat and opens up my pharynx, so important for a singer." Nero gulped his drink and made a face. "And now I must see to my other guests, but Poppaea is certain to amuse you."

Before Justinus could say more about Flavia, the princeps left.

He sipped his wine. Caecuban, the best as promised. And hardly watered. He surveyed the banquet hall, studying the guests—senators who favored Nero's policies and could be bribed, senators' wives (welcome if their appearance was pleasing), aspiring philosophers whose arguments Nero found amusing, a famous gladiator and an actress, an infamous prostitute and her bene-factor. And, of course, Nero's sycophants, including Elissa's cousin, Egnatius Rubrius, a pimply youth of eighteen.

Egnatius basked in the glow of his father's achievements. Neither athlete nor scholar, he was best known for liberal spending of his father's assets. He reclined on a nearby couch; beside him lay a plumpish whore who'd passed into a stupor, and a young buck whose muscles attested to hours spent at the gymnasium.

Egnatius called out to Justinus, "Where's Seneca's nephew, the so-called poet?"

"If you mean, Lucan, he prefers intellectual pursuits."

"Here's a bit of poetry: scribblers who hold themselves above the state will fall."

Egnatius was a viper, and vipers who'd not yet reached matu-rity were the most poisonous. Excusing himself from Poppaea, Justinus wandered to the far end of the banquet hall. A model of the new city Nero planned to build stood on a banquet board. He intended to rename Rome, Neropolis.

"Fantastic isn't it?" Nero's voice startled Justinus. "I call my new palace the Domus Aurea, my Golden House. When my building is complete, I shall finally live like a human being."

What of the rest of us? Justinus wondered.

Nero gazed lovingly at the model and pointed to a minia-ture replica of parkland. "My Golden House includes not only buildings, but woodland and fountains, even an artificial lake where naval battles can be staged."

A gilded colossus of Nero towered over the complex.

"Impressive."

"I'm glad you approve of my project. Friends must stick together, don't you agree?"

"I have a friend that I'd like you to meet. A scholar—"

"I have no use for books these days."

Nero steered Justinus back to the pink couch and Poppaea. He poked his wife, interrupting her conversation. "Take good care of him," he said.

"Of course." Poppaea smiled at Justinus, patted the couch.

He had no choice but to recline beside her.

"And now," Nero clapped his hands, "a special treat—my pipe organ." He nodded toward a contraption fitted with more than a dozen pipes, a board of ivory keys, and a bellows.

"He's been practicing for weeks." Poppaea yawned, revealing sharp white teeth again.

Nero went off to play with his new toy, leaving Justinus with Poppaea. A slave poured more wine, and Justinus settled on the couch, taking care that his thigh did not touch Poppaea's. Her perfume assaulted him.

"Justinus," Poppaea rested her hand on his arm, "what have you been doing with yourself?"

"Not too much," he said. "Managing my land, straightening accounts. I get my greatest pleasure from my apple trees."

"How exciting." Poppaea stroked his arm. "Apples were Adam's downfall, according to the Jews. Will apples be your downfall, Justinus?"

He saw his opening. "You favor Jewish teachings, don't you?"

"You want to talk religion now?" Poppaea rolled her eyes. "I must be losing my touch." She drew her hand away, her demeanor growing serious. "All right, let's talk philosophy. It's true I find the concept of one Almighty God fascinating. I'm interested in the mystical aspects of Judaism."

"And have you delved into the teachings of God's son?"

"Jesus?" Poppaea raised a lacquered eyebrow. "Josephus claims Jesus of Nazareth was a wise man, a great teacher and a performer of wonders—not the Messiah."

135

"Perhaps Josephus is mistaken."

Poppaea studied Justinus with calculating eyes. "Have you been listening to Paul of Tarsus?"

"I've met him, yes. Have you?"

"Not yet." Poppaea plucked a morsel of spiced pork wrapped in grape-leaf from a platter and offered it to Justinus. When he refused, she popped it into her mouth.

"Paul speaks of the one true God, an almighty—'

"Relax," Poppaea said. She refilled his cup, pouring from a small pitcher. "This wine is from my private stock."

Justinus quickly downed his wine, and Poppaea poured again.

"I believe faith in that one God may save Rome from disaster. Faith in—"

"What disaster?" Poppaea let go of a slice of peppered melon to study Justinus. "No god is more powerful than Nero. Let's drink to my husband."

Justinus knocked back the wine, spiced with cinnamon and strangely sweet. He'd bungled everything. Even his stomach rebelled. Hoping to settle it, he reached for a bit of eel, chewed, and wondered if the eel had come alive inside his stomach.

He felt like he was swimming underwater.

What had he been saying?

He rubbed his brow. He'd been talking about Jesus, talking about Paul. He glanced at Poppaea, and she smiled at him, her teeth longer and more pointed.

Nero sat before the pipe organ, cracked his knuckles and pumped the bellows.

Justinus stood, unsteadily. He knew, from experience, once Nero began to play the audience would be held hostage, unable to escape even to relieve themselves.

He had to speak to Nero now.

His knees felt like jelly as he walked. That fool, Egnatius, had abandoned his whores and stood beside Nero, admiring the pipe organ, stroking the keyboard. They laughed as Justinus approached.

"Caesar," Justinus said, attempting to show respect. His mouth formed the words carefully, but they came out slurred, "I mu-must speak to y-you about Fla-fla—"

Nero and Egnatius burst into another fit of laughter.

"I must—"

"Sit down before you fall." Nero turned back to Egnatius. "He stutters like my Uncle Claudius."

"Sh-she w-won't be coming."

"Who?" Nero asked, impatiently.

"Fla-flavia Rubria. Sh-she's betrothed."

"Betrothed to whom?" Egnatius said.

Justinus stared at him. That was a good question; it rolled around his head. For lack of an answer, he blurted, "Betrothed to me."

"That's a lie, you drunk." Egnatius grabbed Justinus by his toga, shook him. "Flavia is mine!"

Justinus batted at him, wildly, and the banquet hall grew quiet.

A voice rang out from the entryway, "I'm not yours, Egnatius! I'm not betrothed to anyone."

Flavia's stola was disheveled, and a tangle of silvery hair fell about her face. But the flush of her cheeks only heightened her beauty, Justinus noticed despite his stupor.

Tigellinus blocked her from entering.

"Let her in," Nero said.

She glided toward Nero, her head high and defiant, her green eyes shining.

Justinus started toward her, intending to drag her away from the banquet hall, away from Nero. But he stumbled and banged into a couch. He shook his head, trying to clear his mind, but the room would not stop spinning.

CHAPTER XVII

The banquet hall was more splendid than Flavia had imagined it—guests in dazzling attire, rose-petals strewn across the floor, banquet boards draped in fine linens and laden with foods she couldn't even name. The princeps walked toward her, arms outstretched in welcome.

"Not betrothed. Splendid news!"

She offered him the smile she'd been practicing.

Justinus walked behind Nero, his gait off kilter. The princeps glanced at him and said. "I thought you were an honest man. This girl isn't betrothed to you."

"You shouldn't have come," Justinus said. "I'll take you home."

"I just arrived, and I intend to stay."

Nero clapped his hands like a delighted child. "Finally, the night shows promise! Welcome to my feast, Flavia Rubria."

As if in a dream, she floated toward him. Everything she saw, everything she touched, exceeded her imaginings. The princeps appeared godlike in his spangled toga, his head crowned by a golden wreath. Anticipation bubbled in Flavia's stomach as all eyes in the banquet hall were riveted on her.

"Caesar," she said, lowering her gaze and noticing his feet—hennaed toes wrapped in golden sandals. "This must be Olympus, for certainly you are Apollo."

"And you are Venus." Nero kissed her hand.

Excitement coursed through her body, and she tingled with a newborn heat. What would it be like to gain the admiration of the most powerful ruler in the world? To have slaves and senators grovel at your feet? To be revered as a goddess?

Nero led her across the room.

"I want to introduce you to Flavia Rubria," he said to a woman who reclined on a couch, her head cushioned by silk pillows, her ample breasts slipping from her stola. She looked like a satiated cow. Flavia had seen Poppaea Sabina in processions, but at close range she appeared older. And fatter.

"So this is your new pet," Poppaea said, eyes sparking with jealousy.

Nero reclined on the pink couch next to Poppaea and drew Flavia beside him.

"Something to drink?" he asked.

"I'll have what you're drinking."

Poppaea snorted, the rude noise of a pig.

Nero offered Flavia his chalice. She peered into the cup at something greenish.

"It's my special elixir," he said. "It won't hurt you."

The slime looked bad and tasted worse. It slipped down her throat, and she stuck out her tongue.

Nero laughed. "Can you touch your nose with that?"

She demonstrated.

"What talent!"

Poppaea groaned.

Nero snapped his fingers and a slave scurried over. Kneeling before Flavia, the slave removed her sandals, then dosed her feet with aromatic oil. Expertly, he massaged her toes, and she giggled.

"Have some wine," Nero said.

Flavia drank it too fast and coughed.

The slave stroked the soles of her feet, his thumbs digging into her arches.

She moaned.

"Good girl," Nero said. "Pleasure is an art, and like any art, it requires skill and practice."

He plucked a grape from a glass bowl, holding the fruit between his forefinger and thumb. "Open your mouth."

She did as she was told.

He pressed the jewel between her lips. "Don't bite, just suck."

She rolled the grape over her tongue, and the fruit oozed sweet juice. Catching the grape between her teeth, she bit.

"I said, don't bite." Nero jabbed an elbow into Poppaea's ribs. "Demonstrate."

Throwing back her head, Poppaea lowered a cluster of grapes toward her mouth. Her tongue flicked at the fruit, circling a purple orb before drawing it between her lips.

"So gifted," Nero said.

"So bored." Poppaea cocked her chin at Flavia. "What shall we do with her?"

"Not we. This one is all mine."

"I see," Poppaea sounded petulant.

"Gallus Justinus seems to be available," Nero said.

Flavia looked to where Nero pointed. Justinus sat slumped on a nearby couch, his head bent over his arms.

At the mention of his name, he looked up. "What game are you playing?" he asked.

"Poppaea wants to show you my glass collection," Nero said. "And I'm sure you'll humor her."

"I'm your wife." Poppaea's voice rose above the din of conversation. "Don't try to shove me off while you indulge your latest whore."

The guests stopped talking.

Flavia's face flushed hot. Did Poppaea refer to her?

"Flavia," Justinus said, rising to his feet. "It's time I got you home."

"For once, I agree with Justinus." Egnatius, who had been sulking, grabbed Flavia's wrist. The pustules on his chin looked ready to explode. "I order you to leave at once."

"You have no right to order me."

"As your future husband—"

"I'd rather die than marry you."

Nero laughed. "The girl has spunk." He motioned to the musicians. "Play something jubilant." Taking Flavia's hands in his, he led her from the couch into the center of the banquet hall. They began to dance.

"Feel the rhythm, Flavia? Let the music rise within you like a snake."

She rotated her hips slowly, uncertain if she did it right.

Nero drew her close. "You're a natural."

The flute and cithara were joined by drums. Dancing girls, dressed only in gilded girdles, shook their hips and swung their hair while they banged on timpani. Bacchus and a host of nymphs played panpipes, while guests stamped their feet and clapped their hands, cheering as the music grew wilder. Nero sent Flavia spinning across the floor, causing guests to scatter to the walls. He whirled her through one archway then another, zigzagging between couches and tables, knocking over food and wine.

She spun past Justinus, he and the banquet hall a blur of color. She felt dizzy.

"Please stop," she pleaded, trying to free herself from Nero.

"We're just beginning."

He crushed her against his chest and lifted her off the ground. They spun and spun and spun, his breath wet against her neck.

"Put me down."

"As you wish."

Scooping her into his arms, he carried her out of the banquet hall. The music faded along with Poppaea's accusations. They entered a vestibule. She tried to scream, but he locked his lips on her mouth. He kicked open a door, and they entered a chamber. The bolt fell into place with a thud.

"This is what you wanted, isn't it?" he said.

She thought it would be different.

A gibbous moon shone through a window, casting his face in eerie light. The whites of his eyes appeared greenish.

"Don't worry, Flavia. I'll be your teacher."

He placed her on the largest bed she'd ever seen, the room's sole piece of furniture. A wolf pelt overlay the coverlet. It smelled musty. She tried to stand, but Nero pushed her down. Leather straps had been attached to the headboard and before she realized what he what he was doing, he'd slipped the straps over her wrists.

She screamed, piercing shrieks that set the palace dogs barking.

She kicked him, and tried to squirm out of his grasp, but he was strong. He secured her ankle with another strap, anchoring her to the base of the bed. Then he grabbed her other foot, forcing her legs apart. Just like Egnatius. What made her think Nero would be different?

"You're not a god," she shouted. "You're not even human. No animal would kill its mother. You murdered Agrippina!"

Nero released the leather strap he'd been tightening. "Don't speak my mother's name."

"Why not?"

He stared at her, his gray eyes dull as slate.

"Agrippina! Agrippina! Agrippina!"

"Shut up!" Covering his ears, he sank onto the bed, his body trembling.

"So the rumors are true," she said.

"She made me do it."

"You're a coward."

"I'm not." He hugged himself, but he still shook. Perspiration glistened on his brow, and he gasped as if he were drowning.

"You sent your guards to do your dirty work," Flavia said.

"Shut up! Shut up!"

"Coward," she said softly. "I see the truth."

Nero staggered to his feet, undid his robe and shook it off his shoulders. The fabric slipped onto the floor. He didn't wear a loincloth.

Flavia could not help staring. She had never seen a naked man, except for statues, Egnatius had kept himself covered. Nero moved toward her, and her courage fled. Heart racing so fast it hurt, she struggled to free herself, arching her body, tugging at the bindings. But that only made them tighter. The leather cut into her wrists and ankles. She tried to scream, but her voice came out in panting breaths.

Nero yanked the wolf pelt out from under her and set the snarling head on top of his. Bending over her, he bared his teeth and growled. Then he curled his fingers into claws, jabbed one hand between her thighs, and pressed his other hand against her belly. A trickle of hot liquid leaked down her leg.

"Piss on me," he said.

"What?"

"Pissss," he sounded like a serpent.

"I can't."

Her body tensed.

"You can."

His tongue slithered between her thighs, and she thought she would explode.

His tongue flicked relentlessly, inflicting torment—or was it pleasure? He jabbed his fist into Flavia's belly. Unable to contain herself, she let go. He raised his head, liquid dribbling down his chin. "Nectar of the gods," he said.

Throwing the full weight of his body onto Flavia, he sank his teeth into her stola, ripping the emerald silk away from her breasts, and latched onto a nipple.

She cried out, but he sucked until she bled.

She became aware of pounding—someone banging on the door, followed by shouting, "Let me in: it's Poppaea!"

Nero stopped sucking and glanced at the door.

It shuddered on its hinges. "I have witnesses! Gallus Justinus and Egnatius Rubrius."

He looked back at Flavia. "I'm sorry," he said in a childlike voice.

She stared at him, saw tears forming in his eyes.

"Undo my bonds," she said.

"I never meant to hurt you, Mater."

Mother? To humor, she said, "You've been a bad boy,"

He nodded. "Very bad."

She raised her voice, "And bad boys must be punished."

"Yes."

"Undo my bonds."

The pounding on the door shook the room. The bed trembled, and so did Flavia.

Nero stood, wriggling off the wolf pelt.

Free of his weight, Flavia inhaled a deep breath, but she had not stopped shaking. Nero untied the leather bindings, and a thousand needles pricked her fingers. Placing her numb feet on the floor, she prayed they'd carry her across the room.

Nero stood in her way, blocking the door.

He removed a horsewhip from the wall. Raising it above his head, he cracked the leather thong. Wielding the whip, he walked toward her.

Flavia backed away from him.

"Punish me," he said. He handed her the whip. "Go on," he said and knelt.

"I can't."

"I order you!"

Tentatively, she raised the whip.

"Do it!"

She brought it down, slashing the thong across his buttocks.

"I'm sorry!" he sobbed. "Sorry, Mater."

She wielded the lash again. It left an ugly welt. Startled at the damage she had done, she dropped the whip.

"Don't stop," Nero pleaded.

"I'm leaving."

Pulling her torn stola over her breasts, she headed for the door.

"Don't leave me." He collapsed onto the floor, weeping, clinging to her ankles.

She shook him off, undid the bolt.

The door flew open. Poppaea, Justinus, and Egnatius stumbled in, flooding the chamber with lantern light.

"Animal," Poppaea shrieked. "Selfish boar, I'll castrate you!" Charging past Flavia, she pounced on Nero. He tried to crawl away from her, but she raked her fingernails across his face.

"Are you all right?" Justinus asked Flavia.

"I'll live."

"Did he—ah—do anything?" Egnatius stammered.

"Of course he did. You're a child, Egnatius. A novice."

Even his pimples blushed.

"I blame myself for what's happened," Justinus said. "I should have—"

"Don't worry, I'm still intact." Flavia glanced at Nero, still trying to escape his wife. "Let's go to the banquet hall," she said. "I want dessert."

CHAPTER XVIII

The moon peeked through the latticework, spinning webs across the temple. Elissa huddled on a stone bench by the fire as night crept toward dawn. She had missed the evening meal, and now her stomach growled. But the emptiness felt more insistent than mere hunger.

Her eyes closed and her head drooped. She shook herself awake, focused on the fire, tried not to think of Justinus, and drifted back into a dream.

Waking with a start, uncertain of how much time had passed, she glanced at the cauldron. The fire had burned down.

A dull ache settled in her back. She stretched, went to the coal bin. Using a wooden shovel, she scooped black lumps into a leather bucket, carried the bucket to the fire, and poured coal onto the embers. A haze of smoke and ash flew into her face. Coughing, she rubbed her eyes with sooty fists, stopped when she heard someone call her name.

"Who's there?"

She turned, searching the shadows. Of course, she was alone. She opened one of the double doors, peered out at the forum, and then closed it.

She stirred the coals with an iron poker. A gust rushed through the room, reviving the fire. Moving closer to the cauldron, closer to the heat and light, she ran her fingers through the flames. She loved the fire's constant change, its power to transform and purify. She gazed into the cauldron, losing track of time, and within the shifting, flickering light, a shape began to form. A torso. Limbs. And then a face.

Elissa, a voice whispered.

Or was it the fire's hiss?

Her brother's face, eyes receding into sunken sockets, appeared within the flames. She closed her eyes, then opened them, and still she saw his face. His body, bruised and battered, rose slowly from the cauldron. He stared blankly at her.

"Are you a lemur?" she asked.

Rome burns.

She rubbed her forehead and wondered if she were still dreaming.

Rome burns and from union unholy the sister will bring forth a son. Her brother's voice sounded hollow. *Save yourself Elissa.*

"Save myself from what?"

From fate. Unravel the prophecy.

"Tell me what it means."

Her brother made a screeching sound. Blood spewed from the cavern of his mouth, sizzling in the flames.

"Marcus!" She reached into the fire wanting to touch him, wanting to draw him back to life, but succeeded only in singeing her fingers. His face melted like a wax death-mask, his eyes becoming wide and empty, before vanishing.

Rome burns, the fire hissed.

Choking on black smoke, Elissa ran to the doors and flung them open. No orange blaze lit up the city, no flames licked the horizon. She heard no frantic screams, no tortured wails, only the incessant clattering of wooden wheels on cobblestones.

Wind whistled through the temple, sent cinders swirling from the cauldron, a thousand souls escaping the womb of the Great Mother. A thousand souls doomed to live and die.

Rome burns....

Covering her ears, Elissa refused to listen to the prophecy.

She sank onto her knees. "Help," she cried, though she had no idea to whom she pleaded.

Paul's words mocked her.

What are we without love?

"Nothing."

She felt small, insignificant. Unloved and unloving. She told herself she must have faith, if not in ancient deities, in Paul's Almighty God and in his son, Jesus.

"My Lord," Elissa whispered, "if you exist, show yourself. If you exist, save Rome from destruction." She pressed her forehead to the floor, waited for an answer, prayed for some sign she'd been heard.

The fire crackled.

She listened to the sound of her own breathing.

Listened for words of wisdom.

The prophecy ran through her mind.

Rome burns and from union unholy, the sister will bring forth a son.

"Help me, please!"

The floor felt cold against her forehead, hard beneath her knees. Her body ached. What if the gods were not just powerless, what if they did not exist? What if her prayers fell, not on deaf ears, but on no ears at all? What if all that mattered in this world was power and brute strength?

She found no comfort in the temple.

None in her beliefs. None in her family. None in her religion.

No comfort anywhere.

CHAPTER XIX

Flavia clung to the chariot as Justinus cracked his whip, urging the stallions to go faster. Bare breasted, hair flying, she imagined herself a goddess—a creature of her dreams. She felt wildly triumphant, no longer a child.

The stallions charged through empty streets. In night's twelfth hour, before dawn, traffic was minimal and so the chariot made good speed. Jaw clenched, Justinus stood as far away from her as possible. Despite her protests, he'd dragged her through the banquet hall, just as a cake, dripping with honey, stuffed with pinenuts and sultanas, was being served.

"You could have let me have my cake," she said.

"Your parents will be frantic when they discover you're missing."

"My parents are asleep." She used her most sophisticated tone of voice, a voice she had practiced, attempting to sound condescending. "When they wake they should rejoice that someone in our family has made amends for my brother's bad behavior and has won Nero's favor."

Justinus grabbed her wrist and squeezed until she thought the bones might snap.

"Stupid girl! Your brother was a hero."

"Drunk!" She tried to break away from him, but his grip tightened. "I'm not a child," she said.

"Only a child would be naive enough to think she held sway over Nero." With a look of disgust, Justinus released her.

"Only a drunk would guzzle enough wine to fall into a stupor at a banquet. You've hurt me." She rubbed her wrist. Granted the bruises weren't from Justinus, but from Nero's bindings.

"Poppaea laced my wine with some kind of potion," Justinus said.

"Why would she do that?"

"Perhaps for her amusement. Who knows why those in power do anything." Justinus focused on the road ahead. "What happened in that room?"

"Nothing."

"Nothing?"

"Nothing I care to discuss."

"Nero can't be trusted. The game you play is dangerous."

"Perhaps I like danger." She shot Justinus a smile, and he returned it with a frown. He was gloomy, and far too serious. He reminded her of Elissa.

"Cover yourself," he said.

She folded her arms over her torn stola, determined to say nothing more. No matter what Justinus thought, Nero desired her. Justinus might think he was wise, but he knew nothing. Had he witnessed Nero's sobs? Seen Nero crawl? Heard him beg for punishment?

Flavia had to admit Nero's behavior was far from what she had expected. All her life she'd heard stories about love. Some of the stories seemed fantastic—princes held under a spell, swans transforming into men, slave-girls rescued by a king—but she had also heard the whisperings of servants and the gossip of her mother's friends. They spoke of men tricking women into bed, wooing them with wine and jewels. They spoke of men who forced women to do their bidding, like Egnatius had done to her. But none of those clandestine conversations mentioned that a man might beg for punishment. She rubbed her breasts, still sore from Nero's suckling, and knew she should find his behavior frightening. But, in truth, the prospect of another encounter excited her.

From her perch in the chariot, she watched the city pass. One day, she vowed, she'd be celebrated. One day, slaves would carry her through Rome in her own palanquin, as they did Poppaea, and crowds would gawk at her passing. But now there were no crowds, only vigiles patrolling the streets in search of fire and a few stragglers from the Meditrinalia festival. Shops were closed, no workmen manned their posts, not even the street sweepers. Most citizens had gone home long ago. Drunken shouting echoed through an alleyway and a gang of toughs appeared. Flavia allowed her stola to fall to her waist, and the young men caterwauled.

"Cover yourself," Justinus ordered her.

"You're no fun," she said.

Thrilled at being out while others slept, she gazed at the stars, yellowish and fading. She wished morning would never come. When her parents learned that she'd attended Nero's feast, they would be furious. No doubt they would keep her under lock and key. But having experienced one night of freedom, she was determined to spread her wings.

And my legs.

She chuckled at her joke.

"Is something funny?" Justinus asked.

"Everything."

Cracking his whip, he urged the stallions up the Esquiline. The chariot approached The House of Rubrius, and Flavia felt her old life closing in. Justinus jumped down from the chariot, secured the horses to a post, and offered her his hand.

She refused his assistance.

In day's first light the world looked colorless and dead.

They walked along the garden path and, before they reached the entryway, barking broke the quiet of the dawn. The door opened and Spurius stood on the threshold, keys jangling at his waist. He held Cerberus on a short leash.

Behind the steward, to Flavia's dismay, she saw her mother.

Constantina pushed past Spurius. "Thank Jupiter you're home," she cried, taking Flavia into her arms.

"I'm fine, Mater."

"Where have you been?" Constantina brushed a lock of hair out of Flavia's face then looked her over. "Your stola is torn. And is that blood?"

"I'm tired, Mater. I want to go to bed."

Constantina grabbed Flavia's hands, examining her wrists. "How did you get these bruises?" She spun toward Justinus, her usually mild manner gone. "I demand an explanation."

"I escaped from my room," Flavia said before Justinus could answer. "I climbed a tree, scaled the roof and got the bruises when I fell."

"You fell? Is anything broken."

"I'm fine, Mater. I went to the palace."

"Gallus Justinus took you to Nero's feast?"

"I-I didn't take her," Justinus said. "I merely—"

"You're no longer welcome in this house." Constantina pointed a slender finger at Gallus Justinus, forcing him backward. "Leave, before I wake my husband!" She dragged Flavia up the stairs and shoved her through the doorway.

"Mater, stop!"

"You don't understand—" Justinus tried to explain.

Spurius slammed the door on him.

"Thank you, Spurius." Constantina said. "I'm sure I can count on you to be discreet."

"Yes, Domina." Keys clinking and Cerberus in tow, the steward shuffled away—back to his morning chores.

Constantina grabbed Flavia's bruised wrist and steered her through the foyer. It hurt, but Flavia said nothing. Never had she seen her mother so angry. Wordlessly, they passed through the vestibule of ancestors, and by the time they reached the atrium, Constantina had regained her composure.

"You will say nothing more about climbing trees or running away," she said. "Gallus Justinus must shoulder the blame."

"Justinus has nothing to do with this."

"Of course he does—"

"Don't be stupid Mater. I saw the missive Nero sent to Pater. If you could read, you'd know I was invited to the feast."

"What are you saying?"

"Nero invited me to the Domus Transitoria, and I went. No harm came of it."

"No harm? What of your reputation? A young girl running around Rome. What man will have you now? When your father learns of this, Gallus Justinus will be charged with abduction."

"He didn't abduct me. This is my fault."

"Of course it's not your fault. You're just a child."

"I'm not a child!" Flavia stamped her foot.

"Quiet, you'll wake your father." Constantina lowered her voice, "There is one way to save your reputation. You must marry Egnatius. And soon."

"No!" Flavia's voice echoed through the atrium. "I won't marry that imbecile, and you can't make me. Are you blind, Mater? I don't intend to marry anyone. I'm Nero's new favorite."

Constantina's slap came as a shock. Flavia rubbed her stinging cheek, her eyes filling with tears. Unsure of why she was crying, she only knew that she felt powerless.

"I'm not a child," she said again.

But Constantina turned her back. She wasn't listening.

CHAPTER XX

Ringing pounded in Elissa's ears.
Bells?

She opened her eyes. The rising sun peeked through the temple's latticework, a cool light in a pallid sky. She rubbed her brow, trying to recall what she'd been dreaming. Paul's words came back to her.

Prepare yourself for God.

She wanted to believe in a loving God, a God who saw what happened here on earth and cared about the plight of people. All night she'd prayed, hoping for a sign from Jesus—assurance that he noticed her. But in the dawn's chill light she felt invisible.

Bells rang, calling the vestals to the morning ritual.

The marble floor made an uncomfortable bed. Elissa rubbed her neck, loosening the sore muscles. She got up, stirred the embers then fed the fire coal, taking pleasure in the newborn flames.

Her tongue felt furry, tasted sour. Finding a jug, she swished water around her mouth and spat it out. She ran her tongue over her teeth, and felt the double incisor. A strange sensation flooded through her body. She felt not fully awake and yet not dreaming. She saw herself as a baby, wrapped in swaddling, held not by her mother, but by someone else. A lullaby ran through her mind. It sounded foreign. Not a song she remembered Constantina ever singing.

Bells drowned the melody, chased away the lullaby.

She squinted at the sky, pink around the edges, and watched it change from lavender to blue—a mirror of life's transience. Nothing lasted forever. Not even gods.

She recalled reading about Re, the Egyptian sun-god who once commanded a following greater than Apollo. Now wind swept through Re's temples and his altars crumbled into sand. But Re was not the only god to perish. Jupiter, god of the Romans, had snatched the throne from Zeus. Did gods depend on people to achieve their immortality?

And what of Paul's almighty God?

An almighty God would exist whether humans had faith or not. An almighty God would dwell not only on the highest mountain, not just among the stars, but in everything and everywhere.

"If God created me then I am part of God."

Stunned by the revelation, she stared into the fire.

Wind blasted through the temple as the doors swung open.

Marcia entered, ruddy-faced and breathless from climbing the seven steps. She was followed by Cornelia, who ran across the room and threw her arms around Elissa's waist.

"Priestess Junia is near to death," the little girl announced, forgetting the rule of silence.

Marcia burst into tears.

"Is this true?" Elissa asked. Old Junia had shown her only kindness, and she hated to think of the poor old woman suffering.

"She won't wake," Marcia said. She drew a handkerchief out of her stola and loudly blew her nose. "Her eyes don't open, and she's barely breathing. Mother Amelia insists she must be removed from the house."

"Will she die soon?" Cornelia asked. "I've never seen a dead person."

"Where will they take her?" Marcia wailed. "Where can she go?"

"Surely she has family," Elissa said.

"Only a younger sister, whose husband has no use for another woman in his house." Marcia twisted the handkerchief around her hand as if binding a wound. "That's why she's stayed on at the temple. She could have retired years ago, but now, when she's old and sick, the priests claim her illness pollutes the House of Vestals."

"Poor Junia," Elissa said.

"Lucky Junia!" Angerona stood in the entryway. "She'll finally escape this prison. I wish the priests would open up my cage."

"You don't mean that," Elissa said.

"Don't I?" Angerona snorted unbecomingly.

"I have no wish to leave," Marcia said. "When my time comes, like Junia, I have nowhere to go."

"I thought you were rich," Cornelia said.

"Oh, yes, I have money. But my family has no use for me."

"Don't fret, Marcia," Angerona said. "You're nearly thirty-seven. Before long you'll have a man between those solid thighs."

"You're disgusting." Marcia's face grew redder than a slab of meat. "You're not fit to be a priestess, Angerona. I have nothing more to say to you."

"But I have more to say to you."

"Enough," Elissa said.

"Enough? Perhaps for you, Elissa. After all, you have Gallus Justinus. You pretend to be pure, indifferent. Meanwhile, you're a bitch in heat, and he hounds you like a lovesick dog."

"That's not true."

"Isn't it?"

Elissa stared at Angerona, the woman who had been her closest friend, the girl she had loved since childhood and trusted more deeply than a sister. "Tread lightly," she said. "Lest you say something you regret."

"Like what?" Cornelia asked, her face rapt with interest.

"Listen and learn, little girl," Angerona said. "I regret the years I've spent locked in this pretty cage. I don't intend to perish in this place, loveless like old Junia. When my thirty years are done, I plan to make up for lost time." She smiled slyly. "You're all welcome to join my brothel. I think I'll name it Holy Whores, or maybe Vestal Prosti—"

"Angerona!" The doors flew open, and the Vestal Maxima stood at the entryway. "How dare you desecrate this sacred ground?"

"I merely sought to lighten our spirits."

"You may find a diet of bread and water elevating."

"Why chastise me for idle words and, meanwhile, allow blasphemous acts to go unpunished?"

"What blasphemous acts?"

Angerona shot Elissa a menacing look. "Apparently, you have your favorites."

"That's enough," Mother Amelia warned. "You're not to leave the house, Angerona."

"You might want to reconsider how you mete out punishment," Angerona said. "Others might take great interest in your discrepancies—The Collegiate of Pontiffs, for example."

Icy fingers squeezed Elissa's heart.

"Are you threatening me, Priestess Angerona?" The high vestal's eyes narrowed. "How dare you question my authority?"

"I'm beholden to a higher power."

"Tigellinus?" Elissa said. "Or should I say Nero?" She spoke his name as if it were a curse. "There is none lower. For the gods' sake, Angerona, he murdered my brother, forced your father to suicide—"

"Shut up!"

"And to think I trusted you." Suddenly, Elissa saw the truth. "You betrayed Marcus, didn't you?"

Angerona's face went pale.

"It's true," Elissa said. "I see it in your face. You're despicable."

Angerona threw herself at Elissa, knocking her onto the floor.

Elissa fought her off, twisting and scratching, trying to get out from under her. "You disgust me," she yelled.

Angerona tore off Elissa's suffibulum and grabbed a fist of hair, yanking till the roots gave way. They tumbled over one another, kicking, clawing, biting, nearly toppling the cauldron and the sacred fire, as Marcia ran around the temple shrieking and Cornelia wailed.

"Stop at once!" Mother Amelia's icy voice was followed by a shower of cold water.

Elissa broke from Angerona, panting and furious.

"Get up," Mother Amelia ordered. She stood over them, in her hands the empty urn meant for holy water. "See me in my chambers now. Both of you."

Elissa hurried to her cubicle, drew the curtain shut, and fell into the chair.

Angerona could not be trusted.

Her impulse was to run to Justinus, warn him of possible allegations. Warn him Angerona was a spy. But first she had to face the Vestal Maxima.

She changed her soaking clothes, making sure her shoes were spotless, her robe immaculate. Straightening her suffibulum, she carefully arranged the veil. But she couldn't stop her hands from shaking.

Angerona had thrown Marcus to his death—the man she'd claimed to love—to save her family. Clearly she would stop at nothing. Elissa wracked her memory, trying to remember anything damning she might have told Angerona. Even the suggestion of a vestal's impropriety would necessitate an inquiry. An examination. Elissa had heard stories about priestesses forced to endure tests—carrying water in a sieve, being thrown into the river to see if she would sink or float, walking barefoot through fire. And if she failed, she would be entombed alive.

Is that what Angerona wanted?

"Jesus, if you're listening, help me now. I promise to sacrifice thirty sheep, two bullocks, a hundred birds to you." That would be more than enough to appease Jupiter.

Bracing herself for her meeting with the Vestal Maxima, and hoping to avoid Angerona, she slipped out of her cubicle. She hurried through the dormitory, past the servants' quarters, and was halfway down the stairway when a shrill wail broke the silence.

Shouting echoed through the atrium.

"Priestess Junia is dead!"

"Death pollutes the House of Vestals!"

Weeping servants ran through the halls.

Elissa sprinted through the tablinum and found the foyer deserted. The front door stood open. A stray dog tore through the doorway, and a kitchen slave chased after it.

Elissa moved toward the door, considered running.

Thais burst into the foyer with a sob. "Death has taken Junia," she cried. "Rome is cursed."

Bells clanged, announcing the disaster.

A vestal's death on sacred ground portended drought, plague, pestilence—all manner of catastrophe.

Junia's death sent the city into turmoil. Over the next month, countless prodigies occurred: a fiery comet streaked through the sky and fell into the Tiber, giants abandoned mountaintops and scoured villages in search of children, a woman gave birth to a goat, a shadow swallowed up the moon, and on the Nones of November all water-clocks were said to stop at night's eleventh hour.

Elissa's routine of quiet meals, scholarly pursuits and working in the garden became a memory. The ten day ordeal of Junia's state funeral took precedence, and the vestals' days were filled with ritual. Each morning at dawn they sprinkled salt along the perimeter of the House of Vestals to drive out demons. Each noon they fasted in silent contemplation. Each evening they offered prayers, sacrificing not only cedar wood and wine, but all manner of animals. Rumor claimed blood ran from the temple like the Tiber, and the sacred fire was sustained by bones.

The altercation between Elissa and Angerona seemed forgotten. But every time Elissa sought to escape the House of Vestals, Angerona appeared close behind her, watching.

End of Part Two

PART THREE

Dark Eternity

She held him, and they nestled tenderly.
He followed her meandering path
trilling his song to her alone.
She wanders down a road, lost in shadows,
from which, they say, no one returns.
I follow, shaking my fist at evil gods.
All beauty is destroyed within your dark eternity.
You, who have absconded with my songbird...

—Catullus

CHAPTER XXI

A month had passed since the awful night of Nero's Meditrinalia banquet, a month since Justinus had been banished from the House of Rubrius.

"When did you last see her?" Akeem asked.

"Who?"

"The girl. The girl you can't stop thinking of. The one who receives your letters."

"Those are documents of state."

"Is that why their deliverance includes a bribe to ensure secrecy?"

Tact was not an attribute in which Akeem excelled. The slave had the annoying habit of saying what he thought. Justinus glanced at the sodden sky.

"It's going to rain."

"In Egypt we have an expression for your affliction, 'Isis has you by the balls.'"

"It's going to rain *soon*."

A creature of the desert, Akeem despised thunderstorms. Throwing Justinus a surly look, he left the courtyard.

Justinus returned to tending his apple trees. He'd wrapped the trunks with muslin to protect them against frost, doused the soil with eggshells, and now he mulched the roots with pine needles. A gust of wind blew lingering leaves from barren branches. A metaphor, Justinus thought, for his barren life.

Akeem was right.

He could not stop thinking about Elissa. In the past month he'd received little news of her, except for what he gleaned from their exchange of letters. According to Elissa's missives, her father had recovered from his bout of apoplexy and a wedding was in store for Flavia. Her betrothal to Egnatius would soon be publicly announced. Once the dowry was settled there could be no change of heart without reparation to the injured party. Justinus felt sorry for Flavia. She was foolish, impetuous, but marriage to Egnatius seemed unjust punishment. But, if life were fair, he and Elissa would be getting married.

He scattered a handful of pine needles, breathing in their sharp, clean scent. Elissa's last letter had been less of news and more of questions. She seemed preoccupied by death, and had asked about the resurrection, wanted to know how it could be possible.

Raindrops began to fall, leaving coin-sized marks on the courtyard's paving stones. Justinus welcomed them. Rain filled the aqueducts, watered fields, quenched his apple trees.

Akeem poked his head outside. "Come in," he called, venturing no further than the edge of the covered portico. A clap of thunder sent him scurrying back into the house.

Storms didn't bother Justinus. When he'd been a soldier in Britannia gray skies had been the norm and rain became a way of life. The Fourteenth Legion had been founded a century ago by Julius Caesar and had been stationed in Britannia for seventeen years, though Justinus had joined them at the finish of the tour. His men despised the endless damp, water seeping through their boots, mildewed clothes and moldy bread. Most couldn't wait to return to the sunny warmth of Italy, but Justinus reveled in the wake of green.

Until that day in June.

Even now he heard the cries for war. Smelled the stench of fallen bodies. A part of him had died that day.

Rain pelted him, but he kept working, lost in memories of war.

Akeem ran into the courtyard, a blanket draped over his head. "Master," he pleaded. "Come in now."

"Rain won't kill me."

"But Priestess Angerona might." Akeem danced from foot to foot, avoiding rivulets.

"Angerona?" Justinus's mood grew darker than the sky.

"She just arrived and waits inside."

With the next lightning flash, like Mercury, Akeem bolted from the courtyard, his soggy blanket flapping in the wind. Reluctantly, Justinus followed him inside. Dripping wet, his boots leaving muddy tracks, he walked through the vestibule and into the atrium. Rain streamed through the open roof, showering the central pool, waking the cat.

"She's in there." Akeem pointed to the library.

Justinus ripped open the curtain and found Angerona sitting in his chair, the chair that had once belonged to his father. He glanced at the cedar chest that housed important documents and stood bolted to the floor, half expecting to find the lock broken, its contents plundered, but Angerona was busy examining her nails. No lictor stood inside the doorway, no escort of any kind. She must have come alone. She looked up with a smile that Justinus did not return.

He bowed slightly, meeting the requirement for good manners. It was possible that Angerona had been sent by the Vestal Maxima on an important matter. Maybe the House of the Vestals required a supply grain for the coming winter, maybe their stable needed horses—

"To what may I attribute the honor of your presence?" he asked.

"Must you always be so formal, Justinus? My reason for coming here is personal."

"How so?"

"A matter of utmost delicacy."

Angerona got up from the chair and walked toward him, hips swaying beneath her stola.

"Do you find me attractive, Justinus?"

"Of course not." Realizing how insulting that must sound, he added, "You're a vestal virgin."

"Not a woman?"

Angerona's laughter sounded sharp as breaking glass. She pushed away her suffibulum, releasing her auburn curls, then lifted her chin in expectation of a kiss. Justinus clenched his fists, held them at his sides.

"What do you want?"

Her lips froze in a smile. "Have you heard from Elissa lately?"

Justinus clenched his fists tighter. "I haven't seen her."

"But somehow you communicate?"

He refused to lie, so he said nothing.

"About a month ago, at Meditrinalia, I followed the two of you into the Subura."

"Elissa told me." He'd said too much.

"Told you, how? By letter?"

"That's not your concern."

"I think it is. Love letters are forbidden to vestal virgins."

"You'd better leave."

"What would you say if I told you I found one of those letters? A letter she meant to send and lost? Do I make you nervous, Justinus?" She moved closer, so close her scent traveled up his nostrils. "Your clothes are soaking wet," she said. "Maybe you should take them off."

"Where is this so-called letter?"

She pointed to her bosom.

"Give it to me," he said.

She pulled away her palla and leaned toward him. "You'll have to fish it out."

He snatched the letter from between her breasts.

She tried to grab it back, but he held it away from her.

"I'm willing to forget that day in the Subura," she said, "deny I saw anything, retract all accusations if—"

"What?"

Using the oil-lamp on his desk, he set fire to a corner of the letter, and watched it burn. The papyrus turned brown, curling around his name and Elissa's, white ash drifting to the floor.

Angerona stood behind him, her breathing shallow and rapid. He felt heat rising from her body. She stroked his neck.

"Make love to me."

"I don't think so."

"Why not?" She ran her fingers through his hair, and he felt himself weaken.

"You're a vestal virgin, remember?"

"That didn't stop you from bedding Elissa."

"Have you lost your senses?" It took all his strength to restrain himself from hitting her.

She backed away. "I only know that since that day Elissa has been different."

"How dare you speak of her?"

"Anyone can see I'm prettier."

"You're revolting. Worse than a whore. Get out," he said quietly.

Her eyes flared with anger. "Perhaps there's something else between you and Elissa. Maybe the two of you are plotting treason," she said.

"Would you have me burned like Marcus?"

She didn't answer.

"I know what you did." He pressed her against the wall, allowing her no escape.

"I had no choice."

"No choice but to destroy your friends?"

"Nero threatened to make my sister his courtesan."

"And you preferred to sacrifice the man who refused to destroy your reputation?"

"I'm only trying to survive—"

"And now you plan to sacrifice Elissa."

"No."

He peered into her frightened eyes. "What have you told Tigellinus?"

Angerona shook her head. "Nothing."

Justinus touched her neck, felt her pulse beneath his finger-tips. "Strangulation is an unpleasant death, slower than you might imagine. First the eyes bulge from their sockets, then the lips turn blue—"

"You wouldn't."

He pressed his thumb against her throat. "Tell me, Angerona, what does Tigellinus want?"

"He says Elissa holds Nero in a spell. He told me to find evidence against her, fabricate it if I have to, something damning to be used in court—" Her voice broke with a sob.

Justinus released her.

"What of me, Justinus?" she asked in a small voice. "I'm so afraid." Her beauty crumbled—a fine statue, disfigured and destroyed.

Justinus jerked open the curtain, nearly ripped it from the rod.

"Goodbye, Angerona."

CHAPTER XXII

Elissa, Marcia, and Cornelia stood before the Vestal Maxima. Elissa's gaze followed the carpet's familiar pattern. Since Junia's death, the colors seemed less vibrant, and she noticed a threadbare spot. Cubbyholes still lined the library's walls, stuffed with books and documents, but somehow they seemed emptier. Death, Justinus had said in his last letter, transforms the soul, preparing us for God.

"We all miss Priestess Junia, but the time of mourning is over." Mother Amelia straightened the wax tablets covering her desk, and settled in her curule chair. "I've called you here to discuss—" She glanced around the room. "Where is Priestess Angerona?"

Elissa glanced at the doorway.

For the past month she and Angerona had barely spoken. When they did, they quarreled over minor irritations—how the fire should be laid, the correct format of a document, whether or not it would rain. They never spoke of Justinus. Never mentioned Marcus.

"She was present at the midday meal," Marcia said.

"I hate pea-soup." Cornelia wrinkled her nose. "I wish the cook would go back to barley—"

"Angerona took no soup," Marcia said. "Only bread and cheese. A little watered wine, I think. No honey. And no almond cake."

"You had a third helping," Cornelia said.

"Little girls should be seen and not—"

"Thank you, Marcia," said Mother Amelia, ending the discussion. "We shall begin our meeting without Priestess Angerona. I'm pleased to announce the Pontifex Maximus and the Collegiate of Pontiffs proclaims our sanctuary purified. It's time for us to continue business as usual."

She dipped her hand into her bowl of sweets, popped a nut into her mouth. "As you know, another priestess must be selected to join our ranks. As is our tradition, the new priestess will be determined by lottery. The Pontifex Maximus has nominated twenty candidates."

"Who?" Marcia demanded. "I know every family of consequence and—"

The curtain opened, and the vestals turned to see who entered. Angerona, her veil askew, her stola rumpled, swept into the library. She bobbed in deference to the Vestal Maxima then took her place, not beside Elissa, as once she would have done, but next to Marcia.

"Where have you been?" Mother Amelia asked.

"Fighting dragons, killing snakes."

Angerona looked at Elissa, and Elissa's stomach tightened.

"Speak in plain Latin," Mother Amelia said.

"I was on a mission."

"To what end?"

"As I've mentioned in the past, but you've chosen to ignore, I suspect corruption within the House of Vestals."

Mother Amelia leaned over her desk. "False allegations will not be tolerated."

"The allegation isn't false. A month ago I followed Elissa Rubria and Gallus Justinus into the Subura—"

"And I haven't seen him since," Elissa said.

"But you've been exchanging letters, haven't you? You and Justinus are lovers."

"That's not true."

"Isn't it?"

"Silence!" Mother Amelia slammed her bowl of sweets on the desktop, and candied nuts went flying. "This meeting is over. Don't stray from the house, Priestess Angerona. After I speak to Elissa, I will speak with you."

"I'm sure our conversation will be stimulating."

"Go." Mother Amelia pointed toward the doorway.

Angerona stalked out of the library, followed by Marcia—redder in the face than usual. Cornelia skipped after them, asking questions.

Mother Amelia nodded at a stool and Elissa sat. "Look at me."

Elissa raised her eyes, expecting to see Mother Amelia's anger, but she saw only weariness. With a sigh, Mother Amelia asked, "Have you seen Gallus Justinus?"

Elissa shook her head.

"But you've been writing letters."

"Yes, Mother Amelia."

"Love letters are—"

"Not love letters, Mother Amelia, scholarly discussions. He writes to me about Paul of Tarsus."

The high vestal looked taken aback. Taking a deep breath, she leaned back in her chair. "His letters pertain to a foreign religious sect? Love letters might have been preferable," she said, more to herself than to Elissa.

"Poppaea favors Jews."

"You are not Poppaea. Followers of The Way are rabble-rousers, and you will have no part of them. Am I understood, Elissa?"

"Yes, Mother Amelia."

"Meanwhile, if Priestess Angerona pursues these allegations, you may face an inquiry, even a trial."

"She has no proof."

"Are you certain? Even if she lacks proof, Angerona holds something far more dangerous, the ear of Tigellinus."

Elissa laughed bitterly. "Now there's a judge of character, a man of high ideals."

"Nevertheless, your fate is in his hands."

Elissa had no argument. Tigellinus, it seemed, determined the fate of everyone.

"Open the shutters, Elissa. We need fresh air."

The window looked out on the courtyard's garden—neat rows of winter vegetables, patches of herbs, stalks of dying flowers. Summer's abundance had given way to roots and kale—hearty fare that could endure November's dropping temperatures. Fingers of blue-black clouds stretched across the sky, promising more rain—the heavy hand of Jupiter.

"Come here, Elissa." Mother Amelia reached out her hand, knotted by arthritis and spotted with age. "All my life I've done my best to take care of my girls."

"You've been a mother to me."

"Have I?"

"More than Constantina," Elissa said wistfully. "I hardly know my mother, hardly know my family. Sometimes I think of them as strangers."

Mother Amelia's eyes sparkled with tears.

"Is something wrong?" Elissa asked.

"There's something you should know, something I should have told you long ago—"

A clap of thunder made them jump.

"Shall I close the shutters?" Elissa asked.

"Leave them open. I like the smell of rain."

"What were you about to say?"

Mother Amelia shook her head. "Sit down, my dear."

Elissa sank onto the stool. She listened to the beat of rain, steady, persistent, like a memory trying to break through to consciousness.

"There are things that you don't understand, things I hesitate to speak of—" Mother Amelia picked up a stylus, examined the sharp tip, then set the stylus down again. "But I will tell you this: your family is in danger. Nero employs spies..." Mother Amelia's voice trailed off.

"Angerona?"

"One of many." Mother Amelia picked up the pen and twiddled the stylus between her fingers. "Sometimes, to protect the ones we love, we must make a sacrifice."

"What sacrifice?"

Mother Amelia tapped the stylus on her desk.

"What sacrifice?" Elissa demanded.

"Your sister has been named one of the candidates."

"Flavia? But she's fourteen, older than Cornelia, too old to be selected as a vestal virgin."

Mother Amelia tapped the stylus in time with the rain. *Click, click, click.* An unsettling sound. "The Pontifex Maximus has persuaded the Collegiate of Pontiffs to make an exception."

"Why?" Elissa guessed the answer. She had refused Nero's advances, foiled his plan to seduce Flavia and keep her for himself, and now he'd hatched another plan, a new form of extortion. She saw into his mind as if peering through an open window. "My sister can't be named a candidate," she said. "She's betrothed."

"The Pontifex Maximus has offered to pay the groom twice the amount of the dowry as compensation."

"And Egnatius agrees?"

"Apparently." Mother Amelia continued tapping, though the rhythm grew erratic.

Elissa wanted to scream. She wanted to kick the Vestal Maxima's desk, stop the infernal *click, click, click.*

She went to the window, allowing raindrops to bombard her face. Leaning over the sill, she gulped moist air. Her gaze fell on the rows of kale, parsnips, and beet greens.

She looked up at the Domus Transitoria, searching for some sign of Nero. He had no respect for the sacred office of Pontifex Maximus, no respect for the sacred order of the vestal virgins. If Flavia were selected, with no husband or father to object, Nero would use her as he wanted.

Rome burns and from union unholy, the sister will bring forth a son.

What if the prophecy had nothing to do with Agrippina? What if the unholy union referred to the seduction of a vestal virgin? Virgins were often referred to as sisters. What if the prophecy referred to Flavia?

"My sister is unfit to be a vestal virgin."

"The Pontifex Maximus disagrees."

"My parents will never consent."

"They already have."

Elissa turned from the window. How could Mother Amelia sit there, so calmly, tapping her pen? She stalked over to the Vestal Maxima, grabbed the offending stylus from her hand, snapped the reed in half and threw it on the floor. "Don't you see, it's just a ploy? Nero plans to make my sister his whore!"

"That much is obvious, Elissa."

She stared at the Vestal Maxima, saw her with new eyes. "You've been well paid, haven't you? You've orchestrated this arrangement."

"Don't be a fool, Elissa. There's nothing I can do. Nothing anyone can do. Truth be told, Nero can have your sister any time he wants—"

"But if she's a vestal virgin, her corruption will be that much juicier."

"If she's a vestal, perhaps we can protect her."

"How?"

"We can watch over her."

"If you permit this travesty, you're as corrupt as Nero."

"Sometimes we must make a sacrifice—"

"I've already sacrificed my brother. I won't offer up my sister." Attempting to control her rage, Elissa picked up the broken stylus and set the pieces on the desk. "I trusted you."

"Elissa, listen to reason—"

"And if my father refused the nomination, what then?"

"Your family's ruin. Your disgrace." Mother Amelia pressed her hands into the marble desk and leaned toward Elissa. "Spies mark your every move. If you stand in Nero's way, he will turn your friends against you, as proved by Angerona. Stand in Nero's way, and he'll destroy you. Even if you're innocent, he will find you guilty."

Lightening followed by a clap of thunder, portended Jupiter's approval.

"I guess it's settled."

"Yes."

A metallic taste washed over Elissa's tongue, a taste as poisonous as hemlock. She felt the prick of her incisors, imagined plunging sharpened fangs into Nero's jugular. So much for prayers to an Almighty God. So much for miracles and Jesus. No god was powerful enough to wrestle Nero.

Mother Amelia found a stray piece of candy and slipped it into her mouth.

"When will the lottery be held?" Elissa asked.

"At winter solstice. Nero plans to announce our new addition at his Saturnalia banquet."

"Perfect." How suitable for an upside-down decision to be made during that topsy-turvy festival when masters waited on their slaves, senators dressed up as clowns, and fools dressed up as senators.

Elissa stared out the window as rain pelted the withered garden. She shivered. How would she survive the encroaching winter? Perhaps she'd burrow deep into the ground and hide like a root vegetable. Like mandragora root.

Mandragora.

She bit her tongue to stop herself from saying it aloud. Mandragora. Love Apple. Most mysterious of herbs. Old wives claimed carrying the root close to the heart would lure a lover, the berries were an aphrodisiac, and a sprinkling of powder would inspire conception even in a barren womb. Named Devil's Apple by the Persians, mandragora was prescribed to cast out demons, foretell the future, stupefy an enemy. The taproot fattened quickly and could lengthen to four feet. Jews claimed the plant shrieked when uprooted. And everybody knew that boiling mandragora root resulted in a lethal poison.

"If that's all," Elissa said, "I'd like to do some work out in the garden."

CHAPTER XXIII

A leaf swirled through the open ceiling, fluttered through the atrium and settled in the pool. A tiny boat, Flavia thought, drifting out to sea.

"Pay attention," Constantina said, "or your spinning won't improve."

Steadying her left hand, Flavia attempted to keep the distaff, top-heavy with flax, from tipping. In her right hand she held the weighted spindle, a slender rod designed to whorl the flax into thread. Copying her mother, she allowed the spindle's weight to draw out the flax and tried to make an even thread. It snapped.

"Again," her mother said.

"Vestals don't have to spin flax."

"You haven't been selected yet."

"I will be."

Soon, Flavia told herself, she'd be rescued from marrying Egnatius. Just that morning Nero had sent her a handsome gift, a strand of lustrous pearls. She touched the necklace.

"Stop day-dreaming, Flavia."

She took up the spindle again and attempted to whorl another strand of thread.

"Remember yesterday, Mater, when we went to get the flax?"

"Concentrate on what you're doing."

The morning had been chilly. She and her mother had huddled together in the coach, their cloaks wrapped tight and sheepskins snug over their knees. Flavia had pretended they were on a journey to somewhere exciting—Macedonia, where King Titus had turned everything he touched to gold, or Arabia, the land of genies, wishes and magic. She imagined traveling in her private coach, wrapped in silk and fur. But her daydream had been broken when they reached the city gates.

Beyond the wall a crowd had gathered and, as the coach left the city, it seemed a riot might erupt. The coachman urged the horses on, toward open fields and orchards, but a horde of people blocked the road.

"Crucify him," a man shouted.

"Drive stakes into his wrists!"

"The cross is too good for him."

"Look away," Constantina said.

But Flavia could not help staring.

Her mother pointed to the sky. "See that flock of birds flying in formation? That's a good omen for our purchase."

"Ravens flying westward are a sign of death, Mater." Flavia tugged her mother's arm. "What are they doing to that man?"

"Pay attention," Constantina said, bringing Flavia back to the present.

"Ouch." She sucked blood from her finger.

"That's what you get for day-dreaming. Be careful. The spindle's sharp." Constantina drew out a perfect thread, even and strong.

Flavia rolled her eyes. Her mother always made such useful comments. "Why did they crucify that man, Mater?"

"Stop thinking about that man or you'll have nightmares."

"But, what did he do?"

"He was a criminal. A slave. Many slaves are crucified."

"How could you tell?"

"He bore the stigma of a fugitive. He must have run away." Constantina shook her finger at Flavia. "When we don't obey the law, when we are disobedient, we can expect punishment."

"I'm sick of spinning." Flavia dropped her distaff and spindle. A breeze blew through the atrium, damp and chilly. Though steam-heat ran through the floor, the room felt cold. "I'm going out."

"It's nearly time for bed, and it's raining."

"I don't care."

"You're not to leave."

"I'm sick of doing women's work, sick of this house." Flavia ran her hand through her silvery tresses, twisted a strand around her finger.

"Stop pulling on your hair."

"Perhaps I'll pay a visit to the Domus Transitoria tomorrow." She rearranged the necklace Nero had given her, playing with the double strand.

"I want you to return those pearls."

"That would be rude, Mater."

"What of your reputation? Accepting expensive gifts from—"

"I'd rather be whore to Nero than slave to Egnatius."

"Daughter!" Honoratus appeared in the doorway of his library, his face haggard. "Apologize to your mother."

"For what? Speaking the truth?"

"For your impertinence."

"Why do you think Nero wants to make me a vestal, Pater? He doesn't want me to be married. He wants to keep me near."

Her father's shoulders sagged. "I would stop him if I could," he said to Constantina. "But consider what he did to our son."

"What did he do?" Flavia asked. "You said Marcus was a traitor and he committed suicide."

Honoratus and Constantina held each other's gaze. "Things aren't always as they seem."

"You lied to me?" Flavia looked from her mother to her father.

Honoratus stared past Flavia to a place she couldn't fathom. "Your brother paid too much attention to the Greeks—Socrates, Plato, Aristotle. All that talk of democracy, of a republic, gave him ideas—"

"So Marcus wasn't a traitor?"

"Only if ideas are enough to condemn a man."

"We wanted to protect you," Constantina said. She clasped her hands together, and held them in her lap, to stop them from trembling.

"Protect me from what?" Flavia asked, her voice rising in pitch. "From whom?" Her parents' faces provided the answer. "Nero murdered Marcus? Is that what you're saying? He killed my brother without cause?"

"Go to bed, Flavia." Honoratus nodded toward the stairway.

"Answer me, Pater!"

"To bed. You're tired."

"To bed. To bed. To bed, of course!" Bile rushed into her mouth, and she thought she might vomit. Without kissing them goodnight, she raced up the stairs, ripped open the doorway's curtain and threw herself onto her sleeping couch. She pressed her face into a pillow and screamed. So much for dreams of freedom. So much for trusting anyone. Her parents had lied to her, but they would not, never in a thousand years, marry her off to Egnatius.

She hugged the pillow to her chest, and began to formulate her plan: She would be Nero's whore, serve her brother's murderer. Anything to get out of her parent's domus.

She leaned over the chamber pot and retched. Wiping her mouth with the back of her hand, she stumbled to the window and flung open the shutters. The black branches of the fig tree grasped the leaden clouds. Down in the courtyard, she saw her constant watch-guard—since her escape to Nero's feast her parents made sure she could not leave without permission.

Romulus and Remus pecked at their cage.

"There is no freedom in this world," she said.

How long did it take, she wondered, to die on a cross? Hours? Days? She imagined the slave's sinews tearing from his bones, his tongue swollen from lack of water, magpies pecking at his eyes— each moment an eternity. Could a person endure a lifetime of suffering? A lifetime of slavery?

She opened the cage.

Remus shied away from her, but she drew Romulus into her palm and stroked his downy chest. So soft and warm. So trusting. What would he do when she was gone?

She walked to the window, held the dove over the ledge. The bird fluttered its wings anticipating flight. She imagined the dove gliding through the courtyard, soaring high above the house, disappearing into clouds. But winter would be coming soon, and she couldn't bear to think of him frozen and half-starved.

Better to die quickly and put an end to suffering.

Holding the dove against her heart, she whispered, "I'll miss you." And, with a sharp intake of breath, she wrenched its neck. She placed Romulus back inside the cage and reached for Remus.

CHAPTER XXIV

Above the House of Vestals, on Palatine Hill, the Domus Transitoria stood sentinel. The windows stared vacantly at Elissa, mirroring the dismal sky and her even blacker mood.

She picked up her basket and walked along the portico past statues of dead priestesses, past the central pool. A breeze rippled the water, sent shivers down her back. She drew her cloak closer. All her life she'd followed protocol, lived by rules set down by others, and now she ventured down an unmarked path. Today marked Nero's birth, the Ides of December, two days before the festival of Saturnalia—the ideal date to plot his death. Pulling up her cloak's hood, she headed for the herb garden.

Planning someone's eradication required passion, preparation, and devotion. For weeks she had tended the garden—pulling weeds, tilling soil, gathering vegetables. And relentlessly, as a mother cares for a babe-in-arms, she'd nurtured the patch of herbs.

Frost had changed the lush green mint into brownish stalks, and the leaves crumbled at her touch. The basil, named for Basilisk the fire-breathing dragon, had died long ago. But the thyme still thrived. She broke off a sprig, rolled the verdant leaves between her thumb and forefinger, then ran her hands along her arms, anointing herself as soldiers did before a battle. The thyme's keen scent brought back the days of summer—happy days, before Nero had murdered Marcus.

Basket in hand, she pushed past a hedge of rosemary. The plant she wanted preferred shade. Its apple-scented berries had fallen and the shriveled leaves appeared deceptively innocuous, but it was mandragora root.

Elissa found her knife, knelt on the damp soil, and scribed a circle around the plant. "I call on Pluto," she chanted softly, "Lord of the Underworld and his consort, Persephone." According to Pliny, three circles were required for a charm to work. She scribed the second. "May Nero lose his breath, and may poison seep into his liver, stop his heart, turn his eyes to stone." The third circle completed the spell. "May he burn for all eternity."

She removed a vial of wine from her basket, carefully uncorked it, and poured the contents on the ground as Pliny instructed. Wiping perspiration from her brow, she prayed Jesus would forgive her. Surely it could not be wrong to destroy an enemy as evil as Nero.

She crawled around the plant, until she faced west. With both hands, she grabbed the stalk and tugged, but the root clung to the earth. Jabbing the knife into the earth, she rocked the blade back and forth, loosening the dirt. Again, she grabbed the stalk and yanked, fearing it might break. Finally the root gave way. She fell backward, victorious, the mandragora dangling in her hand. There was no scream, as predicted by the Jews, but the root resembled a human being: two arms, two legs, a torso and head.

A shadow fell across the ground. Elissa tossed the mandragora root into her basket, quickly covering it with a handful of thyme. Turning, she saw Angerona.

"What are you doing Elissa?"

"Gardening, what else?" Elissa wiped her earth-caked hands on her stola.

Angerona crouched beside her, peered into the basket. She brushed aside the thyme. "Love Apple," she said. "I might have guessed."

"Is it? I mistook it for parsnip. The two look similar."

"I can guess what you're concocting—"

Elissa licked her lips.

"—a love potion," Angerona said triumphantly.

"Love potion!" Elissa choked down her laughter. "Nothing gets past you."

"Take care, Elissa, or you'll face the Collegiate of Pontiffs. I'm warning you as a friend."

"A friend? The friend who betrayed my brother. The friend who sent Marcus to his death."

"I'm truly sorry, Elissa." Tears filled Angerona's eyes. "I named Marcus to protect my family. If I could take it back I—"

"You can't."

"Forgive me. I beg you."

"I curse the day I met you." As soon as the words left her mouth, Elissa regretted them.

Angerona backed away, her eyes no longer sad, but fierce.

"I don't mean that," Elissa said. "I'm sorry."

"You don't know what sorry is." Angerona turned and ran.

Collecting her basket, Elissa told herself she had nothing to fear. Even if Angerona ran to Tigellinus and he charged her with infidelity, a physical examination would prove her innocence.

Meanwhile, she had business to which she must attend.

According to Pliny, boiling mandragora root would result in the strongest tincture, and the deadliest.

CHAPTER XXV

"Assassination," Lucan spoke in a harsh whisper.

Justinus glanced around the forum. Saturnalia began at sundown and the piazza overflowed with people, animals, and merchants. A market day had been declared, and an exception had been made for traffic—though it was midday, carts laden with amphorae of wine, sides of oxen, and sacks of grain, rolled up the winding road to the Domus Transitoria.

"I won't resort to violence," Justinus said.

He scanned the crowd. The Assembly had recessed early for the holiday and citizens streamed out of the Curia Julia. He nodded to a passing senator, trailed by petitioners. The senator nodded back, then glanced unsmilingly at Lucan. The poet was fast gaining a reputation as a troublemaker. Politicians, wishing to remain in Nero's good graces, shunned him.

"Another of Nero's pawns," Lucan said, loudly.

"Let's get out of here."

They headed across the forum, in search of somewhere quiet where they could talk. Two men sat hunched on the steps of the Basilica Julia playing Terni Lapilli. Justinus stopped to watch and so did Lucan. Alternately, the men moved blue or red chips into hatch-marks scratched into the stone. On another step, four boys challenged each other in a heated game of walnuts. Between shouts and shoves they rolled the nuts into depressions, attempting to knock out the walnuts of their opponents.

"The trick is to be brutal," Lucan said. "Hesitate and you can't win."

They continued walking past a fountain where women knelt to collect water. They entered an alleyway of butcher stalls, and ducked through hanging carcasses of beef, mutton, and pork— the smell heavy and sickening. They turned a corner, and entered another alleyway dedicated to green-grocers. Justinus stopped to scrutinize the rows of tables stacked with carrots, dark green kale, yellowish onions—a collage of winter vegetables.

He picked up a cabbage, weighed it in his palm.

"Can I help you?" a farmer asked.

Justinus set down the cabbage, and the farmer turned to a more promising customer.

"Violence costs the soul, Lucan."

"You've been tainted by that zealot, Paul. What does a prophet know of politics?"

"What does a poet know?"

"I keep my fingers on the pulse of Rome, and I'm not alone in my hatred of—"

"Let's go." Justinus tossed the farmer a coin and took the cabbage.

"Go where?"

"To see Paul."

"Why not? I'm in the mood for a debate."

"Listen to reason, Lucan, before you do something you regret."

"I regret each day that Nero lives."

"Perhaps he will change."

"When pigs sprout wings."

"All things are possible, by the grace of God," Justinus said.

"Then why does evil still exist?"

That was a good question. One Justinus couldn't answer. He wanted to prove Lucan wrong. He prayed Nero might experience a transformation. But, lately, that hope seemed futile. Nero neglected business of state, devoting his days to athletic training, his nights to the lyre and wine. In order to expand his palace, he extorted bribes and depleted the treasury.

Justinus increased his pace, struggling to keep up with Lucan's lanky stride. "I believe there's good in all of us," he said.

Lucan didn't respond. He just kept walking toward the Hebrew Quarter.

श्री

Justinus sat cross-legged on the floor of the tentmaker's shop alongside Timothy and Luke, listening quietly.

"Violence begets violence." Paul's words echoed Justinus's thoughts.

"Sometimes violence is necessary." Lucan's booming voice made the room feel constricted. The low ceiling emphasized the poet's height and, compared to the prophet, Lucan was a giant—in stature if not in temperament. "Force offers quicker results than platitudes," he said.

"Tent-making has taught me patience," Paul replied.

He smiled, and Justinus felt as if a lantern had been lit—the room glowed with his warmth. A panel of sailcloth rested in the prophet's lap, and he used a curved needle to draw waxed thread through the sturdy fabric. Even at the age of seventy, his eyesight remained keen. Justinus had not been surprised to find him sewing. Tent-making had sustained Paul throughout his travels, and with help from Timothy and Luke the shop yielded a meager profit to fund their gatherings. The tent they worked on now was a rainbow colored pavilion that might shelter fifty people. A length of scarlet cloth stretched across the floor and was covered by a translucent sheet of papyrus. Needle pricks in the papyrus outlined a design, thousands of tiny perforations, through which carbon dust was sifted to mark the pattern. The scarlet cloth would then be cut and stitched to the palm-green body of the tent along with intricate designs in yellow, blue, and purple. Paul's income from tent-making was supplemented by gifts from followers—he kept only enough on which to live, distributing the remainder to widows, orphans and the destitute. The prophet's generosity amazed Justinus.

"I would like to learn such patience," Justinus said.

Lucan grunted. "Where's your guard this evening?" he asked Paul.

"I gave him leave to celebrate Saturnalia." Paul drew his needle through the cloth, gently tugged the thread.

"You gave him leave?"

"Tigellinus may employ him, but my guard follows me."

"Instead of sewing you should be planning a way to rid yourself of Tigellinus," Lucan said. "But to rid yourself of a snake, you must cut off its head—in this case, Nero."

Justinus had to agree. The question was how?

Lucan circled the room, restless as a gladiator before the games. He riffled through a store of goatskins that lay stacked in a corner then examined a birch pole, long as he was tall—materials used to construct the type of tent Justinus had carried as a soldier. Finding an earthen jar, Lucan opened it and sniffed.

"What's this?"

"Tung-oil," Paul said. "From China. My secret for waterproofing."

"It stinks."

"Careful not to spill it. Tung-oil is highly flammable."

"An accelerant might be useful," Lucan said.

"For what?" Justinus asked. "Are you planning to burn Nero at the stake?"

"Not a bad idea." Lucan corked the jar of oil. "If we don't act soon, he'll make slaves of all of us."

Paul set down the length of cloth. "Why not turn your talents to the Lord instead of running after demons, most of whom are your creation? God appointed Nero king, and he appointed you a poet."

"How can you be so complacent? You're Nero's prisoner!" Lucan grabbed the tent pole and pounded the floor. "Soon you'll be tried and put to death."

Startled by the outburst, Timothy, Luke and Justinus shifted on their cushions, but Paul calmly returned to his sewing. "I'm a Roman citizen," he said, "awaiting an appeal. Meanwhile, here in Rome, I'm free to practice my religion. Not so in Jerusalem."

"Paul is right," Luke said. A former physician, Luke often provided a voice of reason. "Last spring at Passover the temple's high priest sent his dagger men to murder James."

"James?" Justinus had never heard the name.

"The leader of our congregation in Jerusalem." Timothy chewed his cherubic lips. "James followed Jewish law to the last letter."

"Then why did the high priest have him assassinated?" Justinus asked.

"His brother was Jesus, and James claimed Jesus the Messiah."

"James sided with Paul," Luke added. "He agreed Gentiles in our congregation should be exempt from Mosaic Law, circumcision in particular."

"I curse the Jews," Justinus said. "They crucified their own Messiah."

"Jews had nothing to do with the death of Jesus," Luke said. "Our Lord's death was ordered by the Roman Prefect of Judea, Pontius Pilate. High priests of the Jewish Temple lack the power to condemn a man to death. And crucifixion is a Roman method."

"My mother was a Jewess," Timothy said quietly. He looked at Justinus, but his eyes held no reproof, only sorrow. "Though she refused to recognize Jesus as the Son of God, I've never known a kinder woman."

"Sorry," Justinus said.

"Apology accepted."

Justinus felt the reassuring touch of Paul's hand on his shoulder. "Keep the tung-oil. Perhaps you'll take up tent-making." The prophet gave Justinus the earthen jar.

"Perhaps I'll learn more patience."

"Patience and forgiveness are no virtues when it comes to Nero," Lucan said. "I have none, nor should you. Today Nero tolerates followers of Jesus, but tomorrow he may have you crucified."

"It makes little difference how or where I die," Paul said, "if my heart is with the Lord."

Justinus rotated his shoulders, trying to loosen them. The old war wound ached. He wanted to learn patience and forgiveness, wanted to emulate Paul, but when he thought of Marcus, slaughtered like an animal, he had to agree with Lucan. Nero paid no attention to laws, but acted as he pleased. And some acts were unforgivable.

He got up, wandered to the window and peered through the shutters. Even in the Hebrew Quarter, the street was filled with Saturnalia revelers. Shouting and singing rang through the alleyway. Celebrants wore the soft felt caps of freedmen and carried lanterns to illuminate the dusk. Across the river, lights twinkled on Palatine Hill.

"The festival has started," he said. "I smell smoke from the sacrifice. Soon the banquet will begin."

Lucan and Paul continued arguing, Lucan's voice raised and Paul's voice calm.

Nero had arranged for banquet boards to be set out in the forum. A feast was to be served, more sumptuous than any public meal the urban mob had ever seen, followed by music, dancing, even gambling. Nero would make a brief appearance, basking in his popularity with the plebs, before attending his private celebration at the Domus Transitoria. Justinus had received no invitation; any pretense of friendship with Nero had died at Meditrinalia. Though he despised the excess of Nero's banquets, the obscene waste, he might have gone—to see Elissa. Her last letter had been full of grief over her sister's fate, and he longed to comfort her. Tonight, instead of feasting, he would pray for the House of Rubrius.

"There's no reasoning with you!" Lucan's voice brought Justinus back to the present. "You spew fantastic tales of miracles and divine intervention, but I have faith only in men's greed."

"My faith is in the Lord," Paul said.

"Jesus was a man, like you and me. The 'Lord' you tout does not exist."

Paul set down the panel he'd been sewing. "Sit."

Lucan opened his mouth as if to continue arguing then closed it. Unable to ignore Paul's command, he sat. Justinus sank onto a cushion next to Timothy and Luke.

"I see myself in you, young man," Paul said, rising stiffly. "I've grown old, but I remember being just like you." He winked at Lucan. "Self-righteous and arrogant."

Lucan began to speak, but Paul raised a hand to stop him.

"Hear me out," he said. "Humor an old man." His smile made it impossible for Lucan to disagree. "I was the Pharisee of Pharisees, following Mosaic Law to the last letter. My great joy was to punish followers of Jesus. Who were they to heal the sick on the Sabbath? To feast on unsanctioned meat, and preach to gentiles? Infidels! I would see them dead."

The floorboards creaked as Paul paced the room. He tugged at his gray beard. "Under the highest temple authority, in order to quell corruption, I was appointed to journey to Damascus. The road was tedious and unforgiving. My men were soon exhausted, but I drove them on. Outside the city gates I met my nemesis. An orb burned in the heavens, brighter than sun, blinding me with scalding light. I fell onto my knees as did my men. We prostrated ourselves, as no Jew should, except to the Divine Creator. And a voice said to me, 'Saul,'—my Hebrew name is Saul—'why do you persecute me?'

"You may imagine my amazement. 'Who are you?' I asked.

"The voice answered, 'Jesus Christos, your savior.'"

Paul's face grew radiant, and Justinus stared at him in wonder.

"Three days later I was baptized and my sight returned." The prophet looked around the room with eyes sharp as a falcon's. "I tell you this, so you may learn from my example."

Even Lucan remained speechless.

Justinus wiped his nose, blinked his watery eyes. Within the confines of this room he felt the presence of the Lord. God's love shimmered in the oil lamp's glow, tempering encroaching shadows. Was it possible the light of Christos might dispel a world of darkness?

"In Christos we are one," Paul said. "Roman, Jew, Greek, Egyptian."

"I'll never count myself as one with Nero," Lucan said.

"Hate breeds hate," Paul said. "I don't believe in violence."

"And I—" Lucan got up, walked toward the door. "—I don't believe in miracles."

CHAPTER XXVI

XIV before the Kalends of January

Year IX, reign of Nero Claudius Caesar Augustus Germanicus

Dear Justinus,

I find my mood blacker than these winter nights. The dark of the year is dedicated to Vesta, goddess of the hearth, but tonight her fire offers me no light. I see no way out of this obscurity—

But one.

E lissa touched the vial of mandragora she hid within her stola.

Tonight, as you know, a new vestal virgin will be chosen by lottery at Nero's Saturnalia feast. Some place their bets on Faustina Equita, daughter of a wealthy corn merchant; others favor Claudia Avisia. Astrologers have studied the position of the stars, haruspices have interpreted the splayed entrails of twenty bullocks, but you and I know, Nero will decide the outcome.

She gazed through the open ceiling of her father's atrium. A single star floated in a sea of night. Pigeons cooed in the rafters and the house creaked as water carried heat beneath the floor-boards. She shifted in her chair, unable to get comfortable.

Across from her, Flavia reclined on a couch, her slender legs propped on cushions, her tumbled hair gilded by the oil-lamp's glow.

"What are you writing?" Flavia asked.

"Nothing." Elissa ripped the papyrus in half and fed it to the brazier's flames. She wandered aimlessly around the room and returned to her chair.

"Do you think Pater will get better?" Flavia asked.

"I don't know."

Their father had suffered another bout of apoplexy. Weakness of the heart, according to Doctor Karpos. Elissa had spent the afternoon tending him. Only at her mother's insistence had she left the stuffy bedchamber. Constantina, ever dutiful, would sit vigil by her husband's side throughout the night. Consequently, Elissa had been appointed to represent her family and escort Flavia to the Saturnalia banquet.

"We should go," she said. "Get this over with."

"I don't want to arrive early. I intend to make an entrance."

Elissa sighed.

Spurius shuffled across the room and set a bowl of apples on a small table that stood between the sisters. "A Saturnalia gift from Gallus Justinus. He hopes your parents will accept, and—" The old slave's shaggy eyebrows lowered, and his gaze fixed on Flavia. "He offers his apologies."

"Thank you, Spurius," Elissa said, cutting short his impending lecture.

"It's others should apologize." Spurius left the atrium, his gait decidedly more sprightly.

No doubt he was headed to the kitchen for a helping of food and gossip. The servants would huddle over fish stewed with onions, discussing moral values, whispering about Flavia's impropriety, ruminating on the fate of the House of Rubrius. Later, woes forgotten, they'd go out to celebrate.

Extending her foot, Flavia pushed away the bowl of apples with her toes. "According to Nero," she said, "apples harm the vocal cords."

196

"By all means, let's give him several."

The vial of mandragora felt cold against Elissa's breast.

If only she could be a child again curled in her father's lap, secure within the safety of his arms. If only she could play a game of hide and seek with Marcus or help her mother to spin flax. If only she could live a different life. How pleasant it would be to gather in the evening with her family for a meal, discuss the day's events with her husband, weave bedtime stories for the children.

She glanced at the curtain leading to her father's bedchamber. "I'd better check on Pater."

"He's asleep," Flavia said. "The physician prescribed a potion." Sitting up, she stretched her arms. She bent over the table, examining the bowl of apples, touching each of them before choosing the brightest scarlet apple in the bowl. Falling back onto the couch, she took a noisy bite.

"You just said apples harm the voice."

Flavia shrugged. "Lot's of things are bad for me, but I still like them."

Elissa shot her a disapproving look. "It's not too late to change your mind."

"About what?"

"Marriage."

"I have other plans." Flavia crunched the apple.

"Nero murdered your brother. Burned him alive."

"I'll make sure he gets his punishment."

"How?"

"I have my ways." Flavia took another bite, severing the apple's core.

Sitting straighter in her chair, Elissa studied her sister. When had she become so cold? "How do you think Marcus would feel," she said, "if he saw what you are doing? If he knew you planned to bed the man who murdered him?"

"Marcus is dead. His opinion doesn't matter."

"He died to save your life."

"To save my life?"

"Nero threatened to have you tortured. When Marcus heard that threat, he donned the poisoned robe."

Flavia stopped chewing. "Even if that's true, it doesn't change my plans."

"Of course not. You care only for yourself, your position in society."

"And you don't? You're a vestal virgin. Educated, allowed to own property. You have freedom other women dream about. Would you give up your freedom to marry Egnatius?" Flavia spat a seed onto the floor. "I know what men are, and I know how to use them."

"You think you can control Nero?"

"I know what he wants."

"You have no idea."

Flavia pursed her carmine lips, the color of a prostitute's. "He's a *man*, Elissa. He might select me as a vestal, but I won't remain a virgin. And I'll see he pays a high price for the honor."

"Fool!" Elissa slapped the apple from Flavia's hand, and the fruit bounced across the tiles. "You think you'll outmaneuver Nero?"

"I intend to try."

"Don't go to the feast. I'll make your excuses, explain Pater has fallen ill. A vestal's parents must be of good health—"

"I'm going."

"How can you be so selfish? Marry Egnatius and you may live to be a mother. Marry Egnatius and our parents may survive to become grandparents. Stupid girl!"

"You're the fool, Elissa. Pining away for Gallus Justinus. Do you think he'll wait another twenty years for you? You think he'll want to couple with a hag of forty?" She smiled. "I wonder what it would be like to bed him."

Elissa clenched her jaw, controlling the urge to slap her sister.

"He's well built, I grant you," Flavia said. "No wonder women find him attractive. Have you noticed his bulge? I'm trying to imagine how large his member gets. You know they swell, don't you, Elissa? Grow hard and big, long as a cucumber."

"A cucumber?" Elissa couldn't help but ask.

"And point straight up, like a spear. I'll bet Justinus's phallus is bigger than a bull's, bigger than an elephant's, bigger than—"

"You're disgusting!"

Flavia surveyed the bowl of apples and chose a yellow one. "I think you're jealous."

"Of you?"

"Have you never wondered what it would be like to slide your naked body against a man's, to feel him deep inside of you—"

"Quiet." Elissa glanced toward their father's chamber. She ran her hand over her forehead and noticed she felt feverish. How many nights had she lain awake, imagining?

"Catch." Flavia tossed her the apple.

"Has Nero taken your virginity?"

"Not yet." Flavia started up the stairs, then turned back to Elissa. "Perhaps tonight. I'm going to get ready now."

If Flavia hadn't run, Elissa would have tackled her.

Sinking back into her chair, she examined the apple. Yellow with a rosy blush.

CHAPTER XXVII

Blood dripped from the altar of the Temple of Saturn, pooling on the marble, soaking the priests' robes, while a band of flute-players drowned the victims' squawks and squeals. The Pontifex Maximus had outdone all expectations, sacrificing not only four score of sheep, six score of oxen, a hundred pigs, but black-and-white striped horses from the plains of Africa, Caspian leopards from Asia, flocks of exotic birds never before seen in Rome. Flavia's meager sacrifice of Romulus and Remus could not compare to Nero's spectacle.

She watched Nero, studying the way he stood, the way he spoke, looking for some glimmer of the desperate child, but he kept his weakness hidden. He stood beside the altar, crowned by a diadem studded with pearls and gemstones, Master of Saturnalia, Lord of The Roman Empire. Her brother's murderer. More than anything, she wanted to see him grovel.

"Let the feast begin," he proclaimed, and the crowd broke into cheers.

The plebs adored their Caesar—his charismatic smile, his penchant for spectacle. Flavia could not help admiring his power. Despite his filthy deeds and perverse ways, she felt strangely attracted to him.

"I've never witnessed such extravagance," she said to her sister.

"Wasteful butchery," Elissa muttered.

Elissa took Flavia's arm in hers, steering Flavia away from the bloody altar and through the noisy throng. Above the forum, on Palatine Hill, every window in the palace glowed. The sisters climbed the steps of the Temple of Castor and Pollux. Guards flanking the stairway stood straighter, out of respect for a vestal, as Elissa passed.

Flavia lifted her hem, exposing a slender ankle. Her white robe, meant to be pristine and modest, clung to her body. Having neglected to bind her breasts, her nipples stood erect, demanding the guards' attention. She enjoyed hearing the men gasp, sensed the heat of their desire—assurance that she possessed a power greater than her sister's.

"Cover yourself," Elissa said, pausing to rearrange Flavia's palla.

They walked through the temple to the entrance of the Domus Transitoria. When they arrived at the doors, Flavia shrugged the palla from her shoulders. She was rewarded by a lascivious smile from the prefect of the Praetorian Guard. Tigellinus slouched in a chair, his feet propped on a table.

"Good evening," Elissa said, her tone as warm as ice.

"Priestess Elissa." Tigellinus did not bother to stand up, but slumped lower in his chair. "I see you've brought your not-so-little sister."

"Must I open the doors or will you trouble yourself?"

"No trouble, Priestess Elissa. I'll make sure of that."

Tigellinus snapped his fingers and two slaves lifted the heavy bar. The doors opened with a groan. "Enjoy yourselves," Tigellinus said, his eyes focused on Flavia's chest.

He was a pig by any standards, far too lowly to touch her. Flavia offered him a condescending smile. Breasts bouncing, she trotted after Elissa, reassured of her magnificence.

The courtyard glittered with what must have been a thousand oil lamps. Hothouse flowers lined the walkways, releasing exotic perfumes. Guards stood beneath the portico, watching from the shadows. A harpist played in the central pavilion. Defying the night's chill, three young men, wearing nothing but loincloths, splashed in the fountain. They caught Flavia staring at their well-formed bodies and motioned for her to join them.

She giggled.

Elissa took her sister's hand and pulled her through the garden, through the nymphaeum and its cascading waters. They ascended the double stairs and entered the vestibule leading to the banquet hall. A slave, dressed in the short kilt of an Egyptian prince, announced them. Conversations ceased as the guests strained to see Nero's latest obsession.

Imagining herself a goddess, Flavia nodded to her audience.

Strands of silver beads cascaded from the ceiling, shimmering in the torchlight, rattling like rain. Opposite the entrance, a dais had been placed along the wall and there an empty throne awaited the Master of Saturnalia. Clusters of couches surrounded small tables loaded with delicacies. Some guests wore masks and many had donned costumes.

On Saturnalia rules were overturned. Concubines, dressed as proper matrons, reclined on couches—while matrons, clad as dancing girls, performed. Priests of Saturn poured wine for slave-boys, and slave-boys ordered knights to do their bidding. Licinius Crassus Frugi, Consul for the incoming year, had been assigned the lowly task of collecting urine from guests too satiated to visit the latrines.

"Nero makes a mockery of our most sacred ceremonies," Elissa said. "How dare he hold the lottery for the next vestal virgin amid this carnival?"

"I think it's perfect. After all, Saturnalia is a night for gambling." Flavia sucked in her stomach and stuck out her chest.

"Your nipples blush," Elissa said, tugging at her sister's palla.

Flavia glanced toward the empty throne, wishing Nero would arrive to save her from Elissa. At the far end of the room, high-backed chairs stood against the wall, and there sat the Collegiate of Pontiffs and the other vestal virgins. The twenty candidates reclined on cushions at their feet.

Elissa squeezed Flavia's hand. "Are you afraid?"

"Afraid he won't call my name?"

Elissa frowned. "You would be wise to be afraid."

They walked toward the Collegiate of Pontiffs, and curtsied to the Vestal Maxima. Flavia took her place with the other candidates, settling on a cushion. She surveyed her competition. She sat between Faustina Equita, a sullen girl who wore too many jewels, and Claudia Avisia, a child who could have been no more than seven. Her competition stood no chance.

Brass trumpets sounded and cymbals crashed, announcing the Master of Saturnalia's arrival. The guests cheered, rising to greet Nero as he climbed the dais to claim his throne.

Flavia couldn't take her eyes from him. Dressed in the costume of a musician—stacked shoes that made him tower over other men and robes that sparkled blindingly with every movement. His eyes sought hers. She slid her little finger into her mouth, pulled it halfway out, and smiled. His nostrils flared.

Oh yes, she would make him beg.

Poppaea Sabina stood beside him, her gaze ever-watchful. They said she bathed in asses' milk to preserve her skin, but even from a distance Flavia could see that asses' milk had not prevented her from wrinkling. Poppaea returned the stare, and Flavia's stomach tightened. She saw cruelty in those kohl-rimmed eyes. Much as she hated to admit it, perhaps Elissa had a point. Perhaps she had reason to be frightened.

She glanced around the room, wishing her mother and father had come. The parents of the other candidates appeared anxious. Giving up a daughter to thirty years of service was a dubious honor that could not be refused. Most parents would prefer their daughters to marry, raise a family and live a normal life.

The Master of Saturnalia pounded his eagle-headed scepter, and the room fell into silence.

"Welcome to my home," Nero said in a falsetto voice that set a few guests tittering. "We will open with a song."

Still using the falsetto, he broke into an aria and pounded out the rhythm with his scepter. When he was done guests rose to their feet, clapping enthusiastically—especially the bushy-haired young men, who were trained in the Egyptian method of applause and well paid by Nero. They even had special names: The Bees made a humming sound, the Roof-tiles clapped with hollowed palms, the Brick-bats clapped with flat hands and made the loudest sound. The other guests squirmed in their seats, unsure of how they should respond. Flavia was among them.

"I am King of Misrule," Nero announced. "And tonight I demand all rules be broken. Allow me to demonstrate."

He climbed onto the throne, grinning at his audience. Turning his back to them, he pulled up his robe, exposing his buttocks, and bent over. Upside-down, he peered through his calves. "Anyone who takes this evening seriously will be severely punished." In emphasis he broke wind, and the crowd gasped.

"Let the games begin!"

Panels in the ceiling turned, releasing flowers. Roses rained down on the guests, pelting them with thorns as well as petals. Nero exploded into laughter, and the guests joined him nervously.

With increasing trepidation, Flavia glanced at her sister. She sat between Mother Amelia and Priestess Angerona, rigid in her high-backed chair, her face an angry mask.

⚶

Elissa pinned her gaze on Nero and watched his every move. He stepped down from the dais and wandered through the banquet hall greeting his guests. He spoke to his childhood nurse, Claudia Ecloge, then kissed her gently on the forehead. With some people he showed tenderness, but she couldn't trust him to do the same with Flavia.

He stopped at the table of a prominent merchant. The merchant's smile quickly faded when the King of Misrule ordered him to prance around the banquet hall pretending to be Bacchus. The rotund man did as he was told, sweat pouring from his blotchy face. Nero finally allowed him, out of breath and close to fainting, to sit. The King of Misrule then commanded the merchant's wife to bare her breasts while reciting a bawdy poem. Close to tears, the poor woman complied. Satisfied at the havoc he had wrought, Nero returned to Poppaea Sabina and reclined beside her on the couch.

The atmosphere grew more relaxed. A stage had been erected by the entryway and the orchestra began to play a soothing melody. The flutist was particularly fine, Elissa thought.

The scent of roasted meat wafted through the banquet hall and servants entered, carrying platters of the exotic animals sacrificed to Saturn.

"Pigeon stuffed with sausage then cooked inside a swan," a boy wearing nothing but an earring offered.

"Leopard fried in olive oil with rosemary," said another. "Guaranteed to make you virile."

"Roasted crocodile in pomegranate." A boy, dressed like a Persian harem girl, proudly displayed his platter.

"No, thank you," Elissa said.

Reaching beneath her stola, she touched the vial of mandragora nestled in the crevice of her breasts. She needed only an opportunity to slip the contents into Nero's drink. After ingesting the tincture, he would become at first elated, even delirious. In small quantity, mandragora was an aphrodisiac.

But she planned to be generous.

Josephus claimed mandragora exorcised daemons—if that proved true, the remedy would soon expel Nero from this world. The thought caused Elissa to smile for the first time that evening.

"Where is Justinus tonight?" Angerona asked. Her face was flushed from drinking wine and her palla had fallen from her shoulders. She wore gold bangles on her arms, and they clinked annoyingly.

"How would I know?" Elissa said coldly.

"I'm watching you," Angerona said.

"I'm watching you as well."

Of course Justinus wasn't in attendance at this sham of a feast—this charade meant to mock the vestal virgins. Elissa hadn't seen him since that day in the Subura. To do so would be dangerous. Through his letters, the letters she paid Thais dearly to receive, she knew that he still followed Paul. Sometimes Justinus transcribed a prayer, a phrase she could latch onto. Sometimes he wrote of love. Though she hadn't seen him for two months, not an hour passed that she didn't think of him.

Mother Amelia patted Elissa's hand with oily fingers. "Your mind is on your sister," she said, chewing a lump of chicken drowned in cream. "Never have I eaten fowl this tender." She smacked her lips, before adding, "Your sister will be fine. In our house, Flavia will be protected."

Protected how? Elissa wondered.

With every passing hour, Mother Amelia seemed to become more oblivious. She leaned close to Elissa, imparting a blast of scallions and wine. "After dessert, it will be time to hold the lottery and, you'll see, everything will come out right."

She lived in a world of children's tales.

"Excuse me, Mother Amelia," Elissa said, rising from her chair. "I must find the latrine."

"Downstairs, my dear." The Vestal Maxima waved her greasy hand in the direction of the orchestra. Lifting a honey-poached dormouse by the tail, she lowered it into her mouth.

Elissa headed for the exit. She walked past Nero. He stood on the stage, belting out a song. All eyes focused on him as he screeched.

She saw her opportunity.

His chalice stood abandoned, not far from the stage, on a nearby table. Fishing for the vial within her stola, Elissa edged toward the cup. She glanced at the crowd, making certain no one watched, uncorked the vial and quickly poured the tincture into the greenish bile that Nero drank.

A heavy hand came down on her shoulder. She dropped the vial, and it rolled under the table.

"What are you doing, Priestess Elissa?"

Plastering a smile onto her mouth, she turned to face Tigellinus. "I'm on my way to the latrine."

The purplish scar that cut through his upper lip deepened in color. He glanced at Nero's chalice. So did she. His hand dwarfed the cup as he sniffed the tonic.

"Nasty smell." He pressed the cup beneath her nostrils. "Laced with what?"

"Echinacea? It soothes the throat."

"Take a sip."

Elissa glanced around the banquet hall, but no one seemed to notice them. Nero continued singing. By all appearances, she and Tigellinus might be discussing the weather. Across the room Mother Amelia concentrated on dessert, an elaborate cake requiring four men to carry it from the kitchens. Marcia preyed on a platter of snails dripping in oil. A red dog with a curling tail had found Cornelia and sat beside the girl, tail wagging, as she slipped it bits of meat. Angerona was too busy flirting with a knight to notice Elissa. Elissa's gaze met her sister's, and Flavia started to get up. Elissa shook her head in warning.

"Drink," Tigellinus said.

Perhaps it would be best to drink, to put an end to suffering and join her brother in the underworld. Elissa's lips met the cup's rim. Her tongue tingled then went numb.

Tigellinus watched, curiosity glowing in his eyes. To squelch his fire, Elissa tossed the cup's contents at him.

He pressed his hands against his eyes, green slime running down his cheeks. "You've blinded me!"

Nero stopped mid-song to glare at Tigellinus. "How dare you interrupt my performance?"

Blinking his red eyes, Tigellinus pointed at Elissa who'd edged out of his reach. "That bitch tried to poison you."

"Play on," Nero shouted at the orchestra.

They began a boisterous tune, drowning out all conversation.

Elissa glanced toward the exit, but guards blocked her escape.

Nero leapt down from the stage, landing in front of her. "You tried to poison me? I didn't think you had it in you."

"There's proof," Tigellinus said.

A slave-boy crawled under the table to retrieve the empty vial.

Nero sniffed it. "Mandragora," he announced.

"An aphrodisiac," Elissa said.

"My Saturnalia gift?" Nero spoke so only she could hear, leading her away from Tigellinus. "I require no aphrodisiac to tup your sister."

"Keep your hands off Flavia." She grabbed the vial from him.

"I should kill you now," he said.

"You have no evidence." She dropped the vial and crushed it under her heel.

Nero chuckled. "I enjoy our little game, don't you, Elissa? By the way, I've deciphered the prophecy. It's not about my mother after all."

"I don't care about your stupid prophecy."

"I *am* Rome, am I not? And I *burn* for you."

What nonsense.

She tried to walk away from him, but he stayed at her heels. "From union unholy the sister will bring forth a son. I see the meaning clearly now: I, Rome, burn for you—and your sister will bear my son."

Elissa turned to face him. "You'll have to kill me first."

"But we're having so much fun. Come with me, Elissa, it's time for the lottery, and I want you to draw the lot."

Tigellinus trailed after them, ensuring she followed Nero onto the dais. The King of Misrule retrieved his scepter and pounded the heavy staff until the guests grew quiet.

"Fellow citizens, the moment you've been waiting for has come." He spoke to the crowd's upturned faces. "Priestess Elissa Rubria Honoria will draw the name of the next vestal virgin, Priestess of the Sacred Flame."

Poppaea Sabina handed him a bowl.

The clay lots rattled as he stirred them. He handed Elissa the bowl. "Draw."

She reached her trembling hand into the bowl.

Please God, let it not be Flavia, she prayed, and I promise to devote my life to Jesus. She'd lost all faith in Roman gods.

Her fingers wrapped around a small clay tablet.

"Read the name aloud," Nero commanded her.

Her sister's name swam before her eyes. The lot fell from Elissa's hand and shattered on the floor.

"Most inauspicious," Poppaea said.

Nero thrust the bowl in front of Elissa. "Draw again."

Again?

Was it possible Flavia had escaped, and another girl would be chosen? Elissa reached into the bowl, withdrawing another tablet. Before she could read the name, Nero grabbed the lot out of her hand. He held the bit of clay above his head.

"The gods have spoken," he proclaimed. "Rome's next vestal virgin will be—" He cleared his throat. "Flavia Rubria Honoria."

"It can't be," Elissa cried. But no one paid attention.

All eyes turned to Flavia—so pale, so young, and so afraid.

End of Part Three

PART FOUR

THING OF EVIL

Who can watch, who can tolerate this evil?
Only the shameless, only the voracious gambler,
wealthy Mamurra of Gaul, living in a distant land.
Oh Rome, debauched and decadent,
do you bear witness to these atrocities?
Everything he touches turns to gold,
And, pridefully, he beds them all without discretion.
For this thing of evil, did the brave captain go to war,
for this you voyaged west to that far island?

—CATULLUS

CHAPTER XXVIII

Flavia bent over the copper cauldron and blew on the embers. It was her night to tend the sacred flame, a weekly task she'd come to hate.

When she'd arrived at the House of Vestals, she'd held hope for her new life—imagined, as Nero's favorite, she would have fine clothes, jewels, anything she desired. But instead of feasts and parties, she'd been sequestered within the House of Vestals, as if, knowing he had captured her, the princeps had lost interest. Her days were squandered in the library reading tomes of history, writing legal documents—endless pages of dreary copying—all under the scrupulous supervision of her sister and the Vestal Maxima.

She fed the fire several lumps of coal then wiped her hands on her white robe, leaving sooty smears. What was she, but a glorified scullery slave?

She pulled at the strand of pearls Nero had given her, a forbidden ornament that she hid beneath her robes. After her name had been announced at the Saturnalia feast, she had expected him to claim her as his prize, carry her off in front of all of Rome. Instead, she had been escorted by her sister to the House of Vestals. For days she'd waited for a summons to the palace.

But the summons never came.

At night, alone in her cubicle without even Romulus and Remus to keep her company, she'd cried herself to sleep. Days dragged into weeks, weeks added up to months until winter became spring. Now it was May, the time of Lemuria—when the dead woke from their tombs to walk among the living.

For all she'd seen of Nero, she might be a ghost. Forgotten. Dead. Invisible.

She ran her fingers through her shorn locks, evidence of her position as lowly novitiate. What a fool she'd been to think she might replace Poppaea. Now that Nero held her in his snare, he had no use for her.

Scooping more coal onto the fire, she watched the flames leap. She banked the ashes, coughing as they choked her. Seeking air, she headed for the temple doors. A flurry of moths swirled through the dark like snow and rushed toward the fire, as if begging to be burned.

She stepped outside into the green-smelling air, into spring bursting with life.

Silvery light shimmered on the buildings of the forum. Dawn wouldn't break for several hours, and the constant clatter of cart wheels had finally ceased. An owl hooted in the nearby grove. Flavia glanced toward the House of Vestals—dark and silent. If she left who would know?

She ventured down the temple steps, her slippers whispering against the stone. Circling the temple she gazed up at the Domus Transitoria, wishing she might see a light, wishing Nero would appear. The palace loomed over the forum like a sleeping giant.

A twig snapped behind her and she caught her breath.

"Who's there?"

"Flavia?"

Before she could scream, a hand clamped over her mouth. She recognized his scent. Nero loosened his hold, nuzzled her neck. She shivered.

"Did I frighten you?"

"A little." Her heart still raced. "What brings you here at this hour?"

"Wandering."

"By yourself?" She glanced around, expecting to see guards, or worse, Poppaea Sabina.

"I often wander by myself at night. When else can I be invisible?"

"You want to be invisible?" She cocked her head. "I want to be seen."

He touched her face, traced his fingers down her cheek and over her lips. "You're lovely," he said.

"I thought you would send for me."

"I've been busy, practicing my music. I plan to travel, perform as a citharode. It's a dream I've had."

"I have dreams too."

He smiled and looked quite handsome.

"What do you dream about, little Flavia?"

"Of you."

She lifted her face to his, and he bent to kiss her mouth. His tongue slid between her lips, flicking like a serpent's. She flicked her tongue in response. Meanwhile she considered what her next move should be—this time he wouldn't get away.

According to rumors, after his recent performance in Naples, an earthquake had destroyed the theater. The senate hoped he would view the disaster as an omen, return to Rome and stop performing. The aristocracy considered Nero's concerts an embarrassment. But, Flavia mused, kindling his dream of being a citharode might prove her ticket to escape.

Nero's kisses moved from her lips to her shoulders.

"I want to travel too," she said.

"You have a fine sense of adventure."

"Will you go to Greece?"

His caresses stopped. He ran his fingers through his hair. "My journey to Athens has been cancelled. The Greeks were heartbroken, of course. Now I plan to visit Alexandria. I don't want to disappoint my followers again, but my astrologers insist that I consult my ancestors before making the journey."

"What can ghosts tell you?"

"They'll tell me if the omens are auspicious."

"I want to go with you"

He searched her eyes, and she looked into his—steady and unblinking.

"I'd like you to come," he said.

Heat shot through her body, not from his next kiss, but from knowing she was one step closer to her goal. She wanted him to sweep her off her feet, rescue her from her dreary life, and take her far away from Elissa's hawkish eyes.

"I want to bear your son."

He studied her.

"Willingly, you'd break your vows?"

"For you."

"The penalty for infidelity is death."

"The priests won't question Caesar. You are above the law."

He hesitated. "I'm not the man you think I am."

"I know exactly who you are."

My brother's murderer, she thought, keeping her gaze steady.

"I've done loathsome things." He looked at the sky. "A thousand years from now," he said, "stars will shine as they do now, the moon will rise and set. But who will remember us?"

"Who cares what people think a thousand years from now?" She took his hand in hers, and led him toward the sacred grove.

CHAPTER XXIX

III days after the Nones of May

Year X, reign of Nero Claudius Caesar Augustus Germanicus

Dear Justinus,

I'm glad to hear your studies with the prophet Paul are going well. Each day I say the prayers you have sent me in your letters, and perhaps your prayers are working. The last few months have been blessedly uneventful—Flavia has settled into our routine, my father's health is much improved, and Nero has been gone from Rome. Perhaps Mother Amelia is right, and everything will work out for the best.

But, yesterday, Nero returned from his travels. And now, sleep escapes me.

Yours as Ever,

Elissa

She set down her stylus. The moon stared through the window of her chamber, bright and insistent.

She got up from her stool and peeked into the dormitory. From behind the other cubicles' closed curtains, she heard the steady sound of breathing. She wandered to Cornelia's doorway. The little girl slept on her stomach, clutching the one possession she'd been permitted to take from home—a rag doll she called Lucia. Stealing past the other doorways, she heard Marcia snoring, Angerona mumbling in her sleep.

She parted the curtains of Flavia's cubicle and saw her sister's empty bed. Tonight was Flavia's night to sit vigil by the fire. Why, then, did she feel afraid?

ॐ

Throughout the morning ritual Elissa watched her sister. Flavia yawned as Mother Amelia began the convocation. Her lips barely moved as dreamy-eyed she recited prayers. And when she laid a branch of cedar on the flames, she tripped on her hem and nearly fell. Her robes were smeared with soot, not unusual after tending the fire all night. But what was that stain? According to Elissa's calculations her sister's monthly flux wasn't due for days. Most troubling was the laughter Elissa detected in Flavia's eyes.

Mother Amelia finished the closing prayer, and as the vestals left the temple, Elissa followed Flavia.

"You look different," she said.

"Do I?"

"You look—" And suddenly Elissa knew. "You've been with him, haven't you?"

Flavia's flush provided the answer.

"You've bedded him!"

Before Elissa could stop her, Flavia fled the temple.

Elissa wanted to strangle her sister, pull her flaxen hair out strand by strand—

"Elissa—"

"Yes, Mother Amelia?"

"As you know, Lemuria begins at midnight, and the Pontifex Maximus intends to join us for the ceremony."

"He always joins us for the ceremony." Elissa edged toward the door, hoping to catch up with Flavia.

"The Pontifex Maximus is concerned about the auspices."

"As he should be."

Mother Amelia's eyes widened. "You've had a vision?"

"Many visions."

She often dreamed of Nero's death: his entrails shriveling in the sun, his body writhing on a pyre, his mother greeting him in Hades—arms outstretched, fire flaring from her eyes, smoke pouring from her nostrils. Elissa pushed open the temple door, but didn't see Flavia.

"I have more to say to you, Elissa. The Pontifex Maximus has made a special request. He wants you to call forth—"

"—Agrippina."

"Yes."

"I won't."

"You must try."

Elissa gazed out at the forum. The buildings, dazzling in the morning sun, were no better than a prison. Here she would live, and here she would die.

"Help me, Jesus," she whispered.

"What did you say?"

"Nothing." She bit her lip.

"I forbid you to speak that name. I've warned you to stay away from Messianic Jews. Have you been attending meetings?"

"No."

"Look at me." Mother Amelia raised Elissa's chin, peered into her eyes. "Have you seen Gallus Justinus?"

"No!" She spoke the truth, at least in theory.

She had attended no more of Paul's meetings. But, in her dreams, she often saw Justinus. And, in her prayers, she called on Jesus.

"Are you listening, Elissa? Tonight, when veils between the worlds are thin, you will call forth Nero's mother."

"The dead don't like to be disturbed."

Already, she felt Agrippina's fingers reaching up from Hades, clutching at her ankles.

☙

"The Lord is my shepherd," Elissa read for the hundredth time, "I shall want nothing...."

Except Nero's death.

She refolded the papyrus, placing her last letter from Justinus on top of all the others. Carefully, she rewrapped the letters in silk, tied the blue ribbon in a bow and kissed the bundle, before hiding it between the pallet and the leather webbing of her bed.

Nero had gone too far, coupling with her sister. There was only one solution, and this time she would seek assistance. The aristocracy's discontent with the princeps had been simmering for months and now it reached a boiling point. Dissatisfaction brewed in the Senate. Nero needed no more than a push to send him tumbling from the throne into a roiling stew. The recipe required only a dash of salt, someone to turn up the heat and rally those in power. Who better than Justinus, a valiant knight and war hero?

But visiting his home would be unwise. Since Saturnalia, Tigellinus kept close watch on her, his spies were everywhere, and Elissa was well known on the Esquiline. According to his letters, Justinus spent most of his time studying with Paul. No one would recognize her in the Hebrew Quarter. Her heart raced at the thought of seeing him.

Digging through her cedar chest, she came up with the rags that served so well as her disguise. She drew them on, wishing she could go to him wearing something more becoming. She combed her hair and pinched her cheeks, regretting that she lacked carmine for her lips. Cosmetics were considered an indulgent vanity as were mirrors. She gazed at her reflection in the wash basin, wondering if Justinus thought of her, at this moment, as she thought of him. Touching the double incisors, covering them with her fingertips, she wished she might be beautiful. Pale and perfect like her sister. The water in the basin rippled, transforming her face. And the image she saw was Agrippina's.

The basin crashed onto the floor, splashing water. It crept over the tiles, reflecting memories, pictures from her childhood. She told herself she must be faint from hunger, dazed from lack of sleep.

On her knees, she mopped the water, trying to forget what she had seen.

She placed several cushions on her bed and pulled a coverlet over them. From the doorway, it looked as if she lay sleeping.

At this hour the dormitory was quiet. Her fellow priestesses were partaking of the midday meal. She'd claimed to be suffering from her monthly flux, and told Mother Amelia she needed rest. She hurried past the servants' quarters, down the stairs, and through the atrium. Thais had left her post, and the front door stood unguarded. She glanced around, saw no one, and slipped out.

The sun lurked behind a cloud and shadows fell across the forum washing the white buildings bluish-gray. At midday, most people went home to eat and take a nap, returning to work after several hours. She walked along the near-deserted Via Sacra.

A drop of rain fell on the paving stones, and more drops followed. Jupiter released a bolt of lightning and then a crack of thunder. Elissa ran for cover, finding shelter in a recessed doorway. The downpour drove stragglers into taverns—the only open shops. Further along the street a door swung open. Voices burst out of it, along with the smell of onions and boiled meat. The tavern door opened, admitting two soggy men, and then slammed shut.

Finally the rain subsided. Elissa headed for the river and the Trastevere, hoping to find Justinus in the Hebrew Quarter.

❦

Wanting to avoid her sister's questions, Flavia claimed to have a headache and planned to spend the afternoon hiding in her room. Under no circumstance did she want to speak to Elissa. She had a scare when her sister appeared in the dormitory instead of going to the midday meal. Narrowly escaping an encounter, Flavia had ducked into her cubicle.

Though Elissa guessed her secret, Flavia told herself nothing would come of it. Even Elissa was powerless against the will of Nero. And of one thing Flavia was certain—Nero desired her. Last night had been proof.

She lay on her bed, running her fingers over her strand of pearls, caressing their smooth surface. She ran her palms over her belly, remembering how he'd touched her—here, and here, and even there. Remembering what she'd done to him, and how he'd begged for more.

No one could deny she was a woman now. Not even Elissa.

The smell of goat stew wafted through her window making her mouth water. She regretted missing the midday meal. Her midnight activities had left her ravenous.

Too restless to sleep, she got up, wandered to the narrow window, stared at rain.

Here she was, trapped behind locked doors again, but, after tonight, her life would change. If the Lemurian auspices were favorable, Nero promised he would marry her, take her as a second

221

wife. He'd told her about Ramses the Great, how the Egyptian Pharaoh kept three wives, hundreds of concubines, and had fathered over forty children. Ramses had ruled for sixty years. But Nero wouldn't live that long. Not after Flavia bore his son.

She imagined drifting up the Nile, reclining in a golden barge while slaves fanned her with peacock feathers. She imagined wearing gossamer robes, perfumes from the Orient, treasuries of gold and jewels.

Be Cleopatra to my Antony, he'd said.

What would Elissa say to that? Elissa still thought of her as a child, but Nero saw her as his queen—his empress.

Soon Poppaea Sabina would fade into a memory. She grew old, and her time was running out. She couldn't bear a healthy child. So, what use was she to Nero?

Thrusting aside the doorway's curtain, Flavia left her cubicle. She meandered through the dormitory, past the servants' quarters, toward the front of the house. A bolted door didn't stop her from entering the archives where wills and documents were kept. But she had no interest in musty tomes. Passing shelves of vellum scrolls, sheets of papyrus and wax tablets, she walked the chamber's length and stood before the row of windows, looking out at the Via Sacra.

Barred to keep intruders out, or to keep the vestals in? She pressed her face against the iron grate. The forum appeared quiet. A single figure, dressed in rags, walked along the avenue. Something about the person seemed familiar.

Elissa.

Where was she going?

Determined to find out, Flavia ran to the door. The fall of footsteps on the stairway made her retreat. Peering through the door jamb, she watched Marcia clomp past the servants' quarters and into the dormitory. She might look like a cow, but Marcia had the hearing of a cat. Trying to sneak down the stairway would be risky.

But there might be a better escape.

Returning to the row of windows, Flavia found the one she sought. The iron bars wobbled in the crumbling casement. Easing the grate back and forth, she loosened the plaster, lifted out the grate and set it on the floor.

She looked out at the pouring rain, and saw her sister huddled in a doorway, a ragged palla draped over her head.

Definitely up to something.

She leaned over the window-ledge, ignoring the downpour. Ivy crept along the wall, and the twisted branches appeared sturdy. The ground below looked wet and slippery. Climbing would be difficult, but she enjoyed a challenge.

Veils of mist rose from the Tiber's rushing waters and swirled around Elissa's feet. She walked across the bridge and felt like she was walking through a cloud.

Footsteps, muffled by the fog, tapped softly behind her.

Or was it rain?

She stopped. So did the tapping.

She glanced back, half expecting to see Angerona. Shifting vapors swallowed the river, swallowed everything. Clammy wetness seeped through her palla, and the tunica beneath her stola clung to her back. Brushing a limp strand of hair out of her face, she listened for footsteps, heard only the steady beat of rain.

When she reached the far side of the bridge, a labyrinth of twisting lanes told her she was in the Hebrew Quarter. Here, women remained cloistered in their homes and were rarely seen, men mumbled prayers in Hebrew, and pork was a forbidden meat. The Jews were a strange people, though Elissa saw few of them today. The Day of Saturn was their Sabbath and all the shops were closed.

She wondered which way she should turn. She only knew she sought the shop of a tentmaker. There were no streets signs, no numbers on the houses. Just graffiti. The cobblestones were slick with rain. Reaching out her hand to steady herself, she touched a wall dripping with water, and something slimy brushed her face.

Stifling a scream, she hurried on. Saw no sign of a tentmaker.

Backtracking, she walked along another street.

Fog crept toward her from the river, and she could barely see her shoes. The idea of finding Justinus seemed ludicrous. Commonsense told her to return to the House of Vestals before she was discovered missing.

Or worse.

People often met their death in Rome's deserted alleyways. Just last week a woman had been raped and stabbed. Retracing her steps, she sought something familiar. She would have asked for help, but every door she passed was closed.

She hurried by a stinking pile of rags.

The rags shifted.

From beneath the tattered pile of cloth a gnarled finger appeared, beckoning for her to come closer. She heard a wheezing sound. Blood-shot eyes peered out from the mud-caked rags.

"You seek the truth?" said a rasping voice.

"I seek the prophet Paul."

The gnarled finger extended, pointing a blackened nail.

"But I've just come from there."

"Then you did not go far enough."

"To find the tentmaker's shop?"

"To find what you are seeking." Eyes glinted in an ancient face, though whether male or female, Elissa couldn't guess. A gash festered on the creature's forehead.

"You're hurt," Elissa said.

"An old wound that doesn't heal."

"Maybe I can help you. Tell me your name."

"You don't recognize me?"

"Should I?"

The creature sucked in air. "We met last autumn at the Circus Maximus, but I looked younger then." Opening its mouth the creature revealed double incisors. "My name is Agrippina."

"Agri—"

The gnarled finger beckoned. "Rome burns and from union unholy the sister will bring forth a son. Have you heard these words before, Elissa?"

A chill ran through Elissa's heart. "How do you know my name?"

"I know many things. I know the meaning of the prophecy."

"What is it?" Elissa inched toward the pile of rags.

"Come closer."

She took another step.

"Your answer lies in Book Fourteen."

Bony fingers, cold as death, wrapped around Elissa's ankle. Her scream was followed by a clap of thunder. Breaking from the creature's grasp, she turned and ran. Rain pelted her with icy needles, stung her face, soaked through her palla.

Fog descended, dark and thick. When she glanced back, the pile of rags was gone.

Certain she heard footsteps, she called out, "Is anybody there?"

Within the soup, she saw a face, pale and frightening.

The face was joined by others. Waxen masks of the dead destined to wander from their graves, eyes smoldering within the shadows.

Lemures.

The slippery cobblestones caused Elissa to stumble. Regaining her balance, she sprinted through a twisting alleyway.

"Though I walk through a valley dark as death," she recited, her voice thin and breathless. "I fear no evil for you are with me."

Lemures surrounded her. Mouths gaping, hands outstretched.

Through a shadowy veil, Elissa saw her brother.

"Marcus!"

She ran toward him, tears streaming from her eyes as she threw herself into his arms.

His body felt warm and wonderfully alive.

"Elissa?"

She looked up at his face.

"Justinus?"

"I thought I heard you calling."

She peered into the fog. A sign swung on squeaking hinges above a doorway. It advertised a tentmaker's shop.

Justinus drew her close, and their mouths merged in a kiss, more insistent than the rain.

☙

"Run away with me." The look in Elissa's eyes told Justinus she desired him as much as he desired her.

"I can't run away," she said.

"I have land. We'll move to the countryside, be farmers, tend the fields."

"Grow apples?"

"Would you like that?"

"Very much."

The door to Paul's apartment opened, cutting short their conversation. Justinus expected to see the assigned guard, but instead Timothy greeted them.

"Shalom," he said and grinned, delight sparkling in his eyes. "If you're expecting the guard he's gone forever. Paul has been released."

"That's good news," Justinus said.

"And good news should be celebrated with good friends. Come in." Timothy clapped Justinus on the back then smiled warmly at Elissa. "Your clothes are soaking. Have the two of you been swimming?"

"The river's a bit cold this time of year," Justinus said jokingly. He shook off his cloak and handed it to Timothy.

"Yours as well," Timothy said, holding out his hand to receive Elissa's palla. "The fire will soon dry your clothing." He ushered them into the apartment where a brazier burned cheerfully.

Paul sat at a table stacked with documents. Hunched over a sheet of parchment, he wrote by the light of an oil lamp. Reed pens, meticulously sharpened, were set along the table's edge. Arriving at the end of a sentence, he punctuated it with so much force that the pen's tip snapped off. Without looking up, he reached for another.

"Sorry," he said, glancing at his guests. "I want to finish this letter."

"Paul often writes all night," Timothy said good-naturedly. "Luke and I force him to eat, blindfold him and hold him hostage to get him to sleep."

Usually serious, today Luke seemed light-hearted and he chuckled in agreement.

Paul continued scribbling.

Luke sat cross-legged on the floor sewing a canvas panel. He gave his thread a final tug then set aside his work. "This damp," he said, groaning as he stood, "I feel it in my knees."

"I feel it in my back." Justinus rolled his shoulders.

"Let's sit by the fire," Timothy said. "The warmth will do us good." He unfolded goatskin stools and set them by the brazier. Coals glowed within the metal pan, and a pot of water simmered on the grate.

Justinus soaked up the heat, felt it penetrate his wet clothes and warm his skin. "This is what we want, isn't it Elissa?"

Their eyes met. "Exactly."

The heat he felt wasn't generated by the brazier.

Paul stopped writing long enough to say, "Timothy, Luke, why don't you get our guests something to eat? Just because I feast on ink doesn't mean you have to starve."

"Hungry?" Luke went to the sideboard and rummaged through the shelves. With a grunt, he took down a loaf of barley bread and a lump of yellow cheese. "You'd think with all my years as a physician, I might devise a remedy for arthritis," he said, carving the crusty loaf of bread. "Some say bee-stings help."

"I know a better antidote." Pursing his cherubic lips, Timothy retrieved a flagon from the sideboard and held it up for all to see. "The elixir of youth."

He poured wine into earthen cups, added a spoonful of honey to each, then lifted the pot from the brazier and measured out hot water. He handed Luke a cup and brought another to Elissa. "This will warm you," he said, his eyes shining with good humor. "Have I seen you at our gatherings?"

"I—ah, yes...once."

Justinus leapt to her rescue. "She's wary of being here," he said. "Allow me to introduce Elissa Rubria Honoria."

"The vestal virgin?" Timothy nearly dropped his cup.

Paul set down his pen. "Priestess Elissa." He drew the ink-stained writing glove from his hand, and rose to greet her. "I'm honored. Forgive my rudeness, but thanks to hours of petitioning by Timothy and Luke I've been released from my imprisonment. I intend to leave for Hispania next week, and have much to do in preparation."

"Next week?" Justinus said. "So soon?"

Paul nodded.

"I'm told Hispania is beautiful," Elissa said. "Fields of lavender and sun-flowers—"

"A wilderness," said Justinus. "The natives are uncivilized. They speak no Latin and no Greek, but a kind of gibberish."

Paul laughed. "God has called me on a mission to the world's farthest reaches, and I have no doubt his language will be understood."

"Crossing the sea is treacherous," Justinus said. "The waters are rife with pirates, not the businessmen of the Mediterranean, but rogue sailors and criminals. Perhaps I should journey with you as your bodyguard."

Paul laid his hand on Justinus's shoulder. "You're needed here in Rome, my son."

Justinus stood a good twelve inches above Paul, but he felt like a child. He felt no joy at the prospect of losing his teacher. The prophet had been his anchor in the unsettled seas of Rome.

"I'm curious," Paul said, turning to Elissa. "What brings a vestal virgin to my humble abode?"

"I want—" Elissa glanced at Justinus then back at Paul. "Tell me about Jesus."

"What would you like to know?"

"Did you know him?"

"In the flesh?" Paul shook his head. "My Lord left this earth well before we met, but He is with me every hour of the day, guiding my every action, tempering my every word."

"That must be wonderful," Elissa said. "Roman gods seem so indifferent. I pray, but no one listens."

"God hears your prayers," Paul said.

"Which god?"

"All gods are aspects of the One."

"I don't understand," Elissa said.

Neither did Justinus. The prophet often said confusing things.

"God has many faces," Paul explained, "and can be likened to the seasons. Though we perceive winter as separate from summer, and spring separate from fall, all seasons are but aspects of a single year. So it is with God."

"You have no separation from your God?" Elissa asked.

"How can I, if God created everything?"

"We are all children of God," Timothy said. "And the flame of our creator burns within each one of us."

"That's what Jesus tried to tell us," Paul said. "That's why he called Himself the Son of God."

"Jesus said, 'The Way to God is through me.'" Timothy pointed to his chest. "By that he meant The Way to God is through each of us. We must find God within our hearts."

"But can God's flame burn within an evil person?" Elissa asked.

Luke stroked his beard before speaking. "God dwells in every soul. That's why we must love even our enemies."

Elissa looked as doubtful as Justinus felt.

"Even Nero?" she asked.

Paul's eyebrows formed a single line, making him appear stern, but his voice was gentle, "Anyone can love a friend, Priestess."

Justinus shifted uncomfortably. No matter what the prophet said, never again would he love Nero. His childhood friend had become a monster.

Paul picked up his pen, examining the tip as if he might write something more. His eyes grew distant. "Only God can look into a heart," he said. "It's not for us to judge our fellow man."

Luke tugged on his beard, straining the salt and pepper strands. "Pass no judgment and you will not be judged."

"We must love each other," Timothy said.

"Love even our enemies," Paul echoed him.

Justinus did not agree. At one time he'd believed Nero might be saved, but Nero's actions proved he was beyond redemption. It was easy for Paul to speak in platitudes. He was leaving Rome.

Fog drifted through the window, smothering the oil lamp's glow, and engulfing the room. Justinus glanced at Elissa. She hugged herself, her lips bluish.

"The dead are watching us," she whispered.

"Enough dreary talk," said Timothy. "Let's eat."

He passed around the bread and cheese. Justinus chewed gratefully. He hadn't realized how hungry he was, couldn't remember the last time he'd had a meal.

Paul turned back to Elissa. "Death is an illusion," he said. "Jesus promises life after death, salvation. Would you spend your eternal life drifting in darkness?"

"I find darkness comforting," she said. "It's the womb of the Divine Mother. You speak of God in terms of Him, but what of Her?"

"Ah, the mystery. What holds the flame to the wick?" Paul passed his hand through the lamp's flame. "You're a wise woman, Elissa. Wise beyond your years. I wonder what really brings you here."

"I came in search of Justinus," she said, blushing. "I have hopes that he will help me rally a campaign against Nero."

"Ah," Paul said. "But there is no salvation in revenge. To find salvation you must forgive yourself. Only then can you forgive your enemies."

"Forgive myself for wanting to avenge my brother's wrongful death?"

"You blame yourself for his death, don't you?"

The color drained from her face. "I might have prevented it."

"Do you rival God?" Paul looked at her, his eyes no longer gentle, but piercing. "God called your brother home. Accept the love of Jesus and you will find salvation, peace."

"I don't deserve God's love," she said.

Unable to contain himself, Justinus shouted, "Of course you do, Elissa!" Rising to his feet, he turned to Paul, angry that the prophet had so little understanding, so little of the compassion he liked to preach about. "Elissa's family lives in fear. Nero tortures them."

"And now he has my sister," Elissa said.

"What has he done to Flavia?" Justinus demanded.

"He's stolen her virginity."

"Stolen her—?" Justinus slammed his fist into the wall. "He makes Rome his Whore of Babylon!"

Lucan was right. Nero would have to be destroyed. Not because he'd dipped into the sacred well of Flavia's virginity—in all likelihood the girl had sacrificed herself all too willingly. Besides, Justinus had to admit, if Elissa were to offer the same sacrifice to him, he'd gladly accept the offering. Nero deserved to be destroyed, not for Flavia's ruptured maidenhead, but because he took joy in Elissa's suffering.

The sound of knocking on the door interrupted his thoughts.

"Are we expecting company?" Paul asked.

Timothy peered through the peephole. "It's a girl."

🏵

Flavia burst into the room. Her palla hung limply over her shorn hair, and the hem of her stola had been steeped in muddy water. Elissa stared in disbelief.

"I followed you," her sister said. "I've been waiting outside—"

"You're soaking wet." Elissa found her palla, warm and dry from hanging by the brazier, and wrapped the woolen shawl around her sister's slender shoulders. "Come sit by the fire."

"I followed you!"

Flavia's anger felt like a slap. Elissa backed away.

"You dare to lecture me," Flavia said. "Meanwhile you're meeting him." She pointed at Justinus.

Elissa felt weak in her knees as if she might faint. "I can guess what you're implying, but I've done nothing wrong," she said.

"That's not what Angerona claims."

"We'll discuss this later. This is not the time or place."

"You're a hypocrite Elissa."

Paul raised his hand for silence. "Young woman, I realize you're upset, but—"

"Please forgive my sister," Elissa said. "I'm sure she will apologize."

"For what?"

"For insulting Paul of Tarsus. For entering his home and treating him as if he ran a brothel rather than a House of the Lord."

"What lord?" Flavia glanced at Timothy and Luke. "I see only paupers here."

"Followers of Jesus," Elissa said.

Flavia's mouth dropped open. "Better and better. I'm sure the Vestal Maxima will want to know how you spend your afternoons."

"Let's go, Flavia." Elissa grabbed her sister then turned to Paul. "Blessings on your journey."

With Flavia in tow, she headed for the door. Hand on the latch, she glanced at Justinus and saw the pained expression in his eyes. Her heart rushed toward his—two flames burning in the dark.

Don't go, his eyes pleaded.

But fate had carved her path.

She opened the door and led her sister out to the street. Fog settled in every crevice, thick and heavy, making it impossible to see beyond several feet. Dragging her sister along the alley, Elissa hoped she would find her way through the labyrinth.

"Paul is a man of God," she said, "respected throughout the empire. You should be ashamed of your behavior."

"*I* should be ashamed? You're the one who sneaks out for assignations with your lover. *You* should be ashamed, not me."

Elissa slapped her sister with all the force of her frustration.

Flavia's green eyes glistened. "That was a mistake," she said. "I plan to tell the Vestal Maxima what you've been up to, tell her you've been meeting Justinus, tell her that you've turned against the Roman gods and become a follower of Jesus. Angerona will be happy to corroborate."

"While you're speaking to the Vestal Maxima, please mention you've been bedding Nero, so you and I can die together."

Flavia laughed, tears rolling down her face, her mouth a grimace. "You still don't understand, do you Elissa? He plans to marry me."

"Marry you?"

"He said I'm Cleopatra to his Antony."

Elissa stared at her sister, so young, so innocent. So stupid.

"He called me Cleopatra too."

Flavia's nostrils flared. "Liar!"

"Flavia—"

She couldn't stop her. Flavia ran along the street disappearing in the fog. Despair enveloped Elissa. Ghosts flickered in the shadows.

The restless dead.

The displaced souls.

And she was one of them.

CHAPTER XXX

Cloaked by fog, the House of Vestals had become invisible, and as Elissa walked along the Via Sacra she imagined the white-washed walls had vanished. Not just for the moment, but forever, leaving a void in which she could create a different destiny. She imagined running back to Justinus, leaving Rome, beginning a new life. Raising a family. Her daydream dissolved as the mist parted. Dragging her feet, she passed through the gates of the House of Vestals and, her heart weighted with sorrow, she approached the massive doors.

They opened all too readily.

Thais was at her post, eyes bleary from a recent nap. "Priestess Elissa," she said, her sleepy face surprised. "In this weather you are walking?"

"Family emergency."

"Today no letters," Thais said, her voice conspiratorial. "I think maybe tomorrow."

Pressing a coin into her palm, Elissa slipped past the slave.

Sparrows flitted through the atrium; no other sound disturbed the sanctuary. In preparation for the nightlong vigil of Lemuria, the vestals had retired to their cubicles to spend the evening in rest and contemplation. No lamps would be lit, no torches set aflame, until the midnight hour of Intempesta when pathways opened to the underworld. For three alternating nights, rituals would be held—on the ninth, eleventh, and thirteenth of May. Odd days were luckier than even, and luck was needed when consorting with the dead. But Elissa would need more than luck to deal with Nero—and more than luck to deal with her sister.

She recited the prayer Justinus had taught her. "Divine creator of the stars in heaven, of mighty oceans and verdant earth—" She reached the stairway leading to the dormitory, heard the creak of lead pipes, a breeze whistling through the rafters, nothing else. She climbed the steps. "Your name is sacred on my tongue. Now and for eternity may your will be done." She made it past the servants' quarters and entered the dormitory. The shutters had been closed against the rain, and dim shapes melded into one another.

"Give us this day our share of bread," she whispered. "And forgive us our wrongful deeds—"

She approached her sister's cubicle, touched the doorway's curtain and withdrew her hand. "Flavia," she called softly. "Are you in there?"

No answer. She heard movement inside the room, rustling.

"May I enter?"

"No."

She slid open the curtain. Flavia's eyes were bloodshot from crying, her nose red. "You're safely back," Elissa said.

"Good observation."

"We need to talk."

"You're ruining my life."

"I'm trying to save your—"

"Don't." Flavia wiped her nose.

"Have you seen the Vestal Maxima?"

"Not yet." Her green eyes narrowed, calculating as a cat's. "There's only one way you'll stop me from talking—"

"What?"

"Tonight, make certain the auspices are in my favor. I want to travel with Nero to Alexandria."

"I can't do that—"

"You'd better."

The curtain slapped Elissa's face.

Defeated, she returned to her cubicle. The cedar chest was open, clothes scattered everywhere. The wash basin lay on the floor where she had dropped it. She didn't remember leaving her room in such a state of disarray, but she had been distracted by the thought of seeing Justinus. She had left the shutters open, and a storm wind must have swept through the room. The coverlet had slipped from her sleeping couch, exposing the cushions she had placed there. She straightened the coverlet and rearranged the cushions.

Sitting on the bed, she kicked off her damp slippers. She lay down, closed her eyes, and let her thoughts drift. Her sister understood so little of the world. She might think she held the upper hand with Nero, but there was no winning when it came to tyranny. Poor Flavia.

Elissa turned onto her side and faced the wall. She traced her forefinger along a crack in the plaster. No matter what Paul said, she saw no good in Nero. She dreaded seeing him tonight.

She thought of Justinus, the opposite of Nero—kind and compassionate. She felt his arms encircling her, felt his lips on hers and felt her resolve slipping.

"Deliver me from evil," she whispered and prayed Jesus was listening.

❦

Clouds blotted out the moon, making the night blacker than Elissa's mood. She followed Angerona up the seven steps leading to the temple, climbing slowly, as if condemned to meet her executioner. At the doors each vestal dipped her fingertips into an urn of water drawn from the sacred spring. Elissa sprinkled herself liberally.

The solemn faces of her fellow priestesses flickered in the light of torches as they took their places. Mother Amelia stood beside the stone altar where a bleating lamb, newly separated from its mother, stood tethered. Marcia, having drunk copious amounts of wine at dinner, hiccupped loudly, and Cornelia giggled. Angerona's sullen stare followed Elissa.

Flavia refused to meet Elissa's gaze.

In silence, they waited for the Pontifex Maximus.

Sap popped in the cedar branches as they burned.

A rush of footsteps, made all heads turn toward the entryway. The temple's double-doors opened and guards appeared, followed by the Pontifex Maximus. The doors swung shut behind him, leaving the guards outside. Nero had outdone himself and wore a toga of spun gold. His face had been gilded with gold leaf, and a gem-encrusted diadem crowned his curls.

Apparently, he still hoped to impress his mother, Elissa thought. She glanced at Flavia. Her sister stood transfixed, eyes riveted to Nero.

Mother Amelia nodded and the priestesses bowed in deference to the Pontifex Maximus.

Nero raised his hands in supplication—just a show, Elissa mused. He was far too arrogant to revere any god. "Tonight I play the role of Pluto, Lord of the Underworld," he said, annunciating every syllable. "Elissa Rubria Honoria has the honor of playing my consort Persephone."

She did not return his smile.

Flavia looked sour.

"Tonight," Nero said, ignoring the sisters' reactions, "we journey into other realms. We invoke the hungry ghosts and lay wandering souls to rest."

"So be it," said the priestesses.

Except for Elissa.

She had no intention of putting souls to rest. Quite the opposite. If Nero ordained her to play Queen of the Underworld—holder of the keys to the fields of Elysium and the fires of Tartarus—she would make sure he regretted it.

He played the role of paterfamilias to perfection, spitting black beans around the room for the lemures to feast upon.

"Tonight," he proclaimed, "we seek blessings from those who've walked this earth before. And we make amends—"

Amends to those he'd raped, and wronged, and murdered.

Thunder announced more rain. It battered the temple's roof, and wind brought moisture through the latticework. Damp seeped into Elissa's bones, into the deepest recess of her being. She sensed lemures rising from the underworld. Tendrils of mist snaked through the temple and set the torches sputtering.

The vestals continued the invocation—repeating after Nero, mindless litany. A form took shape within the mist. Eyes peered at

Elissa. A voice spoke, so quietly it might have been a dream, "The fourteenth book."

She stared into a face of shifting shadows.

"Agrippina." She hadn't meant to speak the name aloud.

Nero paused mid-sentence. "What did you say?"

"The dead have arrived."

Angerona snorted. "Where?"

Marcia barked another hiccup, Cornelia clung to Mother Amelia, and Flavia's green eyes bore into Elissa.

Nero's face grew pale. "My mother?"

"Yes."

Agrippina's wraith drifted toward Elissa. Plumes of mist issued from her mouth, and frozen teardrops sparkled in her eyes. The queen breathed her essence into Elissa's heart.

"I'm cold," Cornelia said.

The girl clung to Marcia, shivering. The other vestals shivered too. Their frightened eyes stared at Elissa.

"Where is she?" Nero asked.

"Standing beside you."

The dead queen breathed crystals of ice. Suspended in the air, they shimmered.

"Mater," Nero said, his eyes wide. "Are you really here?"

Elissa nodded. "She wants to know why you have summoned her."

"I have a question."

"Ask."

"Did you bear another child? Do I have a sibling?"

The answer coursed through Elissa's veins, cold as newly melted snow. Her lips moved slowly as if frozen, and when she spoke the voice was Agrippina's, "Yes, I bore another child—a child who will avenge my murder."

Nero's face grew paler. "How?"

"My child will be your nemesis."

"What is his name?"

Nero's voice echoed in Elissa's ears. Frost clouded her vision, and when she spoke her tongue felt like an icicle. "He," Agrippina said, "does not exist."

Nero's voice grew shrill, "Tell me his name!"

"The answer stands before you, but you're blind to the truth."

"Show yourself, Mater. Show yourself to me!" Nero grabbed a torch and brandished the flames.

Elissa drew back from the heat. The dead queen's tendrils loosened, and Elissa breathed more easily. In the torchlight, she saw Nero watching her, as did the priestesses, none more avidly than Flavia. Who was she to disappoint her audience? She would do as Angerona had advised and play the role of Nero's mother. Yes! She would give him Agrippina.

Throwing back her shoulders and straightening her spine, Elissa spoke in a commanding voice, "Look at me. I am your mother. Do you see me?"

"Yes," his voice sounded like a child's.

"I know what you've done."

"I didn't mean to—"

"Silence!"

Tears ran from Nero's eyes. "Please forgive, Mater," he said, sobbing.

"I forgive you under one condition."

"I'll do anything you—"

"Promise me—"

"What Mater?"

"Do not, under any circumstance, travel to Egypt."

Flavia squeaked in protest.

"Go to Egypt and your reward will be derision. Go to Egypt and a cobra will strangle you, eagles will pluck out your eyes, and you will become impotent."

Elissa feasted on Nero's expression, and prepared to bite again.

"I'm warning you—" Flavia said. She tried to charge Elissa, but Mother Amelia held her back.

Elissa raised her voice, drowning out her sister, "Go to Egypt, and you will not return. The earth will quake with revulsion, a wall of water will rise from the sea, fire will rain from the heavens. Go to Egypt, and you will be destroyed!"

Nero stood before her, trembling. Elissa thought he might faint.

"One thing more," she said. "If you value your life, your throne, your empire—have nothing more to do with her." She pointed at her sister.

"Don't listen," Flavia shouted. "Can't you see she's not your mother?"

Nero remained mesmerized. Placing his hand over his heart, he said, "I promise, Mater. I swear to all the gods and to The Roman Empire."

"Good," Elissa said. "You are forgiven."

Nero fell to his knees, kissed Elissa's hem.

Flavia broke free from Mother Amelia and threw herself onto Elissa, pummeling her with fists and feet. "I hate you!" she shrieked.

Mother Amelia and Marcia wrenched her off and dragged her toward the door.

Elissa remained undeterred. Ignoring her sister's protests, she raised Nero to his feet and placed the sacramental knife into his hands, the same pearl-handled secespita he had used to slash their palms. "Seal your promise with the sacrifice."

"And you will reveal my rival's identity?"

"I will."

As one in a trance, Nero cut the lamb's tether.

Elissa sprinkled the animal with salt and flour then poured red wine over its head. She held the lamb over the altar's granite basin. "With this sacrifice I feed the hungry ghosts," she said, "that Rome may thrive."

She nodded to Nero.

He raised the secespita, but his hand trembled.

"Why so nervous?" Elissa said. "You found it easy to sacrifice your mother."

The blade fell from Nero's hand, clattered on the stone.

"Pick it up," Elissa said.

He shook his head.

"Make the sacrifice and seal your promise," Elissa's voice was harsh. "As your mother, I order you!"

The slender blade glinted in the firelight. Nero wrapped his fist around the pearl handle, raised the knife. But instead of slitting the lamb's throat, he stabbed wildly at its gut. The shrieking animal tried to escape, but Nero threw himself on top of it, wrestling the lamb, driving the blade deep into its belly. Entrails spilled into the altar's troth soaking both of them in gore.

Marcia screamed. Cornelia wailed.

Finally the lamb stopped bleating. Its dead eyes stared into Elissa's.

Nero stumbled to his feet, his white robe stained red.

"Tell me the name of my rival," he said.

"Ahenobarbus."

"That's my name."

"And you are your worst enemy."

Nero advanced toward Elissa, the secespita dripping blood. "I want the name!"

"I know no name. I only want you to seal the promise. Swear before the gods that you won't touch Flavia."

Nero aimed the knife at Elissa's heart.

"Would you kill me as you killed your mother?" She splashed him with sacred water.

Nero shook his head as if waking from a dream.

"Elissa," he murmured.

"Put down the blade," Mother Amelia said.

Elissa's eyes stayed focused on the secespita as she reached into the bloody troth, scooped the lamb's liver into her palm, and held it out to Nero. "See how it quivers? Even the gods tremble for you. They tremble for Rome's future."

"The gods will do my bidding."

An icy blast shot through the temple's doors, ripped around the room extinguishing the torches, and chilled Elissa to her marrow. Smoke billowed from the fire and sparks swirled toward the ceiling. The wind threw Nero forward. He clutched the cauldron, and glowing coals rained down on him.

He staggered toward Elissa, pointing. "You're a sorceress," he said. "A practitioner of black magic."

"An adulteress," Flavia shouted. Escaping Mother Amelia and Marcia, she ran to Nero. "I've seen her with Gallus Justinus."

"As have I," said Angerona.

Marcia nodded in agreement.

"I've seen her making potions."

"Riding on the wind."

"Howling at the moon."

"Enough!" Mother Amelia's voice rose above the accusations. "Have you forgotten where you are?"

Wind whistled through the temple. Elissa heard agonizing screams.

Nero's eyes grew wide with terror. "Do you hear that?"

"Your mother," Elissa said. "She's here, and she speaks through me."

"What does she want?"

"The truth."

"I'll give her the truth," Flavia said, rushing toward Elissa. "You're having an affair with Gallus Justinus."

"That's a lie."

"I have proof." Flavia reached into her stola withdrawing a package wrapped in silk. "Love letters addressed to you."

Elissa stared at the strand of blue ribbon binding the papers together, the strand of love tying her to Justinus. She looked around the circle of accusing faces. Even Mother Amelia said nothing in her defense.

The fear in Nero's eyes became a nasty light. "Is it possible the pristine priestess is not a virgin after all? Has the vestal, pure as snow, melted for a man?" He bent close to Elissa and whispered, "Yet you refuse me?"

"I've done nothing wrong," she said.

"Elissa Rubria Honoria," Nero proclaimed. "I, Pontifex Maximus, charge you with breaking your vow of chastity. An inquisition will be conducted, and you will stand trial before the Collegiate of Pontiffs. If you are found guilty, you will be entombed alive. Until then you will be held a prisoner of Rome."

"But I am innocent."

Flavia and Angerona held Elissa firmly by her arms.

"I am innocent," she said again.

But only the lemures were listening.

End of Part Four

PART FIVE

The Final Hour

Here lies your only hope. This battle you must fight—
and be victorious.
You shall prevail. You have no choice, only this—
To win.
Gods have mercy, come to the aid of the wounded,
Help them through death's torment, life's final hour,
Pity my suffering, be savior of the one who's committed no evil.
Purify my essence, make me new and free
of this corruption,
this decay creeping through my blood, my bones, my body.
Spare my heart, so joy may enter me.

—CATULLUS

CHAPTER XXXI

The Ides of May

Year X, reign of Nero Claudius Caesar Augustus Germanicus

Dear Justinus,

I write to you from the confines of the Regia, though you may never see this letter. They allow me ink, but no messenger. No contact with the outside world, except what I view through this barred window.

Today they'll weigh the evidence, decide if I shall go to trial. Pray for me—

Elissa stopped writing. What was the point? Her letter would not be delivered.

She paced the short length of her cubicle. Bolted from the outside, the chamber might have been a prison cell. Overnight, the life she'd known had been destroyed and, like Persephone, she slipped into the underworld. Meanwhile, within these walls, priests prepared for her inquisition.

She'd mulled over the visitation from Agrippina, unsure of what was real and what she had imagined. What if Agrippina had truly borne another child—a sibling to Nero who might prefer his brother dead? Could that sibling be her ally?

Through the window's iron bars she gazed at the forum. Earlier that morning she'd watched Nero enter the Regia's gates, watched as he walked past the pilasters and the sacred spring.

He was here now. Lying in wait.

She glanced toward the door. It remained shut, but it might open at any moment. She told herself the physical examination would prove her innocence—prove she retained that most important virtue: her virginity.

From the window she saw the House of Vestals and, beyond the house, the Via Sacra. No matter what the season the wide artery leading to the heart of Rome pulsated with life. She watched the urban mob, pushing, shoving, eager to get somewhere. Most walked along the raised sidewalk and stayed close to the storefronts avoiding the street where they might be trampled by horses, slaves carrying litters, infantries of twenty or more bodyguards. Young men practiced less precaution, boldly strolling down the avenue, calling out to one another, chasing after pretty girls. Rome was bursting with wealth, and most passersby seemed oblivious to the ragtag children trailing after them, oblivious to elderly men with hacking coughs who huddled in the doorways, oblivious to weary women, their backs bent by grueling work. Romans considered slavery a fact of life, the natural order. But, confined in her cell, Elissa viewed the world differently.

A priest of Saturn, preceded by a lictor, walked through the Regia's iron gates and onto the street. He strolled along the Via Sacra and plebs parted like a frightened school of fish. The priest paid them no attention. Deference was expected. Elissa had often experienced that same power, but today she would have given anything to be lost in the teeming crowd.

The priest entered a door inscribed with an erect phallus. A brothel. If chastity were such a cherished virtue why were men exempt?

Her mother often said a woman's most precious asset was not her dowry, but her purity. Like all exemplary matrons, Constantina upheld the motto: honor, self control, and reverence for the gods.

Meanwhile, her husband saw nothing hypocritical in visiting his concubines. Elissa felt sure there had been plenty. Yet Constantina said not a word against her husband.

No wonder the world lacked harmony. True love between a man and a woman required they be equals. Instruments, finely tuned but different, producing complimentary chords. Only then could music be achieved.

By her mother's standards, Elissa knew her thoughts were blasphemous. But given a second chance she would go to Justinus, lie with him. What union could be more sacred than love between two souls? Purity lay within the mind, within the heart, not within a hollow vow of chastity.

When all hope has fled, and the empty heart meets its desire, fulfillment of the heart—that—that is the greatest joy.

Catullus had understood.

Elissa's eyes clouded with tears. Bowing her head she prayed to Jesus, the loving Son of God, a radiant light in this dark world. Her prayers were interrupted by tapping on the door.

The lock shifted and the door creaked open.

Mother Amelia entered. "Ready for the consulate, my dear?" The high vestal, usually immaculate, appeared disheveled. She offered Elissa a weak smile of encouragement.

"Ready as I'll ever be."

"Your hair is shorn?"

"Marcia has seen to every detail." At dawn Marcia had bathed and anointed Elissa as if she were a bride. She'd cut Elissa's long dark curls and shaved her head as if she were a novice. "Have you seen my sister?"

"Flavia has moved into the palace."

"You said you would protect her."

"She went under order of the Pontifex Maximus."

"And that makes it all right."

Mother Amelia said nothing. What could she say?

"My sister's accusation stands?" Elissa asked.

"Be brave, my dear." Mother Amelia offered another tepid smile.

Elissa leaned against the windowsill and stared at the unflinching sun. Though it was morning, already the day was sweltering. "Angerona's accusation stands as well?"

Mother Amelia touched Elissa's shoulder. "The truth will prove your innocence."

Opening the door, she ushered Elissa out into the hostile world.

❦

The Major Flamine greeted them with a curt nod of his head and led them to the tablinum. "Wait here," the high priest said before leaving the room.

This time they were offered no refreshment. Mother Amelia settled on a high-backed chair and Elissa stood by the window.

"What if I'm found guilty?" she asked.

"According to the law, you're assumed innocent until proven otherwise."

Mother Amelia sank into the cushions.

Elissa studied her. What if Nero used his power to sway the Collegiate of Pontiffs? Sway the Vestal Maxima? Would the high vestal risk her position, her authority? Elissa doubted it.

She trusted no one. Only Justinus.

If Marcus were alive, things would be different. If Marcus were alive, at the suggestion of Flavia's nomination, the first whiff of Nero's foul intentions, he would have rallied Rome's intellectuals and caused a public outcry. Elissa longed for her brother's strength, his courage, his conviction.

The Major Flamine returned. "The Pontifex Maximus will see Priestess Elissa Rubria Honoria alone," he said.

Every muscle in Elissa's body tensed.

"That doesn't follow protocol." Mother Amelia shifted on her cushions. "Elissa is to have a physical examination performed by me, while the Pontifex Maximus stands behind a screen. Only then, if just cause is found, will there be a hearing before the Collegiate of Pontiffs."

"But first a private interview with the Pontifex Maximus," the priest said.

"Then I will act as witness." Mother Amelia stood, preparing to escort Elissa.

"You will not." The Major Flamine snapped his fingers, and two guards stepped into the room.

They blocked the high vestal from the door.

248

"But this is unacceptable—" Mother Amelia said.

"Come." The priest guided Elissa out of the tablinum and along the white marble vestibule leading to Nero's chamber. As they passed the library, she slowed. The sibyls seemed to call to her. The prophecy screamed in her ears.

Rome burns and from union unholy the sister will bring forth a son.

What had Marcus said? Interpret the prophecy, save yourself from fate? She had to find Book Fourteen.

She slumped against the wall, her breathing rapid and shallow.

"Is something wrong?" the priest asked.

"I need to collect myself."

"The Pontifex Maximus is waiting."

"Tell him I'll be there momentarily."

The priest hesitated.

"Please, go. I'm right behind you."

She watched the priest, purple robes billowing, as he walked along the vestibule. He knocked on Nero's door then entered, disappearing from her sight.

The hallway stood empty. Elissa pushed against the library's ornate doors, but they refused to budge. She tried to turn the bolt, but it required a key. Frantically, she glanced down the hallway, expecting the priest to return. The vestibule was starkly furnished, and no artwork graced the walls. A vase sat on a table, and it seemed out of place. Elissa touched the vase and something rattled. A key fell into her hand.

It fit the lock.

Shutting the double doors behind her, Elissa was met by darkness. She took a step, tripped over a stool and fell. She sat still, listening. Heard distant voices, but the door remained shut. Flexing her foot, she winced. Her ankle wasn't broken, but it hurt. She managed to stand, took several limping steps, and bumped into a shelf of scrolls. A flurry of dust tickled her nostrils and she sneezed. She bumped into another shelf. The room was crammed with bookcases. Steadying herself, she touched the shelves on either side and walked gingerly along the row. Her eyes grew accustomed to the dark and seeing became easier. Inching along a wall, she found a window. She fumbled with the latch and the shutters opened. Sunlight poured into the room.

She blinked, blinked again as she surveyed the library. Rows of shelves and cubbyholes filled the room from floor to ceiling. Never had she seen so many books. How could she hope to find the Sibylline Oracles before the priest discovered her?

She limped along honeycombs of scrolls reading the contents of each cubbyhole. Euclid's *The Elements. Commentaries on Metaphysics* by Eudorus. The plays of Euripides—the title *Hercules* jumped out.

"Jesus, help me," she whispered.

Somewhere within this sprawling collection lay the *Books of Fate*. She sought the letter S. A top shelf had been devoted to the oracles. Although most of the original scrolls had been damaged, scholars had rewritten them. Fourteen in all. Following Agrippina's instructions, she sought the final book.

Eleven. Twelve. Thirteen.

Book Fourteen was missing.

She dragged a stool over to the shelf, stood on it favoring her good ankle, and peered into the cubbyhole.

Empty.

Footsteps pounded down the hallway. She stood frozen.

A voice called out, "Have you seen Priestess Elissa?"

She didn't have much time. She gazed through the cubbyhole. Saw a table on the other side. And on that table she saw an open scroll.

"Dear Jesus, please."

She jumped from the stool and nearly screamed with pain. Dragging her wounded foot, she hobbled toward the table.

The fourteenth book.

She scanned the page.

May curses rain on you with flames of fire
Time draws near, for you to meet inferno
Day in, day out for all eternity,
Your false and useless gods—shamed and destroyed

A prophecy of doom referring to the final days of Rome. She glanced toward the door then continued reading.

Those who know the one eternal god of truth
Live forever in the light of beauty
A verdant paradise of fertile fields,
Feasting on starry heaven's honeyed bread

Could the eternal god the oracle referred to be Jesus?

She unrolled the scroll a little more and saw the words she knew so well, the prophecy emblazoned in her memory. Another phrase followed, written in a different hand, not careful lettering, but scrawl:

Darkness cannot prevail within the light of a happy soul.

Below those words she saw a drawing—a large black dot within a circle of light, the symbol of the sun.

To what did it refer? The sun as god? Apollo? Re? The womb of the Great Mother? The longer she stared, the more the symbol appeared to be an eye. A bright eye peering from the darkness. Watching her.

The door burst open, and the Major Flamine rushed in followed by the guards. They stood aside as Nero, dressed in the robes of the Pontifex Maximus, sauntered past them.

"Apparently you're feeling better," he said. "It would be a pity for you to fall ill on this momentous occasion."

Elissa met his mocking gaze. "I do feel better, thank you."

He nodded to the scroll. "Have you deciphered the prophecy?"

"Not yet, but I will."

CHAPTER XXXII

"Rome burns," Nero's voice wafted through clouds of incense, "and from union unholy—"

"—the sister will bring forth a son," Elissa finished.

"The words are useless without meaning," Nero said.

His chamber appeared smaller than Elissa remembered, more cluttered. Sheets of papyrus, scrolls and tablets, filled every surface amidst a jumble of statues and furniture. His armament collection had expanded, covering the walls. Her gaze alighted on a pugio. The dagger's hilt was close enough to touch.

Nero sat on his alabaster throne, his fingers caressing the eagle-headed scepter.

"Am I to receive a hearing?" Elissa asked.

"I will be your jury and your judge."

"My executioner?"

"So you admit you're guilty?"

"I want a proper inquiry and a physical examination."

Elissa pulled the door's handle. It was locked from the outside. The high window above Nero's throne appeared to be the only other exit. Narrow and barred.

"I want to leave."

Nero shook his head. "That won't be possible."

"Let me out!"

"There's no use shouting. I've asked the guards not to disturb us until we're finished."

Turning from the door, she was startled to find Nero standing beside her.

He brushed her cheek with his forefinger, his eyes deader than lumps of gray stone, placed a chalice in her hands, then offered her a plate of honey cakes. "Have one: they're my favorite."

"What do you want?"

"I'm not unkind, Elissa. By nature, I'm compassionate. A fault I've fought to overcome. I might have held your hearing in the forum, made your shame a public spectacle, but I thought you would prefer a more discreet approach."

His gaze traveled her body.

"Remove your robe."

"Remove my robe?"

"For the examination you requested."

Elissa gripped her cup of wine, her knuckles turning white.

"Physical examination is the Vestal Maxima job," she said.

"I've changed the rules." Nero's cool fingers pushed aside her suffibulum.

She tossed the wine into his face.

He barely blinked.

"That was a mistake," his said. "You force me to punish you."

Something in Elissa snapped—the rage she held inside, the grief. With a swift upward jerk, she rammed her knee into Nero's groin. Her wounded ankle screamed, but the pleasure was worth the pain.

With a groan, Nero doubled over and sank to the floor.

That gave Elissa time to grab the pugio. The dagger's hilt fitted snugly in her palm, an extension of her hand. She grasped Nero's mop of curls, yanking his head backward and held the blade against his throat.

"Tell your guards to unlock the door."

"You think you'll win so easily?"

She pressed the knife into his skin. "Call them."

"You're a tigress. I like that."

One slash and it would be over. One slash and his evil life would gush out of him.

"Murder is forbidden by the Ten Commandments of the Jews," Nero said. "Would you go against Jesus?"

"Don't speak His name. You have no right."

"No right? I'm Princeps of Rome, ruler of the empire."

"Princeps, not Almighty God."

"That's debatable."

She pointed the tip of the blade at his larynx. The ribs of cartilage were begging to be pricked.

"Not my vocal cords." He attempted a smile.

"I'll spare your precious vocal cords if you will pray with me. Repeat these words, "Almighty God how insignificant am I in the glory of your presence.""

Nero's lips remained glued.

"Say it." She nudged the blade against his throat pleased to see his face pale. "Repeat after me: I am a lowly pig, a writhing worm, a wad of dung."

"Did I ever tell you," he was careful not to move his neck, "how I took your brother? His buttocks were smooth and well-rounded, just like your sister's—"

Elissa flicked the knife, and Nero winced. She felt the pop of skin, and watched in awe as the blade drew a drop of blood.

With a bellow Nero grabbed her arm and twisted till she dropped the pugio. Pain raged from her elbow to her wrist, traveling through her torso, down her leg and to her wounded ankle. Nero threw himself on top of her, pinning her onto the floor. Clawing at her chest, he pushed aside her stola, ripped open her tunica, and tore away the strophium that bound her breasts.

"Get off!" She kicked at him with her good leg.

Balling up the triangle of cloth, he stuffed the strophium into her mouth. She tried to spit it out, but he slapped his hand over her lips and lay on top of her. His weight made breathing difficult. He didn't move. Didn't speak.

She wondered if he'd fainted.

Slowly, carefully, she wriggled her twisted ankle out from under him. Freeing an arm, she pulled the gag out of her mouth and sucked in air. She glanced at the locked door, the barred window. If she didn't escape, surely he would surely kill her.

Her gaze fell on the pugio.

If she could free her other leg, maybe she could reach the dagger.

"Don't go."

Nero grabbed her arm, flinging her back to the floor. Her head hit the tiles with so much force that she saw colored lights. He climbed back on top of her, rubbing her face with his, nuzzling her breasts.

"Don't go, Mater." His mouth latched onto her nipple.

The spirit of Agrippina rushed through Elissa, filling her with rage, blessing her with courage. She spoke in the dead queen's voice, "Release me now or suffer the consequence."

Nero raised his head, stared at her. He appeared confused. "You look different, Mater. Younger."

"And you look like a crueler version of your father."

"I'll take that as a compliment."

"Don't."

"If you're really the harpy who grew me in your putrid womb, tell your beloved son the joyful story of his birth."

Elissa knew the tale, as did every Roman. "You were born, feet first," she said, "on the Ides of December, and as the midwife placed you on the linen sheet, a ray of sunlight touched your face—"

"Not true, Mater. It rained the day that I was born."

"Perhaps it was raining," Elissa hedged. "In any case, your birth was blessed—"

"My father claimed me cursed. And you, dear Mater, foresaw your death by your son's hand. I merely fulfilled your expectations."

Nero stumbled to his feet, as did Elissa, although her ankle could barely tolerate her weight. She turned from him, bent down to grab the pugio.

He slammed into her, his weight propelling her against a wall. Iron fingers locked around her wounded ankle and she shrieked. She lay prone on the floor, tears of pain running down her face. Somewhere she had read that when confronted with a rabid beast it was best to remain still. Play dead. Nero kicked her ribs and she tried not to flinch.

He crouched beside her, rolled her onto her back. She kept her eyes closed, heard him panting, felt the moisture of his breath, smelled his sweat. As a child she had played hide and seek, searched for a safe place to hide. She pretended she was hiding now, behind the statue of Venus in her father's garden.

Nero's hands wrapped around her throat, and her eyes flew open.

His eyes stared at her.

From the corner of her eye, she saw the pugio lying on the floor. She stretched out her hand, her fingers reaching for the hilt.

"Did you want this?"

The blade glinted as he raised it, came down with a flash of silver, ripping through flesh and bone, pinning her hand to the floor. Pain tore through her palm and lights danced before her eyes. She was falling, hurtling through stars and planets, spiraling from this world to another. She couldn't stop screaming.

"Like your friend Jesus," Nero said.

Fists pounded on the door, followed by loud voices.

"Caesar?"

"Go away," Nero shouted.

"But, Caesar—"

"Leave!"

Elissa slipped in and out of consciousness, felt his hands grabbing her, tried to fight him off. "Justinus," she whimpered, wishing he could save her from this animal, this beast that thought himself a god.

He forced himself inside of her, tearing deep into her soul.

"The first time always hurts," he said.

She felt nothing.

She was hiding in the garden, hoping Justinus would find her. But her fate had been decided. There would be no savior.

Not Justinus.

Not Jesus.

Not even an Almighty God could rescue her from Nero.

CHAPTER XXXIII

The door clicked shut. Mercifully, he was gone.

Elissa lay where she had fallen.

She heard the steady drip of a water-clock. The sound of her own breathing. Outside the window, hooves clattered on cobblestones. A woman shouted and a child began to cry.

Squeezing her eyes shut, Elissa wished that when she opened them she would find herself safe within the House of Vestals. Bells would be ringing, calling her to morning ritual.

The smell of him.

She opened her eyes.

From the high window, dusty rays of sunshine fell across the floor. Her stola lay in a heap, stained and torn. Sliding her undamaged hand down her body, she felt stickiness and gagged.

She moved the fingers of her wounded hand and pain shot to her shoulder. Inch by inch, she rolled onto her side. Her good hand found the pugio and tugged at the hilt. The blade released and blood pulsed from the gash. He'd missed the main artery or she might have bled to death. Finding her strophium, she wrapped the cloth around her throbbing hand.

Her stomach roiled.

Half crawling, half dragging her body, she found a chamber pot.

Someone was knocking on the door.

"Elissa, are you all right?" A voice called.

She vomited into the pot.

The door opened and footsteps rushed toward her.

"What has happened?" Mother Amelia's eyes widened with comprehension. Her sturdy arms wrapped around Elissa, drawing her close, rocking her like a baby, as Elissa sobbed. The high vestal held Elissa till her tears were spent.

"Rest," Mother Amelia said, leading Elissa to a couch.

She lay back on the cushioned seat, heard the clink of pottery and splashing.

"He's gone too far," Mother Amelia said. "He cannot get away with this."

The damp cloth felt cool against Elissa's neck. Water trickled down her back, stinging when it met the welts, the result of his fingernails.

"I'm so ashamed," she whispered.

"It's not your fault."

"I'm no longer suitable for service."

"Purity is not a garment, not a vestment we can don. A true vestal is pure of heart."

Pure of heart? Her heart was poisoned.

Even in attempting murder she had failed. She had disgraced her family in every way. At best, she would be banished, exiled to an island to live out her life in obscurity without even the satisfaction of having killed her enemy. At worst, she would be entombed alive, left to die with only a crust of bread, a jug of water, and shameful memories.

Mother Amelia handed her the cloth. "Clean yourself. A physician will see to your ankle and your hand."

"And then?"

"We must say nothing for a time. Perhaps Nero will be satisfied and we can avoid a trial."

"He raped me. You can testify."

"I didn't examine you before—" Mother Amelia's voice faltered. "Before the incident."

The incident.

Would that be the term used to describe what he had done to her? The incident?

260

Elissa held out the cloth to Mother Amelia. "My blood is proof of my virginity."

Mother Amelia shook her head. "All blood looks the same. And he has witnesses, one of them your sister. If I accuse Nero, he will simply claim you're lying, claim that your virginity was already taken by Gallus Justinus."

"And if I say nothing?"

"Perhaps we can forget all this."

Forget?

Elissa felt her life slip away, quietly, without a fight. Truth buried beneath lies.

"I want a trial."

"There's something I must tell you." Mother Amelia straightened her suffibulum. The coils of snowy wool were limp with perspiration, her forehead furrowed. "I should have told you long ago, but your parents wanted to protect you, and I remained silent—"

"What?"

"Sixteen years ago a child was brought to me, no more than three years old. By order of the highest authorities and with utmost secrecy, I was commanded to find the child a home where she'd be raised with love and security—"

"What does this have to do with me?"

"You are that child."

The high vestal's words tore through Elissa. The wound Nero's dagger had inflicted was nothing in comparison. Her mind raged in disbelief. "That can't be," she protested. "I take after my father."

"And your mother."

"No. My mother is pale, while I am dark. I have nothing of my mother in me."

"Nothing of Constantina."

Elissa stared at Mother Amelia. She had sensed the truth for a long time, felt it, but never had she put what she sensed into words—or even thoughts. "Who is my mother?"

"I've been sworn to secrecy."

"Sworn by whom?"

"Your birthmother."

"Surely she'll want to meet me, now that I'm grown."

"I'm sure she would."

"Introduce us."

"She's dead."

"Dead?"

As quickly as she'd discovered this mother, she'd vanished. An oath to the dead was sacred, and Mother Amelia was bound to never reveal the name.

"And who is my father?"

"Honoratus."

"Then he knows who my birthmother is, and he must tell me."

"Your father and Constantina believe you to be the outcome of his unfortunate affair with a peasant girl who died two years after your birth."

"Constantina knows I'm my father's bastard?"

"She's your true mother, Elissa, the woman who raised you. Don't hurt her more by dredging up the past."

But, of its own accord, the past came back to haunt Elissa. She remembered the words she'd seen scrawled under the prophecy. *Darkness cannot prevail within the light of a happy soul.* The symbol of the sun. Darkness encircled by light. The eye of truth.

Something stirred within her.

A thought. A memory. A name.

She sensed her dead mother, reaching out to her.

In her mind's eye she saw a baby, wrapped in swaddling clothes, held within a mother's arms. "Do I descend from the line of Julius?"

Mother Amelia's nod was almost imperceptible.

Elissa didn't want to believe what her gut told her to be true. Though Mother Amelia swore to keep the name a secret, Elissa guessed her birthmother's identity.

She felt it in her bones. All the pieces fit.

And the despair in Mother Amelia's eyes confirmed Elissa's fears.

CHAPTER XXXIV

Flavia stared into the bronze mirror propped over her vanity. The table was littered with bottles of expensive scent, pots of creams and powders, combs and brushes, jewelry—everything she'd ever wanted. Yet she felt her power over Nero dwindling. He talked constantly about his dead mother, seemed to think she watched him. On one point, at least, he defied Agrippina.

"He won't give me up," Flavia said to her reflection.

But worse than his preoccupation with his mother, was his obsession with Elissa. Flavia had hoped her sister's arrest would put an end to Elissa's meddling, but lately Nero kept asking questions like, "What would Elissa think of this? How would she respond to that?"

Flavia ran a comb through her hair, still shorn as required for a novice, but beginning to grow out. She leaned toward the mirror, examining her face. A pimple had erupted on her chin.

And, thanks to Elissa, all Flavia's plans to travel had been thwarted. After the Lemuria fiasco, Nero sent a notice to Alexandria announcing his trip had been abandoned, his performances indefinitely postponed. Not that anyone would cry about his cancelled concerts, but Flavia wanted to see Egypt. She dreamed about sailing up the Nile as had Cleopatra.

At first, Nero had been an ardent lover. Breaking all the rules, he'd transported Flavia to private chambers within his palace. The senate and the Collegiate of Pontiffs—stuffy old men, in Flavia's opinion—were outraged, as was his wife Poppaea. But Nero said anyone who questioned his judgment must be a traitor to the state. A vestal's vow of chastity, he claimed, was null regarding the Pontifex Maximus. Their copulation should be viewed as a divine fertility rite.

But a month later Nero had lost interest. Flavia hadn't seen him in days.

Desperate to win him back, she'd hired a well-known actress to transform her into Venus—or at least Aphrodite. The actress came from Thrace and was an expert at cosmetics and complicated Grecian hair designs.

Loaded down with sacks and baskets filled with her trade secrets, the actress entered Flavia's dressing room.

"Set them there." Flavia pointed to a table.

The actress looked her over, shook her head. "You're just a child," she said. "And nearly bald."

"Did I hire you to insult me?"

"I'd better get to work. Close your eyes." Using the fur of a rabbit, the actress doused Flavia's face with lead powder.

Flavia shooed away the dust and sneezed. She glanced at the mirror. "I look like a ghost," she said.

"Powder hides your blemishes." The smile the actress offered was as warm as a wolf's.

Wolves populated Nero's court, Flavia had learned. At first, they'd seemed friendly—concerned for the poor virgin held hostage in the palace. But swiftly Rome's aristocracy had turned, circling her with hungry eyes, hearts pounding with envy, drooling for her devastation. She'd clung to Nero, throwing herself into a tidal-wave of banquets, a sea of parties. But, with the summer's heat, Nero's enthusiasm for his paramour had waned. By the Ides of June, his interest had dwindled from a rushing torrent to a dry creek bed.

Flavia was cast into a desert without friends.

But she would win him back tonight.

A three day feast, thrown by Tigellinus, was to begin this evening—the most spectacular banquet Rome had ever seen. Flavia had not received an invitation. Apparently, Nero intended to keep his vestal virgin safely locked away while all of Rome partook of the festivities.

But she had other plans.

"Perhaps a smudge of blush on my cheeks," she said to the actress.

"With your reputation, blushing comes naturally."

Flavia tried to ignore the remark, in the past month she'd become accustomed to people whispering behind her back. She'd become a laughingstock. She promised herself, after tonight, things would be different.

The actress babbled as she worked, but Flavia paid no attention. She had a lot to think about. She'd consulted her astrologer and the haruspices, sacrificed a flock of doves to Venus, and by her calculations tonight proved the ideal date for conception. Bearing Nero's son, heir to the throne, would be her salvation. And her revenge.

"Just make me beautiful," she said.

"You need a wig."

"Before my head was shaved, people said my hair looked like spun gold."

"Looks like new-mown hay now." The actress brushed red ochre on Flavia's cheeks, and the result was garish. She rummaged through her sack, muttering, "A wig, a wig, a wig." Finding a mop of inky curls, she slapped it on Flavia's head.

"Now I look *paler* than a ghost."

"You said you want to be disguised." The actress jabbed a pin into Flavia's scalp to hold the wig in place.

"That hurts!"

"Beauty has its price." The actress tossed her head of curls. "Of course, my mane is natural, though I use a dye of vinegar and leeches to heighten the color. Some hair is thin, some hair lacks shine. But life is unfair, don't you think?"

"I suppose."

"Take you, for example."

"Me?"

"You must know what they say."

"Who?"

"Everyone."

"What do they say?"

"Never mind." The actress wrapped a strand of Flavia's wig around a heated curling tong to make a ringlet.

"Tell me what they say," Flavia insisted.

"They say…" The actress took her time heating the tong. "They say you prostitute yourself to Nero without consequence, and they call you the sacred whore. Meanwhile, your sister is held prisoner with no evidence."

"My sister will stand trial, and have a chance to prove her innocence."

"You feel no remorse for being her accuser?"

"She's guilty."

"And you're not?"

The curling iron slipped.

"Watch what you're doing!" If the woman had been a servant, Flavia would have had her flogged. But the actress was popular at court, especially with Poppaea.

Flavia stared at the mirror. Perhaps she felt a smattering of remorse for having accused her sister. Even now, after a month's confinement, Elissa refused to admit to her guilt. Why did she have to be so stubborn, so self-righteous? To make matters worse, although a physical examination had proved Elissa was no virgin, the high vestal insisted on her innocence.

Flavia frowned at her reflection.

Even her parents had turned against her. Instead of congratulating her on her rise in the world, her mother suffered melancholia and cried constantly. The health of her father had also deteriorated. These days Honoratus rambled on for hours about leaving Rome as soon as he gained strength. He talked about moving to the countryside.

Flavia rolled her eyes.

Did no one in her family consider how their actions might affect her? They were selfish, egotistical. And Elissa was the worst. She had ruined everything.

"I'm not like my sister," she said. "I was chosen by the Pontifex Maximus."

The actress stabbed another pin into the wig.

"Ouch!" Flavia rubbed her scalp. "This wig looks hideous."

"Without it you look like a boy."

"Show some respect," Flavia said. "In case you forgot, I'm Nero's favorite."

"They say he favors cocks. That's why he rarely beds you."

"Get out!"

The actress dodged an earthen pot. It shattered, showering the room with red ochre. A jar of powder followed. Neglecting her curling iron, combs and pins, the actress bolted from the chamber.

"For an encore," Flavia shouted, "I'll have you crucified."

She tore the mop of curls from her head and flung the wig against the wall.

What the actress said was true. Nero flaunted her at parties, flirted with her in front of guests, but when night fell he preferred boys.

How could she conceive his heir if he refused to touch her?

She wiped the powder from her face. Using bear fat, she removed the gray galena from her eyes, the carmine from her lips. Roughing up her butchered hair, she stared at her reflection.

All she needed was the clothes.

She would seduce him as a boy.

❦

Dressed in a soldier's leather tunic and boots—her breasts tightly bound, her shorn locks tousled—Flavia hid within a grove of olive trees. The night air felt smooth and warm, and many guests wore only diaphanous scarves. A full moon lit the sky and torches flared along the lakeshore illuminating gardens and pavilions. On successive days the artificial lake might be filled for mock naval battles or drained for wild beast hunts. Tonight, rafts strung with lanterns drifted on a rippling sea of black and silver, while lesser guests milled on the shore. The largest raft, and the most luxurious, supported Nero's private party.

Tigellinus had spared no expense. A sumptuous feast had been provided along with entertainment—music and dancing, contortionists and fire-eaters. It seemed to Flavia that all of Rome had been invited to the banquet from plebeians to aristocracy. All of Rome, except for her.

The imperial raft drifted close to shore. Festooned with flowers, like a barge of Ramses the Great, the raft was buoyed by empty wine barrels and drawn by tugboats. Slaves, chosen for their beauty as well as their brawn, manned the oars. Sea creatures had been released into the lake: vicious eels, stinging jellyfish, and sharks—though they would not survive for long in fresh water. Nero's guests reclined on couches, nibbling delicacies then tossing scraps into the water to be snatched by predators.

Flavia noted, with satisfaction, that Poppaea was not included in the party on Nero's raft. Nor was any other woman. But her heart sank when she saw Egnatius, pock-faced and flushed with wine. If he noticed her, he might see through her disguise and say something stupid. She hoped he would drink himself into oblivion, lose his balance, and become dinner for the sharks. Nero languished on his couch surrounded by admirers. A young man dressed as a satyr sat beside him. The satyr said something Flavia couldn't hear, and Nero laughed. She gritted her teeth. If not for the sharks, she might have jumped into the water and swum out to the raft.

She had seen the satyr before. He wasn't even a freeman, but a slave Nero called Pythagoras. Unlike his namesake, by no stretch of imagination was Pythagoras a mathematician, he could barely add. But according to the gossip, he had other aptitudes. Unable to square a hypotenuse on papyrus, he excelled at triangles in bed. Flavia doubted Pythagoras could count beyond ten fingers, but his eleventh digit, rumor claimed, was prodigious.

Nero fed Pythagoras a fig, offered him more wine.

The unfairness! Flavia wanted to scream. Did Nero intend to discard her, like a worn-out sandal, and return her to the dreary life of a vestal virgin?

The tugboats dragged the raft further from the shore. Tears stung Flavia's eyes as she watched her hopes and dreams slip from her reach. Despair lured her from the safety of the olive grove. Somehow she'd make Nero pay.

She passed a string of banquet tables where guests stood in line, eager to pile their plates with food. At least a hundred kitchen slaves ran back and forth to the tables, refilling platters of oysters, dishing vegetables from pots, rearranging bowls of fruit and setting out loaves of bread. Whole pigs, stuffed with pigeons, plums, and cherries, turned on spits, dripping fat into the fire.

Jugglers and acrobats vied for Flavia's attention. A girl, about her age, contorted herself into an impossible position, and kissed her own genitals; a man with skin as black as coal lowered a sword into his throat; two dwarfs engaged in lewd demonstrations. Flavia didn't stay to watch.

Laughter and voices spilled out of the pavilions along the lake. Tigellinus had arranged makeshift brothels and filled them with makeshift whores. Placards announced the delights a visitor might find within:

> *THE GOLDEN ASS*—satisfaction guaranteed.
> *THE ODYSSEY*—tantalizing sirens.
> *SECRETS OF SOCRATES*—if you dare.

Whoremongers stood at the doorways, collecting fees and offering credit, while bodyguards held back men fervent to get in. Funds were needed for the treasury, and Nero had decreed all Romans do their duty for the empire. Wives of senators, virgin daughters, widows, mothers, were required to serve as prostitutes. No woman was exempt from service, and every male guest was expected to pay up and perform.

Avoiding the brothels, and hoping to gain Nero's attention, Flavia ventured toward the water's edge, her boots sinking into mud.

"Soldier!" someone called. "Stay back. That lake is treacherous."

She recognized an acquaintance of her father, a senator acting as whoremonger. Screams issued from the pavilion behind him, and the crowd of waiting men howled with laughter.

"Virgins," the whoremonger said. "How much can you cough up, soldier?"

Fearful of being caught, Flavia dug into her pouch.

The whoremonger snatched an aureus from her fingers.

"Make way for a warrior," he shouted. "Stand aside!" Dragging Flavia by the arm, he pushed through the crowd of shouting men. "Don't be afraid, boy," he said to Flavia. "I can tell you're still a virgin. These two will take care of you."

Two girls lay on a pallet. They clung to each other, sobbing. Blood stained the rumpled bed linens. A heavyset man, at least twenty years their senior, kneeled in front of them.

"Time's over," the whoremonger said.

The patron stood with a grunt. "All yours," he said to Flavia.

Clamping her hand over her mouth, she ran from the pavilion. Outside, two men were pummeling each other—cheered on by spectators. Fists swinging wildly, they stumbled toward the water's edge. The larger of the two landed a punch, and blood gushed from the other's nostrils. Hands cupped over his nose, the man staggered to the lake, scooped up water, and splashed it on his face. Without warning, the lake surged, and snapping jaws clamped around the man's ankle. A sea creature, Flavia wasn't sure exactly what, dragged him into the water. Howling for help, he thrashed his arms. Onlookers pushed and shoved, trying to get closer, to gain a better view, but no one offered assistance.

Her heart slamming so hard it hurt, Flavia ran toward the olive grove. Ducking under branches, tripping over roots, she ran to the safety of the trees. Tears streamed down her face.

She felt powerless and stupid.

She ran until the sound of the feast grew distant, the laughter and the music faint. The olive grove gave way to untamed woods. Cypress trees towered overhead blotting out the moon, their weeping boughs barred her way. The scent of cedar filled her nostrils, and each breath pierced her lungs. Torches flickered through the veil of branches. She ran toward the light then slowed. Drawing aside a drooping limb, she peered into a clearing.

Torchlight revealed a gathering of women. They sat in a circle, chanting.

Flavia grabbed onto a low-hanging limb of Cypress and pulled herself into the tree's crook, to gain a better view. The bark chaffed her knees and thighs as she shimmied along a bough. Pushing aside a branch of prickly cones, she peered down at the clearing. Poppaea lay naked on a bed of moss, surrounded by women Flavia recognized from court. They knelt beside the empress, stroking her arms, massaging her thighs, anointing her plump belly.

Stories of Poppaea's strange gatherings ran rampant through the court. Some said Nero's wife dabbled in magic, some said she consorted with sorcerers, some said she practiced the black arts—casting spells to blind, or maim, or even kill.

Flavia inched closer, and the bough dipped toward the clearing. Digging her fingernails into the bark, she struggled to keep her balance.

A priestess of Venus stood before a slab of granite that served as an altar. Smoke spiraled from a fire fed with frankincense. The priestess poured salt into an earthen bowl while the women chanted. Her voice rose above the others, "Great goddess Venus,

we call on you to protect Poppaea Sabina. Set Furies on her enemies. Putrefy their entrails, pluck their eyeballs from their sockets,
and toss their bones into eternal fire." The priestess stirred water
into the bowl.

Flavia watched with fascination.

"We beseech you, great goddess, to bless the womb of Poppaea
Sabina that she may receive Nero's child." The priestess dipped her
fingers into the bowl, touched Poppaea's right eye then her left,
touched each of her ears, each of her nostrils, her mouth, her nipples,
and her navel. She parted Poppaea's thighs, sealing every orifice.

"May her womb be bountiful and bring a son to term," the
priestess said.

The other women echoed her.

The priestess brought a chalice to Poppaea's mouth, and
Poppaea drank. Flavia knew of herbs that might induce a child
into a womb—lemon balm steeped in wine, orchis tuber crushed
into powder and dissolved in goat's milk, even simple watercress.
What if they worked on Poppaea?

Clinging to the branch, she whispered, "Great goddess, Venus,
hear my plea. Curse Poppaea Sabina's womb, allow no seed to ger-
minate. And make my womb fertile for Nero's son."

The priestess moved around Poppaea, blocking Flavia's view.

She edged further along the branch.

"By the power endowed in me," the priestess chanted, "may
Poppaea Sabina bring forth a manchild, heir to The Roman
Empire."

"No!" Flavia screamed. Losing her balance, she tumbled from
the tree and landed in the circle.

Rising on her elbows, Poppaea stared at the intruder. "Who
are you?" she asked.

The women whispered, pointing at Flavia.

Poppaea crooked her little finger. "Come closer, let me see you,
soldier."

Flavia scrambled to her feet.

"Come back here, boy!"

Flavia ran into the woods.

The women followed, shouting, screeching, but Flavia outran
them. Rays of a lantern swung through the dark, casting light on
a patch of earth, a branch, a stream of rushing water. Jumping the

creek, her foot sank with a splash. She stumbled from the water, saw a deer track, and veered onto the narrow path. Clouds cloaked the moon and made the woods a shadow-play. The path grew dense with brambles, and thorns slapped her face.

Behind her, a twig snapped.

She heard breathing.

Not her own.

The panting of a predator.

She ducked into a patch of briars, fell onto her knees, and crawled. The vines clawed her, tore her clothes, but she kept going.

Behind her, she heard cursing.

A cry of pain.

Then nothing.

She stopped, breath catching in her throat, sweat pouring down her neck. She lay prone on the ground, heart pounding against the earth, sweat stinging the scratches on her back and arms, listening. She heard tree frogs. Water running in the creek. The distant sound of shouting and music from the feast. A rock cut into her ribs, but she didn't dare move until she felt certain her pursuers had given up the chase.

Finally, she crawled out of the briar-patch and staggered to her feet.

The lantern blinded her.

"Who sent you to spy on me?"

Flavia recognized Poppaea's voice. She squinted, but couldn't see.

"Nobody sent me," she said.

Poppaea raised the lantern. Lifting Flavia's chin, she stared into her face. "You're not a boy," she said. "You're my husband's whore."

Flavia glanced toward the brambles, wishing she had stayed there.

"After your run, you must be thirsty," Poppaea said.

Flavia swallowed, and her throat felt parched.

Poppaea reached into her robe and found a flask. "Drink."

Flavia sniffed. The contents didn't smell like wine or anything she'd ever drunk.

"Go on," Poppaea urged.

The taste was not unpleasant, sweet and milky. It numbed her throat, warmed her stomach. "What is this?" she asked.

"Poppy juice," Poppaea said. "A specialty of mine. Drink up. I insist."

Flavia finished it and handed Poppaea the flask.

"Feeling better?"

She nodded.

"You see, there's no reason to fear me. Is there?"

"I thought you hated me."

"I don't hate you, Flavia." Poppaea's eyes burned into hers. "Why would you think that?"

"I don't know." Flavia moved her head, and the landscape traveled with her, blurring. The lantern left a trail of light, and her legs felt weak.

"Now, tell me, dear, who sent you?" Poppaea's voice sounded distant.

"No one."

"So no one knows you're here?"

The question floated through Flavia's mind, but she could make no sense of it. She stared at Poppaea. Flames danced in her eyes.

With surprising strength, Poppaea pushed Flavia down, forcing her to kneel. Rocks cut into her knees, but the pain seemed distant, as if this were happening to someone else.

"The female tongue is more agile than the male's," Poppaea said. "And I've heard your tongue is amazing."

"My tongue?"

A halo encircled Poppaea's head. Or was it the lantern's light?

"Your tongue." Poppaea drew her lips back in a snarl.

Flavia watched, in awe, as Poppaea's incisors lengthened into fangs. Her face narrowed, and her nose grew longer. Her paws loosened the cord binding her robe. The silk slipped from her body, pooling around her feet.

Flavia shook her head, trying to wake up.

And Poppaea blew out the lantern.

CHAPTER XXXV

Justinus hadn't shown his face among the aristocracy in weeks, and if he had they would have turned him over to Tigellinus. His domus on the Esquiline stood vacant, while he found sanctuary in one of his tenements. The apartment was above a perfumery, close to the Circus Maximus—a hodge-podge district favored by actors and prostitutes, charioteers, artisans and would be writers—the dregs of society. It suited him.

On the night of Tigellinus's banquet, despite the sultry temperature, he lay on his pallet, fully clothed, a pile of bedcovers drawn to his chin. He studied each twist and turn of the cracks in the ceiling.

Upon hearing of Elissa's impending trial, he had sent Akeem with a message to Nero declaring her innocence, demanding she be released. Akeem had returned with Nero's answer: if Justinus dared to interfere in any way—if, for example, he appeared before the Senate to protest, if he posted notices, or made speeches on the Rostra—he would be arrested. And, if Elissa's trial found her guilty, he would be stoned to death for desecrating a vestal virgin.

Rolling onto his side, Justinus closed his eyes and tried to find a comfortable position. He mumbled a prayer. But since Paul's departure from Rome, his prayers seemed to have no effect. The pallet felt lumpy. He rolled onto his other side. His hand went numb, and he shook his wrist attempting to revive his fingers, vaguely aware of a pounding noise.

Waves crashing on a shoreline.

He looked out at a dismal sea and breathed the smell of putrefying fish. His lips tasted of salt. Barefoot, he walked along a rocky beach. Wind whipped the water into swells, and waves pummeled the shore. He stumbled, falling to his knees. Caught by the undertow, he somersaulted, couldn't breathe.

"Justinus," someone called.

Fighting his way to the surface, he sucked in air. A wave sent him crashing to the shore. He dragged himself onto the beach. Gold sand shimmered in the sun. The gates of paradise appeared before him. He crawled toward them, grabbed the bars and shook the gates with all his might, begging to gain entrance. They opened with a sigh. Jesus sat on a throne of light, surrounded by the twelve apostles.

He spoke to Justinus.

The battle you fight is mine.

The pounding waves grew thunderous, drowning the words Jesus spoke. Justinus strained to hear, but someone kept banging at the gates.

"Justinus!"

He woke with a start. Rubbed his eyes. Found himself entangled in sweaty bedcovers.

The banging persisted.

He glanced toward the door, wishing his unwanted visitor would leave. He'd warned Akeem to stay away. Running his hands over his face, he pressed his palms into his eyes trying to recall the dream. So vivid. More like vision.

Something about a battle.

Hadn't Paul called followers of Jesus soldiers of the Lord?

The door rattled on its hinges, threatening his barricade.

"Open up!"

The voice wasn't Akeem's.

Groping beneath the pallet he found his dagger and wrapped his fingers around the hilt. Falling to the floor, he crawled toward the enemy. He'd honed pugio's blade to a fine edge, prepared to cut through cartilage and bone.

"I know you're in there, Justinus."

Spies. Within his troops.

How else had they guessed his name?

He reached the door. Levering a chair beneath the latch, he fortified his barricade.

"Open up. It's Lucan."

Justinus pressed his eye against the peephole. "How did you slip past the watch?"

"Let me in."

"My troops have deserted me?" He cracked open the door.

Lucan shoved his way inside. He grabbed the pugio and tossed it on the sleeping pallet. "You stink and your beard's as long as a Jew's. When was your last visit to the baths?"

Justinus shrugged.

"This place is sweltering." Lucan crossed to the window and unlatched the shutters. Justinus followed him. The moon, full and bright, poured light into the room. Music and shouting wafted through the window from the street.

"The enemy is close," Justinus said. He slammed the shutters, taking care to latch them.

"You look half-starved," Lucan said. He surveyed the sideboard and found a jar of water. Opening the lid, he made a face. "Let's get out of here. I'll buy you supper."

"I'm not hungry."

"You're delirious."

❦

Justinus sopped the last remnant of gravy with a crust of barley bread. Fat soaked into the chewy grain and tasted wonderful. His first bite of food had left him ravenous. He couldn't remember his last meal.

Lucan snapped his fingers and the tavern maid came running, anxious to serve so prosperous a customer. "More wine," he said, waving his hand over their empty cups. "This time bring a flagon."

Justinus turned away from the girl, hoping to remain inconspicuous—bearded and stinking, he doubted he'd be recognized. Lucan, on the other hand, was clearly an aristocrat. The Fatted Calf's usual clientele were the sort to count every quadran, but Lucan threw around denarii as if he were a gambler. The tavern's tables were placed close together, and from where he stood Justinus could see most patrons ate pastries stuffed with sausages. They watered their wine liberally or drank sludgy ale. But Lucan ordered pheasant and the finest honey wine. The Fatted Calf's proprietor stood behind the food-bar where a variety of dishes, hot and cold, could be bought for dining in or taking out. Through clouds of grease he smiled across the crowded room at Lucan.

Justinus buried his nose in his empty cup. Fatted Calf—Greasy Pig would be more appropriate. If the proprietor smelled a fat reward for turning in a fugitive, no doubt he wouldn't hesitate to run his mouth to the authorities.

The tavern maid refilled Lucan's cup, leaving him the flagon. She removed their plates and wiped down the table.

"Custard for dessert," she asked Lucan, "or snails?"

"Rose pie," Justinus mumbled, licking gravy from his fingers.

The tavern maid smiled winningly at Lucan, then hurried off to fill the order.

Lucan chuckled. "And you claimed you weren't hungry."

"Starved for justice."

The tavern maid returned before he could elaborate. She set the plate of steaming pie in front of Lucan. He slid it toward Justinus. Using a wooden spoon, Justinus dug into the crust, stuffed pie into his mouth and chewed, savoring the delicate flavor of rose petals and baked calf's brains. Wiping his mouth, he glanced at the next table. The neighbors paid him no attention. One of the men broke into a boisterous song, and his companions joined him.

"We need to talk," Justinus said. "Need to make a plan."

"About?"

"I've had it up to here." Justinus sliced his hand across his throat. "And I'm not referring to my dinner."

"There's only one solution," Lucan said.

"We can't get close enough." Lowering his voice, Justinus leaned toward his friend. "He no longer trusts you, and if I so much as show my face—" He pushed away the empty plate. The thought of Elissa, held a prisoner and facing trial, made him sick. "What if she's found guilty?"

"A lot of girls claim to be virgins," Lucan said. "A physical examination has proved otherwise."

"Are you calling her a liar?"

"I'm merely suggesting—"

Justinus slammed his fist on the table and nearly sent the pie plate crashing. "Her whorish sister wrongly accuses her."

"So you and she never—"

"No!"

"If she's pure she'll be exonerated." Lucan calmly sipped his wine.

"With the Pontifex Maximus as judge?" Justinus grabbed Lucan's cup and downed the wine. Heat rushed through his gullet.

Lucan poured another cup. "You have a point," he said.

"I wish she weren't a virgin. I wish we'd lain together when we had the chance."

"Sometimes fate has other plans."

"Fate be damned. I plan to change the course of history."

"How?"

Justinus glanced at the next table. The men were laughing, didn't notice him. "As you've often stated, violence may be required."

"What happened to your faith?"

"I'm a soldier of the Lord."

"What of turning the other cheek?"

"This is war."

CHAPTER XXXVI

Flavia woke from restless sleep. The sky, tinged with lavender, seeped through tangled branches. Something sharp cut into her shoulder-blade. A rock. Her head felt like a lictor's double-headed axe had split it open. Memories bombarded her. A gathering of women. Poppaea Sabina.

Her tongue begged for water.

She pushed herself onto her knees, stood shakily. The woods surrounded her. An owl called out like a lost ghost. Perhaps she'd woken from a nightmare.

Squinting at the newborn sun, she headed toward the lake.

Straining to hear music, shouting, laughter, some remnant of the banquet, she stumbled along a path. Birds chirped in branches overhead. An irritating sound. The woods gave way to an olive grove. Between twisted trunks of trees, she saw the lake. Nero's abandoned raft floated on placid water, a band of crows its only occupants. Overstepping carcasses of sea creatures, she picked her way toward the water's edge. The morning stank of fish and garbage.

Slaves wandered along the shore collecting trash: gnawed bones and apple cores, broken bits of plate, odd pieces of clothing—a woman's veil, stained and torn. The pavilions stood deserted among beds of trampled flowers.

"Boy," someone called to her.

She recognized the acquaintance of her father. No longer playing whoremonger, he appeared to be an upright citizen.

"You disappeared the other night," he said, slapping her on the back.

"Where is everyone?" she asked.

"Gone home. As I soon will be. But as procurator of this district it's my duty to oversee the cleanup."

"What day is it?"

"What day?" He chuckled. "You got your money's worth, didn't you, soldier? Last time I looked, the day of the Sun always follows Saturn's day."

"But the feast began on the day of Venus—"

"Get back to your barrack. Sleep it off." The man's attention shifted to a weary slave who shoveled ashes from a smoldering pit. "Lazy scum! Douse the coals with water then pack them well with dirt. If Rome burns, I'll hold you responsible."

Flavia felt dazed by what the man had told her.

The day of the Sun.

For two nights and a day she'd been in a stupor. Only the gods' mercy had spared her from the elements, from savage beasts or worse.

Her heart fluttered against her ribs like a caged bird, and she realized Poppaea had intended her death. She had to speak to Nero.

✺

Tigellinus stood at the entrance of Nero's private chambers welcoming guests, arms folded over his massive chest, his condescension palpable as he took in Flavia's matted hair, the grubby soldier's tunic, her naked legs. A smile tugged at his scarred lip.

"You make a pretty boy," he said.

Flavia started toward the doors.

"Not so fast," Tigellinus said. "No women are allowed in there."

"I need to see him." She reached for the bronze handle.

Tigellinus caught her by the arm. "You don't want to go there, little girl."

"Why not?"

"Run back to your chambers and hide. Better yet, seclude yourself within the House of Vestals."

The doors burst open, and two senators tripped into the hallway, their togas disheveled, their faces flushed. Laughter followed them.

"Disgusting," one of them muttered. "The nerve, throwing us out."

"Worse than Caligula."

Straightening their togas, the senators slunk down the corridor. Tigellinus followed, ensuring their departure.

Flavia took that opportunity to slip through the doors and into Nero's chambers.

Revelers, still drunk from the banquet, packed the entryway. Some leaned against the muraled walls, others lolled on wine-stained couches, while those too stupefied to stand sank to the floor. The sun had risen hours ago, but the windowless room was as dark as evening, and oil lamps provided flickering light. Rich perfume and rancid sweat smothered any remnant of a breeze.

Making her way through the crowd, Flavia managed to find standing room in Nero's tablinum. The room teemed with men in various states of intoxication.

Music greeted her—tambourines and flutes accompanied by a trilling voice. She recognized a wedding song. The lyrics had been altered and seemed more suitable for an orgy than a marriage.

She pressed through the crowd, attempting to see the singer.

Chairs and tables had been pushed against the walls to accommodate the swarm of guests. They settled on high-backed chairs, leaned against tables, perched on windowsills and cushions, their attention riveted to an enormous marble desk that now served as a stage.

The bride, a substantial girl, stood on the desktop and, to Flavia's amazement, it was she who sang. Flame-colored silk veiled her face, and a bridal girdle jingling with coins encircled her hips. The way the bride moved seemed familiar. The slave, Pythagoras, stood beside her, his satyr's goatskin worse for wear. He shifted from foot to foot playing the nervous groom.

Of course, Flavia realized, this was a pantomime. Bawdy entertainment for the guests. What else could this charade be, but the grand finale to three days of orgies and gluttony? Only Nero was missing.

The bride ended her song with a series of high-pitched trills, and the guests applauded with enthusiasm. With a flourish, she swept aside her flame-red veils and bowed to her audience.

Flavia stared in disbelief. Beneath the elaborate pile of curls, the kohl-rimmed eyes, the carmine lips, she recognized Nero.

"Time for the ceremony," he said, his voice a falsetto.

He yanked the groom into his arms. The kiss was passionate and lingering.

Flavia looked away. She felt dizzy. The room seemed to be spinning. A neighbor's shoulder broke her fall. Egnatius! Hypnotized by Nero's performance, her cousin barely noticed the young man who had bumped into him. Flavia moved away from him, but the room was crowded and she could not go far.

Nero raised a bejeweled hand for silence.

"Good citizens of Rome, in case you think your Caesar mean, I bestow upon my groom a most generous dowry: land, a lavish domus, and a flock of fine servants. As for the wedding sacrifice—" Nero gyrated his girdled hips, making the coins jump, "—I offer up my not-so-virgin ass."

The guests laughed nervously.

Flavia expected Nero to fling aside his veil, rip away the wig of curls, laugh at his outrageous joke. Instead, he grabbed Pythagoras, joining their hands as was customary for marriage vows.

"Do you, Pythagoras, take me as your wedded wife?"

The slave looked frightened as a man condemned to die.

"Answer me." Nero's voice, suddenly a baritone, boomed across the chamber, "Do you take me as your bride?"

"Wh-whatever you desire, Caesar."

"Right answer." Nero flung his bridal wreath of herbs, a symbol of fidelity, out into the crowd. "Now we will consummate the marriage."

"In f-front of everyone?"

"Ravish me, husband."

The bride jumped from the desk, nearly crushing several spectators. A priest broke the wedding loaf over the happy couple's heads and guests scrambled for crumbs to gain good luck. With the resolve of a tragic hero, Pythagoras carried Nero, kicking and screaming like a captured Sabine, into the adjoining bedchamber.

Flavia lurched forward, caught in a wave of people as guests surged after the bride and groom, throwing walnuts for fertility. Oil lamps glowed in every corner, on every table. Nero's sleeping couch had been draped with flame-colored silk and strewn with rose petals. Grunting under Nero's weight, Pythagoras set down his unwieldy bride.

"You brute," Nero said in a falsetto voice.

The reluctant groom tried to escape, but the bride jerked him back onto the bed.

"Be gentle, I'm delicate." Nero rolled onto his stomach and pushed himself onto all fours wiggling his buttocks at Pythagoras. Loosening his girdle, he hiked up his bridal robe. "Deflower me."

"In front of everyone?"

"Rut me like a horny boar."

The guests watched in stunned silence.

It was not unusual for a bridal party to witness the wedding's consummation. Not unusual for one man to take another—members of the aristocracy often enjoyed slaves and boys. But the man in power reserved the dominant position. Why would Nero feign submission?

Flavia knew the answer. He craved humiliation.

And to satisfy his hunger, she planned a feast of punishments. As an appetizer she would bind his wrists and ankles as he had done to her. For the main course she'd tantalize him with the whip. How dare he embarrass her in front of all these witnesses? Already people whispered that she couldn't please a man. Now, not only would she be the brunt of jokes, a laughingstock for all the empire, but a disgrace.

In disgust, she watched as Nero reached between Pythagoras's thighs, found flaccid proof of the slave's lack of enthusiasm, and squeezed. Whether out of fear or stimulation, the shaft grew thick and stiffened.

"Screw me or I'll chop it off!"

Eager to retain his parts, Pythagoras mounted the bride.

"Long live the happy couple," a voice called out.

Flavia turned, and saw Egnatius.

Others took his lead.

"Be fruitful and multiply."

"May the gods grant many children."

Flavia bit her tongue and tasted blood. She despised Nero and hated what she had become—what he had made her.

The crowd cheered as Nero shrieked and whimpered.

"An improvement on his singing," someone said.

Flavia couldn't bear to watch another moment. Blinded by anger, choked by shame, she fought her way toward the door. Halfway to her destination she ran into Egnatius.

"Flavia?" he stared at her. "What are you doing here?"

"Leaving."

"Stay and have some fun." He pressed his cesspool of a mouth on hers.

She bit him and he yelped.

Fists flying at his ugly face, she punched and clawed. Everything was ruined, all her dreams and all her plans. Even her stupid cousin saw her as a whore. Someone grabbed her by the shoulders, pulling her away from Egnatius, dragging her through the crowd and out into the vestibule.

"Let me go," she shouted.

Kicking at her captor, she tried to free herself. But what freedom could she gain? Like her doves, she would be forever caged.

Tigellinus held her firmly, his forearm clenched around her neck. One sharp twist and she'd be dead. "What shall I do with her?" he asked.

"She'll make the perfect pet for me," an all too familiar voice answered.

Tigellinus released her to Poppaea. Crushed against her ample bosom, Flavia struggled to breathe.

"My naughty nymph," said Poppaea. "I imagined you were dead."

CHAPTER XXXVII

F lavia struggled to free her hands from the leather bindings.
"Does Nero know what you're doing?" she asked Poppaea.

"You mean *my* husband? He's got other problems."

Poppaea tightened the straps, bruising Flavia's wrists. A chain ran through an iron eyebolt in the concrete ceiling. She pulled, hoisting Flavia's arms above her head, drawing up her body until, feet brushing the dirt floor, Flavia dangled like a puppet.

"What do you want?"

"Just a chit-chat between girls. I've dismissed the guards, so we can…talk."

"I have nothing to say to you."

"I'll remove your blindfold, so you can fully appreciate your accommodations."

Flavia took in the cave that lay within the bowels of the palace, dark except for light provided by Poppaea's lantern. She didn't want to cry, but her eyes teared. For weeks, she didn't know how many, Poppaea had held her hostage within the Domus Transitoria. Today she'd been stripped and blindfolded, dragged through moldy corridors, pushed down countless steps—to reach this dank hole. The air smelled vaguely of sewage.

Poppaea ran her hands along Flavia's flanks, grabbed hold of her hips and tugged until Flavia's arms strained in their sockets.

"Why. Not. Torture. Pythagoras?" Flavia's voice came in gasps. "He married your husband."

"He poses no threat. Pythagoras is a diversion. But you, my pet, may bear a son."

Flavia struggled against the leather bonds, but that only made them tighter.

Poppaea paced from one end of the cell to the other. She paused to kick a rusted bench fitted with a series of pulleys. "The rack might prove effective," she said. From the filthy floor, she picked up a device that looked like a gigantic claw. "Or the tickler."

"Let me go, and I'll never bed Nero again. I'll return to the House of Vestals—"

"You'll stay right here," Poppaea spat her words, "where I can keep an eye on you. You think you can take my place, but I'm not replaceable." She stood before Flavia's dangling body. "Pity you're so pretty. What a waste."

Flavia felt Poppaea's cheek, soft and warm, against her belly.

The stab was unexpected.

She screamed as pain tore through her cervix, blast through her uterus. She didn't see the knife until Poppaea held the blade before her face.

"You'll never bear his baby now."

Blood ran down Flavia's legs, puddled at her feet. Her bladder emptied, and the sting of urine made her writhe.

"I'll send servants to clean this mess."

"Cover me," Flavia begged.

"You don't deserve that much respect, but I'll leave the lantern."

Poppaea paused at the cell's doorway. "By the way, even as we speak, my husband's at your sister's trial."

The door closed and the bolt fell into place.

Flavia tugged the leather straps. Her arms ached. Kicking only increased the pain. The cramping in her womb became excruciating, shooting up and down her legs. Gritting her teeth, she squeezed her thighs together and attempted to stay the bleeding.

Cobwebs drifted from the ceiling, and something crawled along her back. She heard the sound of water. The sewer ran close by. A rat approached the pool of blood and others followed.

What a fool she'd been. Elissa had been right. About Nero. About everything.

"A stupid fool!" Her voice echoed hollowly.

And if Elissa was found guilty, it would be her fault. Her sister would be sentenced and entombed alive.

Like me.

Don't think like that.

She had never meant to jeopardize her sister's life. She'd only meant to prove her power and keep Elissa at bay. What had she witnessed? Nothing really. A mere kiss. And the letters were mere words, not proof of infidelity. Justinus wrote mostly about the prophet Paul and his god Jesus.

The servants would be coming soon.

They had to be.

"Help!"

Was that the sound of footsteps?

"Get me out of here!"

CHAPTER XXXVIII

"The Collegiate of Pontiffs, the vestal virgins, and the Pontifex Maximus have reached a verdict." Sweat beaded on the Major Flamine's brow. He ran a cloth over his forehead, small defense against July's sweltering temperature.

Riveted by the prospect of a vestal virgin's downfall, all of Rome anticipated Elissa's trial as if it were a battle between gladiators. Nero seized the opportunity to serve cheap entertainment to the urban mob by opening the proceedings to the public. Court had been established in the forum and risers erected to accommodate the spectators. Men and women, even children, packed the stands until the floorboards groaned. The tribunal of priests and vestals looked down at Elissa from a dais set in the center of the small arena.

She sat on a stool before them, cradling her hand. The wound had healed, but left a scar. The stigmata served as a reminder of what Nero had done to her. Curling her fingers into a fist, she prepared to hear the verdict.

Someone laughed. A baby wailed.

Elissa caught a whiff of citron, the scent of pork and onions. It might have been a festival.

Guards stood at the exits, and Tigellinus, in full dress uniform, arms crossed over his chest, stood watching.

Elissa scanned the crowd, thankful that her parents were not in attendance. At her insistence, they had fled Rome for their country villa. To have them witness her disgrace would have been unbearable. Mother Amelia's revelation had preyed on Elissa's mind for the past month, but she had kept the secret close. If the name of her birthmother was made public, would it help her case or go against her? In any case, she lacked proof, and without proof who would believe her? One thing was certain—the revelation would destroy Constantina, humiliate Honoratus, and disgrace her family a hundredfold.

Her gaze moved over the spectators. They came from every stratosphere of Roman society. She didn't blame Gallus Justinus for failing to appear. In fact, she prayed he'd remain absent. Flavia was missing. In her stead, the letters spoke—although they'd proved nothing. But who needed proof? Ultimately, Nero would decide the verdict. Angerona's testimony had been most damning. Elissa tried to meet her eyes, but Angerona turned away.

"All rise for the verdict." The Major Flamine wiped perspiration from his face. "The sentence will be pronounced by the Pontifex Maximus."

Elissa stood. Her feet seemed miles away, and she felt disembodied. Struggling to retain her balance, she focused on the tribunal. Marcia and Cornelia had been crying. So had Mother Amelia, who now seemed bent on strangling a handkerchief. The priests' stony faces held no sympathy. Angerona's face presented a tragic countenance.

Nero sat in his curule chair while slaves fanned him with peacock feathers. He wore a robe of silk, rather than a toga. Upon his head he wore the crown of the Pontifex Maximus.

The Major Flamine handed him a scroll.

"The verdict—" Nero cleared his throat, "Guilty as charged."

A murmur ran through the crowd.

Only determination prevented Elissa from fainting.

Nero raised a hand for silence. "Good citizens of Rome, the vestal virgin, Priestess Elissa Rubria Honoria, has broken her sacred vows and polluted the holy rites with infidelity. She has fornicated, which is deemed an act of treason against Rome. The court finds her guilty of incest. For indeed, an act of fornication by a vestal virgin, is named the lowest deviance."

Shouts of protest were drowned by stamping feet and cheers of approval. No women were more revered than vestal virgins, none placed on a higher pedestal. Romans loved to raise their idols to ever greater heights, but even more, they loved to see those idols fall.

"Order in the court!" Nero pounded his scepter. "Has the prisoner anything to say? Words of repentance? An apology?"

"Yes," Elissa's voice shook. "I do."

She faced the crowd, afraid her courage might fail. The spectators grew quiet as she gazed out at the blur of faces. Even now, she felt their respect, their wonder that she dared to speak. Perhaps they hoped that she, a vestal virgin selected by the gods, might convince fate to find her innocent.

The citizens of Rome deserved better than Nero.

They deserved the truth.

"Good citizens," Elissa said, her voice clear and strong. "Respected priests, women, slaves—I am one of you. A Roman. The Pontifex Maximus asks, do I have regrets? I do. I regret that our beloved Rome has been corrupted by a kind of poison. The venom of greed and arrogance. I regret the Collegiate of Pontiffs swallows lies and finds me guilty."

Murmurs rumbled through the crowd.

"The Pontifex Maximus claims I've committed not just adultery, but incest."

"That is how the crime is viewed," Nero said. He yawned, loudly. "Get on with it. You're boring me."

"And does my sister bore you too, the one whose innocence you took?"

Nero smoothed his robes and flicked away a bit of lint.

"Oh, yes, I forget myself," Elissa said. "The Pontifex Maximus lives above the law." The crowd leaned forward, hanging onto every word. "Meanwhile, I am to be entombed and left to starve—"

"As you know," Nero said, his voice quavering with anger, "entombment is the punishment set down by law."

"The laws of men?" Elissa asked.

"Of course, the laws of men. Who else? Women? Slaves? Perhaps a donkey?"

Laughter, led by Tigellinus, rocked the court.

Elissa's voice rang out above the noise. "There are greater laws than laws of men. The law of truth. The law of justice."

"The law of God," someone shouted from the bleachers.

A pauper peered down from the highest tier, a filthy cloak drawn over his head. His eyes locked onto Elissa's.

Justinus.

She wanted to climb the ropes, scramble up a wooden beam, and throw herself into his arms. His presence strengthened her resolve. She would speak the truth. Death came only once; even Nero couldn't kill her twice.

"Incest," she said, her voice commanding attention, "may also be defined as sexual union between close relations. For example, a daughter and father, a mother and a son. Or siblings."

Despite the heat, Nero's face grew pale. "That's not what we're discussing."

"I think it is."

Anticipation sparked the crowd.

"If I am guilty, so are you." Recognition flashed between them. "After all, we are brother and sister—in the priestly sense, of course."

For once, Nero seemed at a loss.

Pointing the finger of her wounded hand at him, Elissa addressed the crowd. "The Pontifex Maximus took me by force. In other words, he raped me. The act of incest at its worst."

"She's a liar," Tigellinus shouted. "A liar and a whore."

"Then all Romans are whores," Elissa countered. "Like you, Tigellinus. Whores and slaves to Nero."

Coming to his senses, Nero pounded his scepter. "Court is adjourned," he shouted.

"Not before I have my say." Mother Amelia stood, still twisting her handkerchief. A hush fell on the court as all heads turned to the Vestal Maxima. "By the gods I hold sacred, I bear witness to Elissa Rubria Honoria. Despite the evidence this court has brought against her, I know her to be true of heart, immaculate in every way. By my life, I swear she is innocent."

The crowd went wild, screaming, shouting, climbing ropes and swinging from the balconies.

"Sit down," Nero ordered, but no one listened. Brandishing his scepter, he bellowed, "The sentence stands!"

Elissa watched with amazement as men and women stormed the arena, declaring her innocence, calling for justice, yelling obscenities at Nero.

"Tigellinus!" Nero banged his scepter on the dais. "Do something!"

Tigellinus reached under his arm, withdrawing his sica.

Justinus shinnied down a rope and jumped into the arena. He landed in front of Tigellinus, surprising the prefect, and knocked the sica from his hand. Locked in a stranglehold, the two men tumbled over one another. Onlookers surrounded them, pelting the prefect with citrons, eggs, anything they had on hand, and cheering Justinus.

"Guards!" Nero shouted.

Praetorians descended on the chaos. But their efforts to control the seething crowd seemed half-hearted as if they too doubted Elissa's guilt.

The mob scaled the dais, swarming Nero like angry bees.

Using his scepter, he attempted to beat them off, riling them into a frenzy. Stung by the crowd's animosity, Nero leapt from the dais and fought his way through fists and curses, attempting to reach the exit. A child grabbed the hem of his silk robe and the fine fabric ripped as he fled the arena.

Tigellinus was not so easily deterred. Escaping Justinus, he pushed through the mob toward Elissa. He bound her wrists and dragged her from the court. She would be stripped of priestly vestments, beaten, paraded through the streets to the Colline Gate where she would be entombed and left to die.

And yet she felt victorious.

Darkness cannot prevail within the light of a happy soul.

Like all good Romans, she took pleasure in watching Nero tumble from his pedestal.

CHAPTER XXXIV

Flavia ran her tongue over her lips, cracked and dry from lack of water. No servants had come to her rescue.

She no longer felt pain.

Her arms, straining in their sockets, had long ago gone numb. The dying lantern emitted sickly light. She gazed up at her shackled hands, attempting to move her fingers.

She recalled a story Marcus had once told her, one of Aesop's fables. A farmer sewed seeds of hemp in a field where a swallow and a flock of crows were feeding. "Don't trust that farmer," the swallow warned the crows. "Make sure you pick up every seed." The crows paid no attention to the swallow and, after eating their fill of seeds, they flew away. Come spring, the remaining seeds grew into hemp, by midsummer the hemp was woven into cord, and from the cord the farmer made a net. In that net the crows were caught. But the swallow escaped.

Fog drifted through Flavia's memory. The story's moral evaded her.

Death crept toward her like the night, dark and inevitable.

Was she already dead?

She wasn't certain.

With no gold coin to pay the oarsman, she would be forced to swim across the river Styx. Her shade would find no peace in the afterlife, and her soul would wander between worlds.

A lemur.

As she drifted toward darkness, the moral came back to her: Destroy the seed of evil or it will grow and become your ruin.

※

Twelve days before the Nones of August, as the Dog Star moved across the heavens, Justinus paced his room.

Elissa was going to die.

He could think of nothing else.

Although the Vestal Maxima had claimed her innocent, Nero pronounced her guilty. The sentence was unpopular, but the word of the Pontifex Maximus was final. Too cowardly to face the urban mob, Nero and Poppaea fled to their palace in Antium and left the task of entombing Elissa to Tigellinus.

Her funeral would be held today.

Justinus wiped his brow. Sweat poured down his back, soaking through his tunic. Even at this pre-dawn hour July's heat felt oppressive. He opened the shutters, felt the stirring of a breeze. The Dog Days of summer promised no rain. No chance Elissa's funeral might be postponed.

The clang of bells called out the fire brigade. Not unusual. It happened almost every day. The gods' wrath, people whispered.

God's wrath brought down by Nero.

Justinus wished he had killed him when he'd had the chance. But hiding in this tenement, a fugitive, he had no opportunity. *It's not for us to judge our fellow man,* Paul would have cautioned him. Paul didn't understand the politics of Rome. Destroying evil as powerful as Nero required, not patience, but violence.

The Dog Star dipped toward the horizon. Soon it would be dawn, and the city would be waking. Scents from the perfumery, on the building's first floor, drifted through the window making Justinus lightheaded. Jasmine, lotus, orange blossom from the Orient—scents too exotic for this tenement.

The perfumery marked the last of his tenants.

Justinus had always taken pride in maintaining his properties, but over the past months he'd done little to care for them—especially this one where he lived. Pipes, frozen last winter, had never been repaired. The roof leaked, and the ceiling spat bits of plaster. Lately even lack of running water didn't bother him. In turn each of his tenants left. And now the building was condemned.

As was Elissa.

Dawn's light revealed the Circus Maximus. Nero's sordid playground loomed across the street, and from his window Justinus could see the gates Marcus had entered, but never left. There would be no games today. Today, Rome's entertainment would be Elissa's death.

His gaze fell on the cedar chest.

Paul had told him he was needed here in Rome.

An idea formed within his mind, and he could not let go of it. He paced the room, becoming excited as the idea bloomed into a plan. Finally, he understood his mission. He had been chosen by God, not to convert Nero to following The Way of Jesus—a task which proved impossible—but to rid the world of evil. To root it out by destroying what Nero best loved.

The Circus Maximus.

He opened the cedar chest. Flinging aside clothes, discarding a sandal missing its mate, he dug. He discovered a medallion from Britannia, his father's knife, a forgotten figurine. At the bottom of the chest, he found what he needed. The jar of tung-oil Paul had given him.

Accelerant.

All he needed was a spark.

He ran downstairs to the perfumery in search of a flint. At this hour, before shops opened, the business was abandoned. Even in July the perfumer used heat to distill raw materials, and Justinus found embers still smoldering in the brazier.

Conducting an experiment, he poured a small portion of tung-oil on a rag and touched it to a glowing coal. The oil proved more potent than he'd expected, and the rag burst into flames. He dropped the burning cloth and stamped it with his foot, but only succeeded in dispersing the fire. He ran to the fountain where water should have flowed and found it dry—the result of his negligence.

Flames caught hold of a curtain, climbed the fabric, and leapt onto a nearby shelf. The wood ignited quickly and the shelf gave way. Amphorae filled with oil crashed to the floor spewing their precious contents. The air was redolent with clove, lemon, and sandalwood. The fire gobbled up the oil, then looked for more. Flames devoured shelf after shelf. Tumbling jars gushed precious fragrances, splattering the walls, coating every surface with oily fuel and transforming the perfumery into an inferno.

Justinus found a horse blanket and used it to bat the flames, but that only encouraged the fire. Choking on fumes, he bolted to the door and kicked it open. A fireball rushed after him, scalding his back, singeing his hair.

He raced across the street and watched in horror as a flash, more powerful than lightning, blasted through the building. Plaster and timber exploded in a shower of debris as the tenement burst into flames, spewing sooty cinders, painting the sky black, obliterating the rising sun.

He thanked Jesus—thanked the Almighty Father, Jupiter, Apollo, Zeus, any god he could summon—the building had been condemned and vacated of people.

But he hadn't considered the wind.

It swept down from Caelian Hill, fanning flames, encouraging the fire to attack adjoining buildings. Sleepy tenants, roused from bed and still in their nightclothes, rushed from their apartments and out into the street.

Horses whinnied, kicking at their stalls. Chickens escaped their coops and ran squawking underfoot. The screams of women blotted out the wails of children.

Clanging bells announced the arrival of a fire brigade. The vigiles quickly formed a line leading to the Aqua Appia, the nearest aqueduct, and began passing leather buckets of water. Grabbing a bucket, Justinus joined them.

The inferno consumed everything in its path: a grocery, an apothecary, a forger's smithy. The temperature increased until the heat became unbearable, hot enough to melt metal. The apothecary's copper vats spit blue, green, and purple flames, as if conjured by a sorcerer. Choking on smoke and drenched in sweat, Justinus tossed buckets of water as fast as he could muster them, but before the water met the flames it evaporated.

Timbers came alive and fell on fleeing people. A frightened family ran from a collapsing building and faced a blazing wall of flames. The mother, clutching her newborn infant against her breast, narrowly escaped a burning beam.

A small boy stood in the middle of street, screaming, "Mama."

Horses, manes on fire, stampeded toward him. The clomping hooves were deafening as the horses galloped past. Justinus dropped his water bucket and lunged for the child.

Too late.

The boy's skull was crushed.

Sinking to his knees, Justinus cradled the trampled body.

"God forgive me."

Wind carried flames across the street, igniting the Circus Maximus. Fire raged through the entryway, up the wooden steps, and through the spectator stalls.

And as the dawn grew darker, Justinus bowed his head over the boy and sobbed.

CHAPTER XL

Dawn crept across the forum, its purplish light darker than usual, as if a storm were brewing. Wrists bound, head shaved, dressed in a simple tunica, Elissa looked out at the crowd gathered to witness her demise. Haruspices had examined the sacrificial entrails, the position of the stars had been consulted, and the Collegiate of Pontiffs declared the omens favorable for her funeral. Throughout the piazza, myrrh smoldered in copper braziers. Praetorian guards surrounded the Temple of Vesta, and Tigellinus stood at the bottom of the seven steps like the hound of Hades.

All night, Elissa had prayed to Jesus. Only he, who died so cruelly, could understand the injustice of her circumstance. Welts scored her back, inflamed and festering, a reminder of the beatings she'd received from the Pontifex Maximus.

"Your palanquin awaits you." With a gentle hand, Mother Amelia guided Elissa.

The litter—made of solemn alder wood, black curtains rippling in the breeze—had been especially prepared for the occasion. Priests, rather than slaves, had been assigned to carry Elissa through the streets to the Field of Iniquity.

"Daughter," a voice called.

Elissa turned, slowly, as if submerged in water. Her reality had shifted, and she felt like an observer in these final moments of her life, detached and mildly curious.

Constantina wore mourning rags, her haggard face smeared with ashes. Breaking from a cluster of family, she walked toward Elissa, arms outstretched. Her embrace was fierce, and Elissa lacked the strength to respond. She felt like one already dead, a shade among the living.

"Forgive me," Constantina said.

"For what, Mater?" A lump formed in Elissa's throat. Calling Constantina mater seemed fraudulent, but Constantina was the only mother she had ever known.

"I wish you had married; I wish I'd refused the priests when they took you from our home; I wish you'd led a normal life—"

"Don't blame yourself for fate, Mater."

"I blame the gods."

"I'm the one who should be sorry. My existence must have caused you pain." Tears welled in Elissa's eyes. "I know all you've done for me."

Constantina touched Elissa's cheek, lightly as a butterfly. "Then know you have never caused me pain, sweet daughter."

Honoratus stood nearby. Fighting to remain stoic, his face reflected no emotion, but the depth of his anguish was apparent in his eyes.

"My little girl," he said.

"Pater—" Her voice choked with tears.

Honoratus kissed her forehead, took her hands in his, and said, "I know you're innocent."

Tears spilled from Elissa's eyes. She felt like she was five years old.

"There's something I must tell you," Honoratus said. "Something you have a right to know. Something I thought politic to keep a secret—"

"I know, Pater. I *know*."

"Who told you?"

"That's not important."

"My little girl. Where do you get your stubbornness?" Honoratus squeezed her hands.

304

The wind picked up, sweeping dust into their eyes. Or so Elissa told herself when she saw her father cry. She glanced toward her wailing aunts, the solemn faces of her uncles. Egnatius must have come to gloat. He stood apart from the family. The household slaves were in attendance. Spurius loudly blew his nose. The vestals, dressed in their whitest robes, hovered like apparitions.

Marcia approached. "Forgive me," she said.

Elissa touched her round face. "There is nothing to forgive."

"I'll pray for you," Marcia managed to say, before bursting into tears.

Cornelia clutched her rag doll. "I'll miss you, 'Lissa," she said, her pink lips trembling.

Elissa knelt, peered into Cornelia's eyes. "I'll miss you too. Take good care of Lucia."

"She wants to go with you." Cornelia held out the doll.

Elissa shook her head. "It's dark where I'm going. Lucia would be afraid. She needs to stay with you. You're her mother, aren't you?"

Cornelia nodded, her relief apparent.

Before Angerona had the chance to speak, Elissa turned away.

"Where's Flavia?" she asked Mother Amelia.

The Vestal Maxima glanced at Tigellinus. "No one seems to know. She must have gone to Antium with Nero and Poppaea."

The lump in Elissa's throat became painful. "Please tell my sister I forgive her."

"Of course, my dear."

Elissa surveyed the crowd, hoping to see Justinus yet praying he would stay away. Praying he was safe. The crowd had increased in number and, though the mob was strangely quiet, she sensed their anticipation.

She heard Constantina weeping.

The song of birds.

Felt the rush of wind.

"The time has come," Mother Amelia said.

Tigellinus stepped forward. He bound Elissa's wrists, tightening the rope until it cut. A mournful wail emanated from the gathered people, not only for Elissa, but for Rome.

The blindfold made her world go black.

"This way, my dear." Mother Amelia touched her shoulder.

Elissa climbed into the palanquin, her body still aching from Nero's rod and whip. But fury overtook her pain.

She was on the verge of protesting, on the verge of claiming innocence, about to shout that Nero, not she, should be punished, when a gag was stuffed into her mouth. Leather straps bound her to the litter and a pall was drawn over her body. On the count of three, the priests lifted the palanquin and the procession began.

Ululations reverberated through the forum.

Bound and gagged, there was no use in struggling. Elissa lay still. Breathing. Feeling blood course through her veins. Lights flickered beneath her eyelids.

Jesus had carried his own cross.

What was her life compared to his?

A small sacrifice.

She told herself that soon she would see Marcus. He would be waiting by the River Styx, ready to receive her. She heard the rush of water, smelled the river's fecund scent. Was there any difference between birth and death?

The litter bounced along. They must have left the forum. From the crowd's rowdy noise, Elissa surmised they'd reached the Fauces Suburae, an artery that ran past the maze of the Subura. The litter bounced on.

She heard the curtains luffing. Smelled smoke too caustic to be incense. Somewhere outside the city wall farmers must be burning fallow fields.

"Fire," someone shouted.

"Where?"

"The Circus Maximus."

"The brigades will soon appease it."

"It's spreading fast. Wind carries the flames."

Tigellinus barked out orders, and Elissa heard the stamp of horse's hooves as men were dispatched. She listened to the fire brigade's distant clanging and sensed the city's rising panic.

"Let's go," Tigellinus shouted. "This procession doesn't have to take all day."

Smoke stung Elissa's nostrils. Beneath the blindfold, her eyes watered. She heard people coughing. The palanquin tipped precariously as they climbed Viminal Hill. The procession traveled northeast to the far end of the city. Just inside the Colline Gate they came to a halt. The litter and Elissa were lowered to the ground.

Mother Amelia pronounced an invocation. Whether it was long or short Elissa couldn't tell. Her heart thumped louder than a drum. Acutely aware of each inhale, each exhale, she filled her lungs with acrid air. Prayers were said and hymns were sung. Finally the leather straps were loosened, the gag and blindfold removed.

Light blinded her.

"I pray the next world will be better," Mother Amelia said.

She draped a veil over Elissa's face and helped her from the palanquin. Even here, on a hill above the city, smoke was evident. Through the veil Elissa saw a hazy sun. Black clouds choked the western horizon, too dark for a summer thunderstorm.

"Rome burns," she said softly. "And from union unholy the sister will bring forth a son."

"The tomb is prepared," Tigellinus announced.

Mother Amelia led Elissa away from her weeping parents and walked her through the Field of Iniquity. Removing Elissa's veil she mumbled a final prayer.

Elissa faced a mound of dirt. Guards stood at the entryway, where they would remain until her death was certain.

Darkness cannot prevail within the light of a happy soul.

For an instant the phrase made sense. But when she peered into the gaping hole, the dark pit she was to enter, she felt terror.

"My Lord," she whispered. "Why have you forsaken me?"

Tears streamed down Mother Amelia's face as she handed Elissa an oil lamp. In light of day the flame seemed weak.

"I will pray for you," she said.

"Pray for Rome."

Elissa glanced at the sky, gray with smoke, yet infinitely brighter than the tomb. Holding up the lamp, she steadied her foot on the first rung of the ladder and began her descent.

The crypt was windowless. The air smelled of earth. She ran her hand along the wall and felt the porous tufa bricks cut from volcanic stone and, in between the bricks, smooth mortar. She set the lamp on a small table that also held a loaf of bread, a jug of milk, a ration of olive oil.

A rock tumbled through the hole as the ladder was withdrawn. More rocks followed as a slab of stone thumped into place, sealing her inside the tomb, plunging her into darkness more profound than Hades.

The oil lamp sputtered. How many days could she survive? How many hours?

Recently, workmen, excavating a new road, had uncovered a coffin. Inside they found a woman, her face contorted in a silent scream, her fingers worn to bone from clawing.

Elissa breathed in dust and tasted dirt.

She strained to hear sounds from outside the tomb. Surely birds were still singing, her mother weeping, mourners wailing.

Down here, silence ruled.

She walked the tomb's length and counted ten paces. The width was identical and the height seemed about the same. She thought of lions in their cages.

Thought of Marcus.

Thought of Jesus. He had risen from the dead.

Hours must have passed.

Reclaiming the lamp, she lifted the light toward the ceiling. Without a ladder, she couldn't reach the slab of stone.

Her gaze fell on the three-legged table.

She removed the provisions, taking care not to spill the precious oil. Dragging the table across the room, she positioned it under the opening. She hiked up her tunica and climbed onto the table. It wobbled, nearly threw her off. Regaining her balance, she stood on tip-toe. Her fingertips brushed against the ceiling, but offered her no leverage. The stone slab didn't budge.

She climbed down from the table, dizzy and nauseated. Lately she had not felt well, especially in the mornings, and she found eating repulsive. But now hunger tugged at her. She took a sip of milk, already warm and slightly curdled, then glanced around the crypt.

A straw pallet lay on the floor. She grabbed hold of a corner and heaved the pallet onto the table. A few more inches of elevation allowed her to press her palms against the ceiling. The slab blocking the opening was heavier than she'd imagined. She bent her knees and, gathering her strength, pushed upward. The stone shifted slightly, allowing in a breath of air. With a thud the slab fell back into place. Again, she tried to move the stone, with similar results. She continued trying, until sweat streamed down her face and she felt breathless, sick to her stomach.

Was it her imagination, or had the air become thinner?

Exhausted, she climbed down from the table and threw the pallet on the floor.

She tried to think. Tried to conceive how she might lever the stone, dig her way out, tunnel through the earth to freedom.

She yawned.

Maybe if she rested, not for long, just to regain her strength. She sank onto the pallet. Gathering her knees into her chest, she leaned against the cold stone wall, rocking like a child. A song drifted through her memory.

A lullaby.

Her wrists and ankles still ached from Tigellinus's bindings, her arms were sore from pushing at the slab of stone. The sour milk unsettled her stomach.

And the oil lamp grew dimmer.

CHAPTER XLI

Flavia twitched.

Pain stabbed her gut, her spine stretched to the breaking point as she dangled from the ceiling. She gagged at her own stench.

Memories slipped through her mind, and she grabbed hold of one…spinning with her mother—the green scent of flax, the tug of thread, the whirring spindle.

A firebrand poked at her womb, forcing her back to consciousness.

Suspended between this world and the next, she swung back and forth. Vibrations rattled through her arms as if the ceiling trembled. But how could that be possible? She must be dreaming, lost in yet another nightmare.

The ceiling shook, the joists creaked and timbers groaned. She imagined the walls shifting. Imagined a door opening at her command, like the story Marcus had once told her about a magic treasure-trove. The walls rumbled. The shift was unmistakable. Dirt rained from the concrete ceiling. A chip of plaster jabbed her eye. She blinked, trying to dislodge the shard.

The shackles slipped and loosened. With a crack the iron bolt gave way, and she fell to the floor. The boom of rupturing concrete followed as the ceiling collapsed. A hailstorm of wood and sand

and stone pelted her. It grew into an avalanche, burying her until she couldn't move.

Stunned, she lay beneath the weight of wreckage.

Thought she must be dead.

She tasted the paste of plaster, the grit of sand.

Something heavy pressed against her shoulders. She tried to arch her back and the pressure shifted, bringing a new flurry of stones and dirt. But she'd gained more space in which she could maneuver. Sucking in dust, she wriggled her hands out of the leather straps. Blood pulsed through her fingers and brought back feeling. Pain. She pushed herself onto her battered hands and knees, managing to crawl a short distance.

If she hoped to survive, she'd have to surface.

Closing her eyes, she heaved her shoulders through an ocean of debris, kept shoving upward through rocks and plaster. Clawing with broken fingernails, she swam through rubble, fighting her way to the surface. Dust clogged her nostrils, made her cough. She gulped air. Acrid, smoky. Breathed the stink of excrement.

Wiping sand from her eyes, she studied her surroundings.

Light, dancing with particles of dirt, filtered through a hole, high above a mountain of ruptured wood and concrete. Any attempt to scale the pile would cause a landslide. All that remained of the chamber was a narrow passage. And, at the end of the passage: hope.

Crumbling walls revealed a tunnel. The sewer. It ran beneath the palace, met the Cloaca Maxima at the forum and emptied into the Tiber.

Weakened by pain and thirst, Flavia knew she couldn't last much longer. But determination gave her strength. The ceiling sloped down at an angle, grew progressively lower as she crawled toward the sewer's opening. Lying on her sore belly, she wriggled like a snake. She made slow progress, and the stench was overwhelming. Vomit gurgled in her throat.

A rat's eyes gleamed as she approached the tunnel, and she wanted to scream. But her lips were pressed into the dirt and she could barely breathe.

She wished she were home, back at her parents' domus, back in her old life.

But wishes were only granted in tales told to children.

CHAPTER XLII

Justinus knelt within the charred remains of the Temple of Vesta. Head bowed, hands clenched together, he prayed for forgiveness. He had caused this devastation. His hubris. His stupidity.

For days, he wasn't sure how many, he'd wandered through the burning city lending muscle to the vigiles. Using an axe, he'd hacked down walls. He'd strung up boulders with hemp rope, swinging them at plaster to demolish buildings. Anything to arrest the blaze and create a firebreak. But seven thousand vigiles were no match for the conflagration, a fire more enormous than any in memory, heat so intense it transformed statues into puddles. Corpses lay piled in the streets while homeless people wandered through the devastation. The dead haunted Justinus.

He looked up from his prayers.

Skeletal remains of the imperial palace lined Palatine Hill, phantasms of magnificence. Sparks whirled through the blood-red sky, and ancient trees raised blackened limbs pleading to the heavens. Scooping up ashes, Justinus threw them on his head and shouted, "Forgive me, Lord."

But even if God forgave him, how could he forgive himself? He thought of Elissa, slowly starving, asphyxiating. To maintain a shred of honor, his only course was suicide.

"Justinus?"

Angerona hovered over him, robes stained with soot, hair in disarray. More lemur than woman. The last person he hoped to see.

"Go away," he muttered. Stumbling to his feet, he sought escape.

She caught him by the arm. "Hear me out."

"Let go of me."

Her face, usually a placid mask, disintegrated into tears. "Please, forgive me. I did what I had to do to save my family."

His fortitude crumbled. How could he, guilty of the worst atrocities, refuse anyone forgiveness?

"What do you want?" he asked.

"I need your help."

He followed Angerona's gaze and looked toward the smoldering House of Vestals where charred statues of the priestesses stood among the courtyard's ruin.

"Help me to redeem myself," she said.

"I can't help you, Angerona. Redemption comes from God."

"Then help me save Elissa."

With sooty fists, Justinus swiped at his eyes. "Elissa's dead."

"Are you certain?"

"It's been days."

"Come with me to the Colline Gate. In all the confusion of the fire, the guards have fled and no one will notice us. Grant me the chance to prove myself." She held out her hand to him.

Justinus saw sorrow in her eyes, and yearning for forgiveness. Goddess or Gorgon?

It made no difference, if Elissa lived.

CHAPTER XLIII

With bloody fists, Elissa hammered at the tufa bricks. Bits of rubble broke away, rattling down the wall, but her prison remained invincible. Her throat was raw from screaming, her tongue swollen.

She lacked the grace to die like Jesus.

Clinging to the wall with blistered fingers, she tried to stand. Her legs buckled, and she fell onto the sleeping pallet. Straw poked through the fabric, stabbing her. She rolled onto her stomach, pressed her hands into the pallet and raised herself onto all fours. Standing seemed impossible. Exhausted, she sat staring into darkness.

The fragment of a lullaby haunted her.

She drew her knees into her chest, feeling her body's warmth, imagining that someone held her. An unfamiliar touch, a long forgotten scent, tugged at her memory. She squeezed her eyes shut, banishing her birthmother.

Hugging her knees tighter, she hummed the lullaby.

When the end came who would be here?

Not Mater. Not Pater.

Not even the gods.

She rocked back and forth and imagined she was in her father's arms. When she had been a child, she and Honoratus had often walked hand-in-hand along the garden path. Half-running, she had struggled to keep pace with him. When she grew tired, he carried her small body in his arms and held her close. She'd felt safe then. Petals drifting down like snow, whirling on the breeze. White flakes kissing her with ice. But, it must have been spring.

And now it was summer.

Wasn't it?

She pressed her burning cheek against the tufa wall. So cool. So soothing. Inviting her to sleep. To lose herself in sweet oblivion. She sank onto the pallet, lay down and closed her eyes as peace crept through her consciousness.

But sleep meant death.

Forcing her eyes open, she focused on a light.

The oil lamp?

No.

The oil lamp had burned out.

An image stared at her. A dark circle in a ring of light. The sun. The eye of God. A face, kinder than any she had ever known, gazed into hers. Smiling and radiant. A diadem of thorns encircled his head; trails of blood ran down his brow. How he must be suffering.

He had died in pain.

Died for her salvation.

What was her death in comparison? A final breath, a letting go, the last flicker of a flame.

She watched in wonder as the thorns of his crown fell away. The vine turned green and smooth, sprouted leaves then blossomed with roses.

He reached out his hand to her.

Light flowed into her body, pulsing through her heart, rushing through her arteries. Hatred, rage, the need for vengeance, vanished at his touch.

He drew her up beyond the darkness, carried her within his arms. They traveled past the sun, past stars, and through the heavens. When they reached the moon they sat perched on its silver crescent, legs swinging.

Humming a lullaby.

He handed her a rose, pink and blooming.

CHAPTER XLIV

J ustinus ran a cloth over his face. It came away with sweat and soot. Even here, far from the city's center, the fire's heat combined with the day's increasing temperature to create a furnace.

"Over here," Angerona called.

Peering through the smoky haze, he saw her standing by a mound of earth.

Elissa's tomb.

Spikes of purple lupine, yellow-centered asters, and drooping bluebells lay scattered in the dirt and marked her grave. A slab of granite blocked the tomb's opening. Falling to his knees, Justinus tried to lift the stone. Rough edges cut into his callused hands and the slab barely moved.

"Help me," he said.

Angerona's hands were smooth and white. "I don't think I can—"

"On the count of three." Together they heaved, and the stone shifted slightly, enough for Justinus to peer through a narrow fissure.

"Elissa," he called into the darkness.

No answer.

He needed something for leverage. He glanced at Angerona, noticing her palla. "Give me your shawl."

Slowly, she unwound the fabric, exposing pale shoulders, slender arms. Through her stola, he saw the silhouette of her body—she wore no tunica beneath it. She dangled the palla in front of his face. He should have come alone. Should have known she would be trouble.

"When I lift, run your shawl under the slab," he instructed her.

She bent toward the slab, allowing him an eye-full.

He managed to lift the stone enough for Angerona to saw the palla back and forth, creating a sling. Grabbing hold of both ends of the fabric, he tugged, and the slab shifted. Gritting his teeth, he levered the palla over his shoulder and pulled as if he were an ox, moving the stone inch by inch, sweat stinging his eyes. He heard the fabric tearing. The palla ripped and sent him to his knees.

"I see her," Angerona shouted. She knelt beside a crevice large enough to squeeze through.

"Is she alive?"

"I can't tell."

Justinus pushed her aside. In the dim light, he saw Elissa lying on a pallet, unmoving, and her eyes closed.

"We need a ladder," Angerona said.

"They've taken it."

Beneath the opening, Justinus saw a table. Lowering his legs into the hole, his feet found the table's surface.

Pebbles tumbled after him.

The tomb felt dank, stank of sour milk and vomit.

Elissa looked pale and fragile. Afraid if he touched her she might break, shatter like fine glass.

He whispered her name.

Her lips moved silently.

"Elissa!" He reached for her, felt the moisture of her breath. "Do you hear me?"

Her eyelids fluttered open.

"Is this Hades?"

"I think it might be heaven." Justinus smiled, could have laughed. "And finding you is my salvation." He took her in his arms, felt her heart beating against his, and lifted her toward the light.

Elissa weighed no more than a child as Justinus carried her from the Colline Gates and across the Field of Iniquity. Despite the lightness of his burden, his lungs ached. Brown haze settled on the city, crept along Viminal Hill, made his eyes water, his throat raw.

He lay Elissa on a grassy bank and sat beside her, watching the steady rise and fall of her chest. She was not fully awake, but seemed to be gaining strength.

He gazed down at the city. A battlefield. Fire had marched through the Forum Romanum, destroying palaces of senators, claiming granaries and warehouses, plundering the Temple of Jupiter built by Romulus. Then without warning the winds had shifted, and the fire had turned back, ravaging the Subura's twisting streets. Meanwhile, people huddled within the tufa walls of the Forum of Augustus while flames raged around them.

A million lives destroyed.

Angerona appeared over the rise, her face reflecting terror as she stared at the city's devastation. "When will it end?"

Justinus had no answer.

They watched in silence as a hazy sun looked down from midheaven. The air felt heavy, still. Birds had ceased singing.

"Nero has returned from Antium," Justinus said.

"They say, while the city burns he stands on his balcony and plays his lyre. They say he sings of Troy."

"His palace is destroyed. He has no balcony to stand upon."

"Do you think Nero's agents set the fire?" Angerona asked. "Rumors claim he wants to clear the city so he can build his Golden House."

"There are easier methods," Justinus said. "Extortion, threats, forced suicide—" He stopped mid-sentence, remembering Angerona's father.

"Timing is everything." She stole a sideways glance at him. "And I can't help noticing the fire's timing coincided with Elissa's funeral."

Justinus felt his face redden.

Elissa moaned, seemed to be waking.

"She's thirsty," he said, glad to change the subject.

Angerona handed him the water bladder.

He fed Elissa water, prayed that she'd recover soon. Since the death of his parents he'd become used to self reliance. He'd thrown himself into a soldier's life and accepted the post in Britannia as far from Rome as possible. But he could not continue. Not without Elissa.

"Are you crying, Justinus?"

"Smoke." He ran his hands over his face. "The smoke is getting to me."

Angerona settled beside him, touched his cheek and brushed away a tear. "You and I, we're the same."

"How so?" Justinus gazed at the seven hills, studying the drifting smoke.

"We'll do anything to meet our desires. Do anything as a means to our desired end. Wouldn't we?"

"The fire's traveling west toward the river."

"I understand your passion. I sense your longing, and I feel it too."

"I hope the fire doesn't jump the wall and reach the Campus Martius."

"Why can't you love me, Justinus?"

He glanced at Elissa. She had fallen back asleep, one hand held protectively over her belly.

"It always comes down to her." Angerona sounded bitter. "Elissa the chaste, the pure, the perfect. No matter what I do, I'm never good enough."

"It's not that—"

"What then?" Angerona stood, brushing bits of grass from her stola.

Justinus stood as well. Avoiding Angerona's stare, he scanned the seven hills. "The fire hasn't reached the Esquiline. If we walk along the ridge we should manage to reach my domus."

Cradling Elissa in his arms, Justinus leaned against the front door of his domus. It swung open. Strange. Usually the servants kept the front door bolted.

He stepped into the foyer, and Angerona followed.

"Hello," he called.

"What's this?" Angerona pointed to a figurine that lay broken on the floor.

"Must have fallen from the altar."

Justinus kicked the pieces across the mosaic and wondered why a slave hadn't swept up the mess. He carried Elissa through the unlit vestibule. It seemed barren. Busts of his ancestors were missing from their niches. Even the wax masks were gone.

They entered the atrium, and he lay Elissa on a couch. The room's sole piece of furniture. Where were the tables? The high-backed chairs and cushioned benches? Ashes covered every surface and sunlight fell in smoky rays through the open ceiling. Except for the cat, crouching by the central pool, the house seemed deserted. Upon seeing the intruders, the cat jumped down from its perch and bolted from the room.

"Akeem," Justinus called.

Curtains leading to the tablinum rustled, and Akeem peered out, his eyes wide and frightened. "Are you a lemur?" he asked.

"Where are all the servants?"

"Gone." Akeem waved his hand over the room. "All gone. I alone remain."

Touched by Akeem's loyalty, Justinus asked, "Why haven't you left as well?"

Akeem shrugged. "I have nowhere to go, and the wine here is excellent."

"What happened to the furniture?"

"Thieves. I couldn't stop them, except for the couch. Too heavy."

Justinus ripped open the curtain leading to the tablinum. The strong box had been pried open, the desk overturned, and papers lay scattered on the floor. He kept important documents at the House of Vestals, but all those records had been burned.

"Could be worse," he said, allowing the curtain to fall. "At least we're alive."

"Barely. You look terrible, Master."

"Is there anything to eat or drink?"

Akeem retrieved a flagon from behind the curtain. He left the room, apparently in search of cups.

"At least your domus is still standing," Angerona said. She wandered around the atrium running a hand along the wall. She studied her palm then held it out to Justinus so he could see the soot. "Thank the gods, my mother and sisters are safe in the coun-tryside. Our palace in the forum, the domus Nero confiscated, has burned. Nothing remains. Not even my mother's garden."

"Sit down, Angerona. You make me nervous."

"There's nowhere to sit." She peered out of a window to the courtyard. "Your apple trees are still standing."

"My father planted them."

"You never speak of your parents."

"They died long ago."

"Don't you get lonely?"

"Hurry with that wine," Justinus shouted, but Akeem didn't answer. Justinus opened the front door and called again. He saw the slave running down the garden path away from the house. And who could blame him?

Angerona touched his back. "You can count on me."

Elissa moaned.

Glad to escape Angerona, Justinus hurried to the couch.

"Where am I?" Elissa asked.

"You're safe, Elissa. Safe with me." He helped her to sit up.

She rubbed her eyes and looked around the room, her gaze falling on Angerona. "What's she doing here?"

"You have every right to hate me," Angerona said, "every reason—"

"You're dead to me."

Angerona's eyes grew hard. "I should have left you in that tomb."

"So you wouldn't have to face yourself?"

"Elissa, you need to rest." Justinus shot an angry glance at Angerona. "You'd better go."

Elissa touched his face. "Has Flavia returned from Antium?"

"We'll talk about your sister later." He handed her the flagon of water, hoping to delay her questions.

"Apparently, your sister never went to Antium," Angerona said.

"Where is she then?"

"No one has seen her since the fire started," Justinus said.

The flagon fell from Elissa's hands, and a stream ran across floor. "The fire is still burning?"

"For three days with no end in sight." Angerona stared at Justinus. "No one knows exactly how it started, but I can guess."

"Probably an accident," Justinus said.

"By accident or by intent, the result is criminal. In my opinion the culprit should be strung on a cross and burned alive," said Angerona.

Justinus flinched, but said nothing. In his heart of hearts, he agreed with Angerona.

Elissa stood shakily, her eyes unfocused, her complexion pale. "Rome burns," she said, "and from union unholy the sister will bring forth a son."

"Lie down, Elissa," Justinus said.

"The prophecy has come to pass."

"What prophecy?"

She headed toward the vestibule.

"Where are you going?"

"I must speak to Nero."

"Elissa," Justinus said, "If Nero sees you are alive—"

"He'll bury you again," Angerona's voice was sharp.

"I don't think so. I know him better than he knows himself." Elissa's face looked ashen, yet determined. "In any case, the dead protect me. After all, I'm one of them."

"Stay here where you'll be safe," Justinus pleaded.

"You'll find Nero at the Campus Martius," Angerona said, "tending survivors."

"Shut up, Angerona!" If she had been a man, Justinus would have slugged her. "You've done enough damage."

"As have you, Justinus."

"What do you mean?"

"I'm referring to your pyrotechnics."

Justinus edged away from her and ran after Elissa.

CHAPTER XLV

Flavia closed her eyes against the water's sting as the torrent carried her through the Cloaca Maxima. Clamping her lips, she tried not to swallow sewer water. The current became stronger as the tunnel reached its end, sucking Flavia into a whirlpool, before expelling her into the Tiber. Light pressed against her eyelids, and the rush of the river sent her under.

She resurfaced, gasping for air, arms flailing, struggling to stay afloat. A world of smoke and cinders swirled around her. Debris littered the water: remnants of boats, loose papers, orange peels, clothing, broken furniture. Flavia grabbed onto a charred beam. Clinging to the wood, she let the river carry her. Bobbing amongst the wreckage, she passed through an archway of the Pons Sublicus and narrowly avoided crashing into the stone bridge.

Her stomach cramped and her teeth chattered, but the cold water numbed her wounds. Or perhaps her pain was numbed by her sheer will. Having escaped Popaea's torture chamber, she was determined to survive.

The river's current carried her beyond the Servian Walls, beyond the scorched city. Tents of refugees lined the riverbanks. A row of brightly painted caravans displayed a sign advertising pantomimes.

Flavia let go of the beam and found the strength to swim.

"Coming here is madness," Justinus said.

"Not madness, necessity." Elissa held out her hand to him and their fingers interlocked.

"You aren't supposed to touch a man."

"That was before I died."

The floodplain of the Campus Martius lay outside the Servian Wall and ran along the river. Tents crammed every patch of earth and a mob of displaced people trampled the field, churning the grass into mud. To appease rising panic in the city Nero had opened storehouses of corn and set up tents providing meals and shelter.

"Flavia must be here somewhere," Elissa said.

Through the crowd Elissa saw Mother Amelia doling out food to the hungry. The high vestal looked up from a steaming pot, her mouth dropping in surprise. Wiping greasy hands on her apron, she hurried to Elissa.

"How can it be?" Fingers trembling she touched Elissa's face.

Elissa glanced at Justinus, thought of all her prayers. "I had a lot of help."

Mother Amelia turned to Justinus. "Why did you bring her here, young man? If Nero learns she is alive—"

"Exactly who I want to see," Elissa said. "Do you know where I can find him?"

"Let's go where we can talk, my dears."

Mother Amelia led them across the crowded field to a tent. "Come in," she said. "It's not much, but it serves." She motioned to cushions strewn on the tent's floor. "Sit. Make yourselves comfortable." Settling herself beside Elissa she asked, "What are your intentions now?"

"First, I must speak to Nero."

The furrows in Mother Amelia's brow deepened. "My dear, perhaps it's best to let him think you're dead."

Justinus placed his arm around Elissa's shoulders. "Let's leave Rome," he said. "Start a new life."

"Not until I see him."

Mother Amelia shook her head. "What's past is past, Elissa. You can't change fate. The gods have given you a gift. A future.

Officially you don't exist, and your sacred vows have been annulled. This is your chance for a new beginning—as if you'd been reborn."

Justinus lifted Elissa's chin. "Marry me," he said.

Love shone in his eyes, and hope. Could it be possible that something good could be born of misery? Elissa thought of Marcus burning on the pyre, of Flavia's stolen innocence. She rubbed her scarred palm, remembering.

"I can't marry you," she said.

"Why not?"

Finally she faced the truth. The nausea. The absence of her monthly flow.

"I just can't."

"For the gods' sake, Elissa," Mother Amelia sounded exasperated. "This is your chance for happiness."

"There's the matter of," Elissa hesitated, "a child."

"What child?" Justinus asked.

"Mine."

Justinus stared at her, and so did Mother Amelia.

"Now you understand why I have to see Nero, and why I can't marry you, Justinus."

His face darkened, but Elissa wasn't sure if she saw rage or sorrow in his eyes. "You think," his voice broke. "Do you really think I'd blame you for what Nero did? Marry me, Elissa. We'll move to the countryside, far away from here, and raise the baby as our own."

She stared at him in wonder. She'd always known he was good, but he was better than she'd dreamed. She trusted him as she trusted no one else. She knew she could rely on him. And he could rely on her. Might happiness be possible?

"Will we grow apples out in the country?"

Justinus laughed. "We'll grow orchards of them. Whatever you want, Elissa."

"Yes," she said, tears of joy filling her eyes. "Of course, I'll marry you."

"Good." Mother Amelia clapped her hands. "Then it's settled. Somewhere in here, I have wine. This calls for celebration."

As Justinus bent to kiss her, Elissa said, "Now I must go."

"Go where?" Justinus asked.

Elissa knew she could disappear and leave no trace. But she wanted retribution. She wanted to see Nero's face when she told him—everything. She owed that much to Marcus, owed it to herself.

She turned to Mother Amelia. "Please take me to the princeps now."

⁂

Mother Amelia pushed open the heavy doors of the basilica dedicated to Agrippina, and Elissa followed. Nero had opened public buildings to victims of the fire, and survivors lay on pallets strewn across the marble floor. Overworked physicians ran back and forth between their patients, applying cold compresses to their burns, dabbing wounds with honey to ease the pain and stay infection.

"This way," Mother Amelia said.

They walked along a hallway lined with patients. Some called out for blessings, some were crying, others slept.

"By the power vested in me," Mother Amelia said softly. "Vulcan, god of fire, may Rome's suffering end."

Elissa called on Jesus, prayed for strength to face Nero, prayed for courage to speak the truth. From the corner of her eye, she saw Marcus watching. Others lurked behind him.

Two sentries stood before a doorway.

"Young men," Mother Amelia said, although the older of the two rivaled the age of Elissa's father. "We've come to see the princeps."

"No visitors," the older sentry said. His eyes focused on a greasy stain smeared down the front of Mother Amelia's apron.

"I'm not a visitor." She revealed her medallion. "I am the Vestal Maxima." Straightening her spine, Mother Amelia seemed to grow as the guards diminished.

They bowed, allowing her to pass.

Mother Amelia knocked on the door.

"I said no visitors!" Nero's voice pierced Elissa like a knife.

She could leave now, run. Like all of Rome, Nero would assume her dead. Her vision clouded, and she resisted fainting. The air stirred and she shivered. They crept in at the edges, slipping through the shadows. Pleading, crying, begging to be heard.

Marcus, Agrippina, countless lemures. She moved through the dead, toward Nero's voice.

"I said—"

His face blanched when he saw her.

Nero sat on a folding stool, behind a makeshift desk covered with scrolls and sheets of papyrus. Dark circles rimmed his eyes and his cheeks were sunken. Instead of a toga or flowing robes of silk, he wore a simple tunic. He set down his stylus, pushed away the wax tablet on which he'd been writing, and stood.

"As you see," Elissa said, "I have risen from the dead."

He ran his tongue over his lips, riffled through a stack of papyrus, his hands trembling. "Official documents," he muttered, "the history of Rome, all lost."

"Where is Flavia?"

"I don't know."

She gazed into his frightened eyes, and she believed him.

"I bring you a message," she said, "from Agrippina."

Papers fluttered to the floor, and Nero stooped to gather them. "How is my mother?"

"*Our* mother."

Nero looked up, papers flying from his hands. He stood slowly, leaned toward Elissa, his hands pressing into the desk. "You?"

"Me."

"What proof do you have?"

Mother Amelia stepped forward. "I am a witness," she said, "and the Vestal Maxima's word is still sacrosanct, even in Rome. I promised Agrippina I would keep her daughter's birth a secret, but now that Elissa is officially dead, the vow of secrecy has been annulled."

Nero swallowed. "Go on."

"Twenty-two years ago, after Agrippina's exile from Rome and the death of your father, your mother married Passienus Crispus."

"My mother had been banished by her brother, Caligula." Nero looked distant, as if trying to remember. "We didn't live in Rome. She and Crispus were married for three years. I must have been about four years old."

"They quarreled," Mother Amelia said. "And Crispus began to travel, leaving Agrippina alone for months. To amuse herself, she took lovers—some of them aristocrats. When Crispus returned from Asia he found your mother—"

"With child," Elissa said.

"I remember," Nero said, "Crispus died quite suddenly."

"Quite conveniently," said Elissa.

"Soon after his death, Agrippina gave birth to a daughter. Agrippina wanted to return to Rome and could not afford another scandal, so she kept her daughter's birth a secret."

Nero's face had drained of color. He leaned over the desk toward Elissa. "What of your mother? Constantina?"

"My adoptive mother," Elissa said. "Honoratus and Agrippina had an affair and I was the result."

Nero's voice shook when he spoke, "If what you say is true, why claim your heritage at this late date? Do you hope to overthrow me? Seize the throne? Officially you're dead. What can you hope to gain?"

"Retribution."

Elissa didn't see him draw the sica. Nero leapt over the desk, papers scattering in his wake, and held the knife to her throat—the curved blade an evil smile. "You force me to kill you twice."

The blade felt cold and razor sharp.

"Let her go," Mother Amelia said.

"I should kill both of you."

"Yes," Elissa said, "both of us—your sister and your unborn child."

"My unborn child?"

"Rome burns and from union unholy the sister will bring forth a son. Remember the prophecy?"

The blade wavered in his hand.

"Release her," Mother Amelia said.

Shaking violently, Nero withdrew the sica. "A child?" Like a drunkard, he staggered backward and sank onto his stool. "You bear my son?"

"Your child grows in my womb. The prophecy calls for a son."

"And I nearly killed him."

"Murder runs in the family."

"My son." Joy flooded Nero's face as the idea took hold. "Heir to the throne. The perfect bloodline, descended on both sides from Julius Caesar." He clapped his hands. "I shall name him Apollo, for

he will be a god. From Rome's ashes he will rise like the phoenix."
Throwing back his head, he laughed.

"Not your son. Mine."

Nero's laughter ended abruptly. "Don't threaten me. If necessary, I'll hold you captive until my son is born."

"I plan to bear my son in peace."

Nero started toward her.

Elissa grabbed the sica. Fierce as any lioness, she brandished the blade. "Call the guards and you will die."

Nero appeared shrunken, dwarfed by his piles of papers—remnants of his burning empire. How had she ever thought him powerful?

"Before all of Rome, you claimed you never bedded me. Before the Collegiate of Pontiffs you accused me of infidelity. Resurrect me from the dead, and I will be your nemesis. All of Rome will learn your vulgar secrets and know you for a liar. Claim this child and you will be despised."

Still holding the blade, she flung open the door, nearly toppling the sentries.

"Make way for the Vestal Maxima," she said.

The guards bowed, allowing them to pass.

"Stop her!" Nero shouted.

Fog crept through the basilica, copious and clammy. Through the mist, the dead were watching, their eyes bright as stars. Elissa heard them whisper, felt their touch, as she walked along the vestibule.

"I'll claim the gods have raised you from the dead," Nero called. "The priests will pronounce you a goddess."

"Cleopatra to your Antony?"

"Elissa needs none of your proclamations," Mother Amelia said. "She is a vestal virgin in the truest sense."

"Come back, Elissa! Together, we'll become immortal." Nero's voice drifted through clouds of fog, as if from a distant world.

The sica slipped from Elissa's hand. She felt no hate for her half-brother, only pity. His vision afforded him no light, no hope.

Hope.

She felt a spark take hold, felt it kindling the flame she'd kept buried in her heart.

Darkness cannot persist within the light of a happy soul.

She walked out into the evening. The mist parted, and a sunlit path opened before her. A breeze brought the scent of roses, and she swore she heard Marcus laughing.

Justinus waited for her beside a fountain.

Light shimmered in the spray of water, and sparks swirled through the air. The setting sun stained the sky red-orange, cast everything it touched in bronze. He might have been a statue, a hero or a god. But he was human. A beating heart, a thinking mind.

Love burned in his eyes as Elissa approached.

And in that flame she saw her own divinity.

THE END

Acknowledgements

Thanks to my writers' group for all the support over the years: Blake Crouch, Terry Junttonen, Shannon Richardson, Haz Saïd, Dinah Swan, Adam Watson and Douglas Walker. Great thanks and appreciation to my amazing teachers and mentors: Elizabeth Engstrom, Tess Gerritsen, Terry Brooks, John Saul, Karen Joy Fowler, Craig Lesley and Dorothy Allison—to name a few of many. Thanks to John Tullius for creating the Maui Writers' Retreat, which I was fortunate to attend a number of times, as well as the magical Maui tour to Rome. And thanks to Eldon Thompson (fellow traveler to Rome) for his continuous encouragement, and to my fellow retreater, Tory Hartmann. Thanks to my beta readers: Blake Crouch, Terry Junttonen, Haz Saïd, Leah Morgan and Carol Stoner. Many thanks to Jeroen ten Berg for designing the beautiful cover. Thanks to Terry Roy for her exquisite formatting. And last, but not least, thanks to all the great writers and readers on Kindle Boards.

About the Author

Suzanne Tyrpak is originally from New York and now lives in southwest Colorado. She enjoys traveling, skiing, biking, and hanging out at the library.

Find her on Facebook at http://www.facebook.com/pages/Suzanne-Tyrpak/144232238928903

And follow her blog, "Who's Imagining All This?" http://ghostplanestory.blogspot.com/

She'd love to hear from you.

Other Books by Suzanne Tyrpak:

Dating My Vibrator (and other true fiction)

Coming soon

Agathon's Daughter—suspense in ancient Greece:

Born a bastard and a slave, Hestia has a gift—the power to read people's hearts. This gift brings her notoriety and takes her on journey through the upper echelons of Athens. Sold to Lycurgus, a prominent statesman with sadistic tendencies, she becomes his consort. As Hestia's wealth and fame increase, so does her despair. Determined to escape her cruel master, she faces enemies at every turn, but the fiercest enemy she faces is herself. To gain freedom, she must unravel the mystery of her past and confront the demons in her own heart.

9 781460 943144